城市想象和人性救赎：

索尔·贝娄小说研究

Imagination and Salvation in Cities

赵 霞／著

中国社会科学出版社

图书在版编目(CIP)数据

城市想象和人性救赎：索尔·贝娄小说研究／赵霞著．—北京：中国社会科学出版社，2016.4

ISBN 978-7-5161-8367-0

Ⅰ.①城… Ⅱ.①赵… Ⅲ.①贝娄，S.（1915-2005）—小说研究 Ⅳ.①I712.074

中国版本图书馆CIP数据核字(2016)第133313号

出 版 人 赵剑英
责任编辑 冯春凤
责任校对 张爱华
责任印制 张雪娇

出 版 中国社会科学出版社
社 址 北京鼓楼西大街甲158号
邮 编 100720
网 址 http://www.csspw.cn
发 行 部 010-84083685
门 市 部 010-84029450
经 销 新华书店及其他书店

印 刷 北京君升印刷有限公司
装 订 廊坊市广阳区广增装订厂
版 次 2016年4月第1版
印 次 2016年4月第1次印刷

开 本 710×1000 1/16
印 张 11.5
插 页 2
字 数 200千字
定 价 45.00元

前　言

索尔·贝娄（Saul Bellow，1915—2005）是第一位荣获诺贝尔文学奖（1976）的当代美国犹太作家，被认为是美国当代文坛继福克纳和海明威之后最主要的小说家。他的作品包含了丰富的社会内容和深邃的哲理思辨，是一个具有现实主义倾向的现代派作家。他曾三次荣获美国全国图书奖，一次普利策奖；一九七六年他以“对当代文化富于人性的理解和精妙的分析”获得诺贝尔文学奖。

从一九四一年发表第一篇短篇小说《两个早晨的独白》开始，贝娄共出版了长篇小说10部：《晃来晃去的人》（1944）、《受害者》（1947）、《奥吉·马奇历险记》（1953）、《雨王汉德森》（1959）、《赫索格》（1964）、《赛姆勒先生的星球》（1970）、《洪堡的礼物》（1975）、《院长的十二月》（1982）、《更多的人死于心碎》（1987）和他的最后一部长篇小说《拉维尔斯坦》（2000）。此外，贝娄还出版过中短篇小说集《只争朝夕》（1956）、《莫斯比的回忆》（1968）、《口没遮拦的人》（1984）、中篇小说《偷窃》（1989）、《贝拉罗莎暗道》（1989）、《真情》（1997），散文随笔集《集腋成裘集》（1994），散文游记集《耶路撒冷去来》（1976）以及剧本集《最后的分析》（1965）等。

瑞典皇家学院在给贝娄颁发诺贝尔文学奖时所发表的“声明”中，将贝娄的文学创作过程分为两个时期。第一时期以其第一部长篇小说《晃来晃去的人》为始点，第四部长篇小说《只争朝夕》为终点；第二时期则以第三部长篇小说《奥吉·马奇历险记》为始点。“声明”认为，随着贝娄的第一部长篇小说《晃来晃去的人》的问世，美国的叙事艺术开始摆脱了僵硬、雄浑的气息，预示着某种与众不同的创作风格的到来。《奥吉·马奇历险记》的创作，开创了贝娄叙事艺术的新天地。瑞典皇家学院的授奖词中对此的评价是："贝娄以他独特的风格，把丰富多彩的流浪汉小说与当代文化的精妙分析结合在一起，融合了引人入胜的冒险故事与接连出现的激烈行动和悲剧性的情节，其间还穿插着与读者之间富于哲理的、同样十分有趣的交谈。"这种风格在他以后的主要作品中都得到反复的体现。这些作品的结构显然是松散的，但正是因为这一点，使作者得以有足够的机会来刻画不同的社会阶层。

在表现手法上，贝娄善于博采众长，他既继承了西方古典文学遗产，又融合了希伯来文化的传统；既吸收了现实主义的某些长处，又运用了现代主义的某些手法，特别是意识流手法，从而使他得以摆脱时间、空间、逻辑规律乃至伦理习俗的束缚，自由地从各个不同角度窥视人物的内心世界，充分揭示人物的性格和心理，巧妙地表现出他们的种种观念和意识活动。而且，他还善于把内心活动和外在世界、把现实描绘和历史回忆巧妙地交织在一起，使我们得以同时看到主人公的内心世界和他置身的现实世界。

贝娄被认为是 20 世纪美国文坛人道主义理想的代言人。他坚信个人的尊严，坚信人有能力创造一个有意义的生存模式，以及人超越现实的特质。他避免重蹈现代主义作家为艺术表现而写作或把艺术和道德价值分割开的强烈倾向，他反对当代社会中流行的荒原观，他拒绝加入任何由愤世嫉俗或荒原人生观产生的文学运动或政治运动。本书探讨贝娄努力为他的主人公，即当代社会的人们，寻找一个合适的出路，让他走出现代城市荒原，立足于"令人信服的踏实的地面。"

贝娄意识到生活的混乱、无意义和它的短暂性，但贝娄运用他的犹太世界观来阐释他对当代世界的认识。贝娄作品中反映的道德准则也是犹太人宗教观点不可分割的一部分，贝娄相信人具有神性，尽管人在心理和情感上很脆弱，他或她是依着上帝的形象创造的，因此是宏伟的。贝娄关注"人是什么?"这个人生命题，他对这一人生命题的回答显示了一个积极、肯定和乐观的人生态度。他的观点源自犹太教信条，这也成了他小说的主题。他拒绝异化和虚无主义观点，肯定人本身固有的价值。他给予个人极高的价值肯定，认为他或她可以通过奉献他人而实现自我价值，通过丰富广阔的经历来获得人生智慧，通过精神上的自我更新作为手段服务社会，通过获得内心的秩序而实现外部世界的秩序。

贝娄坚信人的高贵品质，无法接受对人的贬低和摧毁。但贝娄也意识到自我隔离的危险。为了权衡这两点，贝娄努力在保持自我和协调他人中保持平衡。最终，他往往会回到人群中，认识到“善在真空中无法实现”。决心成为一个好人，他选择回到同胞中，因为手足情谊才使人具有人性。

本书第一章阐述了贝娄主人公的生存状况。在贝娄的小说中，城市代表着现代人的现实本身。城市是贝娄主人公们的栖息地，他们都在城市长大，适应了城市生活；他们必须认真对待城市，以坚持其自我价值，并在混乱中创造秩序。贝娄认为：“城市作为使人异化和心绪烦乱的力量，既压抑又乏味。作为围困人类的环境，城市是让人无法摆脱的混乱扭曲的目标和价值观的丛林。”他把最后的责任归咎于人类自身：正是人类创造并腐蚀了城市。因此，邪恶并非城市固有，而是源于人之本性。

贝娄的主人公们往往被城市所压抑，受困于噩梦般的城市生活，他们偶尔会突发田园式的梦想，渴望走出城市来到乡村。然而，他们从未把乡村生活当作自己的最终理想，因为他们从未在乡村找到真正的庇护，也没有得到彻底的重生。他们只能待在城市，只有通过城市中的人际交往他们才能找到秩序，保持理智，最终达成心灵的平衡。

第二章探讨了贝娄的生存意识。作为一个犹太作家，贝娄的道德观与犹太宗教观一脉相承，不可分割。他对生命持有积极肯定的态度，在小说中也阐发了同样的世界观。贝娄的小说集中展示了生命个体如何处理困境、如何做出选择的问题。他虽然会抱怨、悲叹、焦急，但他从未对未来丧失过信心。

犹太民族流亡、离散的历史深深烙印在犹太民族的记忆中，经常出现在他们的意识中。这种犹太影响赋予犹太作家（包括贝娄）强烈的生存意识。在他的小说中，读者往往会遇到这样一位主人公：他正面临着生活中的某种痛苦境遇——暂时逃避了社会、经济、离婚或者幻灭思想的困扰。然而，他却超越了有限的物质条件，在现代社会找到了立足点。

贝娄认为，现代作家必须面对并且战胜社会的黑暗。无论人世的遭遇多么痛苦，他始终觉得人生就是个奇迹。尽管贝娄也跟许多现代作家一样，塑造了一些遭受异化、饱受困扰的人物，但他也赋予了他们一种克服外部限制和压力、获得内心尊严的能力。正是通过塑造这样的主人公，贝娄显示了他对人类的强烈信心，认为他可以在现代城市的环境下立足。

第三章分析了贝娄在小说中所展示的生存策略。贝娄的文学创作生涯始于20世纪30年代末。海明威的硬汉小说在当时风靡一时。海明威主人公是行动主义者，他可以凭强力制胜，但不懂得反省，因此无法应付隐形的对手。他对生活也很厌倦，总是想着死亡，对世界表现出异化的态度。贝娄认为这种人生态度是十分有害的，因为这种态度最终会导致自杀或灭亡。

贝娄作品中的主人公往往是历史学家、教授、传记作者或诗人，他们是思考型人物，具有一定的精神追求，而且还十分关注人的内心世界。此外，这些主人公往往积极投身于社会，肩负起自己的社会责任，从而保证他们能在社会中立足。贝娄希望在小说中恢复对思想的阐述，并能对这些思想进行戏剧化的表现。贝娄履行了他作为艺术家对社会的职责，塑造了追求内在价值以挽救人类的主人公。

在他的第三部小说《奥吉·马奇历险记》中，贝娄一改最初两部小说拘谨、局限的态度，采用了一种更加开阔、包罗万象的写作风格，在小说中勾勒了一幅20世纪30年代到二战后的美国社会全貌。主人公奥吉在各种各样的经历中对自己有了更好的认识，通过形形色色的经历巩固了自己的社会地位。

贝娄始终明白低俗现实和高尚原则之间的差距，这是他身为作家必须面对和解决的问题，这个差距也使他的小说在绝望与希望之间获得了持续的张力。然而对这一点的意识并未使他彻底绝望，反倒使他更加接受了这个世界的本来模样。贝娄打算用文学创作中的高尚原则来抵御低俗现实，从而证明作家在社会中的位置。

第四章探讨了贝娄在小说创作中获得的生存启示。贝娄的主人公只有先投入社会、屈从现实，才能超越城市的丑陋、暴力、缺乏诗性和文化等弊端。人类必须超越物质束缚，听从内心世界的召唤，并且赋予内心世界一个崭新的意义。贝娄在小说中也阐述了犹太人生存的基础是紧密的家庭联系这一普遍认同的观点。此外，贝娄表明人对归属感的需求有多么强烈，当他感到自己不是所处社会的一部分时，他就会产生十分巨大的失落感。贝娄十分关注城市中建立起来的那种群体感，人们在这种群体中相互依赖获得生存。

贝娄在小说中表达了一种肯定生命的世界观，这个观点基于人性本善以及生存具有意义的基础之上，因此贝娄的主人公往往以一种犹太人的乐观视角来对待生活，最终在现实中获得了生命的精彩，而不只是发现了种种丑陋。贝娄认为作家的作用就是呈现人类的爱心，就是表达对人类通过创造力而获得生命精彩的赞赏。

本书的结尾部分是结论：贝娄是一个道德家，他认为所有的作家都应该如此。他关注人类的生存状况，对现代人持有积极肯定的态度。作为一个犹太作家，由于犹太人历史上长期的流亡离散经历，贝娄本人也具有很强的生存意识。通过小说的主人公，他探讨了现代城市中人类的生存策略。他积极履行社会责任，放弃海明威小说中主人公的悲观态度；他关注内心世界，寻求人类的真正救赎；他采取包容一切的态度，努力与现代社会达成妥协，以适应社会。贝娄向读者展示了人类生存的出路——只有通过从事和想象力有关的工作才能超越现实，就像《晃来晃去的人》中的约翰·珀尔那样战胜了现代城市。城市中人类生存的基础是紧密的家庭联系和社区的建立。只有对人类的坚定信念才是保证人类生存的根本。

Contents

Abbreviations of Bellow's

Dangling Man	*DM*
The Victim	*V*
The Adventures of Augie March	*AAM*
Henderson the Rain King	*HRK*
Mr. Sammler's Planet	*MSP*
Seize the Day	*SD*
Herzog	*H*
Humboldt's Gift	*HG*
The Dean's December	*DD*

Introduction

Bellow won his Nobel Prize "for the human understanding and subtle analysis of contemporary culture that are combined in his works". His acceptance speech further illustrates what he has been constantly experimenting on: "broader, more flexible, fuller, more coherent, more comprehensive, account of what we human beings are, who we are, and what this life is for" (Bellow, Nobel Lecture). It is just based on his deep concerns about human destiny that Bellow has been experimenting in his fictional world on the approaches towards the final accommodation of human being in the modern reality. The present dissertation tries to analyze Bellow's attempt to find a proper way for his protagonist to find a foothold in this tottering world on the basis of close reading of Bellow's fiction.

In 1924 the Bellow family moved to Chicago, a mid-west city, which provided Bellow a much more expansive life. Bellow received his education in Chicago schools. So Bellow has strong feelings towards this big city, which is taken as the setting for almost all his novels, just as he said, "I grew up there and consider myself a Chicagoan out and out" (Hyland 31). During his more than fifty-year writing career, Bellow has developed a rich and complex body of work of extensive intellectual scope.

Varied as they are in the narrative techniques employed, in the human experience explored, and in the central characters portrayed, all Bellow's novels, from *Dangling Man* (1944) to *The Dean's December* (1982), have one feature in common: each centers upon a character. These central characters share so many common preoccupations that they have become a recognizable character type, the Bellow hero. All Bellow's heroes are concerned with the following questions: What does it mean to be a man, a good man, in the modern city, which is characterized by chaos, clutter, craziness, commercialism, and cultural nihilism? How can one keep intact one's individuality in an anomic, massive, de humanized, contemporary society? By what means can one remain one's sovereign self in the technological, totalitarian, and topsy-turvy modern world?

The struggle for survival is a salient theme that runs through Saul Bellow's fiction. All Bellow's novels focus on a character who struggles for order, love, equilibrium, and the meaning of human existence to maintain his survival in the modern urban world. As a Jewish writer, growing up in a Jewish household, Bellow has a strong awareness of survival due to the long Jewish history of suffering, Bellow's rejection of wasteland view of modernism, and his responsibility as a writer. This dissertation explores the theme of survival in Bellow's major fiction to show how Bellow undertakes his mission to maintain human dignity in the wasteland of modern society.

Bellow is undoubtedly deeply concerned with the fate of Jews and affairs of the Jewish mind from the beginning of his literary life. In each of his novels, he focuses on the life of one man, who is experiencing a kind of suffering-temporary alienation from society, financial problems, divorce, and disillusionment. Nevertheless, he never gives up his faith in life, obtains the true meaning of life in suffering and finally achieves the moral sublimation. This protagonist just reflects the Jewish people who think that they are the chosen people by God. However, those chosen people suffered from all kinds of extremely misfortunes: the long history of exile and Diaspora, the expulsions in Spain in the late 1400s, the brutal pogroms by the Russian Czar in the 1880s and the German Nazi Holocaust. Jewish people endure all of these and live stubbornly in many places of the world, keeping their religion and customs. Suffering is a permanent part in Jewish people's life. As God's chosen people, and established the contract with God, Jewish people believe they are suffering for human sin. The earthly suffering is a special test of the Jewish people, is a necessary experience to obtain the true meaning of life to achieve the moral sublimation. It is viewed as a method of correcting wrongs and evils; a punishment sent by God to his chosen people to strengthen and purify them and it is also a test and a sign of greatness and strength for survival. Indebted to these Jewish experiences and belief in suffering, Bellow depicts in his novels the protagonist, who obtains the strength and illuminations for survival during his personal suffering.

Bellow has dissociated himself from the company of those writers who accept the belief that modern society is frightful, brutal, and hostile to whatever is pure in the human spirit, a wasteland and a horror. Bellow wishes to take a stand in opposition to the cultural nihilism of the twentieth century-in opposition to the tendency in Dada and in writers of the Wasteland, to denigrate human life in modern society. Bellow rejects the tradition of alienation in modern literature, and his fiction emphasizes the value of brotherhood. In "The Writer as Moralist" Bellow argues, "Either we want life to continue or we do not. . . . If we do want it to continue. . . in what form shall life be justified?" (59) To answer this question is the writer's moral function. Certainly it is the function Bellow takes on in his fiction. Bellow has taken the role of "divine literatus," and he affirms the possibilities of meaningful individual life and takes cognizance of its difficulties and costs.

IfBellow, like most modern writers, writes of burdened, alienated, impotent people, he believes that a man ". . . should have at least sufficient power to overcome ignominy and to complete his own life. His suffering, feebleness, servitude then have a meaning" (Bellow, "Distractions of a Fiction

Writer" 14). Bellow does not avoid conditions of alienation and despair; but he insists that through them, the power of the imagination "should reveal the greatness of man" (14). He insists that we are "... not gods, not beasts, but savages of a somewhat damaged but not extinguished nobility"①. It is this firm belief in not extinguished nobility of human being that encourages Bellow to depict a protagonist who finally survives in modern wasteland. So it is quite clear that survival is the important theme in Saul Bellow's fiction. The present dissertation conducts a systematical analysis of the theme of survival in Saul Bellow's fiction, which will be helpful in deeper understanding of Bellow's literary oeuvre.

Saul Bellow is one of the most important figures in the study of western literature. Bellow and his heroes are analyzed from different perspectives, such as Jewishness, feminism, transcendentalism, existentialism, humanism and so on. Books have been written on his nihilism, his comic vision, his debt to Jewish tradition, his treatment of history, his position in relation to modernism. Since the 1950s, scholars have produced over 50 criticism monographs and over 3, 000 scholarly essays②, which attest to his importance. In addition to the annual meetings, The International Saul Bellow society started *Saul Bellow Journal* in 1981 and the official website in 1988, regularly issuing the related research information. According to the statistics of Saul Bellow Society, over 90 doctorate dissertations in the world took Saul Bellow and his works as the subject of their study. Gloria Cronin and Blaine Hall's *Saul Bellow: An Annotated Bibliography* (*Second Edition*) involved 46 criticism monographs, and 1, 200 criticism papers among which 32 on *Dangling Man*, 32 on *The Victim*, 74 on *The Adventures of Augie March*, 90 on *Henderson the Rain King*, 151 on *Herzog*, 64 on *Humboldt's Gift*, 90 on *Mr. Sammler's Planet*, 73 on *The Dean's December*, 20 on *To Jerusalem and Back*, 46 on short stories, and 18 on plays.

Bellow is usually considered as a traditional writer and Mohammad Quayum regards Bellow first of all is a new transcendentalist. In *Saul Bellow and American Transcendentalism*, he focuses on Bellow's four works to reveal the similarity between Bellow and Emerson and Whitman, for all of them advocate an integration and fusion of the opposite laws governing individualism and society, and advocate of the human soul and yet they maintained faith in the union of body and soul. John Clayton's *Saul Bellow: In Defense of Man* discusses the paradox of Bellow's personal despair and romantic idealism, his Jewish humanism and Jewish guilt and self-hatred. Clayton concludes that Bellow, like his heroes, is life-affirming, love-affirming, and individual-affirming. Bellow persistently refuses to

---

① Probably by Bellow, although unsigned, in "Arias," *The Noble Savage*, IV, (Chicago: Meridian, 1960). p. 5. Keith Botsford was second editor.

② Statistics comes from Liu Wensong. *Saul Bellow's Fiction: Power Relations and Female Representation*. Xiamen: Xiamen University Press, 2004.

devalue the self even in the midst of the pressure of a vast public life. Furthermore, from Dostoevsky to Sartre and Camus, nearly all representatives of Existentialism in different periods have corresponded to Saul Bellow's different novels. Bellow's heroes are absurd and alienated characters, who also alienated themselves. They are " 'chosen people'-chosen, yet suffering; highest, yet lowest" (Clayton 36). David Galloway analyzes the absurd hero of Bellow's novels in his *The Absurd Hero in American Fiction: Updike, Styron, Bellow, and Salinger (Revised Edition)*, in which he recognizes three stages of development in an absurd hero, and the final stage is the one in which joy accompanies the absurd hero's struggle to achieve a value system, in which his experiences become a comic sequel to his tragic situation, in which victory may be questionable but defeat is not final. Additionally, Judie Newman interprets Saul Bellow from the perspective of history. In *Saul Bellow and History*, she discusses the historical elements in Bellow's five major novels, which are history, nature and freedom, such as *The Victim* is the reflection of Anti-Semitism of that age, and *Herzog* is a history of mental disorder.

In China, there are three main schools in Bellow research: Jewishness, Humanism, and Existentialism, but the research on Bellow is not as productive as that abroad. From 1979 till 2009, there appeared about 181 papers on Bellow-83 academic journal essays, 92 master's theses, 6 doctoral dissertations. Among them, there are 24 theses and 3 journal articles from the angle of Existentialism. *Herzog*, as the best-known masterpiece of Bellow, enjoys an amount of critics and researchers' appreciation. However, the attention to some of his other novels is scare.

Zhu Ping is one of the Chinese scholars doing research on Saul Bellow, with seven journal essays and one doctoral dissertation, analyzing, combing and summing up the criticism on Bellow. His papers are mainly about the morals of Saul Bellow's works. Zhu Ping claims due to Bellow's complicated themes and methods, criticism on Bellow is pluralistic during the past half century. As to categorizing Bellow into existentialist school, some scholars state it in their papers, such as Deng Hongyi's "Brief Analysis of the Source of Saul Bellow's Existentialist Thoughts in His Works". All these essays have pointed out the relationship between existentialism and Bellow.

Qiao Guoqiang, the professor of Shanghai International Studies University, published his monograph *Jewish American Literature* in 2008. His critical papers give a systematical and authoritative analysis on Saul Bellow's novels. They are "The Shift of Saul Bellow's Jewishness in *Ravelstein*", "A Tale of Two Cities: Saul Bellow's *The Dean's December*", "On Saul Bellow's *Bellarosa Connection*", "Saul Bellow, Trosky and Jewishness" published in *Foreign Literature Review* in 2012, "Two Basic Types of Characters in American Jewish Novels", "On the Subject of History in Saul Bellow's Fiction", and "American Saul Bellow Studies in the New Century", in which he gives an complete introduction to Bellow studies in America in new century. According to him, it seems that the enthusiasm for Saul Bellow in America in the new century has abated, which finds expression in fewer essays and works produced and the narrowing of scope in Bellow studies. During this period, the selection and publication of the source materials dominate the field, such as *Saul Bellow Letters* edited by Benjamin Taylor. James Atlas published *Bellow: A Biography* in 2000, and Gerhard Bach and Gloria L. Cronin edited *Small Planets: Saul Bellow and the Art of Short Fiction* in 2000, giving critical analysis on Bellow's short fiction. Additionally, Gloria L. Cronin's *A Room of His Own: in Search of the Feminine in the Novels of Saul Bellow* (2001) is the first monograph to give a systematical study on the female characters in Saul Bellow's novels.

Based on the researches scholars have conducted both in China and abroad on Saul Bellow's fiction, this dissertation aims to establish the argument that the struggle for survival is an important theme that runs through Saul Bellow's fiction. Saul Bellow is a spokesman for human right, and he is trying to find a proper way for his protagonist, that is, whole human being, to go out of wilderness of modern wasteland and get the foothold to survive in this tottering world in his literary works. The present dissertation will comb the survival theme on the basis of closing reading of Saul Bellow's fiction.

Bellow's writings epitomize the moral vision that is an integral part of the Jewish outlook. He believes in the divinity of the individual, that although a person may be psychologically and emotionally fragile, he/she is created in the image of God and is, therefore, majestic. This colossal creature has the ability to overcome obstacles that challenge or impede human endeavor and to determine its own destiny. Bellow believes in the worthiness of life which is also God-given, and that one should partake and enjoy the kaleidoscopic experiences one encounters. It is a positive approach to existence and is reflected in his novels that are generally optimistic and affirmative. Such beliefs have served as armor against the despair resulting from the blows inflicted on the Jewish community throughout history. Maurice Samuel uses the Yiddish word bitochon, meaning certainty, assurance, trust; he writes that bitochon, an "... instinctive faith in every form of life was part of the equipment of survival" (43). "What was it," Samuel asks, that made them predominantly cheerful in the midst of such discouragements as no other people has ever faced for half so long a period of time? What gave them bitochon? "Chiefly, it was their boundless love of life" (36).

Daniel Fuchs has noted that Bellow has been going against the grain of Modernism ever since he published his first novel in 1944. Although in his youth he was strongly influenced by such Modernist as Joyce, Lawrence, Eliot, Yeats, and Hemingway, as early as the 1940s Bellow began to question the validity of the Modernists' estimates of man and society. Underlying Bellow's rejection of Modernism is his strong disagreement with the Modernists' attack on the self. Bellow does not believe in the extinction or bankruptcy or disintegration of the self in the modern world, even though he realizes the lurking danger of the self. Bellow celebrates the Emersonian sovereign self, especially its virtues of independence, self-reliance, freedom, and sanctity. Like Emerson, he is convinced that each individual contains within himself the means to truth: for his high school class oration, Herzog quotes Emerson: "The main enterprise of the world, for splendor ... is the upbuilding of a man. The private life of one man shall be a more illustrious monarchy ... than any kingdom in history.... Everyman should be open to ecstasy or a divine illumination" (*H* 198—199).

All Bellow's heroes live in the modern urban environment. Bellow critics, from Alfred Kazin to Daniel Fuchs, have singled out the importance of the city in Bellow's fiction. Almost all of them agree that Bellow is one of the greatest city novelists of this century. Chester Eisinger points out that Bellow's characters "struggle in the iron-bound landscape of urban America" (Eisinger, Chester 341). Although he sees "the city as oppressive and stultifying, as a force of alie nation and distraction, and as a setting in which man is caught up in a confusing jungle of distorted aims and values" (Dutton 191—92), Bellow hero has to come to grips with the city, in order to assert his selfhood and to create order out of chaos. Bellow does not complain about the city per se as he knows that it is created by and made up of by people. Weighed down by an oppressive urban environment and haunted by a nightmarish city life, the Bellow hero occasionally entertains idyllic dreams or has pastoral impulses. Despite his ambivalence toward the city, the Bellow hero never seriously considers the country an ideal place to live in, because he never finds genuine refuge or gain complete recuperation in the countryside. To him, escape from the city into a rural environment is never a viable alternative. In general, the Bellow hero either remains in the city or eventually returns to the city after brief excursion out of the city.

From the beginning of his writing career, Bellow is concerned with the internal world of his protagonist. Instead of expressing heroism through the displays of physical courage just like Hemingway hero, Bellow's hero struggles to "salvage something of the self under the crushing pressures of urban life, of modern materialism and self-indulgence" (Hyland 18). Like Bellow, his protagonists are all involved in a struggle to assert themselves as individuals, and to know their own identity in a hostile world that does not value the "colony of the spirit" and will deprive modern man of all significant inner life.

Bellow turns away, for the most part, from ponderous introspection, Flaubertian standards, and oppressive environments which characterized his two earlier novels, in his third and fourth full-length novel *The Adventures of Augie March* and *Henderson the Rain King*. With *Augie March* Bellow introduces a new dimension into his fiction with its multifarious adventures, characters and settings, revealing Bellow's adoption of all-inclusive attitude towards reality. By attempting to achieve expansiveness and inclusiveness reflected in the novels with an abundance of characters, scenes, and details, Bellow and his protagonist reject darkness, closure and limitation and embrace cosmic optimism instead.

The Bellow hero is acutely conscious of the integrity of his self in the massive, dehumanized modern world, and realizes that he is "a child of this mass and a brother to all the rest" (*H* 248). Mysteriously, he feels that he is "always, and so powerfully, so persuasively, drawn back to human conditions" (*SP* 118). That is to say, even though his selfhood is endangered by the city en masse, the Bellow hero is at the same time greatly concerned with moral responsibility and the brotherhood of humankind, because he believes that only in society, despite its faults, can he become truly human, and he takes society for granted as the ground of his humanity. He zealously guards his own individuality lest it be engulfed by the mass, and also dismisses the vogue of alienation and isolation, which, to his mind, are almost tantamount to selfishness and irres ponsibility. On the one hand, the Bellow hero fears the oppression of modern society (as symbolized by the modern city) ; on the other, he embraces humanity as a whole because they are "his brothers and sisters" (*SD* 92).

All Bellow heroes, like their author, try to explore what it means to be human. In increasingly baffling circumstances, they try to grapple with the key questions of human existence with a view to discovering liberating and ennobling truths. Bellow persistently uses his imagination to create artistic works which are the best proof against the fragmentation, depersonalization, and pollution of the city. As an artist living in the city, Bellow always looks at the facts of the city without recoil and tries to redeem the ugliness and chaos of the city with his art. Despite the degradation, clutter, dismalness, and annoyances he sees in the modern city, Bellow knows that only by the transcending power of poetry, art, or imagination, can man save himself, the city, and the whole civilization from decay or destruction. In *Dangling Man*, John Pearl, Joseph's artist friend, contends that "the real world is the world of art and of thought. There is only one worthwhile sort of work, that of the imagination" (*DM* 90—91). Like Citrine in *Humboldt's Gift*, Bellow admits that he is "sentimental about urban ugliness" (*HG* 72), but he, like Citrine, decides to ransom "the commonplace, all this junk and wretchedness, through art and poetry, by the superior power of the soul" (*HG* 72).

Although he may be, consciously or unconsciously, telling a story about the Bellow hero in the modern city all his life, Bellow the ever-conscious artist tries hard to surpass himself each time. Accordingly, he has created better novels which adopt different perspective and portray myriad faces of humanity. Despite their common concern with human existence in modern society, Bellow's urban protagonist differs in their various efforts to explore modern society and achieve human dignity by transcending the reality.

The present dissertation tends to see how Bellow portrays his characters in their relations to the modern reality and map out the transformations, modulations, and variances in his eight novels *Dangling Man*, *The Victim*, *The Adventures of Augie March*, *Henderson the Rain King*, *Mr. Sammler's Planet*, *Herzog*,

Humboldt's Gift, and *The Dean's December*, and indicate the way Bellow tries to outdo himself by changing the character－type from one novel to another therein to show their struggle for survival in his fictional world.

Chapter One Reality for Survival

City is important to Bellow's imagination and fiction, and all of his novels are set in the city. The city comes to stand for reality for his hero and modern people. Joseph in *Dangling Man* (1944), alienated from society and from the city, staying in his six-sided box during most of his free time, wants to bolt for nature to escape the city. Nevertheless the city offers the opportunity to find individual fulfillment to be what he is to the limit for unban habitants in *The Victim* (1947). And Bellow finally works his characters slowly and painfully toward a full acceptance of the city in *Herzog* (1964). City is the society, the modern world, and the habitat of Bellow hero, who manages to retain some remnant of his humanity.

Bellow begins his writing career during 1940s, and World War Ⅱ disrupts the continuity with the past for Bellow, as well as for other American writers. The technological surge in America creates an industrial society accompanied by ugliness, boredom and spiritual trouble, which is reflected in Bellow's novels. Herzog witnesses the violence and human degradation of various human dramas that are set in the city. Mr. Sammler in *Mr. Sammler's Planet* (1970) feels humanity victimized while seeing the black pickpocket perpetrate a crime on the bus, and sees in Angela Gruner, his nephew's daughter, gathered several of the characteristics that are for him a clear indication of everything that has gone wrong with modern society. Life on the earth is so corrupt that Sammler longs to start life anew preferably on a new planet. Bellow depicts the modern world filled with images of filth, debris, noise, crime, and death to contribute to a symbolic view of the society as either a wasteland or an inferno.

Bellow depicts the environment of the city charged with fear and terror in his fiction, but he thinks it is humanity, not the environment per se, that produces the in-humanity. City is created by and made up of people. While Bellow criticizes the city as an entity, he places the final responsibility on the individual human being, who corrupt the city, and hence evil not being inherent in cities but in the nature of man.

Weighed down by an oppressive urban environment and haunted by a nightmarish city life, the Bellow hero occasionally entertains idyllic dreams or has pastoral impulses. Nevertheless, the Bellow hero never seriously considers the country an ideal place to live in, because he never finds genuine refuge or gains complete recuperation in the countryside. To him, escape from the city into a rural environment is never a viable alternative. In general, the Bellow hero either remains in the city or eventually returns to the city after brief excursions out of the city. Bellow's deep connection with the city produces in him an ambivalence toward the city and, even though he often treats the city quite negatively, he has not treated the country in wholly favorable terms. Bellow hero has to stay in the city to acts and reacts to other human beings and only through all these human interactions can he strive to find a sense of order, maintain his sanity, and achieve equanimity.

1. Modern Urban Environment with No Escape to Nature

Almost all Bellow criticism calls attention to Bellow's "urban-ness" and the importance of the city to his imagination and to his fiction. Opdahl says that Bellow uses "the city the way earlier American writers used the forest or sea: the city symbolizes the world's destructive power. Bellow shifts to an urban primitivism in which the city represents reality itself" (Opdahl, *The Novel of Saul Bellow* 63). Marcus Klein devotes many pages to Bellow's "city imagination" and concludes that Bellow, "unlike the past masters, Hemingway and Faulkner, is entirely a city writer" (Klein 47).

Bellow himself has acknowledged the influence of both the literary city and the real city upon his imagination. He claims that the three most important literary influences upon his work have been Whitman, Dreiser, and Dostoevsky, three men who are the first, in their respective genres, to acknowledge the force of the city. The actual city of Chicago is certainly at the very center of his imagination. "I grew up there and consider myself a Chicagoan, out and out" (Kunitz 73). In a *Partisan Review* interview, Bellow said it quite simply: "I don't know how I could possibly separate my knowledge of life, such as it is, from the city" (Harper 65).

Bellow's characters are urban-bred and urban-oriented. Their native habitat is "the modern metropolis-cities of elevated trains, overheated apartment, traffic, universities and museums, slums and suburbs, city parks and anonymous cafeterias, the subway rumbling underfoot and the smog polluting the upper air" (Rovit 14). Bellow is intimately acquainted with every facet of urban life and he uses the city in a variety of ways in his novels.

It is particularly fitting that Bellow's first novel *Dangling Man* (1944) be set in Chicago. Just as Chicago is first in his imagination, it is the first of his recreated literary places. Joseph, the protagonist of the first novel, spends most of his free time brooding and meditating in his Chicago room, what he calls his six-sided box. Chicago in winter, cold, raw, and gloomy, just fits Joseph's wintry mood. In a city where one has lived nearly all his life, it is not likely that he will ever be solitary, and yet, in a very real sense, Joseph is just that. The room where Joseph spends most of his time is the first and most important image related to the city motif in this novel. So claustrophobic is Joseph's single room that he feels himself imprisoned: "I, in this room, separate, distrustful, find in my purpose not an open world, but a closed, hopeless jail. My perspectives end in the wall. One room holds me" (*DM* 61). He is alienated from society, generally, and from the city in particular. Joseph's increasing social isolation constitutes the general drift of the novel. This first novel contains the germ of many of the urban-related themes that Bellow explores in different ways in every one of his novels.

> Joseph describes his growing alienation from other people. He begins with the city of Chicago, his society, and proceeds to lose increasingly personal relationships. . . . . By the middle of the novel he is alienated from his in-laws, his friends at the party, his brother, his mistress, and his wife, because Joseph is solitary except for a few minor acquaintances and an alter-ego he calls Tu As Raison Aussi-a second self with whom he quarrels alone in his room-the novel narrows from society to the self. (Opdahl 36)

What Joseph viewed from his city window is the street, the yards, the masses of snow like dirty suds. Joseph's initiation into the real world is an initiation into the urban world of filth, poverty, deformity, sickness-a repugnant mixture of city buildings, animals, and humans.

A dominant theme present in each of Bellow's novels is the question of man's position in the modern world, his relationship to the complex environment in which he finds himself in twentieth-century America. In the course of his novels Bellow gradually raises the city to a symbolic level. It becomes, as Nadon rightly suggest, representative of "society, the modern world, and a reflection of the modern human condition. It is the world dominated by technology, mechanization, and mass man" (407). As Joseph gazes out of the window at the Almstadt's home, he reflects upon the ugliness of the city, "these ruins before my eyes···. There could be no doubt that these billboards, street tracks, houses, ugly and blind, were related to interior life" (*DM* 24). Joseph's concern with the relation of "billboards, streets, tracks, houses, ugly and blind" to the" interior life" is a concern for man's place in the modern world, which the city in microcosm reflects and represents. It is a concern which every Bellow protagonist shares.

However alienated Joseph may in fact be, he refuses to subscribe to a doctrine of alienation. He thinks that he is involved with people. Whether he likes it or not, they are his generation, his society, and his world. Bellow has consistently refused to assume a posture of hopelessness, disgust, and despair with the modern urban world in which he and his characters find themselves. Escape from the city to a rural environment is never in Bellow a viable alternative. The ugliness, the "lack of the human in the too human" setting is frightening and makes man wish to "bolt for nature". Yet, Joseph says, "cities are 'natural,' too" (153). Man must come to terms with modern life, with the city itself that is now a "natural" part of modern life. The condition of the 20th century is that of modern technological urban society, and the city is its most representative manifestation.

In *The Victim* (1947), Bellow's second novel, there is further exploration of the theme of man's place in the modern world. The issue of man's adjustment to the demands of modern urban life is dramatized. Asa Leventhal, living in the midst of metropolitan New York, strives to preserve his individuality by withdrawing from social commitment. Asa is described at the beginning of the novel as "unaccommodating" and indifferent. In a city of swift and constantly changing stimuli, reserve has become a means of self-preservation. So Leventhal preserves himself, but at a high cost. He is lonely, and when his wife Mary is called away for a few weeks he suddenly becomes aware of how alone and isolated he is. The Allbee confrontation changes Leventhal. He realizes that if people shut themselves up, not wanting to be bothered, then they are like bears in a winter hole, or like a mirror wrapped in a piece of flannel. And like such a mirror you are in less danger of being broken, but you don't flash either. But you have to flash. That is the peculiar thing. Everybody wants to be what he is to the limit.

The city provides the opportunity to find fulfillment, identity, and allows freedom for great achievements. There is a pervading acknowledgment that the city is really amoral, not immoral. The person can do "hideous things" or "great things." The city offers the opportunity for both. When you don't want to take trouble with people, you find the means to turn them aside. Well, the world is a busy place.

This description of Leventhal in *The Victim* embodies the essential ingredients and strategy of the urban psychology. Human being's need for community is recognized, but there is acknowledgement of how exhausting it would be to respond in human fashion, with human feeling, to the mass of people that inhabit the urban complex. One needs a refuge, an escape into self. Yet, to be "like a bear in a winter hole" is also to be something less than human. There is something in man that has "to flash." Bellow's use of the "flash" of the mirror to represent individual fulfillment is particularly apt for the urban setting. The "flash" captures the ambiguity of the urban personality, the meretricious effect we associate with being "flashy", and the electric brilliance that is needed to distinguish oneself in the urban complex. Bellow develops the risk involved in being exposed to the city's forces, as opposed to the safe comfort of remaining wrapped in flannel.

The risks and fears of urban living, modern living, are further developed in the passage which can be called the "parable of the egg", which goes as following-There is something in people against sleep and dullness, together with the caution that leads to sleep and dullness. People are all the time taking care of themselves, laying up, storing up, watching out on this side and on that side, and at the same time running, running desperately, running as if in an egg race with the egg in a spoon. And sometimes people are fed up with the egg, sick of it, and at such a time would rather sign on with the devil and what they call the powers of darkness than run with the spoon, watching the egg, fearing for the egg. Here we have the life style of the city presented in images of caution and daring, running and balancing, protecting and threatening. In essence we have two life styles presented side by side, both of which are possible in the city: playing it safe or challenging life. Although the imagery of the city in *The Victim* is generally negative, there is little attempt to either escape it or deny the city.

Bellow skillfully uses the city as means of creating an atmosphere appropriate to the story. The city scene in *The Victim* is realistic, and oppressive. It is oppressive in its style of life, its rushed pace, its crowded conditions that result in men living like strangers. And it is oppressive in its physical details. On the first page of the novel, Leventhal "alighted hurriedly from a Third Avenue train. In his preoccupation he had almost gone past his stop" (*V* 3). The black door of the ancient car was already sliding shut, and Leventhal struggled with it, forcing it back with his shoulder, and squeezed through. He is left on the station "breathing hard" and "cursing." The sights, sounds, and movements of the city are harsh and strident.

As real as the city as place is, there is in the imagery an element of strangeness that corresponds with the nature of Leventhal's experiences and so lends support to the atmosphere of the story. The opening paragraph of the novel establishes the tone of events as taking place in the heart of New York City: "On some nights New York is as hot as Bangkok" (3). The comparison of the heat of New York with the heat of Bangkok sets a perfect tone for the events that follow. They are as strange as if they had taken place in strange lands among "barbaric fellahin." Bellow stresses the "foreign" several times in the course of the novel. Later in the novel he again compares the New York heat to that in foreign ports-The sun is surely no hotter in any Singapore or Surabaya, on the chains, plates, and rails of ships anchored there. Leventhal experiences feelings of bewilderment, confusion, and disbelief at the events that he is experiencing. By introducing Leventhal in conjunction with the suffocating heat, Bellow makes the atmosphere a reflector of Leventhal's interior suffocation.

Like *The Victim*, *Seize the Day* (1956) also has New York City as its setting, in this case the neighborhood of the upper West Side. The protagonist, middle-aged Tommy Wilhelm, lives on the twenty-third floor of a New York apartment hotel, surrounded by retired people with whom he has little in common, and finds himself in an extreme situation as the novel opens. He is out of a job, and he is separated from his wife Margaret who has been making increasingly heavy financial demands which Wilhelm cannot meet. His father, a retired doctor, also lives at the same hotel, but there is little communion between them. He is denied either emotional or financial aid from his father. He has invested and is about to lose his last seven hundred dollars on market speculation in partnership with Tamkin. He feels that his financial obligations are crushing and destroying him. He senses the emptiness of the life that he is leading and yearns for "some useful advice" that would "transform his life" (*SD* 72). In the last scene of the book, as Wilhelm stands and weeps over the body of a stranger, he is indeed "at the end of his tether," "threatened by the void." Although the most obvious occasion that triggers off the chaotic events of the day is Wilhelm's need for money, the city itself plays again a major role in embodying the elements of the human condition which victimize Wilhelm at every turn.

Wilhelm's personal misfortunes are intensified by the pressures of that giant pressure cooker, New York City. The noise of the city keeps him awake at night, and every little thing is a strain. He is reluctant to use his car lest he lose his parking place. The pace of life is too fast in the city. There is too much push here for people. The upper West-Side New York scene is brilliantly described from the huge and gloomy hotels to the barbershops, the steam baths for the tired, flabby businessman, and the local branch of the stock market which is the nerve center of this overdressed and overfed segment of middle class urban society.

The dominant value in Wilhelm's world and the creator of many of the pressures of urban life is money. Tamkin warns him against catching "the money fever," the type of activity filled with hostile feeling and lust, as Tommy Wilhelm well knows. Everyone with whom Wilhelm comes into contact has the "fever": Dr, Adler (his father), Perls, Rappaport, even Tamkin himself. Wilhelm thinks how they love money. They adore money! It is getting so that people are feeble-minded about everything except money. As Wilhelm anxiously stands in the brokerage office watching the stock market ticker tape as it swallows his last seven hundred dollars, he resolves to leave New York. He has to get out the city. No, first he has to pull out his money. Wilhelm is involved in three relationships from which he cannot disentangle himself, with his father, Dr. Adler, with his wife, Margaret, and with Tamkin. All three relationships are rooted in money. Wilhelm cannot make himself and his needs understood to those who recognize only one need: money. The lines of communication between people are broken. You have to translate and translate, explain and explain, back and forth, and it is the punishment of hell itself not to understand or be understood. You have to talk with yourself in the daytime and reason with yourself at night. Who else is there to talk to in a city like New York?

New York City is an alien urban world to Wilhelm. Like the protagonists in Bellow's first two novels, Wilhelm can not play the urban game, or at least certainly not well. Unlike Augie, however, who can operate in the urban complex, Wilhelm is much more like Leventha-lonely, victimized, and defeated, in recoil. New York seems to have become impossible for him to deal with. It is that he is not used to New York any more. For a native, that's very peculiar. "It was never so noisy at night as now, and every little thing is strain" (33).

Like Augie, however, Wilhelm is surrounded by Machiavellian, urban types who use him only to satisfy their own emotional or financial needs. The manager of a brokerage to whom Wilhelm turns for advice is wise in city ways, ways in which Wilhelm is not. The broker tells him that he cannot stay outside of the system if he is going to succeed. One must take a specimen risk so that he feels the process, the money-flow, the whole complex. To know how it feels to be a seaweed he has to get in the water. In a very short time he will take out a hundred-per-cent profit. It is, of course, Wilhelm's fear of becoming a piece of seaweed in the urban sea that prevents his becoming a success. This fear of succumbing to the values of the city, in this case, money-values, is an old city fear that most of Bellow's protagonists share.

Seize the Day, says I. Howe, is "a masterpiece, a work in which many of the pressures and problems that seem unique to contemporary life are fiercely dramatized" (Howe, *Classics of Modern Fiction* 457). Bellow focuses in this novel on the materialism that pervades the modern world, using the city as a symbol of modern life. Geismar recognizes this when he says that "this whole New York City scene is of course an ironic parody of American society as a whole" (19).

In contrast to the well-wrought, Flaubert-like construction of *Dangling Man* and *The Victim*, *The Adventures of Augie March* (1953) is very loose and episodic, what most critics identify as picaresque. This shift from a tight form to a much looser, freer form indicates a shift, as well, in Bellow's attitude toward the city. It seems almost as if Bellow wants to make amends for his earlier treatment of the city as a fearful, suspicious place by writing a novel that celebrates the city, exalts its great variety and energy, and praises the freedom which it engenders. "I am an American, Chicago born-Chicago, that somber city and go at things as I have taught myself, free-style, and will make the record in my own way ..." (*AM* 3); thus speaks the hero of *The Adventures of Augie March*. This announcement not only reveals Augie's larky and independent character but pinpoints his tie to his native city- "Chicago, that somber city." Augie, as the main character, from the first sentence to mid-book accepts the city uncritically, allows himself to come under its aegis, and submits to the many forces and personalities that the city offers. As Augie says early in the novel, "All the influences were lined up waiting for me. I was born, and there they were to form me, which is why I tell you more of them than of myself" (*AM* 46).

More than half of this novel deals with Augie's adventures in that somber city, Chicago. Bellow has Augie experience the infinite variety of the city. His picaresque adventures take him to almost every corner of the city and he experiences the different walks of like, from the well-to-do to the down-and-out. He is acquainted with a wide variety of urban personalities, from the city's intellectuals to its criminal. He tries his hand at many different types of jobs. To name just a few: delivering newspapers, selling papers, magazines, and candy at a newsstand, working in a department store, delivering flowers, peddling rubberized paint, and being a union organizer. He is quite at home anywhere and everywhere in his city. He touches all sides, and nobody knows where he belongs. Augie drifts from job to job, from experience to experience, a picaro on the loose. The city offers a multiplicity of roles and jobs and Augie drifts through them all. He learns from his experiences, chameleon-like, adjusts himself to each new set of circumstances and gets an invaluable democratic education in Chicago. With its sprawling backdrop and variegated people, the city, rather than being a bleak, smothering, naturalistic environment, turns out to be an open sphere for Ague's adventures. Throughout much of the novel, Augie remains youthful, innocent, optimistic, dynamic, and adventurous and is able to accept his city as it is, including its squalor, vice, and shortcomings.

The fact that the novel presents an atmosphere of endless possibility and countless opportunities has led most critics to interpret the novel as Bellow's eloquent statement of affirmation. I. Howe writes that with Augie March Bellow "made a sharp turn, casting aside the urban contemplativeness and melancholy of his previous work, and deciding to regard American life as wonderfully 'open', a great big shapeless orange bursting with the juices of vitality" ("Odysseus, Flat on His Back"). Bellow affirms the urban world by celebrating the color and vitality of many different scenes and characters. Bellow's brilliance in creating living, unforgettable characters is never more evident than in *The Adventures of Augie March*, where dozens of characters make quick entrances and exits and impress the reader with their unique qualities, their life-like idiosyncrasies, and their zest for life. Jimmy Klein's family buys everything on the installment plan, and Jimmy and Augie are sent around the city to make payments on the phonograph, on the Singer machine, on the mohair suite with pellet-filled ashtrays that couldn't be overturned and etc. The interests and life-style of the Kleins are captured in this brief description. Bellow uses his intimate knowledge of the city to breathe life into each of his characters and to create characters with uniquely urban characteristics.

Augie's ultimate aim is to seek a worthwhile, higher, and independent fate, and finally he discovers the "axial lines with respect to which you must be straight" (*AM* 454). He doesn't want to be determined by his environment or to become what other people want to make of him. Nevertheless, Augie is still on the way to learn to live by them. The protagonists of Bellow's next novels go on searching for the "axial lines" of their lives, but only the aging Mr. Sammler in Bellow's *Mr. Sammler's Planet*, seems to have found them.

Augie sometimes laments the non-existence of an Arcadian life to which all youth are entitled before facing up to the realities of maturity. This universal experience of idyllic childhood has been denied him in Chicago. Augie has been in "deep city aims," and nevertheless he always dreams that there are "silken, unconscious, nature-painted times, like the pastoral of Sicilian shepherd lovers, or lions you can chase away with stones and golden snakes who scatter from their knots into the fissures of Eryx" (89). Augie doesn't have shepherd – Sicily and no free-hand nature painting, but the deep city vexation helps to deepen Augie's personality and he has discovered his own identity.

Marcus Klein, who states that Bellow "is entirely a city writer", as mentioned earlier, says that *Henderson The Rain King* (1959) "takes place mostly in Africa, but not in the green hills of Africa. It is an Africa teeming with people and political intrigue and with furniture, an Africa urbanized" (Klein 47). Klein points out that "the city's steaming pavement becomes the strange, obscurely threatening 'calcareous' rocks of King Dahfu's country. The heat of the city becomes the boiling African sun" (49). Henderson

> puts forth effort to escape, but the city stays with himnonetheless. In Africa he talks city talk. . . . He thinks, in Africa, in city metaphors and of city events. The city maintains its pressure, and alive within his other speculations is the city idea of other people, nameless, faceless, billions of other people with whom no communication is possible. (49—50)

Henderson can not escape the city too. Bellow just has Henderson make this exploration of the culturally primitive past to still forever the haunting, nostalgic appeal of the return to the simple life. Cultural primitivism is out, however. Africa is just as culturally complex as twentieth century urbanized life. Our mythic idealization of the past is false. A pure state of nature never existed. Or, if it did, it is more brutalizing than the worst of modern society. Henderson, never really able to feel very much at home with Dahfu's pet, tame lion, and these experiences seem at first hand the authentic just beast - There is a snarl and Henderson looks down from the straw perch into the big, angry, and hair -framed face of the lion. It is all wrinkled, contracted and within those wrinkles is the darkness of murder. The lips of the lion "were drawn away from the gums, and the breath of the animal came over me, hot as oblivion, raw as blood. I started to speak aloud. I said, 'Oh my God, whatever you think of me, let me not fall under this butcher shop'" (*HRK* 271). Nevertheless, Dahfu falls under this "butcher shop," is castrated, and dies of his wounds. Such is the original natural world.

After Henderson's experience with the lion, he turns down the opportunity to be king and eagerly returns to the United States. He says to a consular member, "Yes, I saw a few things in the interior. Yes, I did. I have had a look into some of the fundamentals" (293). Armed with this vision of "the heart of the matter," Henderson is last seen cavorting around the America-bound aircraft as it refuels in Newfoundland- "running, leaping, leaping, pounding, and tingling over the pure white lining of the gray Arctic silence" (301) -refreshed and restored, ready to take up the burden of modern life.

Mr. Sammler in *Mr. Sammler's Planet* (1970) also lives in New York. In its physical aspects the city is appallingly ugly. Public phone booths serve as public urinals. The public paths are invariably dog-fouled. From his window

Sammler sees "a soft asphalt belly rising, in which lay steaming sewer navels" (*MSP* 9). The city is ugly. Even nature is despoiled. Although Mr. Sammler is surrounded by the same violent city as are all of Bellow's other characters, he basically remains untouched by it. Sammler begins the novel as a fully developed character, a man in his seventies, who does not develop or change in the course of the novel. Sammler is a man with a past, a past that is always with him and that is a constant reminder of death's omnipotence. Sammler, having once stood at death's door, is extremely conscious of time and of the importance of making each moment count. The unpleasant details of city life are philosophically contemplated by Sammler. They affect him, but never have the same impact on him that they have on most of Bellow's characters like Leventhal or Wilhelm. Age and experience have given him the "privileges of remoteness." Sammler is "a meditative island on the island of Manhattan" (75). He understands that if one wishes to be happy, one mustn't contradict one's time: "Just don't contradict it, that's all. Unless you happened to be a Sammler and felt that the place of honor was outside" (73).

Bellow uses the particular urban sights and scenes as opportunities for Sammler to speculate and philosophize on various aspects of modern life. Each of Sammler's city experiences is another opportunity for meditative reflection by the "meditative island on the island of Manhattan." Sammler's ride through the streets of the city leads him to reflect that "truth was now slummier and called for litter in the setting" (279). He deplores the "modern individuality boom" in which every individual insists on the gratification of his every desire: "A full bill of demand and complaint was therefore presented by each individual. Non-negotiable. Recognizing no scarcity of supply in any human department" (34). Watching the "human types" on Broadway while bound for the bus- "the barbarian, redskin, or Fiji, the dandy, the buffalo hunter, the desperado, the queer, the sexual fantasist, the squaw; bluestocking, princess, poet, painter, prospector, troubadour, guerilla, Che Guevara, the new Thomas a Becket"-affords Sammler opportunity for a lengthy contemplation of the madness that he feels characterizes the age. After experiencing the horrible Holocaust during World War II, Sammler witnesses the madness of the present age, and he feels that civilization is again threatened by total collapses: "you could smell decay" (33).

In reflecting upon the corruption of the city, Bellow regards the city once again, as in *Seize the Day*, as a symbol of modern civilization. He sees "the suicidal impulses of civilization pushing strongly" (33); the "emancipated masses of New York, Amsterdam, London" were adopting "the sexual ways of the seraglio and of the Congo bush" (32). Thus it is not the city per se which Bellow is criticizing but rather contemporary life. New York makes one thing about the collapse of civilization, about Sodom and Gomorrah, the end of the world. The end wouldn't come as surprise. Many people already bank on it. And Sammler thinks that he doesn't know whether humankind is really all that much worse. . . . He is not sure that that is the worst of all times. But it is in the air that things are falling apart.

Despite Bellow's pessimism about modern civilization, he remains affirmative about the possibility for transcending the situation: "There is still such a thing as man . . . . There are still human qualities" (305). Modern life is mad and chaotic; "a human being, valuing himself for the right reasons, has and restores order, authority" (45). There is a bond between man and his fellow man that must be continually asserted. Man, says Bellow time and time again in his novels, must realize himself within and in spite of the urban world in which he finds himself.

Herzog (1964) begins with the protagonist Herzog, a city-bred Jewish intellectual, a successful academician and letter writer to the world, in retreat from the events of the previous two months, rusticating in his big, dilapidated house in the Berkshires. Eating packaged bread, beans from the can, and American cheese, sleeping on a bare mattress, Herzog's return to the pastoral life is neither triumphant nor idyllic. It is in this setting, however, in recoil from chaotic events, that Herzog reexamines his life. Most of the book is a recounting of the mixed events, ideas, and notions of Herzog's past life, but most of the present action of the work recreates the by-now familiar world of the big city. As Tanner says:

> …we can really feel the background against which the modern mind works, and has to work. Herzog feels part of the New York mess, and indeed there seems to be at times an intimate connection between the city and his thoughts. Perhaps the teeming confusion of its chaos agitates his mind into a state of overexcited emulation – the city triggering off the spasms of unrelated thoughts, just as the thoughts sometimes grind to an inconclusive halt in the congestion of the city streets. (Tanner 92)

Herzog has, indeed, not escaped the city in the Berkshires. The city has become internalized, has become part of his very being: in short, reality.

In *Herzog*, Bellow confronts the full challenge his city world offers to a man of both uncommon sense and sensibility. Like Tommy Wilhelm, Herzog suffers all the decisions gone awry that have brought him to sorry middle age. He, too, is a separated husband and an unsuccessful father, suffering distraction, confusion and humiliation at the hands of more worldly, more cynical friends and counselors. Caught in the predicament, Herzog feels an urgent need to explain. In a frenzy, he is writing letters, most of them mental and almost all of them unmailed, to all sorts of people, living and dead. During this period of near delirium and chaotic turbulence, Herzog relives his past selves as a father, son, husband, friend, lover, scholar, intellectual, college professor, and citizen. Finally he comes to terms with life and reaches a state of rest.

During Herzog's quest for order and sanity, the city plays a very significant role. Although the novel begins and ends in a rural setting, it is to the city that Herzog's life, physical and emotional, is intimately attached. The key scenes of the novel-those leading to his direct confrontation with reality and eventually bringing about his recovery-take place in the city. Three cities figure prominently in Herzog's life: the Montreal of his childhood, the Chicago of his extended adolescence and manhood, and the New York of "his creative crises, liberating deliverances and destructive undergoings and apprehension" (Marcus 234). Herzog's general response to the city is not essentially different from his predecessors'. Like Joseph, Leventhal and Wilhelm, he feels threatened by the urban forces. His lonely fellow New Yorkers are no less desperate than those in *Seize the Day*. On the streets or in public places he is overwhelmed by the city's vastness, populousness, interminability, anonymousness, and terrifying madness. Despite all the negative aspects of city, Herzog identifies himself with the city and he does in fact feel at home. The city in *Herzog* is not only the main setting but a decisive force in the protagonist's life, forming his sensibility, affecting his psyche, prompting his thought-chains and presenting naked reality to him.

At the end of the novel, Herzog's mistress Ramona reaches him by phone in his Berkshire retreat and he cannot resist her offer to visit him. The last few pages of the novel finds Herzog tidying up the house at Ludeyville, picking wild flowers for the candle -laid table, and chilling the wine in the spring-all in anticipation of the restorative powers of Ramona, who is, to some degree, the symbol of the city, not those of the surrounding countryside.

Herzog's nostalgia for the American landscape is, perhaps like his interest in Romanticism and Christianity, an intellectually acquired taste. His most deep-seated response is still for the slum street of his childhood. It was in the street that he came first to know reality. And it is in the street, the city street, that one feels Herzog's destiny lies. As he says, "Out in the streets, in American society, that was where he did his time" (*H* 369).

Herzog's acknowledgment of both the street and American society indicates the distance that Bellow has traveled in his fiction from his first novel, *Dangling Man*. To get Joseph, Bellow's first protagonist, out of his six-sided box and deposited in the street of American society seems like a most modest accomplishment. Given the intensity of Joseph's sense of alienation and the circling, in-and-out, engagement-disengagement strategy which subsequent Bellow heroes employ in their relationships with society in general and the city in particular, the distance actually travelled is great indeed. Bellow has, in the course of his novels, worked his characters slowly and painfully toward an acceptance of the city.

Bellow's use of the city is not static. Just as Bellow's central characters change from the early victim-type heroes to the later wise-observer heroes, the city in Bellow's oeuvre also undergoes transmutations. It changes from the early indifferent, anomie – ridden, unaccountable, and hostile environment for such protagonists as Joseph, Leventhal, and Wilhelm to the epitomization of modern society such wise observers as Sammler and Herzog perceive. The protagonists are threatened by its enormous evil forces and vicious social problems, but Herzog, who believes that brotherhood is what makes a man human, thinks that the modern city-humanity in microcosm-is where he fees at home and attached.

Bellow is the only writer who raises the city to the level of symbol. The city comes to stand for reality itself. In addition, it is also society, the modern world, and a reflection of the modern human condition. It is the world dominated by technology, mechanization, and mass man. Bellow is also the only author who uses the city as a setting in every novel, including *Henderson the Rain King*. Bellow's urban hero has to come to grips with the city in order to assert his selfhood and to create order out of chaos. Every Bellow hero fights the city. Although his heroes never win the battle, neither do they lose. They always manage to retain, battered and shredded perhaps, some remnant of their humanity. Man must come to terms with modern life, with the city itself that is a "natural" part of modern life.

Weighed down by an oppressive urban environment and haunted by a nightmarish city life, the Bellow hero occasionally entertains idyllic dreams or has pastoral impulses. Wieting has pointed out that the pastoral is a cohesive motif in Bellow's fiction: "in each of the novels one finds a corresponding pastoral element, an excursion, either physical or mental, to an environment that is free from the clutter and chaos of the protagonist's urban existence" (359). On the other hand, David Galloway writes that Bellow heroes "must work out their destinies against the brutalized cityscape; they have no recourse to the fishing trips, the rural idylls, or the pastoral dreams of the Anglo – Saxon imagination" (Galloway, *The Absurd Hero in American Fiction* 21).

Despite his ambivalence toward the city, the Bellow hero never seriously considers the country an ideal place to live in, because he never finds genuine refuge or gains complete recuperation in the countryside. To him, escape from the city into a rural environment is never a viable alternative. In general, the Bellow hero either remains in the city or eventually returns to the city after brief excursions out of the city. It is in the urban setting that the Bellow hero acts and reacts to other human beings and it is through all these human interactions that he strives to find a sense of order, maintain his sanity, or achieve equanimity.

The Bellow hero's attitude toward the city and the country reflects the author's own attitude. Bellow himself is both attracted to and repelled by the city. He does not like the city's chaos, madness, crime, ugliness, and philis tinism, and he thinks it is good to go to the countryside to get fresher air. How ever, he does not believe that escape from the city can solve modern man's problems.

Faced with adverse urban environment, the traditional response to it is denied: the escape from the city into nature, or as Joseph puts it more forcefully, "we bolt for 'Nature'." However, country life never provides a viable alternative to the urban-oriented Bellow hero, who remains in the city or returns to the city after brief excursions away.

In *The Victim* Bellow moves further toward a rejection of the efficacy of nature as a means of palliating the harsher aspects of the city environment. The frequent park scenes serve not as a refreshing interlude for either Asa or the reader from the oppressive, debilitating effects of the city, but rather they reveal with increasing intensity the intrusion of people upon nature. The first park scene, early in the novel, is composed primarily of negative imagery-Leventhal passes through a small park where the double circle of benches is jammed. There are lines before each drinking fountain, the warm water limping and jetting into the stone basins. On all sides of the green square, the traffic of cars and cabs whips endlessly, and the cumbersome busses crawls groaning, and steering down from the tall blue oblong of light at the summit of the street through a bluish pallor. In the bushy, tree-grown corners, children play and scream, and a revivalist band sings and drums and trumpets on one of the sidewalks.

Near the end of the novel Asa again seeks relief in the park-the crowd is extraordinarily thick that night. The same band of revivalists is on the curb. A woman is singing. Her voice and the accompaniment of the organ are very dim, only a few notes emerging from the immense, interminable mutter. . . . The trees are swathed in stifling dust, and the stars are faint and sparse through the pall. The benches form a dense, double human wheel; the paths are thronged….

The parks with their green suggestive of a country-like scene, fail to give the solace and coolness Leventhal needs, because they are usually as densely packed with humanity and as full of hustle and bustle as the city streets. Furthermore, his visits to the parks are often thwarted or affected by Allbee's ubiquitous apparition-like intrusion. Instead of giving Leventhal the soothing effect normally associated with the countryside, the parks, like other physical constructs of the city, oppress Leventhal. Perhaps his job as a trade magazine editor confines him to the city and offers him no alternative. Perhaps his urban Jewish background has educated him to be at home in the city. In any case, Leventhal never entertains the dream of leaving the city for the country.

Augie also expresses preference for nature in the novel: "In the world of nature you can trust but in the world of artifacts you must beware" (*AM* 467). Being in nature brings the same kinds of thoughts and words that occurred to Emerson, Thoreau and Whitman-Augie soaked in the heavy nourishing air and the befriending atmosphere like rich life-cake, the kind that encourages love and brings on a mild pain of emotions; a state that lets people rest in their own specific gravity, and where they are not a subject matter but sit in their own nature, tasting original tastes as good as the first man, and are outside of the busy human tamper, left free even of their own habits.

Meanwhile the clouds, birds, cattle in the water, things, stay at their distance, and there is no need to herd, account for, hold them in the head, but it is enough to be among them, released on the ground as they are in their brook or in their air... How is it that human beings will submit to the gyps of previous history while mere creatures look with their original eyes? At the middle part of the book, disillusioned and exhausted by the city, Augie also makes his "bolt for nature." With Thea, a wealthy, married, young society type who wants to go to Mexico to get a divorce and to hunt lizards with an eagle, Augie makes his escape to the jungles of Mexico. On their way to Mexico, Augie does experience some moments of union with nature. For example, while camping near the Mississippi, which Augie is eager to see, Augie is as terribly excited as Huck Finn and he experiences an Emersonian moment. They lay beside a huge tree. "Such a centuries' old trunk still had such small-change of foliage .... And soon you distinguished the sound of the leaves, moved by the air, from the insects' sound" (326).

At moment such as this Augie regrets having grown up in the Chicago of junkyards and El pillars. However, Mexico does not only provide Augie with idyllic escape or arcadian pleasure. Augie tries to adjust to the world of snakes, insects, and lizards, but finds himself instead "hanging around the dizzy town where things were even more dangerous" (*AM* 416). The Mexican scenes-kaleidoscopes of fiestas, bands, Cossack chorus, Indian circus, card playing, and drinking-give Augie neither solace nor comfort. Finally his love affair with Thea also sours. Mexico does not provide Augie with an alternative to his city life in Chicago.

After knocking around for some time, Augie longs to have a place of rest and to be still. He dreams of establishing an academy for foster children in some Walden-like place. He aims to get himself a piece of property and settle down on it. He would like get married and set up a kind of home, and then he would get his mother out of the blind-home and his brother George up from the South. He carries his dream of the foster-home academy into his marriage with Stella, a beautiful aspiring movie actress with a very obscure past. However, Augie's and Stella's private vision of what the reality of that dream will actually be is quite different for each of them. What Augie has in mind is the private green place like one of those Walden or Innisfree Wattle jobs under the kind sun, surrounded by velvet woods and bright gardens and Elysium lawns sown with Lincoln Park grass···. But he already knows what Stella thinks the academy would look like-a beaten-up frame house of dead-drunk jerry-builders under dusty laborious trees, laundry boiling in the yard, pinched chickens of misfortune, rioting kids, his blind mother wearing his old shoes and George cobblering, him with a crate of bees in the woods.

Augie wishes to withdraw to a pastoral setting, work the land, raise children, and stay away from the noise of the city, but these ideals never materialize. The nostalgic impulse for the pastoral life is rejected as preposterous in the twentieth century world. At the end of the novel, Augie is far removed from the pastoral world of the nineteenth century. Augie is at home in the city, and he is the city's child, its own product. Augie, who is literally fatherless, is fathered by the city. Augie's coming to know the city-father is an urbanized version of the old mythic quest for identity. Augie's dislike of the mechanized, highly technological life in the cities does not mean that he will actually choose a life close to nature. Chicago, with all the implications it has for him, is after all, the place he always goes back to. At the end, after the war, we will find him living not in any pastoral retreat, as he had dreamed of, but in Paris, where he has moved with Stella (his argument being that Paris, after all, is the City of Man).

Henderson the Rain King, Bellow's only major work without a dominant city setting, presents the adventures of a representative modern man who attempts in the middle of the twentieth century that "bolt for 'Nature'" at the heart of Africa. For the first time, Bellow does not introduce as the protagonist of a major novel a city man and a city Jew. Instead, he introduces Eugene Henderson, a "millionaire wanderer and wayfarer" and "heir to a great estate" (*HRK* 22). For the first time, Bellow does not present as the setting of a major novel either of the great cities of Chicago or New York. Instead, he presents Africa. Bellow imagines a protagonist with the bulk of a football player and the color of a gipsy, finding when he thinks of his "condition at the age of fifty-five... all is grief" (*HRK* 7). He is despised and rejected, a man of sorrows and acquainted with grief. He is driven into the heart of Africa by a ceaseless voice in his heart that says "I want, I want". He senses that in Africa he might find things "which were of old", and which might make his body and spirit whole again.

Together with a single native guide he travels on foot into the interior of Africa. The first tribe of Africans, the Arnewi, he encounters in the heart of Africa has a serious problem: their cows are starving because some irrational custom forbids them to water the beasts from a cistern abounding with frogs that have mysteriously appeared from nowhere. With his superior technological know how he insists on helping them to solve theirs. Henderson, then, is only too eager to help the Arnewi. But the explosion of the bomb he constructs from rifle shells and his flashlight, not only destroys the frogs but the cistern as well, depriving the Arnewi of their only water supply. Henderson's contact with the primitive Arnewi has resulted in disaster.

Mortified and heart-broken he decides to move on still deeper into dark Africa. Next, he goes to the even more primitive tribe of the savage Wariri. Received with hostility by these Children of Darkness and virtually imprisoned by them, he is even forced to dispose of a dead body placed by the Wariri in the hut assigned to him. Invited to attend the rainmaking-ceremony, Henderson watches the king Dahfu of Wariri perform in a contest of skull-throwing, in which the contestants are to pay the ultimate price if one of them dropped the skull. After moving the statue of the goddess Mummah for the Wariri, the only condition to be fulfilled to make it rain, Henderson is made, inadvertently, the Sungo. He is driven round, naked, by a bunch of huge black women as their new Rain King, flung into the muddy cattle pond, hauled out, driven on again, yelling, feet pounding, and stamping out. During the final episode of Henderson's stay in the African wilderness, the huge lion, mistakenly assumed to be Gmilo, the incarnation of king Dahfu's father, is finally caught. All Henderson is able to hear in the snarling of the ferocious animal is the voice of death, a voice which "was like a blow at the back of his head", and truth to Henderson always comes in blows. This time it is Dahfu's death. Henderson finally finds himself only involved in the equally complex, equally sinister tribal communities of Africa.

After his adventures in Africa, Henderson returns. What he brings back from his exploration of the natural environment is apparently his acknowledgment that society is inescapable, and that his true home is, after all, society. There is no question whether he is prepared to take up, once again, the common life. The answer is explicit in his commitment to begin his education as a medical doctor. Examining Henderson's quest to "burst the spirit's sleep" (67), Bellow confirms that he cannot "possibly separate my knowledge of life, such as it is, from the city" (Harper, "The Art of Fiction" 190).

Tommy Wilhelm tries to flee urbanism by an attachment to the land which is made via his house in Roxbury that is magnified into a pastoral symbol. The need to escape from the city is always acknowledged in urban environment, but Wilhelm recognizes all escape as impossible. He tells his father that he "can't take city life any more, and I miss the country. There's too much push here for me. It works me up too much" (*SD* 44). Later in the novel he complains that "things were too complex, but they might be reduced to simplicity again. Recovery was impossible. First he had to get out of the city. No, first he had to pull out his money. . . . " (78) And, of course, he can not get his money out of the city.

He often recalls his simpler life as a salesman, living in a two room apartment in Roxbury-two rooms in a large house with a small porch and garden. On mornings of leisure, in late spring weather, he used to sit expanded in a wicker chair with the sunlight pouring through the weave, and sunlight through the slug-eaten holes of the young hollyhocks and as deeply as the grass allowed into small flowers. This peace (he forgets that that time has had its troubles, too), this peace is gone. It must not have belonged to him, really, for to be here in New York with his old father is more genuinely like his life. His father is a "city boy" and Wilhelm unconsciously recognizes that the recognition of his father and the city are related acts. His father does tell Wilhelm to get out if he finds city hard on him, and Wilhelm says he will "as soon as I can make the right connection" (44). Wilhelm makes only the wrong connections, however.

A more covert rejection of the escape to the country is the fact that in one way the country is what seals Wilhelm's doom: he loses the last of his money in the commodities market, on lard and rye. In addition, the city has corrupted the country, transformed the peaceful family farm into a part of the complex "chicken industry." Wilhelm recalls the glimpse he has had of the chicken industry. On the road, he frequently passed chicken farms. Those big, rambling, wooden buildings stand out in the neglected fields. They are like prisons. The lights burn all night in them to cheat the poor hens into laying. Then comes the slaughter. Pile all the coops of the slaughtered on end, and in one week they'd go higher than Mount Everest or Mount Serenity. The blood can fill the Gulf of Mexico. The chicken shit, acid, burns the earth. Cut off from a return to nature, broke, and denied by both his father and his former wife, Wilhelm discovers at last one truth-suffering, the human condition.

Even though there is no pastoral retreat for Sammler in *Mr. Sammler's Planet*, there are discussions of Wells' utopianism and moon colonies, another version of the pastoral. This theme is brought forth by his daughter Shula's theft of Dr. Lal's manuscripts. Sammler is no longer interested in the Bloomsbury group, but his eccentric daughter Shula is still obsessed with Sammler's plan to write a memoir about H. G. Wells. She steals Dr. Lal's *The Future of the Moon* for the sake of her father's project and thus brings Dr. Lal and Mr. Sammler together for a long dialogue on the Bloomsbury group and their conception of Utopia, the necessity of colonizing the moon, technology, and the problems of the world.

For Dr. Lal, the journey into space is the ultimate adventure. Sammler's answer to Lal is, "As an engineering project, colonizing outer space, except for the curiosity, the ingenuity of the thing, is of little interest to me" (*MSP* 237). Sammler wonders: should man concentrate his activities upon improving life on this earth, or is this earth so corrupt that it is unredeemable and that he must seek to start life anew preferably on a new planet? To Sammler, it is a nihilistic attempt to escape the human condition on the earth.

Herzog's first wife Daisy is the embodiment of country nostalgia, and he can still reconstruct his first glimpse of her on the carbolic-reeking platform of a Chicago streetcar. "From her bare neck and shoulders he inhaled the fragrance of summer apples. Daisy was a country girl, a Buckeye who grew up near Zanesville" (*H* 157—158). It is because of Daisy and his desire to write a definitive work on Romanticism and Christianity that he ventures into the Connecticut countryside, where he almost succumbs to the climate and the stultifying natives. When the local minister tries to convert Herzog, Herzog fears for his sanity and makes his escape.

With Madeleine, his second wife, Herzog makes his second attempt to live in the country. "For a big-city Jew he was peculiarly devoted to country living" (148). But taking his new bride to Ludeyville is one of Herzog's "biggest mistakes" and he admits that he was "stupid-a blockhead" (53). Although he ostensibly goes to the Berkshires to continue his scholarly work on the Romantic spirit, he admits near the end of the novel that there were other motives as well. He refers to Ludeyville as his folly, monument to his sincere and loving idiocy, to the unrecognized evils of his character, and symbol of his Jewish struggle for a solid footing in White Anglo-Saxon Protestant America. The countryside in the Berkshires is rich in natural beauty. Herzog's well-situated estate commands a gorgeous view. Occasionally he is able to appreciate its beauty: for instance, while Shapiro and Madeleine engage themselves in intellectual dialogues, Herzog does not join them but, instead, observes his surrounding. He minutely takes in all of nature's objects, which like the repetitious details of the urban scenes, are both exciting and distracting.

Herzog admits that he has succumbed to the agrarian impulse. Herzog, who during his first thirty years knew only the slums of Montreal and the West side of Chicago, falls victim to the pastoral ideal of WASPish America. As one of his friends puts it, in answer to Herzog's comment that he hoped that Maddy and he would settle down in Ludeyville: "Out in the sticks? Don't be nuts. With that chick? Are you kidding? Come back to the home town. You' re a West Side Jew" (114). Herzog discovers that he is "at home" in Chicago, but the knowledge comes much too late to save his marriage. Maddy is dissatisfied with country living from the very beginning and deserts Herzog and becomes the mistress of Herzog's best friend.

The house in the Berkshires has cost him a pretty penny: his father's twenty thousand dollar inheritance. But life in the country never satisfies. He is always uneasy in the middle landscape. Although he often thinks of himself as "Squire Herzog" or as "the old Jew man of Ludeyville, with a white beard, cutting the grass under the washline with my antique reel-mower, eating Woodchucks" (64), the Thoreauvian primitivism never works out for him, in spite of its great appeal. Even his final return to Ludeyville at the end of the novel is acknowledged to be only a temporary respite from his present cares - he is in Ludeyville only to look things over. Like Augie's rejected dreams of an academy in an arcadian, Walden-like setting, Herzog comes slowly to recognize that his dreams of nineteenth century Emersonian self-sufficiency in the countryside cannot sustain his need for something beyond his "rotten dreams of peace" (393). Ludeyville has cost him his father's inheritance and his second wife, Maddy. It is a great price to pay. In spite of the overwhelmingly negative impression given by the urban environment, Herzog takes the edge off of its negative force. He finds the city strangely neutral and feels in fact at home in it.

Humboldt, the main protagonist Citrine's poet friend in *Humboldt's Gift* (1975), moved from Greenwich Village to rural New Jersey with his newlywed wife Kathleen late in the Forties. However, Humboldt, growing up in New York City, is essentially an urbanite. His ideas about the pastoral are mostly derived from books: Plato, Proust, Virgil, Marvell, and Stevens. Living in the New Jersey back country did not make a hermit of him; instead, he traveled to New York several times a week on business. To his friend Citrine's mind, it is a great irony and contradiction for Humboldt-" a man of powerful social instincts" (*HG* 284)-to bury himself in the dreary countryside. Humboldt lived in the countryside not simply for pastoral beauty: he wouldn't even allow Kathleen to grow flowers around the cottage. His motives were complicated. Like Herzog's buying the Ludeyville house, Humboldt's move to the barren backlands gave him a feeling of entering the American mainstream.

Humboldt knew that to be a poet meant he was doomed to be solitary. Yet, when he retreated to the countryside, his craving for active life and social activity killed him. No longer able to produce "poems of great wit and beauty" (25), he felt terrible. Consequently, the place "sometimes looked like Arcadia to him and sometimes looked like hell" (25).

For Humboldt and Kathleen, life in rural New Jersey brought no simplicity, productivity, or contentment. What's even worse, the paranoid Humboldt suffers illusionary anti-Semitism. As a son of Hungarian-Jewish immigrants, Humboldt suffered "keen Jewish terrors in the country" (27), because, as Citrine reflects, "he was an Oriental, she a Christian maiden, and he was afraid. He expected the KKK to burn a cross in his yard or shoot at him through the window as he lay on the Castro sofa reading Proust or inventing scandal" (27). His fear of his back-country neighbors gave him nightmares. In his nightmares his neighbors buried his house, he shot it out with them, and they lynched him and carried off his wife. As in his other novels, in *Humboldt's Gift* Bellow does not let the country speak more eloquently than the city. Humboldt's country life fares no better than his urban life, as far as its effects upon his emotions, creativity, and marriage are concerned.

Although each of Bellow's characters comes to recognize the inefficacy of nature to heal with any permanent balm the human need expressed in Henderson's phrase, "I want," each employs nature in some fashion for a momentary respite from the press of the urban world. Henderson goes further and experiments with the nature-related alternatives of the rural life (pig farming) and cultural primitivism (flight to Africa). Neither is successful, however.

Bellow's deep connection with the city produces in him an ambivalence toward the city and, even though he occasionally treats the city quite negatively, he has not treated the country in wholly favorable terms. In his view, the country in its present version is not a place for the pastoral ideal and is not a symbol for nature. He thinks that "America is now all city" (Bellow, "A Writer from Chicago" 183); under the influence of modern technology, the countryside of the present has become almost as modernized and mechanized as any city and it has been invaded by many problems which used to be located in cities only. In other words, Bellow does not believe in a popular theory in American intellectual history, the dichotomy between the natural world of God in the countryside and the artificial world of man in the city. He does not resolve the city - country dialogue in favor of the country.

2. Darkness in Modern Society with Evil in the Nature of Man

The existential dilemma of our modern time can be credited to the monumental atrocities such as World Wars Ⅰ and Ⅱ, the Holocaust, and the current spate of genocides and so we can understand Bellow's concern for the fragility of the human condition both as an artist and a Jew. In his acceptance speech for the Nobel Prize, he laments on this condition as though he is speaking from the pulpit: "Let me take a little time to look more closely at this travail. In private life, disorder or near-panic. In families-for husbands, wives, parents, children-confusion; in civic behavior, in personal loyalties, in sexual practices further confusion. And with this private disorder goes public bewilderment" (Bellow, *It All Adds Up* 93). This is the state of affairs that concerns Bellow the artist as he cautions us about the distressing predictions that confront us, our history of disorder, and our vision of disintegration; this source of upheaval Bellow attributes to, "The unending cycle of crises that began with the First World War has formed a kind of person, one who has lived through terrible, strange things, ... an ability to live with many kinds of madness" (Bellow, The Nobel). It is against this background of disorder that he admits our existential turmoil: "... we stand open to all anxieties. The decline and fall of everything is our daily dread, we are agitated in private life and tormented by public questions" (Bellow, The Nobel).

Bellow's fiction encompasses the American experience from the Depression in the thirties to the automation and conformity of the fifties. Chester E. Eisinger comments on the situation at that time:

> Everymajor social phenomenon of these decades has in common the drift toward human effacement and individual anonymity. The growth of big government and big labor, the development of the massive military establishment, the technological depersonalization of industry, ... these and many other phenomena were equally crippling to the human personality. (179)

World War Ⅱ for Bellow, as well as for other American writers, meant "the disruption of continuity with the past" (Podhoretz 208) and its aftermath meant for his characters an alienation resulting from the depletion of cultural resources replaced by the mass culture of a technological surge in America.

> A powerful nation of unparalleled energy and practicality created an industrial society without precedent in history. The accompanying ugliness, boredom and spiritual trouble are also without precedent. Parts of society seem mad... The peculiar difficulty of the artist in this situation is

that he is obliged to take a commonsense view of things. What are his alternatives? (Bellow, "Culture now: Some Animadversions, Some Laughs" 177)

Within the past two centuries, massive industrialization, technological and scientific advances, wars, diseases, failures in social systems, and religious, ethnic, and political conflicts have produced an existential angst that has saturated the collective consciousness of modern man. The atrocities of World Wars I and II induced European and American authors and artists to confront this state of disillusionment, anxiety, loneliness, fear, and dread; consequently, much of our modern literature reflects this nihilistic darkness.

Bellow's first novel *Dangling Man* written in 1944, though mainly about Joseph's existential problem, shows the collective psyche affected by the distant battles and reflects the contemporary political and social atmosphere, which is why it has been considered a novel about World War II despite the absence of combat. Edmund Wilson praised it as "one of the most honest pieces of testimony on the psychology of a whole generation who have grown up during the war" (78). Although the novel, like all Bellow's novels, centers upon the consciousness of a single individual, the gloomy environment as represented by war-time Chicago is a haunting force in his life. Joseph, having resigned his job at a travel agency to be ready for military induction, really has nothing to do but wait. Examining his present life Joseph finds himself suffering from a "narcotic dullness"; life is a loathsome burden to him. There is nothing for him to do but wait, or dangle, and grow more and more dispirited. Compared with his older self, he is deteriorating, storing bitterness and spite which eat life acids at his endowment of generosity and good will.

It is in the street that Joseph in *Dangling Man* has a "prevision" of urban man's fate, the blackness of death which strikes suddenly without warning. Joseph, on his way to meet his wife to celebrate their sixth wedding anniversary, finds a well-dressed, middle aged man suddenly collapse in front of him in a smoky alley along side of the library. The victim of some kind of unknown attack, he labors for breath as Joseph and others stand helplessly by. The police, in business-like fashion, attend the man to an ambulance while Joseph vividly recalls the last few moments of his own mother's agonizing death. His mother's last words were smothered by the weight of a hysterical aunt of his who had thrown herself on the deathbed, clawing at Joseph when he tried to pull her from the dying body, and leaving a deep scratch on his forehead, a scratch which he now feels smarting again. It is then that Joseph has his "prevision" of the accidental forces of urban life which in a moment make man a victim. "To many in the fascinated crowd the figure of the man on the ground must have been what it was to me-a prevision. Without warning, down" (*DM* 77). A stone, a girder, or a bullet lashed against the head, and the bone gives like a glass from a cheap kiln or a subtler enemy escapes the bonds of years; the blackness comes down; we lie, a great weight on our faces, straining toward the last breath which comes like the gritting of gravel under a heavy tread. Such an incident, fraught with a mythic quality, gives Joseph a "prevision" of urban man's fate, the blackness of death which strikes suddenly without warning.

Mr. Fanzel, the tailor, used to sew Joseph's loose buttons to his coats gratis. He now charges fifteen cents, although he knows that Joseph is not working. It is the war that has corrupted Fanzel's kindness. If Fanzel is to make money while he can, secure his share in order to cope with rising prices, he has to keep up with the spiritual climate of the time. He is even convinced that this is as it should be. More will be better for everybody if business is booming, and since this is the case there is no need to make small gestures of human kindness any longer.

People like Myron, whom Joseph knows, once felt genuine friendship for him, back out of their promises to find a job for him, because they fear that Joseph in his new situation might prove an embarrassment to them.

At the Servatius party Joseph watches how his friend Morris, invited to entertain the people in his capacity as an amateur hypnotist, submits his old flame Minnie to a series of insults while she is under hypnosis. He perceives that even in his own circle of friends, his "colony of the spirit" , life's nastiness and brutality are not absent. Joseph, in short, awakens to the realities of life which tell him that sudden death, corruption, cruelty and hate are an integral part of existence, knowledge which up to now he had carefully chosen to ignore. He not only dislikes what he sees in others, he also ceases to be satisfied with his own self, for, as he come to realize, the treasons he saw at the Servatius party were partly his own.

When one Sunday the landlord shuts of the heating in order to carry out repairs, Joseph flies into a rage and running down to the basement he starts a fist fight with him. This is "not like" Joseph. But it is "an early symptom" of the changes that are taking place in him. At a dinner party in the home of his older brother, he allows himself to get involved in a disgraceful quarrel with his family. Provoked by his teenage niece, Etta, over a trivial incident, he loses control of himself and starts beating the girl, an act which acquires added significance if we bear in mind the reference that is made to the physical similarity between Joseph and Etta. Joseph may dislike Etta for what she actually is-a vain, spoiled nuisance-but by punishing her he also seems to punish himself, the old Joseph who was so expert in planning his life, the man who used to keep a tight control on himself. Joseph even falls out with his wife, Iva, whose new position as the sole breadwinner rapidly increases her awakened sense of independence, a situation detrimental to his old certainties. When in retaliation he tries to renew the relations with his former mistress Kitty Daumler, he discovers that he has already been replaced in her affections by somebody else, and, humiliated, he realizes that there was nothing in his old existence that could really be taken for granted. He starts have bad dreams full of violence and dread.

It is not accidental, therefore, that the title of Bellow's second novel is *The Victim* and that the protagonist, Asa Leventhal, is a middle-aged, moderately successful, happily married "everyman" kind of figure who is a victim not only of anti-Semitism, but, as Tanner puts it, of the New York city atmosphere with its "lurking fear of vague powers which can destroy the individual in a moment" (Tanner 30).

The first scene in which Leventhal squeezes through the shutting door of a moving bus is a fit index to his position in that densely-packed metropolis, to his efforts to find a foothold in that tottering topsy-turvy urban world. The city of New York, with its huge crowds of people, oppressive high-rise buildings, and lurking, unnamable forces, has always been an ominous, suffocating threat to him. This summer, however, his feelings of loneliness, alienation, and insecurity are intensified by the enervating heat, the constant noise, and the cluttered, unrelated density of New York. He has the feeling that he really does not know what goes on about him, what strange things, and savage things. His feeling of "overwhelming human closeness and thickness" brought about by the crushing presence of Allbee and the "too-humanness" of the city makes him feel that there is not a single part of him on which the whole world does not press with full weight on his body, on his soul.

Asa, an editor of a small trade magazine, temporarily left alone in New York, is suddenly accosted by a remote acquaintance, Kirby Allbee, who is now little better than a bum. Allbee insists that Leventhal was responsible for his losing his job, and thus for his subsequent fall into the social deaths. Leventhal denies the charge as fantastic, the lunatic accusation of an anti-Semite at first, but gradually comes to acknowledge some relationship. "I haven't thought about you in years, frankly, and I don't know why you think I care whether you exist or not. What are we related?" (*V* 210) And Allbee's answer-"By blood? No, no…. heavens!" opens up the central theme of the book. How is man related to man? The corollary to the theme of man's relationship to man is man's relationship to the big city, the city which embodies the anonymous mass of men. How can and how does man relate to man in the "deep urban comp lexes"? Tanner points out that Asa fears not only the threat and hostility of Allbee but that Asa's deeper fear comes from an uncertainty about his position and stability in the cruel, indifferent chaos of the modern city.

In the city the old traditional means of establishing identity are washed away, leaving only two classes: the successful and the failures. French sociologist Durkheim's "anomie" is the chronic disease of the city, says Tanner. "To drive home this basic atmosphere of alienation, insecurity, and the desperate, graceless motion and collision of this competitive, anomic age, Bellow powerfully evokes the crowded unrelated density of New York" (Tanner 29). "Now this atmosphere is crucial, not incidental" (30) says Tanner. It is in this fearful, unrelated urban environment that Asa must discover how he is related to other men and how to escape himself from victimization. The oppressiveness of the urban atmosphere is evoked at once in the very opening lines of *The Victim*-On some nights New York is as hot as Bangkok. The whole continent seems to have moved from its place and slid nearer the equator, the bitter gray Atlantic to have become green and tropical, and the people, thronging the streets, barbaric fellahin among the stupendous monuments of their mystery, the lights of which, a dazing profusion, climb upward endlessly into the heat of the sky. It is not only the oppressive heat, but the anonymous mass of people, the "barbaric fellahin," who, like Asa himself, are lost in the mysterious skyscrapers that press about him and make him "bitterly irritated."

Even the park, that hoped for oasis of nature in the heart of the city, offers Asa no respite from the press of humanity. The trees in the park are swathed in stifling dust, and the stars are faint and sparse through the pall. The benches form a dense, double human wheel and the paths are thronged. There is an overwhelming human closeness and thickness, and Leventhal is penetrated by a sense not merely of the crowd in this park but of innumerable millions, crossing, touching, and pressing. In fact, the park only leads Asa to Allbee, who is identified as one of the city "failures," a Hurstwood-like figure who is being defeated by the naturalistic forces of the city. The bond that links Asa and Allbee is that each is the other's alter-ego. Each represents the only two identities which the city recognizes: the successes and the failures.

The presence of Allbee confronts Leventhal with the degradation of poverty which he has managed to keep himself from, and Allbee also voices views which Leventhal has chose to ignore in his effort to survive and achieve a modicum of security and social comfort. When, in one of their early confrontations, Allbee remarks that people are not gods, people are only creatures, and the things people sometimes think are permanent, they aren't permanent. So one day people are like full bundles and the next people are wrapping-paper, blowing around the streets, and Leventhal angrily shuts him up, telling him that he won't stand for such talk. What Allbee touches upon is again something Leventhal dreads and with which he has yet to come to terms: the arbitrariness, the element of chance, which seems to govern the course of one's life in the urban environment. It undermines one's sense of security, and devalues the individual effort, severely detracting from the dignity of human achievement. To Asa, Allbee is the personification of all his city fears made flesh and blood. Leventhal fears the irrationality which is at the bottom of Allbee's disorderly behavior: the inhumanity, whose ultimate manifestation is death. He cannot accept it; it represents a darkness in man and life, a horror and evil which clash with his views that life should be devoid of "the harsh things, the things difficult to stand".

Early in the novel, even before meeting Allbee, Asa's imagination has limned the portrait of the unlucky ones who do not succeed: "the lost, the overcome, the effaced, the ruined" (*V* 20). Later in the novel when Asa is beginning to recognize the outlines of the success – failure city types which he and Allbee represent, he fills in the picture of the defeated men in flophouses and imaginatively places himself in their places—there rises immediately to Leventhal's mind the most horrible images of men wearily sitting on mission benches waiting for their coffee in a smeared and bleary winter sun; of flophouse sheets and filthy pillows; hideous cardboard cubicles painted to resemble wood, even the tungsten in the bulb like little burning worms that seem to eat up rather than give light. Better to be in the dark. He has seen such places. He could smell the carbolic disinfectant. And if it were his flesh on those sheets, his lips drinking that coffee, his back and thighs in that winter sun, his eyes looking at the boards of the floor?

The dominant quality of the city in *Seize the Day* is not like that of the earlier novels, fear and suspicion, but rather madness, insanity-Everybody in the Hotel Gloriana, where Wilhelm and his father live among those "having-nothing-to-do-but-wait-out-the-day" retirees, has a mental disorder, a secret history, and a concealed disease. The wife of Rubin at the newsstand is supposed to be kept by Carl, the yelling, loud-mouthed gin-rummy player. The wife of Frank in the barbershop has disappeared with a GI while he is waiting for her to disembark at the French Lines pier. Everyone is like the faces of a playing card, upside down either way. Every public figure has a character – neurosis. Maddest of all are the businessmen, the heartless, flaunting, and boisterous business class who rules this country with their hard manners and their bold lies and their absurd words that nobody could believe. They are crazier than anyone. They spread the plague.

And again, that sick Mr. Perls at breakfast has said that there is no easy way to tell the sane from the mad, and he is right about that in any big city and especially in New York-the end of the world, with complexity and machinery, bricks and tubes, wires and stones, holes and heights. And is everybody crazy here?

The complexity and the madness of city have a peculiar form, centering on the inability to communicate and the historical and intellectual trappings with which everything must be properly draped. Every man speaks a language entirely his own, which he has figured out by private thinking. Everyone has his own ideas and peculiar ways.... You have to translate and translate, explain and explain, back and forth, and it is the punishment of hell itself not to understand or be understood, not to know the crazy from the sane, the wise from the fools, the young from the old or the sick from the well. The fathers are no fathers and the sons no sons. You have to talk with yourself in the daytime and reason with yourself at night. Who else is there to talk to in a city like New York? The Tower of Babel, heterogeneity, complexity, insanity, incomplete relationships, not knowing who is who, and worst of all, being driven into the self-here we have the familiar, destructive forces of the city that make communication and community impossible.

Denied the escape into nature and driven into the streets, desperate Wilhelm gives us the last cityscape before he is swept into the funeral parlor where he is going to weep for an anonymous corpse-On Broadway it is still bright afternoon and the gassy air is almost motionless under the leaden spokes of sunlight, and sawdust footprints lie about the doorways of butcher shops and fruit stores. And the great, great crowd, the inexhaustible current of millions of every race and kind pouring out, pressing round, of every age, of every genius, possessors of every human secret, antique and future, in every face the refinement of one particular motive or essence. The sidewalks are wider than any causeway; the street itself is immense, and it quakes and gleams and it seemed to Wilhelm to throb at the last limit of endurance. And although the sunlight appears like a broad tissue, its actual weight makes him feel like a drunkard.

It is for this urban mass-as it is experienced in the street, with its separateness, its anomie, its segmented, driving, hopeless aspiration for individual fulfillment that threatens the very street that can barley contain it-it is for this too human, inhuman scene that Wilhelm weeps.

Moses Herzog in *Herzog* is an intellectual, a professor, a writer. He has made a name for himself in the academic world. Yet his personal life has been a failure: two failed marriages, a series of inconsequential love affairs, and a career as a professor which was on the decline (he has even temporarily abandoned his teaching position), an acute sense of failure both as son and father. At the beginning of the novel, he is at the point where his world has collapsed, where he attempts to grasp hold of himself and his life, to pick up the broken pieces of his personality and see what is left. Herzog has come to Dr. Edvig, the Chicago psychiatrist, at his second wife Madeleine's insistence. It is her condition for their remaining together. Yet, Edvig has forgotten, or betrayed, his obligation to his patient, for Edvig has fallen in love with Madeleine. Madeleine, knowing that, has been able to use the doctor in her conspiracy against Herzog.

Valentine Gersbach is an early friend of Herzog's. Herzog describes him as a "charming man," heavy, with a thick chin, flaming copper hair that literally gushed from his head. He walks on a wooden leg, gracefully bending and straightening like a gondolier. When Madeleine becomes dissatisfied with the solitariness of Ludeyville and decides that they must leave, she insists that Herzog find a job in Chicago for the Gersbachs, too. Valentine has been a radio-announcer, and a disk-jockey in Pittsfield. Herzog finds him a job as educational director of an FM station in the Loop. Herzog naively acts as Valentine's benefactor, all the while ignorant that Valentine has taken from him more than has been offered. Herzog resents Valentine's lack of refinement, but never suspects him of adultery with his wife. He tells his friend, Lucas Asphalter, that Gersbach is the only reliable person on the scene. Herzog trusts him. He's been an awfully good friend. Herzog finds Lucas's tale of Valentine's perfidy incomprehensible.

After his second wife Madeleine throws him out, Herzog goes to see the Chicago lawyer-friend, Sandor Himmelstein. He is a short man, misshapen from the loss of part of his chest, a dwarf and hunchback. He is also presented as garrulous and vulgar. Herzog hires him to look out for his interests, but he prevails upon Herzog to acquiesce to all of Madeleine's demands and betrays him professionally, because she has beguiled him with her beauty. He suggests that Moses face the reality of the whorelike quality of existence in which justice, righteousness, compassion play no part. Herzog's personal troubles become symptomatic also of chaos and disarrangement in the city in general. Herzog reiterates the impingement of the city upon man's sensibility, creating a "wild internal disorder" (247). The modern condition is again described in terms of the city and what it embodies-Herzog is quivering because he let the entire world press upon him. For instance, what it means to be a man in a city, in a cen tury, in transition and in a mass, transformed by science, under organized power and subject to tremendous controls. In a condition caused by mechanization, a society that is no community and devalues the person, owing to the multiplied power of numbers which makes the self negligible, spends military billions against foreign enemies but would not pay for order at home, and permits sava gery and barbarism in its own great cities.

In addition to the soot, gas, noise and other harsh elements that dominate most of the city scenes, Herzog is aware of the violence and human degradation of various human dramas that are set in the city as well. While waiting for an appointment, he wanders into a New York courtroom. He becomes a witness to a judge abusing a Negro accused of assault. He sees the insulting treatment given to a young intern whose career in medicine is threaten by the charge of having committed an unnatural sex act in the men's lavatory of Grand Central Station. Herzog's sympathies go out to the young man as he says that you don't destroy a man's career because he yielded to an impulse in that ponderous stinking cavern below Grand Central, in the cloaca of the city where no mind can be sure of stability.

He is sickened by the details of the case of a male prostitute accused of a holdup to procure drugs. But the "monstrousness of life" and the inability of the court to be either merciful or just are demonstrated in the case of a woman on relief who beats her young child to death (because she cannot toilet train him) by hurling it against a wall while her lover watches idly from the bed. Herzog says, "Lying down to copulate, and standing up to kill, then cry. Others, not even that" (*H* 294). These scenes are evidently very common to lower class city life.

WhenSammler in *Mr. Sammler's Planet* takes bus back home from the Fifty-Second Street Library, he stands in the crowd, taller than everyone else, and peers down on a crime being perpetrated by a black man, but he is unable to do anything about it because no one is interested in curbing the crime. The victims do not feel victimized themselves and the law enforcement agencies are apathetic to this offense. Those who show any interest do so out of curiosity and not from a sense of outrage. Humanity is victimized while Sammler watches helplessly. This is symbolic of a world condition. Originally, Sammler is fascinated by the audaciousness of the offense, but then he is appalled by the apathy of those who should be concerned. Sammler's observations focus on the madness and folly of the age.

The elegantly sinister Black pickpocket reflects the sick society that is within the sublunary orbit of Mr. Sammler's planet and the problem of crime and the pervasiveness of madness in it. He is a powerful Black dressed with extraordinary elegance in a camel's – hair coat and a homburg. He wears dark "Dior shades" of "gentian violet banded with lovely gold" (*MSP* 9) and a single gold earring. He has certain majesty about him, and his face "showed the effrontery of a big animal" (9). When Sammler is accosted by the Black, he reflects that he is never to hear the black man's voice. He no more speaks than a puma would. The Black is a megalomaniac, but possesses noblesse nevertheless. He reflects the primitiveness and barbaric nature of modern man who, behind the external façade of elegance and regality, is really no more than a beast. In the jungle of New York City, he preys upon his unsuspecting quarry. The black exposes his penis as a means of intimidation when he realizes that Sammler notices his thievery. The Black is "an analogy for those dark forces of limitlessness, lawlessness, madness, and chaos that threaten to overcome the discipline and civility to which Sammler pays hard tribute" (Russell 95).

In addition, most outdoor telephones are smashed and crippled. They are urinals, also. New York is getting worse than Naples or Salonika. It is like an Asian, or an African town, from this standpoint. The opulent sections of the city are not immune. You open a jeweled door into degradation, from hyper-civilized Byzantine luxury straight into the state of nature, the barbarous world of color erupting from beneath. It might very well be barbarous on either side of the jeweled door. Sexually, for example. "The thing evidently, as Mr. Sammler was beginning to grasp, consisted in obtaining the privileges, and the free ways of barbarism, under the protection of civilized order, property rights, refined technological organization, and so on" (*SP* 10—11).

The "barbarism" of the larger environment (New York, its inhabitants in general) is an expanded version of chaos in the modern world. The external aspects often become a projection of the character's mind in Bellow's novels, and yet they may also be directly responsible for the character's actions and reactions. In Sammler's view, the outer dirt, confusion, and disorderliness are just a reflexion of the inner state of each individual: "A human being, valuing himself for the right reasons, has and restores order, authority. When the internal parts are in order. They must be in order. But what was it to be arrested in the stage of toilet training!" (21)

Sammler sees in Angela Gruner, his nephew's daughter, gathered several of the characteristics that are for him a clear indication of everything that has gone wrong with modern society. She represents, in exacerbated form, the looseness, the lack of moral order, more specifically, the sexual freedom that even though present in previous decades also (Sammler thinks of his own father, of

Picasso, even of H. G. Wells, whom he admires so much) has now reached almost uncontrollable levels. Sammler says that a sexual madness is overwhelming the Western world, and Angela, with her many lovers, her free language, her microskirts and sexual experiments, is a typical representative of this madness. It is while looking at her, talking to her, in the last scene of the novel, that Sammler draws the parallel between New York and the two Biblical cities destroyed for their moral laxness-New York makes one think about the collapse of civilization, about Sodom and Gomorrah, the end of the world. The end wouldn't come as a surprise. Many people already bank on it.

On his way home from a lecture given at Columbia university, Sammler once more sees the black pickpocket whom he has already reported-but to no effect-to the police. Sammler is followed and cornered by the black man. This time the attack is silent, yet the content and approach are still the same. Without saying a word the pickpocket exposes himself to Sammler-Sammler is directed, silently, to look downward. The black man has opened his fly and taken out his penis. It is displayed to Sammler with great oval testicles, a large tan-and-purple uncircumcised thing. Sammler is required to gaze at this organ over the forearm and fist that hold him. No compulsion would have been necessary. He would in any case have looked. The man's expression is not directly menacing but oddly, serenely masterful. The thing is shown with mystifying certitude.

The episode confirms Sammler's worst doubts. Not only have order and dignity disappeared ("Who had raised the diaper flag? Who had made shit a sacrament?" [45]), authority and power have been transferred to the "genitalia". There is the man's organ, a huge piece of sex flesh, half-tumescent in its pride and shown in its own right, a prominent and separate object intends to communicate authority. "As, within the sex ideology of these days, it well might. It was a symbol of superlegitimacy of sovereignty. It was a mystery. It was unanswerable. The whole explanation" (54).

It is this primitivism, equating man and animal, the abandonment of higher, nobler views of man that Sammler cannot accept. Is this earth so corrupt that it is unredeemable and human being must seek to start life anew preferably on a new planet?

Charlie Citrine in *Humboldt's Gift* (1975) suddenly finds his life in great disorder. His successful life in Chicago has taken various turns for the worse. His home is no longer his retreat, and sanctuary. He is harassed by a minor Mafia figure, Rinaldo Cantabile, enchanted by his mistress, Renata, tormented by his litigious ex-wife, Denis, and racked by cannibal lawyers. Citrine is also obsessed with the question of death, particularly that of his poetfriend Von Humboldt Fleisher, who "acts from the grave" (*HG* 6) to change Citrine's life. Although both Herzog and Citrine are tormented by divorce, they suffer in different ways. In *Herzog* Madeleine dumps Moses whereas in *Humboldt's Gift*, Citrine drops Denise. However, like Tommy Wilhelm in *Seize the Day*, he has to pay dearly for his freedom, because Denise is litigious, an aggressive subtle resourceful plaintiff. After the breakup, they are engaged in endless alimony battles. In a sense, Denise has taught Citrine an important American lesson, for "Real Americans are supposed to suffer with their wives, and wives with their husbands" (42). With the collaboration of cannibal lawyers ("the sharks of Chicago" [173]), Denise squeezes away money from Citrine and forces him out his seclusion to face the chaotic, skirmishing urban world. From his dealing with these people, Citrine learns how universal the desire to injure your fellow man is. He has to face reality- the "Chicago condition"- without recoil. Around him are agents of distractions, unremittingly or potentially detrimental to his gift, well-being, sensibility, and equanimity. Because of them, he cannot lead a serene life nor can he concentrate on his essays on boredom and other subjects.

Affected by his manic-depressive tendencies and by great social forces, Citrine's poet friend Humboldt cannot recover his enchantment and write beautiful poetry again. When his scheme to get himself a chair at Princeton aborts and his wife Kathleen deserts him, he starts to degenerate and never fully recovers. The unproductive, maniacal Humboldt begins to make scenes in New York. He repeatedly threatens a young literary figure whom he suspects is Kathleen's lover. Consequently, he is arrested and sent to Bellevue. As the police put him into a strait jacket and rush him to Bellevue, he has diarrhea. The event leads Citrine to ponder the fate of the poet and artist in American society. "Was this art versus America?" wonders Citrine, to whom "Bellevue was like the Bowery: it gave negative testimony" (155). If brutal Wall Street stands for power and the nearby Bowery and Bellevue, weakness, should poets, like drunkards and misfits and psychopaths, sink into weakness and find themselves among the wretched and busted? With his talent gone and his mind fallen apart, Humboldt ends up as a bum living in a flophouse in Manhattan.

The Bucharest story about Dean Corde's visit to his dying mother-in-law tells grim facts about orderly but oppressive life behind the Iron Curtain in *The Dean's December*. Bucharest is cold, grim, dismal, and imprisoning, while Chicago is hot, chaotic, corrupt, and murderous. In *The Dean's December* the Chicago story begins with the death of Rick Lester, Corde's student, who is bound, gagged, and pushed out of a window to his death by a Black prostitute and her pimp. Lester's violent death is highlighted by "the crying ugliness of the Chicago night" (*DD* 48). Corde remembers it is a "rotten night" when he is called to identify Lester's corpse. Seeing Lester, barefoot, in the morgue, Corde cannot understand why the youths of Chicago are so ignorant or naïve about the dangers of their city. The Lester episode brings out several themes of the novel: sexual anarchy, robbery, murder, the Black "underclass," student militancy, and the news media's noise.

Bellow's frequent cityscapes are predominantly negative, containing images of filth, debris, crime, noise, and heat that contribute to a symbolic view of the city as either a wasteland or an inferno. It is the real living condition of modern man. As a responsible writer with Jewish moral vision, it is undoubtedly Bellow's mission to find therapy for modern human beings.

A child, growing up in a Jewish home, has probably heard, at some time or another, the saying that "in every human being there lives a good angel and a wicked one." Isaac Bashevis Singer's fictive worlds are full of angels and devils. His creations are marvelous portrayals of shtetl life wherein this saying is very real. Sometimes the angels are inside of man and at other times they are outside him. If a man does not come home for the Sabbath, it is because the bad angel delays him, and if he prospers it is because the good angel is watching over him.

John Pearl, an artist friend of Joseph's writes to Joseph to express his deep distaste about his "peeling environment" in New York in *Dangling Man* -peeling furniture, peeling walls, posters, and bridges and everything is peeling and scaling in South Brooklyn. Pearl goes on writing in the letter that they move there to save money. But he is afraid they' d better start saving themselves and move out again. It's the treelessness, as much as anything, that hurts him. The unnatural, too-human deadness. Joseph acknowledges the validity of Pearl's condemnation of the city, but he rejects the easy dismissal of the city as "unnatural". Joseph is sorry for Pearl. He knows what Pearl feels, the kind of terror, and the danger he sees of the lack of the human in the too-human. Joseph acknowledges: "We find it, as others before us have found it in the last hundred years, and we bolt for 'Nature'. It happens in all cities. And cities are 'natural', too" (*DM* 101). Pearl thinks he would be safer in Chicago, where he grew up. It is sentimentality! He doesn't mean Chicago. It is no less inhuman. He means his father's house and the few blocks adjacent. Away from these and a few other islands, he would be just as unsafe.

What Joseph acknowledges and what he denies is crucial to Bellow's attitude toward the city. The evil, that is to say danger of the city, inheres not in its being unnatural, but in the human condition, the all too-human condition. It is humanity, not the environment per se, that produces the in-humanity. Bellow does not deny that the environment of the city is charged with fear and terror. He denies only the cause of that pernicious atmosphere.

Bellow uses the sinister images in *The Victim* to suggest the fear which Asa senses in himself as well as in others in an episode describing Asa's trip on the Staten Island ferry-The towers on the shore rise up in huge blocks, scorched, smoky, gray, and bare white where the sun is direct upon them. The notion brushes Leventhal's mind that the light over them and over the water is akin to the yellow revealed in the slit of the eye of a wild animal, say a lion, something inhuman that doesn't care about anything human and yet is implanted in every human being too, "one speck of it, and formed a part of him that responded to the heat and glare, exhausting as these were, or even to freezing, salty things, harsh things, all things difficult to stand" (*V* 51).

First there are the "towers on the shore"-the buildings of the city evoked in their most bleak aspects, objects signifying for Asa the gigantic city unconcerned about the individual. Furthermore, they lend the light above them a sinister quality as it is likened to the yellow "in the slit of the eye of a wild animal." Opdahl points out that Bellow sees evil "as a force which is impersonally destructive in the universe and malevolent in animals. . . . [and] he equates this force with the instinctual drives of the species and the impersonal force and cruelty of the human will" (Opdahl, *The Novels of Saul Bellow* 64—65). These sinister images serve as a continual commentary on Asa's attitude that most people have fear in them - fear of life, fear of death, or life more than of death, perhaps. When the fear is uppermost they don't want any more burdens. It is this kind of selfish fear that Allbee has already accused Asa of: ". . . you people take care of yourselves before everything. You keep your spirit under lock and key" (*V* 146). Asa himself concedes the truth of this accusation when confronted with the crisis of his nephew's death, acknowledging to himself that he has used every means, and principally indifference and neglect, to avoid acknowledging it, that is, his failure to commit himself wholly to another's welfare. Bellow uses the animal analogy to suggest the depravity of man, but he also means to suggest the possibility of man's transcending such a state by discovering his humanity as he becomes involved with others.

Leventhal refuses to acknowledge in others as well as in himself the irrational, the dark and dangerous passions, the inhuman, with which one has to come to terms if one is to accept oneself for what one is-a human being, not an "ideal construction". Nevertheless, the event which serves to exemplify that he also has the darkness inside himself is the one on the final night of the relationship between him and Allbee when Leventhal comes home to find the door locked and Allbee with a woman. He does not heed Allbee's urgent appeal to wait but smashes his way in and sees, horror-struck, Albee, naked and ungainly beside a woman who was dressing in great haste. Her hair covered her face; nevertheless Leventhal thought he recognized her. Mrs. Nunez! Was it Mrs. Nunez? The horror of it bristled on him, and the outcry he had been about to make was choked down. When he next discovers that the woman is not Mrs. Nunez but a stranger, Leventhal feels "enormously lightened". Now why is it that he is unable to show the common decency to wait till Allbee is ready to open the door, and why is he, once inside the room, so relieved when the woman turns out to be a stranger and not Mrs. Nunez?

There are, in the novel, a number of images which subtly reveal Leventhal's suppressed sexual feelings.① One day he awakens from a nap by thunder, and looking across the street into a window he sees a woman lying on a sofa: ". . . one arm bent over her eyes. At the next sound of the retreating

① I acknowledge a debt here to John Jacob Clayton's analysis of *The Victim* in his excellent *Saul Bellow: In Defense of Man* (Bloomington, 1968; rpt 1979), pp. 139—65.

thunder she moved her legs" (116). The following exchange between Leventhal and Mrs. Nunez, occurring a few pages later, illustrates how Leventhal focuses these unconscious sexual desires on the janitor's wife. Asked whether Mrs. Leventhal will soon come back, Leventhal answers: "I don't think so." "Oh, too bad, too bad" (126), she said in her light, flat, rapid way. Leventhal often paused at Nunez' door to listen, entertained, to their quick-running Spanish, not a word of which he understood. "Too bad," she repeated, and Leventhal, with a glance of surmise at her small face under the white brim, wondered what hint her sympathy might contain. There was a burst of music above them and the window was thrown open. What the music seems to symbolize is Leventhal's hidden passion; the open window, an invitation to satisfy it. Leventhal's mad urge to break into the house becomes understandable now. What he must see is Allbee do what he himself desires to do but has to deny himself, while at the same time it enables him to blame Allbee for what he actually blames himself: his unconscious desire for Mrs. Nunez, which becomes clear from the relief he feels when he realizes that Allbee's pick-up is not Mrs. Nunez but a stranger.

Augie goes toMexico with Thea to tame the eagle, Caligula to hunt giant lizards in *The Adventures of Augie March*. The eagle embodies for Augie darkness and cruelty. As he reflects-if Caligula's motive is rapacious and everything is based on the act of murder, he also has a nature that feels the triumph of beating his way up to the highest air to which flesh and bone could rise. "And doing it by will, not as other forms of life were at that altitude, the spores and parachute seeds who weren't there as individuals but messengers of the species" (*AM* 341). It's the same will that Augie finds in the Simons, Einhorns, Villars and Magnuses, in Thea herself, people whom he thinks he has to admire-and does admire initially-and whom he is eager to emulate. For life to them, the daring, the energetic, the restless, seems to offer endless possibilities, and they all have one goal: to make their will felt in the world, to impose upon the world and its citizens their ideas of man and reality in order to increase their sense of power and as a consequence their sense of personal uniqueness.

It's undoubtedly Thea Fenchel, who most cogently illustrates this. She tames her eagle-that is, exerts power-not because she loves the bird, but, as Augie puts it, because "The motive of power over her, the same as afflicted practically everyone I had ever known in some fashion, ... carried and plunged us forward" (341). Although Augie may allow himself to be modeled on an eagle tamer, even wants to be an eagle tamer, it does not mean that he can really become one. You might begin to love the defenseless lizards employed to train the eagle instead, as Augie does, and thus incur Thea's wrath about his inveterate inclination to humanize fierce nature and the world in general, just as in the end the eagle incurs her wrath and contempt when Caligula proves himself very definitely a coward by refusing to fight the giant lizards. What Augie learns from the experience is that "power" can not make you overlook "the part of nature", that is to say, it is impossible to impose upon the bird a version of reality which is alien to his nature. If one insists he begins to act unpredictably, just as Augie's own actions become unpredictable when, despite his love for Thea, he lets himself become involved with Stella. So Thea's will to increase her sense of power fails in taming eagle and keeping Augie's love because she imposes upon them a version of reality alien to their nature.

Tamkin in *Seize the Day* has all the attributes of Tommy's "bad" angel. He appeals to Tommy's rational and emotional needs, as would the devil. Tommy needs money. Tamkin explains to him how it can be made on the commodities market. "You have to act fast—buy it and sell it; sell it and buy again. But quick! ... You don't want to be a fool while everyone else is making" (*SD* 13). They become "equal" partners in a commodities venture. He needs someone to help him, and Tommy feels that Tamkin would be able to get him through the crisis and bring him to safety also. Their symbiotic relationship is emphasized when Wilhelm observes that he "was on Tamkin' back" (104). Tommy needs sympathy, and Tamkin fulfills this need. "At least Tamkin sympathizes with me and tries to give me a hand, whereas Dad doesn't want to be disturbed" (15). He would like to feel that someone cares about him. Tamkin makes him feel that way. Tommy would like an understanding with his father. Tamkin explains the problems involved. It's the eternal same story and the elemental conflict of parent and child. It won't end, ever. "Even with a fine old gentleman like your dad.... All the same, you should be proud of such a fine old patriarch of a father" (68). Tamkin corroborates Tommy's attitude about Margaret's (his wife) destructiveness by putting it in terms of a generalization concerning all women. He tells Tommy: "Innately, the female knows how to cripple by sickening a man with guilt. It is a very special destruct, and she sends her curse to make a fellow impotent. As if she says, 'unless I allow it, you will never more be a man"' (106).

Tommy is guilty about his past and is anxious about the future. Tamkin assures him that the past is no good. The future is full of anxiety. Only the present is real—the here-and-now. Seize the day. Tommy doesn't understand himself. Tamkin attempts to explain human behavior in terms of the "real soul" and the "pretender soul." He then goes on to say: "biologically, the pretender soul takes away the energy of the true soul and makes it feeble, like a parasite. It happens unconsciously, unawaringly, in the depths of the organism" (78). Tamkin is the other half of Wilhelm, his alter ego, his bad angel, who tells him all the things he likes to hear.

Tamkin possesses the power of words. His ability to use and misuse the language gives him a mastery over the impuissant Tommy. Tamkin's words are not used to communicate ideas, but to seduce his listener. And Tommy is caught. Dr. Adler Tommy's father, a strong man, is not deceived by Tamkin. He recognizes that he is "clever," "cunning," "a liar," and an "operator," and not to be trusted. Tommy lacks his father's strength of character. He recognizes

Tamkin as a charlatan, but is beguiled by him nevertheless. Tamkin inveigles Tommy so that he goes along with him on his speculative venture. Ultimately, Tommy falls prey to this enticement. After losing Tommy's money, Tamkin disappears to seek his next victim in a new territory. Tommy is lack of awareness and vigilance-defences necessary for survival in the city. There is the recognition, however, that the city jungle is the product of man's being, spun out of his own substance. It is for this reason, because of this intimate interrelationship, that man can not deny the reality of the city. The city is his creation as he is the city's creature.

In *Mr. Sammler's Planet*, the idea of man's animality, man's descent, and the survival of the fittest is evoked with the thief's appearance: He spoke no more than a puma would and his face showed the effrontery of an animal. Furthermore, he seems like a great black beast, seeking whom he might devour. And as Sammler looks at him, he feels an immediate descent. Finally, when he exposes himself to Sammler, he asserts Freud's theory of sexual power symbolized by the phallus: "At any rate, there was the man's organ, . . . a prominent and separate object intended to communicate authority. As, within the sex ideology of these days, it well might. It was a symbol of superlegitimacy or sovereignty" (55). One reviewer goes so far as to call the exhibitionist episode "an image for the novel as a whole: reason and decency confronting law, lawless, primordial threat. Civilization facing disintegration" (Gross 154).

Bellow does not complain about the city per se as he knows that it is created by and made up of people. While criticizing the city as an entity, he places the final responsibility on the individual human being: it is human beings who create or corrupt the city, and hence evil not being inherent in cities but in the nature of man.

Chapter Two Bellow's Awareness of Survival

Despite Bellow's depiction of the modern world filled with images of filth, debris, noise, crime, and death, Bellow, as a Jewish writer, whose moral vision is an integral part of the Jewish outlook, holds a positive attitude to existence and expresses generally optimistic and affirmative views in his writings. Bellow believes in the divinity of the individual, and he or she is created in the image of God and is, therefore, majestic. He or she has the ability to overcome obstacles that challenge or impede human endeavor and to determine his or her own destiny. His views, which stem from the tenets of Judaism, become the themes and perspectives of his fiction.

Bellow deals with freedom of choice, social responsibility, the lifestyle of a good man, brotherly love, the uniqueness of the individual, and the dignity and divinity of man in his fiction, the beliefs deriving from Jewish perspective. His novels focus on the individual, the options available to him, his preferences and judgments, and his capabilities in dealing with his present predicament. His characters may grumble, lament, fret, and complain, but they do not despair about the future. Bellow, indebted to his Jewish Weltanschauung, fulfills his responsibility to show human beings' ability to overcome the darkness in modern wasteland.

The Jewish people have a long history of exile and Diaspora. Those terrible experiences are deeply imbedded in the memories of the Jewish people and constantly turn up in their consciousness. The Jewish influences endow the Jewish writers, including Bellow, with a strong awareness of survival. In each of his novels, he focuses on the life of one man, who is experiencing a kind of suffering-temporary alienation from society, financial problems, divorce, and disillusionment. Nevertheless, he transcends his material existence of limitations and finds a foothold in modern society.

Bellow believes that the modern writer must confront and overcome the darkness of this world. In his repeated defenses of the modern novelist, as John Clayton notes, Bellow assumes the position of "a kind of priest bringing value to the world, a mad world which rejects the individual" (Clayton 247). Bellow rejects the contemporary condition of unaccommodated alienation of the individual, and his fiction emphasizes the value of brotherhood and community.

Bellow himself claims vigorously that the writer can no longer dream of an age when the artist had real acceptance, and enjoyed a vital harmony with his surroundings. Rather he must accept his present age for what it is and confront it as best he can with his imaginative gifts. To Bellow, life is a miracle, no matter how intense is the suffering on earth. That is why Bellow believes in the here-and-now and tries to live his life fully in a big city cluttered with confusion and ugliness, sordidness and madness.

Bellow never tires of exposing the purely commercial aspects of American society which often promote "mass culture" and obstruct the "interior life" which the writer seeks to satisfy. Bellow's primary concern as a writer is to have a moral purpose as a justification for his art. Because the moral idea is shaped in the human psyche, Bellow depends ultimately on his characters to convey his value judgments. For in all his novels moral discovery is made in the protagonist's attempt to overcome his alienated condition.

Although like many modern writers Bellow may write of alienated, burdened characters, he gives them the capacity to attain inner dignity despite external restrictions and repressions. Their dignity is realized as they achieve community with others by transcending the all-important Me and becoming concerned for others. It is through this very concept of character that Bellow counteracts "crudity, disorder, ugliness, and lawlessness" of modern life, dramatizes the human quest for the realization of freedom, community, individual choice, order and historical perspective, and make sure that human being can survive in the modern urban environment. .

1. Bellow's Moral Responsibility as a Writer

Our contemporary world is plagued with moral ambiguities and more and more as we lose our compass in life and as dogmas befuddle and distort our consciousness we need to continuously seek the redemptive powers of art and literature. Here Bellow sees the contemporary predicament of our time: "... we stand open to all anxieties. The decline and fall of everything is our daily dread, and we are agitated in private life and tormented by public questions" (Bellow, *It All Adds Up* 92). The moral and ethical blueprints that have sustained the standards for human conduct in Western Civilization can be traced to the poetry and philosophy of men such as Homer, Horace, Socrates, Plato, and Aristotle. The pursuit of the good life in search of truth and wisdom by means of an intellectual inquiry and moral self – discipline was mostly the domain of philosophy but it was literature and the arts that really defined our aesthetic sensibilities and moral responsibilities.

From the epic tales of poetry and drama emerged literature with its flowering of irony, metaphors, and allusions; the art of this new prose also followed the ancient tradition honoring the moral values of mankind. Bellow, too, has paid homage to this tradition: "He [Bellow] believed that literature should hew to one of its original purposes-the raising of moral questions-and his own works remained indebted to those he had studied as a boy: the Old Testament, Shakespeare's plays and the great 19th-century Russian novels" (Kakutani,

"Heart break," E. 1). Keith Opdahl also notes the recurring theme of man's religious and moral needs: "One of the most striking characteristics of Bellow's work is his view of the personal and the metaphysical as a continuum, in which personality finds justification in a universal principle or moral order which it reflects" (7). In his non-fiction collection It All Adds Up, Bellow titles his opening chapter "Mozart: An Overture" in which he strives to explain, among other things, why the world should be indebted to the wondrous and mystical music of Mozart. In the closing sentences of the chapter, we can see how deeply Bellow feels about the role of art as a conduit for our deep mysteries: "In him [Mozart] we see a person who has only himself to rely on. But what a self it is, and what an art it has generated. How deeply (beyond words) he speaks to us about the mysteries of our common human nature. And how unrestrained and easy his greatness is" (14). In a later chapter titled "An Interview with Myself" in this same text, Bellow alludes to the function of art as a tonic for the soul: "The power of a work of art is such that it induces a temporary suspension of activities. It leads to contemplative states, to wonderful and, to my mind, sacred states of the soul" (84). It seems clear that from his early studying of *The Old Testament* and later understanding the play of art, Bellow would gravitate toward those writers that were imbued with a moral imperative. It falls in place, then, that in his first novel and in the words of his character John Pearl, Bellow is ruminating on the value of art: "The real world is the world of art and of thought. There is only one worth-while sort of work, that of the imagination" (Bellow, *Dangling Man* 91).

For writers like Bellow, this function of literature to raise and adjudicate moral questions has become increasingly significant in the last century as we have witnessed the fragmentation of our moral foundation; the record of man's evil conduct representative in incessant wars, greed, and genocides speaks for itself. Thus the function of art on a general level is important, not only as vehicle to produce works of aesthetic principles based on the beautiful, but to argue that moral conduct of the good must be a prerequisite for all forms of art. This moral conduct is differentiated from institutional and religious dogma and instead is grounded in the precepts of the cardinal virtues such as truth, beauty, wisdom, courage, temperance and justice.

From the inception of communal living, all civilizations and their cultures needed to determine and establish parameters and standards for moral behavior, ethical principles and artistic values. Through various processes, each culture, irrespective of geography, formulated social, political, and economic systems to control and manage the wild impulses of its population previously prone to savagery. However, it was only after centuries that these systems, through trial and error, were firmly planted as standard institutions in the civilized lands of the world. It was the implementation of moral, ethical, and artistic codes that lubricated the machinery of civilization. The framers of these systems were first concerned that for society to function on some level of equality and respect for the rights of all people, it was important that from a governing and moral point of view that the architects of society should construct a body of obligations, rules and duties to serve as prescriptive standards for ethical human conduct. In addition to these codes, the institution of art, in its various forms of poetry, literature, painting, sculpture, architecture, and cinema, and so on, supplemented society with standards of aesthetic principles of the beautiful and appealing. It can be argued that art, in producing an aesthetic value in the form of beauty, can be considered a barometer for moral conduct should we follow Keats' formula that "Beauty is truth, truth beauty." Perhaps, indeed this is all we need to know.

The discussion of whether a work of art should have a moral value and the question whether a work of art can be admired on a moral ground and at the same time be aesthetically satisfying, has been debated for centuries. Morris Dickstein, in the preface to his book, A *Mirror in the Roadway*: *Literature and the Real Word*, aptly references Wordsworth and Walter Benjamin as he explains the role of poetry and the emerging influence of literature:

> Wordsworth saw poetry as an instrument for the education of the feelings, a means of nurturing our decency and humanity, rescuing our fellow feelings from the numbing effects of modern life. Walter Benjamin echoed Wordsworth (and in a sense anticipated the Internet) when he described the impact of daily journalism, with its overload of information, in dulling the sensibilities of its readers. But where Wordsworth appealed to poetry for resistance, Benjamin looked to storytelling, with its links to an oral tradition. By the middle of the nineteenth century, the novel had effectively begun to replace poetry as a means of repairing tattered human bonds. (XIII)

More and more we will notice that as the anxieties and turmoil of modern life numbs us, the more humanity turns to the arts for relief. Not dissimilar to television of today, the novel in the hands of such masters like Dickens, Tolstoy, Dostoevsky, and Hemingway provide a hallucinatory escape from the harsh realities of daily life. On the other hand, as Dickstein points out, there are the reality instructors such as Kafka and Beckett who craft their stories to probe "the limits of human endurance and disorientation, surreal situation made all the more credible by their dark comedy and precise circumstantial detail" (XV). As Martha Nussbaum later explains in this chapter, it is the poetic language of literature that profoundly affects us; this is the art form that can transform our world from the opaque to the intelligible. As a universal agency, literature has the power to inscribe, dye, and stitch the moral fabric of the tapestry that we call life.

From the time of man's consciousness as he looked upward to the stars, he must have searched for words to describe his feeling of awe as he pondered the sublime of the universe. In his own way, whether his words rhymed or not, his cognizance of something divine and beautiful must have ignited the first spark that would later determine his moral orbit. I believe it is this same awareness that within man's limited consciousness, there is a perception of a larger harmony that dictates that human conduct should be dedicated to the interest and well – being of his fellow man. It is possible that this very same acknowledgement of the sublime inspired the likes of Homer, Aeschylus, Dante, Chaucer, Shakespeare, and Whitman to have colored our world with beauty, imagination, and intelligence. This coloring has molded our ethos to elevate humanity from our base instincts to a more civilized community of man. These are the virtues of poetry that have reinforced our sense of moral conduct; in the realm of the beautiful we are inspired to be good. Tzvetan Todorov, in his essay "Poetry and Morality," examines the relationship between poetry and morality. Todorov in his first paragraph reminds us that this debate between poetry and morality extends over 2, 500 years ago; not only has this argument been the domain of philosophers, but historians, artists, and critics as well have engaged in this never-ending disputation. This dialectic inquiry, according to Todorov, has been divided into three groups: the first suggests that poetry should yield to morality; secondly, that morality should bow to poetry, and finally, that the two fields should be separate and independent. Todorov argues in favor of the second domain as he cautions us that we can be trapped in dogma when we subscribe to the first classical argument which suggests:

> Poetry should place itself in the service of moral principles, that esthetic values should be subject to ethical ones. As we all know, this position is expressed in Greek Antiquity by Plato, who, once he deemed that poets did not satisfy the demands of morality, repudiated them by banishing them form the city. It is also the dominant position of Christian esthetics, which places art in the service of religious doctrine. But history has reversed things; what seemed self-evident two thousand years ago we find shocking today.

In her essay "The Sovereignty of Good Over Other Concepts," the philosopher Iris Murdoch argues that in the branch of moral philosophy the most prominent activity in the human psyche is the natural inclination to be selfish. The psyche, in pursuit of self, prefer not to face the dark and threatening realities of our everyday life and even how much we strive to believe in a higher power, the human animal, at all costs constantly seeks consolation through a fertile imagination where self is inflated. Murdoch, in the following passage establishes her hypotheses to suggest an end can justify the means:

> We are anxiety – ridden animals. Our minds are continually active, fabricating an anxious, usually self – preoccupied, often falsifying veil which partially conceals the world. Our states of consciousness differ in quality,

> our fantasies and reveries are not trivial and unimportant, they are profoundly connected with our energies and with or abilities to choose and act. And if quality and consciousness matters, then anything that alters consciousness in the direction of unselfishness, objectivity and realism is to be connected with virtue. (198)

Murdoch contends that there is no external point in human life that guarantees us relief from our anxieties; this existential state often gives us license to create a parallel consciousness that allows us to move from our pre-occupation with self to that communal level of unselfishness. Murdoch believes that the production of art is in direct consequence of this other consciousness that employs the imagination to blanket our anxieties and to replace this state with a framework of moral decency and accountability. In this same vein we can appreciate the how the art of Impressionism was in direct consequence to the atrocities of World War I.

Murdoch reinforces her theme by citing Plato's concept of beauty which propounds that we all possess the capacity to instinctually recognize and love beauty on a spiritual level. From this awareness we can therefore transform the beauty in nature to the beauty in art. However, Murdoch cautions us that we must differentiate between good art and fantasy art (self – consolation), for moral conduct is predicated by good art which instructs against the pursuit of selfish obsession: "It invigorates our best faculties and, to use Platonic language, inspires love in the highest part of the soul. ... Art then is not a diversion or a side – issue; it is the most educational of all human activities and a place in which the nature of morality can be seen" (Murdoch 199—200). Murdoch further points out that it is art that punctures the cloak of our darkness, and it is through this opening we are able to perceive and interpret our realties beyond appearances. These realities, however, are not trifling and mundane but are the high virtues that determine the essence of our morality. Arriving at this plane is possible when "we examine what are essentially the same concepts ... such as justice, accuracy, truthfulness, realism, humility, courage, as the ability to sustain clear vision, love as attachment, or even passion without sentiment or self" (Murdoch 200).

Besides the concepts such as truth, love, and beauty that drive the passion for art, so too does man's injustice against his fellow man create the need for art to howl in pain and to record these iniquities for posterity. The function of such a record is not necessarily only to indict the perpetrators of these atrocities such as genocides, but to document that such unbelievable acts of evil that seem beyond our humanity have indeed occurred. Such art serves as a moral museum to remind the world not so much that man is capable of evil but to what extent we can prevent this evil from recurring. It is no wonder then that Bellow's literary production constantly references the horror of the Holocaust: "Bellow and his friends were the children of the Holocaust rather than the ghetto. They did not write about the recent events in Europe-they hadn't directly experienced them-but those horrors cast their shadow on every page of their work, including the many pages of desperate comedy" (Dickstein 171). We must not forget that "desperate comedy" is itself an art form as Murdoch alludes to earlier as the "falsifying veil which partially conceals the world." Thus we can understand the prominence of Jewish self-parody and humor not necessarily as an avenue to entertain the "others" but as the only available too to deal with the horror of being a Jew in a time and place when six million Jews were systematically annihilated as the "civilized" world looked on.

There is a general belief that a major function of narrative art is to postulate a framework of moral values. The themes in such narratives are supposed to lift us out of our restricted and limited spheres of experiences in pursuit of various levels of enlightenment. Through our immersion of the text we become cognitive of the forms representing ideal standards leading to the moral high ground. Thus, as participants of the text, we are affected by plot, characters, themes, style, diction, setting and so on, to a point that the author is often relegated to obscurity for the simple reason that the narrative has taken on a life of its own. However, Longinus, in his treatise "On the Sublime," suggests that the narrative should be an extension of the author and that any work of sublime and moral value must be in direct relation to the elevated language of the author. According to Longinus, there are five major requirements for elevated language: the first is that the author must be capable of "the power of forming great conceptions" (79) followed by the narrator possessing "vehement and inspired passion" (79). The other three prerequisites demand the author's expertise in figures of speech, noble diction, and elevated composition. In relation to the writer as a conduit for moral direction relative to the power of "forming great conceptions," Longinus suggests that as writers we must

> ... nurture our souls to the thoughts sublime, and make them always pregnant, so to say with noble inspiration. Sublimity is the echo of great soul [and] ··· the truly eloquent must be free from low and ignoble thoughts. For it is not possible that men with mean and servile ideas prevailing throughout their lives should produce anything admirable and worthy of immortality. (79)

This idea of noble inspiration has been the universal call of the muse and from both an artistic and moral point of view it is perceptive how Bellow's canvas covers both the sublime and the ordinary: "Instead, Bellow turns these monologues into aching meditations on what makes us human. But late Bellow is often great Bellow, in part because of this current rumination on ultimate things, on the stark contrast between the little disturbances of man and the cosmic chill of constellations ... " (Dickstein 211). Longinus further explains in his treatise that for authors to understand the form of the sublime, it is imperative that in their studies of the great and accomplished writers like Homer and Demosthenes, they should practice the art of emulation and imitation, "For many men are carried away by the spirit of others as if inspired" (83). On another level, Longinus stresses the need for an author to immerse himself in the sublime for "sublimity raises them near the majesty of God" (94); this is the awareness of awe that will connect the author to a sense of divinity that will invariably instruct his work.

Saul Bellow was nine years old when his family moved from Montreal to Chicago, where he lived most of his years, and it is from the backdrop of this city that many of his novels are developed. As much as Bellow has maintained that he is not a Jewish writer as he has indicated in his interview with Kulshrestha, it is undoubtedly that his immersion and early upbringing as an Orthodox Jew in urban Montreal and Chicago, not far removed from the Jewish ghettoes of Eastern Europe, centrally influenced his work. The only gentile protagonists in Bellow's Jewish oeuvre are Eugene Henderson in *Henderson the Rain King* and Clara Velde in *A Theft*. Bellow's Yiddish background has remained a constant and formative influence in his work as Alfred Kazin, in his essay "My Friend Saul Bellow," observes: "he had been brought up as an orthodox Jew; and he had a proper respect for God as the ultimate power assumed but the creation" ("My Friend Saul Bellow" 4). It is this unflinching respect for God and faith in the ancient texts that has anchored Bellow's ethical and moral standards:

> He was brought up in a deeply Jewish spirit and with the Yiddish language, the life-thread of a cultural and religious tradition in Eastern Europe ... This is Bellow's tradition, and of the many interesting and talented novelists of Jewish background in this country, there is probably no other who feels so lovingly connected with the religious and cultural tradition of his Eastern European grandfathers. (Kazin, "My Friend Saul Bellow" 7)

This reverent connection to his Judaic heritage has nurtured and sustained Bellow's writing; from this seemingly ordinariness Bellow has illuminated the dramatic undercurrents in a culture that honors tradition and ancestral values. From this quotidian, Bellow extracts and magnified the personal and domestic struggles and suffering of Jews who are acutely aware of their place in history. However, as much as Bellow is steeped into the circumstances of his culture, his work speaks to both Gentile and Jew.

In his book *Bellow*, James Atlas commences his first chapter with a quote from Bellow's "The Jefferson Lectures": "The living man is preoccupied with such questions as who he is, what he lives for, what he is so keenly and interminably yearning for, what his human essence is" (3). To a great extent, this observation summarizes the recurring subject pervasive in much of Bellow's fiction that investigates the idea of isolation, spiritual fracture, and the potentiality of human renewal. Many of Bellow heroes are men stranded in the middle of some spiritual crisis, are overwhelmed with too many options in the world, and are not equipped to deal with their awareness of death. Bellow heroes do not sink into easy despair nor do they fall victim to easy optimism. Bellow's fiction is philosophically instructive as we will see that as an artist bent on honoring ancient and trusted codes, his art not only makes sense of the painful realities sapping the energies of the modern man, but digs deeper into understanding and reconnecting that ancient spirit that grounds man with the mystery of his being.

Saul Bellow is a unique spokesman for humanitarian ideals in American literature in the twentieth century. There can be no doubt that Bellow was deeply concerned with the fate of the Jews and affairs of the Jewish mind from the beginning of his literary life. He expresses in his writings his moral vision that is an integral part of the Jewish outlook. He believes in the divinity of the individual, and he or she is created in the image of God and is, therefore, majestic. He or she has the ability to overcome obstacles that challenge or impede human endeavor and to determine his or her own destiny. Bellow believes in the worthiness of life which is also God - given, and that one should partake and enjoy the kaleidoscopic experiences one encounters. It is a positive approach to existence and is reflected in a literature that is generally optimistic and affirmative.

Critics have attempted to link Bellow's affirmative approach to man and to life to various streams of literary expressions. Charles Eisinger, for example, attempts to link Bellow's attitudes of love and joy in life to the principles of Hasidism. He says: "Aware as he is of his Jewish heritage, accomplished as he is as a translator of Yiddish stories, Bellow yet offers in his work no evidence of either the theism or mysticism of Hasidism. He is a secular Hasid, whether he knows it or not" (C. Eisinger, 343). Bellow clearly declaims against this careless classification. He is just Jewish rather than Hasid, and his joy of living expresses his deeply rooted Jewish orientation.

Bellow's Jewish Weltanschauung is expressed clearly in his essays, which reflect his philosophy and represent a key to his fiction. Bellow is concerned that modern writing has presented a negative and destructive view of man. Bellow suggests that the negative should be diminished and the positive accentuated. Over and over again, Bellow stresses that the writer's problem is perspective, that he must present a more positive approach to life, based upon a love - relationship with humanity and a belief in the value of existence. It is the writer's function, according to Bellow, to dispel the current misanthropy found in literature, and through his creativity, to project the love of human - kind and the appreciation of the grandeur involved in man's minutest endeavors.

Bellow says that the only thing that matters for the writer is that he cares and believes in the existence of others, that he manifests a love for man. Bellow embraces both the affirmation of man and the infinite mysteries of life. He suggests that literary attitudes undergo change, but the mystery of man is constant, and writers should reflect this in their works. Bellow denigrates writers of the absurd and says that he believes "the moral function cannot be divorced from art…. either we want life to continue or we do not. If we don't want to continue, why write books? .... But if we answer yes…. we are liable to be asked how. In what form shall life be justified? That is the essence of the moral questions" ("The Writer as Moralist" 58—62).

The ideas expressed in these essays provide an insight to the reading of Bellow's fiction. He is a moralist as he believes all writers should be. He is concerned with the question of "What is man?" and his answer reveals an attitude which is positive, affirmative, optimistic. His views, which stem from the tenets of Judaism, become the themes and perspectives of his fiction, and they in turn, affect the tone, character, and style of all his works.

Bellow's novels deal with freedom of choice, social responsibility, the lifestyle of a good man, brotherly love, the uniqueness of the individual, and the dignity and divinity of man. His overall approach to life, as stated above, is affirmative and optimistic. In presenting these ideas as themes of his works, Bellow makes use of his Jewish background and his knowledge of the Old Testament and some of its exegetes.

For example, the biblical statement, "And God created man in His own image" (Genesis 1: 27) suggests that the human, by its very nature, possesses an aspect of the Divine. Bearing the Divine image, there is something unique in man; he has no exact duplicate, and it is incumbent upon him, therefore, to express his uniqueness and individuality. While expressing his individuality, man is given the freedom of choosing between good and evil, but he is encouraged to choose good, which is equated with both life and with God (Deuteronomy 30: 15, 19). This distinction between good and evil becomes the eternal problem for man's decision, but it is the good which echoes like a theme throughout Scriptures, indicated what man's choice should be. The first chapter of Genesis states "and it was good" six times and ends with the declaration: "And God saw everything that He had made, and, behold, it was very good." From the beginning to the end, the focus is on the good, which Milton Steinberg defines as a "quality objectively present in men and their conduct" (Steinberg 62). It also appears to be a quality present in all that God created, and therefore, it becomes an obligation to enjoy life as an acknowledgement of God's presence in the world. Jewish sages say: "He who sees a legitimate pleasure and does not avail himself of it is an ingrate against God who made it possible" (Steinberg 73). This does not mean that man's approach to life should be hedonistic or completely sensual. It does suggest that any withdrawal from life is unnatural. Man is a composite of both spirit and flesh, and both need to be gratified. Steinberg suggests that "Judaism views voluntary abstinence from marriage as a triple sin—against the health of body, the fulfillment of soul, and the welfare of society" (75). Similarly, asceticism, or even isolation of any sort, is seen as immoral and selfish. The isolate has taken all from society — life, language, ideas — but gives nothing in return. The dictum: "separate not thyself from the community" becomes a vital injunction in Judaism. Only as a social being can man affirm the goodness that is in life and his love for his neighbor, for he, too, was created in the image of God.

Furthermore, the most striking characteristic of Jewish prophecy is its relentless demand for morality. Social behavior, religious attitudes, personal development, learning, all are closely connected to the moral dimension. Morality is very carefully and clearly defined by the prophet; namely, it is the ability to distinguish between good and evil and to do the good. It is important to point out that for the prophet evil is as real as the good and that man has to consciously do battle with evil and, hopefully, conquer it. This kind of moral concern for man is at the center of Jewish culture. Art is never, Howe explains, "... its own excuse for being." Beauty is not separated from good; "one spoke not of a beautiful thing but of a beautiful deed or event...." (Howe, "Introduction" 8) Nor was intellect separated from morality. Related to the Jew's moral concern for others, the writer's moral concern for those he writes about①, is the Jew's belief in community. If the Jew is an aboriginal alienatee, he is also the product of an ingrown community. Howe notes that the Jewish child was loved and was beaten, was turned into a little mench terribly young-but was never ignored. ② The strong family ties and the community are responsible for the fact that the Jew of Bellow's generation may despair, may be filled with childhood guilt, but they are not hollow men isolated from one another.

In addition, social responsibility as a foundation of society is suggested at the beginning of the Old Testament in the early narrative concerning Cain and Abel. When God queries Cain: "Where is Abel thy brother?" (Genesis 4:9), it is not that God does not know the whereabouts of Abel. But He wants Cain to realize that he is his brother's keeper, that he is responsible for his actions, and these actions become the core of societal structure. The preservation of society rests upon the proper choice between good and evil.

Joseph in *Dangling Man* has been called up to the army, but because he is a Canadian by birth, though an American citizen, he has not yet been inducted. He has left his job, moved out of his apartment, but for almost a year has lived in a situation of "dangling" between two worlds, being neither a soldier nor a civilian. He is alone ten hours a day in a single room. He no longer sees friends, and his relationship with his family is no better. He is free. He has all the time to do all the things he previously never got around to doing. Yet he feels more imprisoned now than ever before. As he says that he is separate, alienated and distrustful in the room, and that finds in his purpose not an open world, but a closed, hopeless jail. Joseph finally realizes that to be totally and fully unattached and uncommitted is an imprisonment. Real freedom would seem to consist in the ability to choose that which you prefer to do. Bellow

---

① See Bellow, "Distractions"

② See Howe, "Introduction," pp. 41—42.

leads Joseph into the recognition that there is no such thing as abstract freedom. Freedom is relative. You are free from something, or free to do something. You have freedom of thought and freedom of movement, but suspension and stasis are not freedom. Man does not and cannot exit in a vacuum. As Joseph says, man is part of the world, whether he likes it or not. The ending of the novel is significant. When he says that he is in other hands, relieved of self - determination, and freedom canceled, he is referring to the kind of freedom that created a "dangling man," in which "self - determination" was no more than a "narcotic dullness". When he says that hooray for regular hours and long Live regimentation, he means freedom lies in the choice of responsibility, which confirms his relationship with society. This concept of freedom just reflects the basic tenets of Judaism.

Social responsibility is further expounded in *The Victim*. Social responsibility is not only a pillar of Jewish thought, but also an accepted norm of universal social behavior. Asa Leventhal is a man, who, we are told at the very onset of this work, feels a kinship with all of humanity. He is constantly faced with the question whether he is his brother's keeper. And in answering the question, he may grumble, but he never declines the responsibility. He is cognizant of his duty to his family and to his friends. When his brother's family needs help because his nephew is sick and his brother is in Texas, for the first time in his life Asa leaves his job early, goes to Staten Island in response to Elena's (his sister in law) frantic phone call, and becomes his nephew's surrogate father.

While Asa is troubled with the problems of his brother's family, another malady erupts to further disturb his equilibrium. Kirby Allbee, whom Asa has met briefly, accuses Asa of being the cause of the loss of his job, and, therefore, insists that Asa assume the burden of responsibility of Allbee and his regeneration or his reentry into the societal structure. Asa's intuitive reaction is to reject any responsibility for Allbee's degeneration, but his deeply humanistic outlook sympathizes with his fellow man's misfortune, and he proceeds to inquire about the events that had transpired. All the answers he receives seem to indicate that he is the indirect cause of Allbee's loss of position. Asa knows that Kirby's claim is ridiculous, but he feels a slight tinge of guilt because he senses the antipathy between Jew and Gentile and thinks he may have wanted to hit back at an offending Gentile to prove that the Jew is not a weakling, and that he personally is manly. To be human, one must think and one must feel, but the controlling factor at all times, must be that of one's own dignity. This becomes the key to social responsibility. It is also the solution to the dilemma of how a good man should live. Asa himself says that he has a strange and close consciousness of Allbee and a feeling of intimate nearness.

In a sense, Asa andKirby are antagonists and alter egoes. What fascinates Asa about Kirby is that although he appears as his antagonist, the Gentile, the ruined, the oppressor, Kirby mirrors Asa's fears and resentment: the fear of being blacklisted, the fear of being unemployed, the fear of emasculation, the fear of the loss of his wife, the fear of being a societal outcast, and the resentment against society for being in this position and against others who are not in a similar situation. Asa permits him into his apartment when Kirby says he has no place to sleep, feeds him, and gives him his clothes. Kirby attempts to assume Asa's role, makes himself a key to the apartment and comes and goes as if it were his own. But Kirby goes too far when he brings a woman into Asa's home. Asa feels the moral and personal effrontery and absolute disgust towards Kirby for having brought a strange woman into his bed. It is as if, he, himself, were committing adultery. This point, when Asa's dignity is debased by a threat to the sanctity of his home, is the moment when social responsibility becomes more than an abuse. Asa ejects Kirby from his domicile. Asa possesses characteristics that have been associated with the Jewish people: he is intellectual, a family man, and a surrogate father to his brother's family, and possesses a close feeling of kinship in his relationship to his brother.

The socialresponsibility is evident in Augie's immense involvement with others, which, of course, is reflected in his compassionate and sensitive nature. Augie never withdraws from people, regardless of the setback he may encounter at the time. His comment regarding Rousseau stresses the importance of man's recognition of himself as a social creature, and notes that the only way he can affect society, if that is what he seeks to do, is in its midst, not by withdrawal and objective recollection. Augie comments that you take that poor Rousseau and in the picture he leaves of himself, stubblefaced and milky, in a rope wig, while he wept at his own opera performed at court for the monarch and how he was encouraged by the weeping of the heart – touched ladies and fancied he' d like to gobble the tears from their cheeks. This sheer horse's ass of a Jean – Jacques who wouldn't get on with a single human being, goes away to the woods of Montmorency in order to think and write of the best government or the best system of education. Augie goes on, "I can mention many others, less great, but however worried, spoiled, or perverse, still wanting to set themselves apart for great ends, and believing in at least one worthiness. That's what the more deep desire is under the apparent ones" (*AM* 367).

One can only understand and respond to society's needs if one is a vital part of the community because the ideal is very far from the real, the abstract far from the concrete. Augie's dream is to establish an "academy foster – home" to care for children, to teach them, to help them. Even though finally his dream seems to have eluded him, the point, however, is that his thoughts are not egocentric. At no time is he arrogant, cruel, misanthropic, or unloving. He is a happy social creature who refuses to lead a life of "quiet desperation" or even just a disappointed life.

In Bellow's first novel *Dangling Man*, Joseph asks himself, "How should a good man live; what ought he to do?" (39). This is the major question that has driven Bellow in search of moral parameters to frame his overall quest for humanity. This quest, as Clayton points out, is part and parcel of the Yiddish/Judaic divinity steeped in wondrous awe of the ordinary where the Jew pines for the arrival of the final Sabbath when the Redeemer will come and until that day, every Sabbath is sacred in anticipation of the joy and holiness that will pervade the world upon the arrival of this Redeemer. The Judaic sense of spiritual arrival is not a vertical journey to the heights of heaven but is attained in the horizontal immersion of the ordinary and the common life. Thus it is easy to understand why Bellow's recurring themes are closely tied not to the powerful, but to the struggling everyday man: "The Jew totters between the everyday world and the miraculous one at hand" (Clayton 31). Bellow, as a Jew, understands that suffering, joy, and redemption are not worlds apart but are immediately present in the tension of daily life. As Clayton tells us that the Jew has the power, at least according to the Hasidic tradition, of making the everyday actions of his life sacred by the manner in which he performs them. The zaddik teaches Torah by the way he ties his shoes, washes dishes, dances. Hasidism teaches that common life itself can be sanctified, *what is* can be made *what ought to be*. "Through the piety of the Jews the redeemer will come. In Jewish fiction this duality accounts for the combination of a realistic portrayal of everyday life with a fervent idealism" (Clayton 31—32). Bellow, as the student of Judaism is aware that the sanctity of life is in direct consequence of observing and respecting the everyday ordinariness and it is in this celebration in enduring that the pious Jew understands, as Clayton informs, that even a beggar can be the redeeming Prophet. Thus Bellow's characters are not inclined toward the lofty heavens but gravitate toward a sense of holiness and celebration of the common life.

The beliefs expressed above constitute the Jewish perspective. They become ingrained early into the psyche of the Jewish child and remain as his Weltanschauung in his more mature years. This is the effect that Bellow's Orthodox Jewish childhood has had upon the type of literature he creates. Also, Leo Baeck, a German - Jewish religious philosopher, who lived through and survived the Holocaust, states that the distinctiveness of Judaism, which it has passed on to the rest of mankind, is its ethical affirmation of the world: Judaism is the religion of ethical optimism.

> In Judaism this optimism becomes a demand for the heroism of man, for his moral will to struggle. It is an optimism which strives to realize morality in practice…. The optimism of Judaism consists of the belief in God, and consequently, also a belief in man, and the belief in mankind. (Baeck 86)

This "heroism of man" can be traced to the biblical narrative of Jacob's struggle with the angel and his refusal to yield to the strength of his unseen adversary. This is the kind of heroic optimism we find in Bellow's protagonists.

This essentially optimistic perspective and Bellow's knowledge of the Bible affect the style of his fiction. The Jewishness of Bellow's style has been noted by most critics. The Yiddish influence upon his language, the idiom, the gesture, the prolixity of his characters, is readily discernible and requires no special attention at this point. His novels focus on the individual, the options available to him, his preferences and judgments, and his capabilities in dealing with his present predicament. His characters may grumble, lament, fret, and complain, but they do not despair about the future. The desire to complain, however, lends itself both to the first -person narrative and to the memoir or confessional. *Dangling Man*, *The adventures of Augie March*, *Herzog*, *Henderson the Rain King* and *Humboldt's Gift* are written in this manner. It is also a major characteristic of Bellow's works to suggest various aspects of the comic mode in its attitude towards the universe and in its incongruous correlation between appearances and reality, what the individual thinks his station in life should be and what it really is, or in the inaccurate assessment by the individual of his abilities, his needs, and his situation. In addition to this, Bellow makes use of specific biblical narratives that express Jewish philosophy and perspective.

Bellow uses two biblical incidents that are specifically Jewish to express the main ideas of his works, that of Abraham smashing his father's idols and Jacob wrestling with the angel. Abraham is referred to both as the father of the Jewish people and the father of monotheism. He is important to the Jewish people because he was the first to recognize God as a Supreme Being. He is the first of the Jewish patriarchs, and his act of smashing his father's idols — which earned him the ire of King Nimrod who had him thrown into a fiery furnace from which he was saved by the angel Gabriel — ushers in a new perspective, a new way of viewing the world. With this act, he rejected the old form of worship, paganism, and instituted, in its place, monotheism.

However, even more than Abraham, Jacob symbolizes the Jewish ethic because the children of Israel ultimately are called - House of Jacob. The epochal trauma in the life of Jacob is envisioned by the scene in which he wrestles with the angel. Left alone on the night before his encounter with his arch -rival, Esau, the Bible tells us — "a man wrestled with him" (Genesis 32: 25). A well-known biblical commentator identifies this man as Samael, angel of darkness, deceit, perfidy, as an element in Jacob's own personality with which he must contend and overcome in order to acquire the spiritual stamina which will enable him to emerge the victor in his encounter with Esau. He achieves this but leaves the scene limping. The triumph is complete. He masters the struggle of conscience, but the trauma leaves its mark. His limping, however, makes him one with the rest of limping humanity. The Bible tells us henceforth his name is called Israel, suggesting man's dual role: master of himself and servant of the Lord. As a servant, Jacob is humbled and his limp remains a perpetual reminder that though he may rise to the celestial sphere of communication with the Most High, in essence, his life remains bound to the real world.

Bellow weaves these two biblical incidents so that together they constitute the fabric of his novel. In his writings, he views himself as an Abraham figure, while his protagonists are invested with the posture of Jacob. Bellow, in this patriarchal role, feels it incumbent upon himself to smash the idols of contemporary literature and to dispel its negative influence. In place of these destructive idols, he seeks to erect a tribute to man that will be beneficial to him, that will express the profundity of existence, the wonder of life, and the singular significance of the individual. The individual himself, Bellow's protagonist, is constantly engaged in a battle with a superior power: his conscience, his alter ego, and his fantasies. As in the narrative of Jacob, these forces assume the shape and form of adversaries so that he must struggle and reevaluate his position as a human being.

Bellow has said of the Jewish feeling within him that resists the claims of twentieth century apocalyptic romanticism; it rejects, that is, the belief that man is finished and that the world must be destroyed. The world is, on the contrary, sanctified. "Appearing after Hitler's obliteration of humanism, Bellow's works strive to reestablish the foundation of a society by reaffirming the world's need for morality, for the return to the humanism of Judaism" (Goldman, "Saul Bellow and the Philosophy of Judaism" 53). It is quite understandable that after the Holocaust, Bellow would more so instruct on the brotherhood of Jews as Goldman observes: "The quest for most Bellovian heroes is basically the same. It is not a search for identity, as some critics suggest. It is rather a quest for a significant existence that would embrace their own identity, such as it is" (58).

Bellow's fiction is moral fiction. It is not concerned with style "for its own sake" nor even psychological revelation for its own sake. It considers such moral – metaphysical problems as that of the demarcation of human responsibility (*The Victim*) and the relationship of the individual to the world of power (*Herzog*). Always it seeks to know why. Always it is concerned with the question of goodness-the failure or success of the sympathetic heart. It believes in man and in the potentiality of holiness and joy within the common life, the possibility of meaningful existence.

Bellow believes that literature should hew to one of its original purposes – the raising of moral questions-and his own works remain indebted to those he has studied as a boy: the Old Testament, Shakespeare's plays and the great 19th – century Russian novels. For Bellow, this function of literature to raise and adjudicate moral questions has become increasingly significant in the last century as we have witnessed the fragmentation of our moral foundation; the record of man's evil conduct representative in incessant wars, greed, and genocides speaks for itself.

Bellow, in his short piece "The Writer as Moralist" says: "The writer in any case finds that he bears the burdens of priest or teacher. Sometimes he looks like the most grotesque of priests, the most eccentric of teachers, but I believe the moral function cannot be divorced from art." As much as Bellow thrives on Jewish culture, especially going back to his Yiddish inheritance, his themes are steeped in a moral conviction universal to all cultures. Bellow's view is that of a

Jew, yet he is speaking of all men:

> Remembering that he spoke Yiddish before he spoke English or French, we assume that he assimilated the Jewish heritage with his mother's milk. He assimilated "the virtue of powerlessness, the company of the dispossessed, the sanctity of the insulted and injured," as Irving Howe has put it-the great themes of Yiddish literature. And because of this, Bellow speaks for all voices or powerlessness, humiliation, and weakness everywhere. (Walden 145)

Bellow, in his short piece "The Writer as Moralist" implies a relationship between art and morality: "The writer in any case finds that he bears the burdens of priest or teacher. Sometimes he looks like the most grotesque of priests, the most eccentric of teachers, but I believe the moral function cannot be divorced from art."

2. Jewish Culture Heritage

Jewish historic journey was one suffering afteranother, but yet, as a group of people, they were able to influence the world of science and medicine. Harold Heifetz quotes Albert Memmi who reinforces the perspective on this defining aspect of Judaism:

> My delight in Jewish history has never been more than a gloomy delight, the reminder of an endless succession of disasters, flights, pogroms, emigrations, humiliations, injustices . . . I have only to open a book of Jewish history. . . What is called Jewish history is but one long contemplation of Jewish misfortune, despite the extraordinary originality of Hebraic thought, (and) its astounding impact on the world. (Heifetz 9—10)

"Saul Bellow's defense of man has been made in the cultural confluence of two main streams: the Jewish experience and the American experience" (Clayton 30). Of the two experiences, the Jewish experience has been crucially more determinative for Bellow as his heritage, as it frames the Jewish culture, unequivocally instructs on the belief of man and his allegiance to the natural right to life. We can understand how this value and respect for the sanctity of life has evolved over the centuries to shield against unmitigated persecution, genocide, and despair of Jews. And as Clayton poses this question, "How has the Jew said yes to the grimmest facts" (31). The Jewish history is the reminder of an endless succession of disasters, flights, pogroms, emigrations, humiliations, and injustices. What is called Jewish history is but one long contemplation of Jewish misfortune.

Bellow began his writing career just about the end of World War II and he was cognizant of Hitler's gas chambers and death camps. In addition, Bellow was born in North America in 1915 of parents who had escaped from Russia and the pogroms against Jew. Finally, Bellow would have grown up learning about the historic persecution of Jews; even up to the middle of the twentieth - century in America Jews were still considered second - class citizens. And so having grown up understanding the present and historic suffering of his fellow Jews, Bellow has a strong awareness of survival.

The experience of suffering is inherent in Bellow's world. His protagonists, who are all men, are not happily married nor are they found in setting indicative of community; on the contrary, these men are solitary figures who live in their own minds and whose collective existence is unbearable with the suffering of daily life. Similarly, the Jewish people have a long history of suffering of exile and Diaspora. The exilic experiences are repeated throughout Jewish history so that the struggle for survival has long become a subconscious theme in Jewish writings.

According to the Bible, the earliest exilic experience can be dated back to the ancestors of human beings, when Adam and Eve are expelled from the Garden of Eden because they transgress against God's rule in eating the forbidden fruit. They are put in exile on the earth, tilling the ground. And human beings are also unable to return to Eden, and have to live in a state of exile, forever in the struggle for survival.

As recorded in the Bible, the Pharaoh in Egypt is afraid that the Israelite people in Egypt are more numerous and more powerful than the Egyptians, so he increases the burden on the Israelites and even orders that the any boy born to them be killed at birth. Moses, the great forefather of the Jewish people, unable to stand one of his kinsfolk being maltreated by an Egyptian, kills that man and flees into the desert. Later he leads his people out of Egypt through the wilderness to the land of Canaan, the land of milk and honey promised by God, after surviving various hardships.

But historical and biblical studies reveal that most miserable of all is the deportation of the Israeli people after the fall of the Israeli kingdom because of foreign invasion. In 722 BC, the Neo - Assyria Empire conquered the Northern Kingdom of Israel and deported more than 20, 000 Jews. In 587—586 BC, the independent Hebrew states were captured by the Babylonian king Nebuchadnezzar. The Holy Temple in Jerusalem was destroyed and an even larger number of Jews were taken into exile. Some Jews returned to Jerusalem after Cyrus, the Persian king, defeated the final Babylonian king in about 540 BC, but most remained in exile. In 73 AD, Jerusalem fell again at the hands of the Romans and was never to be constructed again until 1948, when Israel was founded. Although Jews kept going back to Palestine at different times, most Jews remained scattered throughout the world in Diaspora until the present.

The exile involved severe and traumatic experiences. Suffering went hand in hand with exile. The Jews were hurled into foreign lands, experienced the pain of separation from the homeland, and suffered from alienation, slavery, oppression, expulsion, and pogroms on the foreign land. Thousands of Jews lost their lives in the exile. With the long history of exile and sufferings, the theme of the struggle for survival is constant in Jewish culture. Human beings, who have been away from the Garden of Eden since the time of Adam and Eve, are forever in the exile to struggle to survive in the wandering and suffering.

In addition, the Jewish people have faced anti-Semitism, persecution and pogroms ever since very ancient times, which is recorded in the Bible: "They have said, Come, and let us cut them off from being a nation; that the name of Israel may be no more in remembrance" (Psalms83: 4). With the destruction of Jerusalem, the Jewish people became homeless and roamed the face of the earth, waiting for the Messiah to come. But the hostility towards the Jews turned out to be universal. Wherever they inhabited, they were regarded as strangers, Christ-killers, and enemies throughout history, forever pursued by antagonism, expulsion, and persecution. In the Middle Ages, the crusade was the turning point in the persecution of the Jewish people in that, unlike previous persecution limited to a small number of Jews, it began a holocaust on a large scale.

The development of modern civilization did not stop such cruelty. The whole European world bore a grudge against this people. Whatever serious trouble occurred, the Jews were taken as scapegoats and were blamed for it. One of the practices was to accuse them of blood libel: the Jews were accused of using the blood of Christian children in a special Jewish ritual in repetition and in mocking of the crucifixion of Jesus Christ.

The situation for the Jews in Eastern Europe had always been much worse than in Western and Central Europe. The Russian Jews had always been severely discriminated against and persecuted, and pogroms occurred frequently. The first pogrom on a large scale took place in 1881, when the assassination of the Russian Czar Alexander II was blamed on the Jews. Between 1881 and 1884, more than 200 Jewish towns were raided, and almost 20, 000 Jews were expulsed. Two other pogroms occurred respectively between 1903 and 1909, and between 1917 and 1921. In the later case, more than 60, 000 Jews were killed. In other Eastern European countries such as Hungary, Poland, Romania, Bulgaria, the Jewish people also underwent increasing persecution. A most atrocious example is recorded in history as the Chmielnicki massacre in Poland between the years 1648 and 1650, in which about 60, 000 Jews lost their lives. Persecution reached its unprecedented peak in the Nazi concentration camps in Germany during World War II, in which almost six million Jews were cruelly killed.

Even the United States as the Promised Land for the American Jews does not guarantee that Jewish people will not suffer, especially with a Jewish cultural heritage that is informed with universalism and sufferings for the hope of life in an ideal land. The American Jews realize that, with its reality of confusion, America is not quite the ideal land for them and suffer from the disillusionment about the United States as the model of democracy. When the Puritans first crossed the Atlantic Ocean to settle in the American land, they dreamed of establishing a New Jerusalem, but the sacred land gave way to a secular one. And the American society proved to be in conflict with the traditional system of democratic values as reflected in the Declaration of Independence and the Federal Constitution. The American Jews are among those who discover painfully that there is a gap between the American dream and what they have actually discovered in the American dominant culture. Even their cultural assimilation does not guarantee the disappearance of anti－Semitism. In *The Victim*, Bellow describes the awkward situation of Leventhal, a descendant of the immigrant Jews who is kept out the dominant society as an outsider. Harold Heifetz comments that:

> My delight in Jewish history has never been more than a gloomy delight, the reminder of an endless succession of disasters, flights, pogroms, emigrations, humiliations, injustices … I have only to open a book of Jewish history …What is called Jewish history is but one long contemplation of Jewish misfortune, despite the extraordinary originality of Hebraic though, (and) its astounding impact on the word. (9—10)

Those terrible experiences are nightmares for the Jewish people. Those experiences turn out to be an inevitable part of Jewish history, which is forever deeply imbedded in the memories of the Jewish people and constantly turns up in their consciousness. But why is it that the Jewish people, who consider themselves as God's chosen people, had to be in constant exile and sufferings? The Jews were puzzled at the reasons why a God of justice and righteousness, a creator of love and grace, allowed His chosen people to suffer, and why a God so powerful should have allowed such evils and sufferings as the Holocaust to exist. The Bible, the Torah and the Talmud have been trying all the time to make sense of exile and suffering. Jewish philosophers, such as Philo (25 BC－50 AD), Moses Maimonides, Spinoza, Mendelssohn, Cohen, and Buber, have also been trying to tackle the problem. And some of their theories and explanations prove illuminating to anyone concerned with the issue of human suffering.

Suffering is viewed as the punishment from God, and God is using foreign power to execute judgment against the Jews because of their sins and transgressions against God's Commandments, which mainly include polytheism and idolatry, fornication, bloodshed, and oppression of the weak and powerless in their own land. In the Bible, such prophets as Isaiah, Jeremiah, and Hosea give warnings of the destruction of Jerusalem on account of Israel's sins: "But rebels and sinners shall be destroyed together, and those who forsake the Lord shall be consumed" (Isaiah 1: 28). Isaiah and Jeremiah predict foreign invasion and prophesy devastation, deportation, and diaspora on the Israeli land respectively in Isaiah and Jeremiah.

Since it is a punishment for human sins, suffering is also considered to be of purgational function, and it is viewed as a way of correcting wrongs and evils. It was believed that the adversity that Israel underwent was to rinse the sinners of their sins, to bring repentance to the Israelis, and to bring correction or modification in Israel's way of thinking.

In the Bible, Isaiah talks of the purgation of judgment:

> Whoever is left in Zion andremains in Jerusalem will be called holy, everyone who has been recorded for life in Jerusalem, once the Lord has washed away the filth of the daughters of Zion and cleansed the bloodstains of Jerusalem from its midst by a spirit of judgment and by a spirit of burning. (Isaiah 4: 3—4)

And Jeremiah persuades the Israelis to repent of their sins and to mend their ways. And the prophets reveal God's promises of restoration and the ingathering of the dispersed after their repentance: "Lift up your eyes and look around; they all gather together, they come to you; your sons shall come from far away, and your daughters shall be carried on their nurses' arms" (Isaiah 60: 4).

Suffering is also a discipline of the people so that people can overcome evils and better themselves. The existence of suffering is supposed to be an education. Suffering usually comes from human evil. And where does human evil come from? They believe that a better world without evil and suffering was not created, because the Creator had to make do with the flawed material at hand in creating the world, which determines that the world is unable to receive more of the divine influence. So evil results both from man's selfish and inaccurate judgment and from inappropriate human desires and greed. However, human beings have free will and sometimes choose to act in immoral ways out of their own desires and intentions. But there is no good without evil. Through evil and suffering, human beings can seek to transcend their physical limitations, raise their spiritual characters, and come round to good.

Moreover, suffering is the importance of individual efforts and intellectual attainments in avoiding and facing human limitations from which suffering stems. Should one wait for God to right the wrong of the innocent for us? Instead of waiting for divine intervention in our sufferings, Maimonides argues, we should try to transcend our material existence of limitations with intellectual thought. We must "take responsibility for our own lives and we should try to perfect ourselves by improving our ability to reason and to develop intellectually" (Leaman 77).

The constant exile, suffering, and struggle for survival recur in the Hebrew Bible and other writings so that they have long become archetypes in Jewish writings, which have always played an important part in the life of the Jewish people. These archetypes are kept and passed down from generation to generation through the Jewish tradition, religion, and stories. C. G. Jung implies in his theory about the "collective unconscious" that there are a lot of archetypes in the cultures of different peoples, which survive in the collective unconscious of these peoples and are expressed in myth, religion, dreams and in the works of literature. And according to Northrop Frye, "myth is the archetype, though it might be convenient to say myth only when referring to narrative, and archetype when speaking of significance" (Frye 15). The archetypes are in fact important contents and carriers of collective unconscious. It is only reasonable that the memory and meaning of the nightmarish experiences of exile, suffering, and struggle for survival permeate Jewish culture so that a Jew does not have to be Judaic to take over the cultural and ethnic heritage. In fact, the Jewish influences endow the Jewish writers, including Bellow, with a strong awareness of survival.

Saul Bellow was nine years old when his family moved from Montreal to Chicago where he lived most of his years, and it is from the backdrop of this city that many of his novels are developed. As much as Bellow has maintained that he is not a Jewish writer as he has indicated in his interview with Kulshrestha, ("Conversations . . ." 58), I will explain how his immersion and early upbringing as an Orthodox Jew in urban Montreal and Chicago, not far removed from the Jewish ghettoes of Eastern Europe, centrally influenced his work. The only gentile protagonists in Bellow's Jewish oeuvre are Eugene Henderson in *Henderson the Rain King* and Clara Velde in *A Theft*. Bellow's novels alternate between the urbanized setting of Chicago and New York City; the families, friends, acquaintances, and adversaries all tend to be Jewish middle-class of some intellectual worth (some more or less than others). There is no doubt that Bellow is deeply concerned with the fate of Jews and affairs of the Jewish people at the beginning of his literary life. In each of his novels, he depicts the life of one man, who is undergoing a kind of suffering-temporary alienation from society, financial problems, divorce, and disillusionment with the reality.

In *Herzog*, the protagonist Herzog suffers from the discovery that reality is different from his ideal and contrary to his good will. He discovers that the government is not trustworthy and that democracy is an illusion. The government emphasizes material production and turns the individual into business. It's a businessmen's government. Modern science creates material wealth that may improve living conditions, but the government ignores its double-edged blessings. Pollution of industry, chemical pesticides and radioactivity threaten human life. Automation accelerates unemployment and creates social insecurity. The problems of delinquency, overpopulation, poverty, and racial conflicts overflow.

He is also experiencing suffering in his personal life. His best friend Valentine cuckolded him, his second wife Madeleine throws him out, and his career as a professor is on the decline (he has even temporarily abandoned his teaching position). At the beginning of the novel, he is at the point where his world has collapsed, where he attempts to grasp hold of himself and his life, to pick up the broken pieces of his personality and see what is left.

Nevertheless, he tries to transcend his material existence of limitations with intellectual thought. Herzog, the history professor, writes numerous imaginary and never sent letters to both famous and familiar people, both living and dead, intending to struggle for order in his chaotic personal life, and hence to "construct a significant order of right and wrong, to pinpoint with unequivocal sharpness truth and falsehood" (Bryant 359). Herzog learns to overcome evils, gets education and betters himself in these sufferings, which just strengthen his belief that "the extent of universal space does not destroy human value, that the realm of facts and that of values are not eternally separated" (*H* 106), and that "The main enterprise of the world, for splendor... is the upbuilding of a man. The private life of one man shall be a more illustrious monarchy ··· than any kingdom in history...." (*H* 198—99). This belief in the human value and the deeply imbedded suffering memories give Bellow strong awareness of survival and inspire him to explore in his fictional world the ways for human being to survive in the Waste Land of modern society.

Bellow's Yiddish background has remained a constant and formative influence in his work as Alfred Kazin, in his essay "My Friend Saul Bellow," observes: "he had been brought up as an orthodox Jew; and he had a proper respect for Gad as the ultimate power assumed but the creation" ("My Friend Saul Bellow" 4). It is this unflinching respect for God and faith in the ancient texts that has anchored Bellow's ethical and moral standards:

> He was brought up in a deeply Jewish spirit and with the Yiddish language, the life-thread of a cultural and religious tradition in Eastern Europe ··· This is Bellow's tradition, and of the many interesting and talented novelists of Jewish background in this country, there is probably no other who feels so lovingly connected with the religious and cultural tradition of his Eastern European grandfathers. (Kazin, "My Friend Saul Bellow" 7)

This reverent connection to his Judaic heritage has nurtured and sustained Bellow's writing: from this seemingly ordinariness Bellow has illuminated the dramatic undercurrents in a culture that honors tradition and ancestral values without forgetting its comedic imperfections. From this quotidian, Bellow extracts and magnifies the personal and domestic struggles and suffering of Jews who are acutely aware of their place in history. However, as much as Bellow is steeped into the circumstances of his culture, his work speaks to both Gentile and Jew. From the ordinary Joseph in *Dangling Man* to the intellectual Herzog in *Herzog*, we easily recognize the everyday confrontations of Bellow's heroes which are: "made up of love and sex and marriage, of common apprehensions ... of the struggles between parents and children, between victims and persecutors, between love and hatred, between life and death" (Kazin, "My Friend Saul Bellow" 8).

The more we read Bellow, the deeper we will recognize the Jewish influence that drives his work. He has admitted that he was learning that trade writing *Dangling Man* and *The Victim*, but once he had passed his qualifying exams, he discovered the allure of his heritage, "I had found a new way to write a book. It was my very own. I had no control over it." (Roudane 81). L. H. Goldman, in her essay "Saul Bellow and the philosophy of Judaism," gives a brief history of Judaism and it is interesting to learn that Hillel, the earliest Jewish humanist philosopher had boiled down the entire Torah to this simple aphorism: "What is hateful to you do not unto your neighbor; this is the entire Torah" (Goldman, "Saul Bellow: Novelist of the Intellectuals" 52). Goldman points out that Bellow's source of inspiration is not necessarily from the Jewish philosophers: "Bellow goes back to the original source, the Bible … Appearing after Hitler's obliteration of humanism, Bellow's works strive to reestablish the foundation of a society by reaffirming the world's need for morality, for the return to the humanism of Judaism" (53). It is quite understandable that after the Holocaust, Bellow would more so instruct on the brotherhood of Jews as Goldman observes: "The quest for most Bellovian heroes is basically the same. It is not a search for identity, as some critics suggest. It is rather a quest for a significant existence that would embrace their own identity, such as it is" (58).

It is important that as much as Bellow thrives on the stories of his culture, especially going back to his Yiddish inheritance, his themes are steeped in a moral conviction universal to all cultures:

> Bellow's view is that of a Jew, yet he is speaking of all men. Remembering that he spoke Yiddish before he spoke English or French, we assume that he assimilated the Jewish heritage with his mother's milk. He assimilated "the virtue of powerlessness, the company of the dispossessed, the sanctity of the insulted and injured," as Irving Howe has put it-the great themes of Yiddish literature. And w because of this, Bellow speaks for all voices or powerlessness, humiliation, and weakness everywhere. (Walden 145)

3. Bellow's Rejection of Modernism

Critics believe that few authors can match Bellow's mixture of tragedy with comedy, and it is this vision that illuminates and separates his themes from the nihilism dominant in much of the literature of modernism which deviated from the established classical from. Modernism, dominant between the late nineteenth and early twentieth – centuries was characterized by "alienation, fragmentation, bread with tradition, isolation and magnification of subjectivity, threat of the void, weight of vast numbers and monolithic impersonal institutions, and hatred of civilization itself" (Fuchs, *Saul Bellow: Vision and Revision* 75). However, allusions to modern as a time frame will be restricted to Bellow's literary production between 1944 and 1970. Thus, it is from this background that Bellow confronts the Romantic inclination for liberation and pursuit of self in favor of community. Bellow acknowledges the darkness, but does not sink in it since as a believing Jew, as Antonio Monda points out, Bellow understands that salvation is possible through the honoring of scripture, not necessarily from the pulpit but from the quietness of moral and ethical action.

Born in Lachine, Montreal in 1915, Bellow began his literary career when such modern writers as Joyce, Lawrence and Eliot were past their creative peaks and becoming a fixed orthodoxy in the universities. Thus, it was these great modern writers who shaped Bellow's consciousness as a young man and greatly influenced the content and style of his first two novels, *Dangling Man* (1944) and *The Victim* (1947). These early novels strongly reflect existentialist premises and modern literary techniques in their respective presentations of alienated heroes functioning in hostile environments and trying to find meaning in apparently absurd worlds. But, even here we sense the beginnings of Bellow's break with Modernism, and by the time *The Adventures of Augie March* was published in 1953, we see Bellow's first open rejection of the tradition.

The world had not come to an end as Joyce, Lawrence and Yeats had predicted it would. The disintegrating self of early modern literature had actually survived two world wars, the holocaust, the technological revolution and the effects of mass society. And even though the typically modern phenomenon of the alienated hero, the wasteland and the absurd world continue to appear in twentieth – century literature right up to the late decades, many writers, of whom Bellow was one of the first, began as early as 1940 to question the validity of Modernist estimates of Man and Society. This questioning begun tentatively in the *Dangling Man* and *The Victim*, becomes a major theme of all subsequent novels through to *Humboldt's Gift* in 1975.

Taking as his major theme the origins, nature and effects of the modern movement, and in particular its destructive attack on the self, Bellow attempts, in both his novels and his essays, to reclaim some of the lost nobility and shaken dignity of the self.

Uprooting Modernist philosophical fallacies, he attempts to describe what has gone wrong with our civilization, and just where we might seek for truth and restoration. In novel after novel he attempts to restore our faith in the integrity of the ordinary people, to revise our social system and to reestablish our connections with a decent and satisfying moral order.

Beginning in 1953 with *The Adventures of Augie March*, Bellow depicts a series of heroes, men of sensibility and often of learning, who are in the process of "becoming"-people who are resisting self – division and nihilistic attacks on their integrity. Each hero comically fights his way through fallacious Modernist estimates of Man and Existence, through perverted ethical systems, through cynicism, alienation and rationalism, to his inner core-to a deep mystical confirmation of the value of Self and Existence, and a personal knowledge of the sacredness of social contract.

Hence, instead of providing us with variations on the wasteland ideology and its crisis ethics, Bellow depicts heroes who learn to reject agreed-upon Modernist estimates of social history, and to recover belief in the moral order which Bellow believes undergirds human existence. Bellow reminds us that since civilization won't burn and rise phoenix-like from the ashes, man must employ his deepest spiritual and intellectual resources in purifying himself and preserving the quality of the social order.

Modernism reached its peak between 1910 and 1925. The dominant mood of the period, as reflected in Modern thinkers' books, was one of great metaphysical despair causing W. H. Auden to label the period "The Age of Anxiety." (Auden) The effects of the anxiety created by all of these modern thinkers were far-reaching. The very structure of society was called into question, history was interpreted in a reductive way, science seemed to have removed the element of mystery from nature, and religion was subverted by a Freudian psychology which robbed moral conscience of its meaning. Added to this, the first half of the century saw two world wars, the holocaust, a massive world depression, and the advent of the atom bomb. It is not hard to see, therefore, why modern literature is so preoccupied with the impotence of man, secularization, and possibility of individual and collective annihilation. The dominant mood of despair in modern literature derives primarily from existentialist premises, and some other philosophical and historical views, one of which sees the twentieth century as the terminal point in history. This historicism engendered in modern fiction a sense of the futility of the human endeavor. On the first page of *Lady Chatterley's Lover*, Lawrence writes that since things have collapsed about us we must each put together some kind of life.

Against this Weltanschauung of futility, absurdity and fragmentation, the modern writer writes of the absurdity of the human endeavor, the separation of the artist from society, and the destruction of traditional aesthetics and morality. Bellow's personal opinions about the nature, origins and effects of Modernism are recorded throughout all of his essays and interviews. They range in style from erudite analyses of Joyce's *Ulysses* to highly entertaining general comments on the history, philosophy and effects of modernism. As early as 1944 Bellow had begun to question the failure of faith in the twentieth-century novel. In the *Times Literary Supplement*, in July of 1960, he summed up his basic attitude-that "disappointment with its human material is built into the contemporary novel." (Bellow, "Sealed Treasure" 414) In particular, he observes that the American novel is "filled with complaints over the misfortunes of the Sovereign Self." (Bellow, "Keynote Address" 2—3) The cause of all this despair he attributes to the legacy of the early modern fathers, Joyce, Mann, Proust, and Lawrence.

This elegiac modern literature, according to Bellow, portrays twentieth century life as divisive and fragmented. Its celebrants claim that the fragmentation and disorder are finally too great to be overcome, and that the novel itself is dead. Such proponents, Bellow complains, draw elaborate and ugly pictures of the breakdown of society, mass culture, centerlessness and the splintering of the individual consciousness without questioning the truthfulness of this view. They have lost their faith in man and can only portray him as an impotent victim of overwhelming forces beyond his ability to comprehend or control.

A good portion of modern despair Bellow attributes to the "historicist" premises which lie at the base of most modern novels, and which serve to generate the despairing modern image of man. Historicism is that view which sees the twentieth century as the terminal point in history. In modern American literature, Bellow sees writers expressing the attitude that America is a fraud and all is blackness, bitterness and hopelessness, and denounces this as a simplistic and rationalistic view. While Bellow is the first to admit to the magnificent artistic achievements of the moderns, he is also the first to quarrel with their philosophy. And very frequently he accuses contemporary writers of adopting the "wasteland mentality" because they feel the need to follow the orthodoxy established by Eliot and Joyce. Such writing Bellow calls "historicism" or "warmed-up" academic leftovers with a set of phony avant-garde attitudes.

However, the most negative aspect of modern literature, according to Bellow, is its presentation of a fragmented self instead of a unitary, noble, human being with the power to achieve at least some of its aspirations. Bellow attempts to account for what has happened to the self in twentieth century fiction. He notes that the First World War, with its unprecedented number of corpse; the Russian Revolution, with its hatred of bourgeois idealism; and the Second World War, with its atomic blasts and reduction of millions of Jews to "heaps of bone and mounds of rag and hair" (Bellow, "Some Notes" 22), has greatly contributed to the questioning of novelists about the viability of individual existence in the present age. Bellow wants to restore the "I" to its rightful position in contemporary literature. He sums up in one sentence what he has been trying to say through his own heroes since the advent of Augie March and Herzog: "There is man's own greatness and then there is the greatness of his imbecility – both are eternal" (Bellow, "Distractions of a Fiction Writer", 9). In an attempt to break the power of rationalistic and scientific estimates of man, which seem to hold sway over the modern imagination, Bellow finally declares that there are avenues into which technology cannot lead us. These avenues are those of the imagination, which Bellow believes to be an organ of truth superior to modern intelligence and likely to provide us with truer estimates of man and experience than the rational formulations of the physical and social scientists.

What all of this amounts to is a growing disgust on Bellow's part with the legacy of dark despair bequeathed to contemporary literature by the early moderns. He decries most forcefully the attitudes of the existentialists, the apocalyptic nihilists and the naturalists, all of whom he sees dragging the sewer for evidence of the decline of western civilization. And this denial of the "wasteland mentality" becomes a major theme in his later novels. In the first three novels we see Bellow as the direct literary heir of the moderns, mining the wasteland vein and espousing many of the principal tenets of existentialism. In his subsequent novels we watch him begin an extensive examination of the fallacies of modernism.

In *Dangling Man* and *The Victim*, Bellow is applying and using typically modern fiction formulas to examine the existential tenets of modernism. Each of the heroes suffers increasing alienation and estrangement from his social and intellectual world. Unable to find any sustaining moral values or satisfying metaphysical answers, each suffers extreme anguish over the burden of responsibility imposed on him by his existential freedom. Each hero is estranged from nature and exists in a modern urban wasteland where he tries desperately to free himself from the metaphysical cul-de-sac into which his modern skepticism has steered him. Yet even in these modernist – formula novels we see the beginnings of Bellow's rejection of modernism. By the end of *The Adventures of Augie March* and *Seize the Day* we perceive Bellow beginning to severely question the premises of the existentialist thinkers.

As Bellow moves from the existential tenets of modernism, he also begins to free himself from the tight, highly aesthetic formalist structures of the early novels. *The Adventures of Augie March* experiments metaphysically and structurally with totally new formulas of affirmation. It is in this novel that Bellow begins to find his comic voice as an alternative to the pessimism and philosophical dread of the earlier works. While the heroes of the first three novels finally acquiesced to the social order, mostly out of sheer exhaustion, Augie March remains socially uncommitted and quite undaunted. He does not know what truths govern the world, but he can identify and resist untruths. Augie eschews all "ready – made" modernist formulas of history and society. He is undaunted by pessimism, world views which preach annihilation, and people who offer him phony, established modern lifestyles. While Augie evades moral and metaphysical, however, he makes a higher kind of commitment to himself. He will explore honestly the vast possibilities life holds out to him, and he will not settle for easy modern formulas and half-truths. The book represents a great liberation for Bellow, for though he lost artistic control of it, he began to find his own fictional style and make a major break with the fiction formulas of modernism.

Though still a despairing and absurd hero, Tommy Wilhelm discovers, in addition to the alienation, effrontery and charlatanism of the commercial world, the literal "holiness of the heart's affection," and his spiritual kinship with his fellow human beings. The ending of this book is a sign that Bellow is beginning to be done with the "fiction of complaint" and is seriously seeking real formulas of social and metaphysical accommodation which will fit the real facts of existence.

This liberating process took a major step forward with the advent of *Henderson the Rain King*. In this novel Bellow has constructed an elaborate parody of the modern hero, modern philosophy and modern literary style. *Henderson the Rain King* is one of the earliest American novels in which we see open parody of the modernist fictional philosophy and formulas. It is Bellow's most formal announcement of his break with the modern tradition.

In *Herzog*, the *Ulysses* of American literature, Bellow has taken as his major theme the survival quest of the embattled romantic individualist in the modern period. Herzog, the believer in family, paternalism, sexual love, God, social contracts and personal altruism—the self—has his romantic impulse severely tested in what appears to be a world dedicated to his destruction. Herzog is the nineteenth-century romantic individualist who has survived on into the modern period which no longer believes in the unified romantic self.

Although the ending of this book is highly ambiguous, there is a tentative affirmation that the modern period, with its apocalyptic expectations and theories of wasteland alienation and existential absurdity, has not entirely managed to defeat romantic individualism.

With the arrival of *Mr. Sammler's Planet* in 1970, we see Bellow attacking modernist philosophy even more overtly. Modernism and its metaphysical validity becomes the major theme of the book. Mr. Sammler, fastidious Polish-Oxonian, and one-time member of the Bloomsbury intellectuals (arch-modernist British writers) is literally raised from the grave of the holocaust and transplanted to New York during the height of the hippie revolution. He is the Lazarus of Modernism returned to examine his modernist premises and manners in the post-modern world. Through his fascinating character we are able to assess the legacy of modernism against the values of the contemporary period. Through this elderly modern scholar, Bellow shows us an early modern who has had to cast off inaccurate, outworn, modern formulas of apocalyptic nihilism, even though he encounters much evidence of distraction and chaos in the contemporary world. Sammler casts off his preoccupation with alienation ethics, formalist manners and aesthetics, and modern metaphysics in order to undergo what Bellow has called that mystical, Heraclitan process of listening deep within oneself for the ultimate truth about human nature and life.

In spite of the moral revolution, his personal neuroses and prejudices, and the barbarous nature of New York in the late sixties, Sammler learns that while his new world may appear absurd and fragmented there is a moral design. The knowledge of one's social contract must and can be found. He arrives at a knowledge of his personal commitment to family and fellow man through an intuitive process of meditation carried out in the midst of apparent chaos. He cannot "cop-out" (Bellow's term) by adopting the alienation ethics in face of apparent social breakdown. Neither can he take the easy mental stimulants of apocalyptic nihilism and existentialism, all of which he examines in the course of the novel. Truth can be arrived at in the old romantic, intuitive ways. His final insight comes in a prayer over his nephew's body: "For that is the truth of it - that we know, God, that we know, that we know, we know, we know" (286).

In his latest novel to date, Humboldt's Gift, we see a fictionalized account of the elaborate process of destruction perpetrated upon a generation of modern American poets and writers. Humboldt is modeled specifically upon Delmore Schwartz and John Berryman, close friends of Bellow. Through tracing Humboldt's passage as a modern poet, and Charlie's alternate formula for survival in the modern world, Bellow manages once more to bring into focus the whole modern period, its ethics, metaphysics, literary and historical premises, sociology and moral impact. As Humboldt dies in the early hours of the morning over his garbage pail in the gutter outside his slum apartment, he becomes a symbol of what the modern age finally did to its artists. He has enjoyed brief success as a late romantic lyric poet, suffered all the ravages of acute paranoia (symbol of what modernism has done to romantic individualism), sojourned in Bellevue (like Pound and so many other paranoiac modern American poets) and finally understands what has happened to him.

On the other hand, Humboldt's disciple, Charlie Citrine, manages to survive the modern period. Charlie is neither a romantic nor a modern skeptic. He is Bellow's contemporary artist - intellectual, who, through his experiences with Humboldt, has managed to steer clear of the Scylla of modernism and the Charybdis of Romanticism. Through moderation, prayer, formal meditation and realistic compromise, Citrine finally discovers the terms of survival in the contemporary world of philistinism and finance capitalism. In spite of all the distraction of the apparently chaotic contemporary experience, Citrine believes firmly in life after death and the responsibility the living have to the dead. He retains his idealism and innocence in spite of all of his experiences and therefore survives. He is Bellow's most recent testimony of the power of self to survive the present age.

Beginning his literary career in the 1940's, when the tide of nihilistic existentialism was running high in American intellectual circles, Saul Bellow even then began to question the current modernist preoccupation with death ideology, absurdist ethics, psychoanalytic premises and defeat of the self and private existence. Refusing to see the twentieth - century human endeavor in historicist terms, Saul Bellow has made a concerted effort to purge our thinking of reductive modernist thinking, an effort which resulted in his being awarded the Noble Prize for Literature in 1976.

Next to this recognition, Daniel Fuchs has perhaps paid Bellow the most intelligent compliment when he said this in 1974:

> … no one has so persistently gone against the grain of modernism, which is still a kind of orthodoxy in the universities and even the quarterlies. In this respect Bellow is the modernist par excellence in that his very inspiration often comes from a resistance to its celebrated aesthetic ideology

> with its tendency toward monumentality, and its perhaps inevitably concomitant tendency toward coldness. (Fuchs 67—68)

Certainly no one could accuse Bellow of coldness or despair when immersed in the humane Fieldingesque exuberance of his last seven novels, and certainly no one could accuse him of fatuous Yea - saying. Like any post-modern writer he has had to assume the realities of the post-war period and modern history, documenting with mature insight not only such phenomena as the decay of humanistic values, the near disintegration of society, the holocaust, and the crisis mentality, but also the undermining nature of Modernist radicalism, aestheticism, rationalism, naturalism and their concomitant, a hedonistic sex ideology. But, unlike the modern writers, he has not assumed these to be the only windows through which to view reality. All of his fiction asserts the existence of higher, more powerful realities perceivable only to the imagination and spirit.

In fact the major thrust of nearly all of his novels has been against the dangers of the rationalistic viewpoint, the most predominant legacy of modernism. Pitting the strength of the human spirit against that of a machine age, Bellow has avowed the equal power of the imagination as a source of truth, claiming with Emerson and Thoreau that beyond the material reality of things lies an order of spiritual reality perceivable by anyone who will ready his soul to perceive it. Further, he freely confesses to having a "shamanistic character," to being "something of a medium" who receives "impulses" from some unknown source. Thus with Henderson he dances the dance against the bleak greyness of an arctic sky, assuming the bleakness to be merely the backdrop against which we can discover also the joy of life. With Herzog he affirms the worth of private existence in the face of anguish. With Sammler he spurns rationalistic scientific humanism and prefers the higher reality of his "God adumbrations." With Humboldt and Citrine he affirms a kind of Platonic belief in a home - world, and in literature as a powerful humanizing force which must maintain its integrity in spite of what he has called the "blaring of the technological band" (Bellow, "Mystic Tradition and the American Novelist").

Hence, in novel after novel, Bellow affirms both the potential meaningfulness of private existence and the integrity of the self, asserting "It would be worthwhile to induce [the individual] to see himself as a true subject, not some ninety - eight cents of minerals which will disappear forever into a 1500 dollar coffin" (Simmons 31).

In fact, one of his most eloquent tributes to the spiritual nature of man comes in his adaptation of some words from the Russian writer Rozanov:

> A million years passed before my soul was let out into the technological world. That world was filled with ultra - intelligent machines, but the soul after all was a soul, and it had waited a million years for its turn and did not intend to be cheated of its birthright by a lot of mere gimmicks. It

had come from the far reaches of the universe, and it was interested in but not overawed by these inventions. (Bellow, "Machines and Storybooks")

And though Bellow is far more openly affirmative in his essays than he is in his novels, the final impression left with the reader of his fiction is one of renewed hope in the human enterprise. Though his affirmations are often couched in strange or comic ways, masked in farce, or put into the mouths of buffoons, cranks and eccentrics, they continue to undergird every novel, so that the radical discontinuities and ambiguities the critics seem to dwell on are no more than those same radical discontinuities which Richard Chase identifies as one of the major characteristics of the American literary tradition. Leaving most of his characters trembling on the brink of love, inner contentment and the great mystery of existence which lies beyond materialism and facticity, Bellow consistently affirms with Herzog that "The light of truth is never very far away, and no human being is too negligible or corrupt to come into it" (382).

Certainly then, the major thrust in Bellow fiction is the rejection of nihilistic modernism and the embracing of an essentially religious and mystical nineteenth - century American romanticism, or perhaps at times even an idiosyncratic Christian humanism which gathers into fuller meaning the social, psychological and historical data of the novels and restores to it the light of mystery and joy that was somehow lost in the nihilistic existential novel. In fact speaking in the vein of Christian humanist Mr. Sammler, Bellow pays the ultimate anti-modernist tribute to the self in an important interview with Jim Douglas Henry:

> I don't think that fashion is going to kill the virtues, and I still think that people must consult their own deepest feelings—their hearts if you like, the government of these feelings has not yet been over - thrown. I suppose that very early in my education I accepted a sort of Tolstoyan explanation of these things, and I've clung to it all through my life. I really believe in a good deal of that. I think the individual has some permanent balance within himself, that he understands what is in his own heart and in the hearts of others, somehow. That he knows right and wrong. That there's an inner voice that keeps him performing certain duties, that makes him recognize certain human obligations, that restrains him from the commission of certain crimes. People know certain things, they know them very well. They know their duty to their children in a sort of natural way. They know that it is a crime to kill. They know certain kinds of theft are offensive. They know that to humiliate another human being is wrong. I don't think there things are very easily eradicated by any fashion (Bellow, "Mystic Tradition" 705—07).

4. Bellow's Effort to affirm Human Value in Modern Society

Our modern time witnesses the monumental atrocities such as World Wars I and II, the Holocaust, and the current spate of genocides and so it is easy to understand Bellow's concern for the fragility of the human condition both as an artist and a Jew. In his acceptance speech for the Nobel Prize, he laments on this condition as though he is speaking from the pulpit: "Let me take a little time to look more closely at this travail. In private life, disorder or near – panic. In families – for husbands, wives, parents, children – confusion; in civic behavior, in personal loyalties, in sexual practices further confusion. And with this private disorder goes public bewilderment" (Bellow, *It All Adds Up* 93). This is the state of affairs that concerns Bellow the artist as he cautions us about the distressing predictions that confront us, our history of disorder, and our vision of disintegration. Bellow attributes this source of upheaval to, "The unending cycle of crises that began with the First World War has formed a kind of person, one who has lived through terrible, strange things, … an ability to live with many kinds of madness" (Bellow, The Nobel). It is against this background of disorder that he admits our existential turmoil: "… we stand open to all anxieties. The decline and fall of everything is our daily dread, we are agitated in private life and tormented by public question" (Bellow, The Nobel).

Two particular events during World War II have helped to effect the fundamental change in the consciousness of twentieth – century man: the extermination of six million Jews, and the actual use of the atomic bombs dropped on two Japanese cities. The significance of these two atrocities exceeds by far the willful destruction of human life. It is not only the scale on which it was done, but also the realization that after this there is nothing that man would not do to man, that accounts for this significance. Millions of people have been slain. These two events have destroyed the human value, and have effected a fundamental change in human consciousness. It is basically this change which lies behind Bellow's effort to save human dignity in the despair atmosphere of the post – World War II period.

Bellow believes writers are influential because they are greatly respected. The intelligent public is wonderfully patient with them, "continues to read them and endures disappointment after disappointment, waiting to hear from art what it does not hear from theology, philosophy, social theory, and what it cannot hear from pure science" (Bellow, Nobel lecture). He refers to Conrad at the end of his Nobel Prize lecture. "What Conrad said was true, art attempts to find in the universe, in matter as well as in the facts of life, what is fundamental, enduring, essential". Undoubtedly, Bellow undertakes his responsibility as a writer to explore what is fundamental, enduring, and essential in the facts of life in the despair atmosphere of the post – World War II period.

As much as Bellow respects and admits his love for the Modernist writers, he challenges this sinking lamentation of existential stasis and he is one of the first American writers to have bridged the gap from Modernism to the tradition of contemporary American literature. From the time Bellow discovered his own voice, he has been battling the established tradition of the Modernist consciousness which implies that the modern man is somehow doomed to an existential wasteland but like other Jewish writers he "rejects the devaluation of man, knowing in his heart … that man is a profound and holy mystery. The 'legacy of wonder' from the Jewish religious tradition is a counterweight to despair over the insignificance of man" (Clayton 33).

Bellow has raised his voice in defense of man and against a merely fashionable pessimistic stance that modern literature has promoted in statements after statement — be it in essays, interviews, or the novels themselves. The idea of the devaluation of the self in and by modern literature finds in Bellow one of its most fervent and active opponents. In a speech given at the Library of Congress (1963), Bellow made his position clear:

> Writers haveinherited a tone of bitterness from the great poems and novels of this century, many of which lament the passing of a more stable and beautiful age demolished by the barbarous intrusion of an industrial and metropolitan society of masses or proles who will, after many upheavals, be tamed by bureaucracies and oligarchies in brave new worlds, human anthills. . . . There are modern novelists who take all this for granted as fully proven and implicit in the human condition and who complain as steadily as they write, viewing modern life with a bitterness to which they themselves have not established clear title. (Bellow, *Recent American Fiction* 7)

"The question nevertheless remains," Bellow says. "Man is something. What is he?" (Bellow, "Some Notes on Recent American Fiction" 29) In the Nobel Prize speech he takes up the subject again. He thinks that literature has for nearly a century used the same stock of ideas, myths, and strategies. Essay after essay and book after book confirm the most serious thoughts — Baudelarian, Nietzschean, Marxian, psychoanalytic, and etc. How weary people are of them, of these most serious essayists. How poorly they represent us. The pictures they offer no more resemble us than we resemble the reconstructed reptiles and other monsters in a museum of paleontology. "We are much more limber, versatile, better articulated, there is much more to us, we all feel it" (Bellow, Nobel Lecture).

From the time Bellow discovered his own voice, he has been battling the established tradition of the Modernist consciousness which implies that the modern man is somehow doomed to an existential wasteland but like other Jewish writers he "rejects the devaluation of man, knowing in his heart . . . that man is a profound and holy mystery. The 'legacy of wonder' from the Jewish religious tradition is a counterweight to despair over the insignificance of man" (Clayton 33). In his repeated defenses of modern human being, as John Clayton notes, Bellow assumes the position of "a kind of priest bringing value to the world, a mad world which rejects the individual" (Clayton 247). Believing that the modern writer must confront and overcome this world, Bellow identifies, to a large degree, with those late nineteenth century writers who "nourished on romantic individualism, find that they are obliged to cope with the results of industrial collectivism… [in which] the individual, the single, separate self, feels severely limited, oppressed by the weight of numbers, by nature, by the conditions of life" (Bellow, "Literature" 137). The attempt to come between the individual and this "collectivism" is, for Bellow, the moral function of the writer.

Bellow rejects the contemporary condition of unaccommodated alienation of the individual. As John Clayton puts it, "Bellow rejects the tradition of alienation in modern literature, and his fiction emphasizes the value of brotherhood and community; yet his main characters are all masochists and alienates" (Clayton 3). What Clayton means is that Bellow portrays his characters as only temporary alienates, for in the outcome they are accommodated to their society. Albeit they do feel "severely limited" by their social conditions, they refuse to go down in the muck of circumstances, to make a myth of hopelessness and futility out of their ostensible alienation.

Essentially, this refusal of defeat on the part of his characters is Bellow's only tradition. He disagrees with the conviction "that the world is evil, that it must be destroyed and rise again. ... I don't see that we need to call for the destruction of the world in hope of a phoenix. If I am not a romantic, it's for this reason" (Steers 37). Neither can he be affiliated with the early twentieth-century tradition of determinism nor with the post-War II writers of the Left who denigrate the value of the individual: "I cannot agree with recent writers who have told us that we are Nothing. We are indeed not what the Golden Ages boasted us to be. But we are Something" (Bellow, "A Word from Writer Directly to Reader" 19). So when Allbee, a down and out, who persists in intruding upon Leventhal's privacy, holding him, Leventhal, responsible for his coming down in the world, says "the day of succeeding by your own efforts is past. Now it's all blind movement, vast movement, as the individual is shuttled back and forth", Leventhal cannot agree after his achieving through strenuous efforts a modestly comfortable kind of middle-class existence. He simply cannot admit to himself the idea that it might be irrationality that largely governs human destiny, just as he cannot admit to himself something inhuman that doesn't care about anything human and yet is implanted in every human being. As one critic observes, Bellow intends "nothing less than [to] possess our minds with a portraiture alternative to the alienated Waste Land figures of earlier twentieth-century literature" (Poirier 265).

As Bellow puts it, "We live in a technological age which seems insurmountably hostile to the artist. He must fight for his life, for his freedom, along with everyone else-for justice and equality, threatened by mechanization and bureaucracy" (Bellow, "The Thinking Man's Wasteland" 20). Bellow himself claims vigorously that the writer can no longer dream of an age when the artist "had real acceptance, and enjoyed a vital harmony with his surroundings" (20). Rather he must accept his present age for what it is and confront it as best he can with his imaginative gifts: "We can either shut up because the times are too bad, or continue because we have an instinct to make books, a talent to enjoy, which even these disfigured times cannot obliterate" (20).

To Bellow, life is a miracle, no matter how intense is the suffering on earth. As Schlossberg in *The Victim* exclaims, "If a human life is a great thing to me, it is a great thing" (*V* 122). "Since it is fitting to approach a great thing with dignity, one is free to choose dignity rather than anything else, free to hoke it up with greatness and beauty rather than anything else. And only those who strive to enact these qualities can really be called human" (Bakker 42). Life's nothingness could be filled with the love Leventhal feels surging up for his brother Max when Leventhal takes leave of Max at the station and Max returns his embrace, an experience which makes him faint "with the expansion of his heart". It's this expansion of the heart that can lend human dignity to man's nothingness, enabling him to face the "immense blackness" that stretches beyond the towering lights of the city. Life is worth living notwithstanding many woes and tragedies in human life. That is why Bellow believes in the here-and-now and tries to live his life fully in a big city cluttered with confusion and ugliness, sordidness and madness. That is also the reason that Leventhal in *The Victim* admits that he might owe Allbee something, and offers him money and a place to sleep despite his contempt for Allbee. As Bellow writes in the Introduction to *Great Jewish Short Stories*,

> We are all such accidents. We do not make up history and culture. We simply appear, not by our own choice. We make what we can of our condition with the means available. We must accept the mixture as we find it - the impurity of it, the tragedy of it, the hope of it. (14)

The Adventures of Augie March (1953), Bellow's third novel, shows the space and openness of the novel of adventures, the outgoing picaro, and the outburst of exuberant affirmation. Man, in *The Adventures of Augie March*, is willed "with a capital M, with great stature…", and "the low view of life", as held by Moulton, the view that the individual is despicable in his littleness and that life's possibilities are limited and constraining, is firmly rejected. What Bellow wants to emphasize in this novel is the belief that man's greatness is not a thing of the past but can still be realized in the present. Throughout the book Bellow compare the characters in the novel to great figures of the past. Augie's grandma Lausch is one of the "Machiavellis"; his mother is compared to "those women whom Zeus got the better of in animal form. . . "; Einhorn is likened to Caesar, Ulysses, Machiavelli, Pope Alexander; when Augie carries him on his back, they become Aeneas and his father Anchises; Lucy is compared to Phaedra; the eagle is named after a Roman emperor, Caligula; the relationship between Augie and Thea becomes that of Leicester and Elizabeth, and at the end of the novel Augie compares himself to Columbus. Bellow shows greatness of these characters to will man with a capital M.

Bellow was attempting to establish himself as a young Jewish writer in America in early 1940s. However, as Bellow himself has avowed, he was not writing exclusively of the Jewish experience. In a 1972 interview he refuted such a notion, "claiming that he portrayed his Jewish protagonists in proper relation to the rest of those American alienatees in large urbanized areas like Chicago and New York" (Kulshrestha 13). These characters of disengagement were the products of a mass culture rather than of an ethnic minority. As Leslie Fiedler wrote in support of Bellow's contention, Bellow "emerges at the moment when the Jews for the first time move into the center of America culture . . . and must be seen in the larger context" (Fiedler 104). This larger context is defined by Irving Howe as mass society, and he asserts that no social scientist had yet produced a satisfactory theory of such a society:

> By the mass society we mean a relatively comfortable, half welfare andhalf garrison society in which the population grows passive, indifferent and atomized; in which traditional loyalties, ties and associations become lax or dissolve entirely; in which coherent publics based on definite interests and opinions gradually fall apart; and in which man becomes a consumer, and values that he absorbs. (Howe, "The New York Intellectuals" 8)

Despite the mass culture and postwar disparity, Bellow is one of those postwar writers who intend that values are to "be realized in America and in relation to the actuality of American life" (May 40). So his protagonists struggle to sustain their integrity as individuals. Their response is what Marcus Klein has described as an "act of accommodation . . . when there were no orthodoxies to speak of to restrict one's freedom, and when all theories of society had been shattered" (Klein 29). The ultimate goal of this "accommodation," Klein remarks, is "the elimination of the distance between self and society, the perfect union of self and society" which means "the perpetual necessity of killing adjustments" (30). This is another way of saying that the individual is confronted with the task of adjusting himself to a society whose values, according to Howe, have been diffused in the postwar era.

Bellow creates an internal protagonist in his novels to carry out private quest for inner values, resulting in the contemplation of the fundamental questions, which Bellow himself as an artist raises in one of his essays: "Why were we born? What are we doing here? Where are we going? In its eternal naiveté the imagination keeps coming back to these things" (Bellow, "Distractions of a Fiction Writer" 19). Bellow's questioning of the purpose of human existence in a diffused, mass society suggests the importance of personal values in his novels, to which external social values remain largely subsidiary. This concern in Bellow's fiction conforms to Jerry Bryant's assertion that "The overwhelming moral and metaphysical preoccupation of the western mind in the twentieth century is the integrity of the individual, because that is where reality and value are deemed to lie" (Bryant 284). In this respect John Clayton is most accurate in his observation that Bellow "stands as a spokesman for our culture, as a defender of the western cultural tradition" (Clayton 3). Bryant has given close attention to Bellow's achievement as a writer concerned with inner values.

When Bellow made a trip to an Illinois town to gather material for an article, he asked an inhabitant of the area how people spent their time there, he received this answer: "They go to club meetings. Or to the drive-in movie. They pitch a little. They raise a little hell. They bowl. They drink some etc." And when Bellow informed this individual that he intended to write an article about this place and needed information, he was struck by the blunt reply: "Gosh, you' are barking up the wrong tree. There ain't nothing here to write about. There's nothing doing here or anywhere in Ellenois. It's boring." Bellow comments: "I had a score of conversations like this one" ("The Sealed Treasure 414").

While Bellow probablyreconstructed this script from composite of such circumstances for reader interest, his real intention is to charge American democratic society with its failure to create cultural incentives for the individual and to charge the latter with the failure to create his own cultural resources in the absence of those incentives. Although Bellow goes on to tell us in the article that he is pleased to find that good books in the library are in much demand, and that some people there does read Plato, Tocqueville, Proust, and Frost. He wonders what use "these isolated readers were making of the books they borrowed. With whom did they discuss them? At the country club, the bowling league, sorting mail at the post office or in the factory, over the back fence? . . . Ordinary life gave them little opportunity for such conversation" (Bellow, "The Sealed Treasure 414").

Mass culture not only separates the artist and intellectual from his natural audience, but it also removes the mass of people from the kind of art which might express their human and aesthetic needs. The tendency of mass culture is to exclude everything which does not conform to popular norms. Mass culture creates and satisfies artificial appetites in the entire populace; it has grown into a major industry which converts culture into a commodity. But whatever the future may promise, there is no doubt that America is a nation where at the same time cultural freedom is promised and mass culture produced. This paradox creates many difficulties for American writers and intellectuals who are trying to realize themselves in relation to their country and its cultural life.

To compensate for the cultural inadequacy, Bellow thinks that an artist should seek to lead the individual inward, away from externalities. To achieve this, he began with the introspective protagonist who represents the turn inward. Such was his attempt in his first published story entitled "Two Morning Monologues," which appeared in the *Partisan Review* in 1941, heralding the theme with which Bellow was to concern himself in his subsequent work: the criticism of a society which provides the individual with no cultural resources, a society which, as the *Partisan Review* editors expressed, "converts culture into a commodity." While the cynical young man of the story waits for his draft call, he projects a façade of introspection — "I know a great deal about myself, in as well as out" —but ironically admits at the same time that he is "very nearly sunk" because he cannot turn inward to find value in his social existence. Rather his world, as he views it, is a conglomeration of commerce. Bellow, of course, is disparaging the emptiness of modern life in the city.

Bellow never tires of exposing the purely commercial aspects of American society which often promote "mass culture" and obstruct the "interior life" which the writer seeks to satisfy:

> Still, the main facts of American life are productive. The overwhelming fact is that of a manufacturing and business civilization. Money, production, politics, planning, administration, expertise, war—these are what absorb mature men. This is what society as a whole is manifestly about. Most writers cannot expect to get easily into the minds of a people absorbed in such matters—a public, one should add, influenced by the mass media. (Bellow, "Skepticism and the Depth of Life" 14)

These are some of the "distractions" which Bellow expounds on at length in "Distractions of a Fiction Writer" (1957). There he calls them "the giant producers of goods ... news and information ... [and] bad art." These distractions the writer must counteract with the imagination — "The great outer chaos which drives us inward" (Bellow, "Distractions of a Fiction Writer" 3—4). Only through the imagination, Bellow insists, can the writer make his claims on worldly men's attentions in this state of affairs. In this role, he perceives the writer as the "divine literatus" who replace the priest.

The writer, Bellow contends, overwhelms the present distractions of society through creating a protagonist who seeks to pursue an inner life over the harassment of mass culture and materialism, through producing order out of disorder by revealing to us our humanity, and all these are carried out through "an unknown process of the imagination":

> "I loafe and invite my soul," says Walt Whitman. Well, perhaps his counterpart today does too. Perhaps. I hope so, because his imagination requires the tranquil attitude. But chances are that he is working, bitterly working, in an effort to meet his brothers of the office and factory sympathetically. The odds are good that he is literally a brother and comes out of the same mass. And now for some strange reason he is trying to throw a bridge from this same place, from a room in Chicago to, let us say, Ahab, to Cervantes, to Shakespeare, to the Kings of the old Chronicles, to Genesis. For he says, "Aren't we still part of the same humanity, children of Adam?" so he invites his soul away from distractions. (Bellow, "Distractions of a Fiction Writer" 10)

To be able to create characters in the imagination to show us our common humanity, our bonds with the past, is to compensate for the distractions of "mass activity, industry, and money". Bellow expresses not only dissatisfaction at American culture from which intelligence, soul, and community are missing, but additionally his awareness of how much he needs to compensate for.

Bellow's primary concern as a writer is not to be associated with any particular literary tradition either by ideology or by style, but to have a moral purpose as a justification for his art. He feels that he, as well as any good modern writer, must take a stand in his art. Bellow asserts that the writer must make a "moral commitment" (Bellow, "The Writer as Moralist" 62). Having such a purpose can ultimately be Bellow's only "tradition." It is the "tradition" which separates him most notably from the post-Worid War II writers who view society as brutal and destructive to the individual and who consequently lack a moral purpose in their refusal to offer the individual any alternatives to his condition. Bellow commented on such writers in his 1963 Library of Congress address. He says that writers have inherited a tone of bitterness from the great poems and novels of the twentieth century, many of which lament the passing of a more stable and beautiful age demolished by the barbarous intrusion of an industrial and metropolitan society of masses or proles who will, after many upheavals, be tamed by bureaucracies and oligarchies in brave new worlds, and human anthills. Bellow continues commenting that there are modern novelists who take that all for granted as fully proven and implicit in the human condition and who complain as steadily as they write, viewing modern life with a bitterness to which they themselves have not established clear title. And it is this unearned bitterness that Bellow speaks of. Bellow answers these complaints with the writer's moral function:

> Either we want life to continue or we do not…. If we want it to continue … in what form shall life be justified? That is the essence of the moral question. We call the writer moral to the degree that his imagination indicates to us how we may answer naturally, without strained arguments, with

a spontaneous, mysterious proof that has no need to argue with despair. ("The Writer as Moralist" 62)

Thus Bellow's attack on the posture of despair proves ultimately to be his only real "tradition" as a modern writer. For Bellow, not to despair means to affirm the possibilities of a meaningful individual existence despite the sometimes wasteland atmosphere in American life. His obligation, asserts John Clayton, involves taking a stand "against the cultural nihilism of the twentieth century: against Dada, against the Wasteland, against the denigration of human life in modern society" (Clayton 3). This is a difficult thing to do, Bellow acknowledges, as he confronts the contradictions inherent in mass urban life, in a society indifferent to significant moral ideas.

Bellow disparages the philistines who are hostile to significant moral ideas as expressed in art. As an artist himself, Bellow does not justify ideas for the sake of ideas, nor does he believe that significant ideas can be anachronistic. When Bellow emphasizes that the moral function cannot be divorced from art, he is not asking the writer to be didactic. Bellow thinks the writer must use his imagination to convey his moral ideas. That is, they must be conveyed convincingly through a fictional character's actions and dialogue or monologue and through a setting which provides the appropriate atmosphere as a genuine test for the ideas. This involves a process of the imagination to carry the reader from disorder to order, from disillusionment to recognition, to build bridges between the present and the past to show us our humanity.

"If a novelist is going to affirm anything," Bellow says, "he must be prepared to prove his case in close detail, reconcile it with hard facts, and he must even be prepared for the humiliation of discovering that he may have to affirm something different" (Bellow, "The Writer as Moralist" 60). For instance, while Herzog insists on the nineteenth-century romantic concept of human dignity, he finds that merciless child abuse is a real fact of his present world. Yet this knowledge does not bring him to a dead-end despair, but to an acceptance of his world for what it is. Such is the imaginative process of Bellow's fiction through which he justifies himself as a writer in an affirmative mode. Just as Clayton has demonstrated that Bellow has to affirm a changed life if he is going to affirm the possibility of meaningful individual life in contemporary America. If life as it is offers cause for despair and if the individual is both product and producer of this life, then the individual must be redeemed. Through his redemption society will be redeemed. So Bellow affirms not the present individual and the present society but their possibilities.

Because the moral idea is shaped in the human psyche, Bellow depends ultimately on his characters to convey his value judgments. For in all his novels moral discovery is made in the protagonist's attempt to overcome his alienated condition. Bellow believes in the character who can go outside the concern wholly with oneself—the "all-important Me" —and become open, or receptive, to the innumerable possibilities in his personal experiences, one who has the capacity to go beyond himself to realized his community with others. Jerry Bryant finds the pattern which Bellow formulates in the characterizations of the protagonist in his works:

> The salient pattern of Bellow's novels is comprised of the main character's attempt … to free himself from the limits of his condition in order to achieve a "superior" life, some "higher fate" or "grand synthesis". He is then confronted with the impossibility of that achievement. In the confrontation, the issues become a question of whether the protagonist will reach that higher consciousness which will illumine the paradox and show him the way toward affirming it. (Bryant 342)

Bellow's protagonists are open, because their achievement of a "superior life" ultimately depends on not only "the recognition of the nature of the self—its contradictoriness, its freedom, its limitations, its subjectivity," but also "on a recognition of one's environment, upon which the self relies for the quality of his existence" (344), so they experience the recognition of the self in reacting to the environment and try to balance hope with despair. Although like many modern writers Bellow may write of alienated, burdened people, he gives them the capacity to attain inner dignity despite external restrictions and repressions. Their dignity is realized as they achieve community with others by transcending the all-important Me and becoming concerned for others. It is through this very concept of character that Bellow is able to dissociate himself from the modern writers of despair, those who depict modern society as deterministic and destructive to the human spirit. By realizing his concept of characterization, Bellow feels that he can justify himself as a writer in society. As he states more than once, character delineation is the true product of the imagination.

Bellow is clearly outraged at the "crudity, disorder, ugliness, and lawlessness" of modern life, and he intends to counteract these facts by depicting a protagonist who makes his moral discovery while overcoming his alienated condition. Bellow perceives the difficulty of ennobling the individual in an age in which so many millions became hair, gold teeth, and ashes; in which whole populations were sacrificed to "make the world safe for democracy" (Bellow, *Recent American Fiction* 2) or to build socialism. Nevertheless Bellow is determined to take character and setting, the stock elements of any literature, and manipulate them through his imagination to dramatize the human quest for the realization of freedom, community, individual choice, order and historical perspective. He will be another Walt Whitman who in *Democratic Vistas* "exhorted the poets of a democracy to create archetypes, images of the American citizen, and charged writers with the highest of moral duties" (Clayton, 5—6).

Chapter Three Fiction as Survival Strategy

Bellow, with Jewish outlook, awareness of survival, and moral responsibility as a writer, explores the survival strategy for human being in his fictional world. Bellow began to write at the end of the 1930s, when 'hard - boiled' school of writing associated with Ernest Hemingway was current then. The Hemingway hero, a man of action, and of instinctive behavior, can shoot his opponent but is "unpracticed in introspection" and therefore cannot handle unseen adversaries. He is also bored with life, preoccupied with death, and in general displays an attitude of alienation to the universe. Bellow viewed this as a philosophy detrimental to the individual because ultimately it leads to annihilation, or suicide, as was the case with Hemingway.

Bellow reveals that the stance of the Hemingway hero is untenable, that man cannot live that way in his works. In its place Bellow project the Jewish outlook, which is more positive and humanistic. The typical Bellow's protagonists, usually historians, professors, biographers, and poets are men of reflection and of intellectual pursuits, who are concerned with the internal world of the human being, which Bellow think is the real salvation. In addition, Bellow heroes get their involvement in society and undertake their social responsibility, which ensures that they can find the foothold in the society. They also go out of his "self-enclosed world" to outside world and get accommodation finally.

Following the first protagonist, Joseph in *Dangling Man*, who talks about his problems in order to deal with them, the internal battle that each one of Bellow's protagonists has to fight to come to accept both himself and the social reality in which he is placed forms the core of his novels. A search for and recognition of values in a given social context is the spring that sets these characters into motion. Bellow wishes to restore the exposition of ideas in the novels as well as the dramatizing of them and has kept his commitment to society as an artist, by portraying his protagonists in pursuit of a private quest for inner values to save humanity.

"How should a good man live?" (*DM* 23) is the question that Joseph poses to himself and is also a recurring theme throughout all of Bellow's works. The answer, of course, is that goodness can only be achieved in the company of man, not by isolating oneself in a room or in a drunken stupor or by going off on a safari to Africa. Bellow, abandoning the tightness and limitation of the earlier writing, adopts expansive and inclusive attitudes in his third full-length novel *The Adventures of Augie March*, and offers a social panorama of the American society from twenties to the post-war years, showing readers characters from different origins, classes and interests. Augie touches all sides and accumulates knowledge of himself through his multiplicity of experiences.

Bellow is always aware of the gap between the high principles and low facts which he must confront and resolve as artist, and this gap gives his fiction its sustained tension between despair and hope. Yet this knowledge does not bring him to a dead-end despair, but to an acceptance of his world for what it is. One way of accepting the real world is to assert the ascendency of art over life. Bellow intends to counteract the low facts with "high principles" as conveyed through the imagination and by doing so to justify the place of the writer in society.

1. Untenability for Hard-boiled Hero to Survive

Bellow began to write at the end of the 1930s, when 'hard-boiled' school of writing associated with Ernest Hemingway was current then. But "Bellow was concerned to stake out a position for himself in the American literary tradition, one that embraced feeling and sensitivity" (Hyland 17). Bellow apparently felt novels of ideas were needed in American fiction which has to a great extent emphasized externalism, as epitomized in Hemingway. As Bellow said in his article on the future of American fiction,

> ... in the masterpieces of the twentieth century the thinker usually has a weak grip on life. But by now an alternative, passionate activity without ideas has also been well explored in novels of adventure, hunting, combat, and eroticism. Meanwhile, miracles, born of thought, have been largely ignored by modern literature. (Bellow, "Where Do We Go from Here: The Future of Fiction")

Saul Bellow's novels are not action-packed and his protagonists do not carry big-bore rifles to hunt lions or rhinoceros on the African plains and jungles, nor are they fighting a civil war in the hills of Spain and honoring masculine codes of bravery. On the contrary, Bellow's men are urbanites who constantly wage war with themselves in the introspective realms of their souls. This mode of solitary, existential introspection runs deep in Bellow's people. In the beginning page of his first novel, *Dangling Man*, Bellow lays the methodological foundation of self-examination as a blueprint for his later novels. Bellow, in this first page, immediately challenges the masculine codes that categorize introspection as a weakness; these codes bent on individual honor are antithetical to his recurring themes that stress community and humanity. Here is Bellow in 1944:

> There was a time when people were in the habit of addressing themselves frequently and felt no shame at making a record of their in-

> ward transactions. But to keep a journal nowadays is considered a kind of self – indulgence, a weakness, and in poor taste. For this is an era of . Today the code of the athlete, of the tough boy . . . that curious mixture of striving, asceticism, and rigor . . . is stronger than ever. Do you have feelings? There correct and incorrect ways of indicating them. Do you have an inner life? It is nobody's business but your own. Do you have emotions? Strangle them. To a degree, everyone obeys this code . . . . (9)

Bellow is aware of the themes of honor, virtue, courage, and duty that havedefined the American literary hero especially through the stories of Hemingway. However, Bellow challenges these prerequisites for the typical "code hero" by ignoring the mold of the silent, strong, and tough typecast; instead, his characters are babblers who break down. Thus, Bellow's insistence to "talk" about feelings instead of strangling them begins this therapeutic methodology consistent with his characters' determination to accept and face their weaknesses. As victims, Bellow's protagonists have no other choice; they are not groomed in the codes of armoring themselves like the hard-boiled. The Bellow man, instead of facing a charging lion, faces his internal turmoil armed to the teeth with dialogue, but his words, like bullets, never explode but implode into a mass of introspection that scatter in all directions.

Instead of expressing heroism through the displays ofphysical courage, Bellow's hero struggles to "salvage something of the self under the crushing pressures of urban life, of modern materialism and self-indulgence" (Hyland 18). So from the beginning of his writing career, Bellow tried to be concerned with the internal world in his first novel, which was immensely introversive both in content, primarily the protagonist's mental experiences, and in form, the tight journal form, which was just appropriate to focus on the protagonist's internal consciousness.

Bellow is turning away from Hemingwayism in the opening paragraph of *Dangling Man* (1944). He rejects the code of Hemingway in the first entry, asserting that he will expose the inner life through introspection. In contrast to the Hemingway style of the dramatic presentation of the camera which maintains a strenuous reserve in regard to delving into the consciousness of the individual, Bellow's protagonist keeps a journal in order to talk about his feelings and perhaps better understand his situation. In the first journal entry of *Dangling Man*, Joseph writes that this is an era of hardboiled – dom, and that the code of the athlete, of the tough boy is stronger than ever. "Do you have feelings? There are correct and incorrect ways of indicating them. Do you have an inner life? It is nobody's business but your own. Do you have emotions? Strangle them" (*DM* 1). To a degree, everyone obeys this code. And it does admit of a limited kind of candor, a close-mouthed straight-forwardness. But on the truest candor, it has an inhibitory effect. Most serious matters are closed to the hard-boiled. They are unpractised in introspection, and therefore badly equipped to deal with opponents whom they cannot shoot like big game or outdo in daring. If you have difficulties, grapple with them silently, goes one of their commandments.

> To hell with that! I intend to talk about mine. . . . In my present state of demoralization, it has become necessary for me to keep a journal—that is, to talk to myself—and I do not feel guilty of self-indulgence in the least. The hard-boiled are compensated for their silence; they fly planes or fight bulls or catch tarpon, whereas I rarely leave my room. (*DM* 1)

The Hemingway hero is the strong, hard-boiled athlete who can shoot his opponent but is "unpracticed in introspection" and therefore cannot handle unseen adversaries. He is also bored with life, preoccupied with death, attempts to order his life by means of an "ideal construction" or a "code," is not responsible to anyone, and in general displays an attitude of alienation to the universe, which is either totally indifferent to him or which he views as a trap. Hemingway manages in *The Sun Also Rises* to depict the empty and aimless groping for direction of the post-World War I expatriates, while Bellow has in *Dangling Man* captured the mood of philosophical malaise which marked the generation of World War II. Bellow reveals that the stance of the Hemingway hero is untenable, that man cannot live that way in his first work and his subsequent novels. In its place Bellow will project the Jewish outlook, which is more positive and humanistic. There is of course one essential thing that the Hemingway hero and Bellow's protagonist do have in common, and that is the compelling need to solve the problem of identity in a society that no longer provides ready-made answers. But they differ in the ways in which they try to reach their solution to this problem.

Since Hemingway's prose is stripped free of cant and the frills of sentimentality, it does not lie. But, says Ruth Wisse, "the absence of lies is not synonymous with truth. The intricacies of rich personality cannot be explored without recourse to the emotive and intellectual probing of sentiment and conscience that Hemingway so consistently avoided" (Wisse 80).

Bellow's protagonists are intellectuals who love to talk. They all have problems, but one way of resolving them is to discuss them with others: friends, associates, and lawyers. Jews have always believed that there is a power in words. Bellow talks about this in his Introduction to *Great Jewish Short Stories*, and, in his travelogue, *To Jerusalem and Back*, he makes discourse the sole preoccupation of all his characters. When the Jews were physically battered, a power which was cultivated and which could not be conquered by the strongest armies or the most vicious pogroms was the power of speech, whereas the Hemingway hero will retreat into silence. So effective is this power that the Jews believe that by their supplication to God they can avert the Divine decree. Bellow bestows upon his protagonist this verbal strength. They don't drink or engage in bullfighting, and they imbibe life excessively.

Bellow attempts to break the hold that Hemingway has over the style and minds of American writers and the reading public from his first work, *Dangling Man*. He discusses the influence of Hemingway in his Nobel Prize Lecture:

> I belong to a generation of readers that knew the long list of noble or noble-sounding words, words like "invincible conviction" or "humanity" rejected by writers like Ernest Hemingway. Hemingway spoke for the soldiers who fought in the First World War under the inspiration of Woodrow Wilson and other rotund statesmen whose big words had to be measured against the frozen corpses of young men paving the trenches. Hemingway's youthful readers were convinced that the horrors of the 20th Century had sickened and killed humanistic beliefs with their deadly radiations. I told myself, therefore, that Conrad's rhetoric must be resisted.

The most logical way for Bellow to turn away from Hemingway is to use a protagonist who is the opposite of the WASP figure. Bellow's method is to use a Jewish protagonist, in a typical Jewish situation, and to allow him to react according to his intellection and upbringing. In Bellow's first novel *Dangling Man*, Joseph resigns his job and expects to be drafted shortly. Nevertheless the moment of actual induction is postponed for months as a result of some quirk in the bureaucratic machine. Joseph's present status as a "dangling man" between civilian and military life is indicative of how the Jew is viewed in society.

One of the most important aspects of Joseph and one which distinctly removes him from the Hemingway hero, is his involvement in society, his feeling of social responsibility. Joseph tries to move from his isolate status, in which his humanity is debased, to a position whereby he recognizes the need to become involved with others. Joseph is aware that at one time he was a social creature, he loved society, but he wanted to be what Schlosberg, in *The Victim*, would term as more than human in attempting to work out his life "according to a general plan" (*DM* 29), in attempting to create a "colony of the spirit" (40) to defend oneself against the dangers and brutality of the world.

At the beginning of *Dangling Man*, Joseph is in the state of limbo, which causes him the loss of his job, the loss of self-confidence, the loss of his manhood, the loss of initiative, and the loss of incentive, and he has a general feeling that life is dull. Consequently, he is lonely, solitary, distracted, misanthropic, unemployed, embarrassed by his position, and denigrated by himself. This is stressed by his movement away from contacts with people. He can no longer endure the society of his friends, and they, in turn find him irascible and shun his companionship. His relationship with his family is no better. The slightest offense sparks an explosion. He does battle with all those with whom he comes in contact. His state of disjunction is amplified by Joseph's not having a last name. His surname is never mentioned in the novel. Although he once had a family (he recalls his mother and father), currently he belongs to no one and nothing, serves only himself, and has an orphaned or hermitlike relationship with the world.

The difference between Bellow's character and Hemingway's is that this estrangement from society is only an interim state for the Bellow character, who realizes that this is an unnatural position for man, and that he is the only one who can lift himself out of this demoralizing circumstance. The world is not his enemy. In fact, Bellow tells us that Joseph is not severe toward the world. Theories of a wholly good or a wholly malevolent world strike him as foolish. Of those who believe in a wholly good world he says that they do not understand depravity. As for pessimists, the question he asks of them is, "Is that all they see, such people?" (*DM* 29) For him the world is both, and therefore, it is neither. In a sense, everything is good because it exists. Or, good or not good, it exists, is ineffable, and for that reason, marvelous. For Joseph the world is marvelous, full of wonder and if at the present time he "suffers from a feeling of strangeness, of not quite belonging to the world" (30), the problem is with him, one that he must deal with and that he must resolve. It calls for a solution rather than capitulation. As an intellectual person, he knows that discussion with another person is the only way to understand and then to resolve his difficulties. Finally he realizes his isolation by indulging in this estranged situation, resolutely gives it up and goes back to embrace life by getting enlistment immediately to find foothold in the life and undertake his social responsibility.

After Leventhal has achieved through strenuous efforts a modestly comfort able kind of middle-class existence, he feels that he has made it on his own, and that the hard way he had to go entitles him to the belief that those who have failed to make it have only themselves to blame. It absolves him, he thinks, from acknowledging responsibility for others. Leventhal, when the novel opens, feels and acts in conformity with the social and economic reality of his environment, the big city, harsh and indifferent, to which he has learned to accommodate himself. However, despite his determination to live by this knowledge, so painfully acquired, a disquieting sense of guilt remains. Somehow he cannot get rid of the feeling that he has not really deserved his position, that he has "got away with it", while others have not, for as he realizes there "was great unfairness in one man's having all the comforts of life while another had nothing" (*V* 69). When Allbee, the man who had lost his job, and as a consequence his wife, and who had become down and out, persists in intruding upon Leventhal's privacy, holding him, Leventhal, responsible for his coming down in the world, Leventhal cannot refuse.

When his brother's wife frantically calls for his help when her little son Mickey falls ill, Leventhal's first impulse is to refuse to get involved. But when

Leventhal does go, obeying his sense of familial duty, the seriousness of the young boy's illness forces him to become actually involved in the lives of his sister-in-law Elena (of Italian extraction) and her two sons Philip and Mickey. And when Leventhal gets to know them personally, as individuals, and from liking his nephew Philip starts to love him, he firmly takes charge of their affairs and derives the emotional satisfaction from this involvement. After Mickey actually dies, in the subsequent brief meetings with his brother Max he learns to see his brother as an individual in his own right as well, and to appreciate him as a man who has taken life's beatings without losing his essential humanity. When Leventhal calls the nurses in the hospital fools because Max, on entering the hospital, found the dead body of his little son lying in an empty room, unattended, Max is still able to find excuses for them: "All the nurses didn't know. It's a big place." What Max's responses reveal is regard for other people's individuality and great tolerance of their weaknesses, the kind of humanity which Leventhal had learned to suppress in his obsessive determination not to remain at the bottom steps of the social ladder.

Since the period of Leventhal's involvement with the affairs of his brother's family coincides with Allbee's intrusion upon his private life, it is not too farfetched to assume that Leventhal's awakened sense of responsibility and his growing love for his nephew Philip and Max himself should make him more accessible to Allbee's ludicrous demands. He even tries to find out whether the man's claims are justified. Although Leventhal tries to absolve him of responsibility for others to accommodate in the harsh and indifferent big city, he still can not escape it. His involvement with his brother's family and Allbee illustrates his growing awareness that human beings are individuals, and that they are to be treated as individuals, not abstractions. It also teaches him what, in fact, is contained in the parable of the slaying of the Ifrit's son, the first epigraph with which the novel opens: even for those events for which one can scarcely be held responsible directly, one cannot in the last analysis escape responsibility. The stones which the merchant threw so carelessly can hardly have killed the Ifrit's son, but he died, and for his death every human can expect to be held responsible.

Augie, this laughing creature whose adventures we share, appears to signify a total break from the morose characters created by the adherents of naturalistic fiction so prevalent in American literature in the early part of the century. For example, the characters in Ernest Hemingway's novels rarely smile. Life for them is a deadly serious matter. The Hemingway character can never say, as does Augie:

> "What's so laughable, that a Jacqueline [or man], for instance, as hard used as that by rough forces, will still refuse to lead a disappointed life? Or is the laugh at nature—including eternity—that it thinks it can win over us and the power of hope? Nah, nah! I think. It never will" (*AM* 599).

Hemingway's characters, as well as those of other naturalistic writers, are completely controlled by nature, helpless in their encounter with what they consider ineluctable forces. Bellow's Augie March, on the other hand, suggests an approach to life which is unique, and uniquely Jewish. Humor is an essential ingredient in the character of the Jew. It is not the humor of the belly-laugh, though that may be present at times. Jewish humor is a perspective on life, which is generally optimistic even in the extremely adverse situations, and which assures the hold onto the life.

Hemingway's disparagement of life, his love of death, and his even greater love of nothingness, are contrary to all the teachings of Judaism. Bellow viewed this as a philosophy detrimental to the individual because ultimately it leads to annihilation, or suicide, as was the case with Hemingway.

Despite the external trappings of an adventure story in *Henderson the Rain King*, Bellow is still reacting against the Hemingway externalism which Joseph rejected-this time, in the form of explicit satire. Seeking the darkest continent as the source for spiritual renewal and recalling a similar trip he has read about, Henderson is dismayed that the natural world symbolized by Africa is only a game land where the sportsman may prove his physical prowess. It is undoubtedly Hemingway who bears the brunt of Bellow's ridicule:

> I had bought the. 375 especially for this trip to Africa after reading about it in *Life and Look*. A fellow from Michigan who had once went to Alaska as soon as his vacation started; he flew to Alaska and hired a guide to track a Kodiak bear; they found the bear and chased him over cliffs and marshes and shot him at four hundred yards. Myself, I used to have a certain interest in hunting, but as I grew older it seemed a strange way to relate to nature. What I mean is, a man goes into the external world, and all he can do with it is to shoot it? It doesn't make sense. (*HRK* 94)

If Bellow is satirizing Hemingway, there is some irony in the fact that his own hero holds the basic Hemingway tenets-that "Truth comes with blows" (67) and that "the biggest problem of all ... was to encounter death" (276). As Bellow himself stated in a 1964 interview, "But what Henderson is really seeking is a remedy to the anxiety over death. What he can't endure is this continuing anxiety: the indeterminate and indefinite anxiety" (Steers 38). But while satirizing the Hemingway hero, Bellow is nevertheless using the African journey motif to his own purpose, as Opdahl's excellent insight clarifies:

> By sending his hero after African game, actually symbols of the internal opponents his early heroes confronted, Bellow takes his fiction out of the self-enclosed world of his protagonist's mind. He overcomes the difficulties of subjective issues by converting Hemingway's world into his own.

(Opdahl, *The Novels of Saul Bellow* 125)

Bellow realizes that, Joseph, locked in a single room, musing in the journal form, will get his humanity debased in such isolation, so Bellow leads his descendent out of his "self-enclosed world" to natural world to get accommodation in the modern society.

Bellow breaks away from Hemingway's hard-boiled codes by creating a typical Bellow hero, who is male, often an intellectual, a scholarly or literary figure, like Bellow himself and has frequently been taken as mouthpieces for Bellow's own views. He is anxious about self, "concerned with exploring its inward claim, and about 'mind', which may be our salvation or the real source of our suffering" (Bradbury 29). He bears his social responsibility and gets involved with other people, and hence obtains his position in the modern world.

2. Quest for an Inner World, the Real Salvation

Among the many statements Bellow has made throughout his career about the art of fiction and the function of the novelist, one comment, short and witty as it is, and perhaps for this very reason often overlooked by Bellow's critics, becomes of vital importance for the understanding not only of the method used for his own writings, but also of his general attitude towards contemporary life and culture:

> The realistic method made it possible to write with seriousness and dignity about the ordinary, common situations of life. In Balzac and Flaubert and the great Russian masters the realistic external were intended to lead inward. I suppose one might say that now the two elements, the inwards and the external, have come apart.
>
> In what we call the novel of sensibility the intent of the writer is to pull us into an all sufficient consciousness which he, the writer, governs absolutely. In the realistic novel today the writer is satisfied with an art of externals. Either he assumes that by describing a man's shoes he has told us all that we need to know about his soul, or he is more interested in the shoes than in the soul. (Bellow "Facts that Put Fancy to Flight" 1)

The dissatisfaction expressed with the modern versions of both the "realistic method" and the "novel of sensibility", with the dissociation between 'externals' and 'internals' is reflected in Bellow's conscious effort to bring together these two elements in his novels. Bellow's whole career can be seen as an effort to correct the necessary failures brought by the separation of externals and internals, of focusing exclusively on either shoe or soul. Martin Corner notes: "... there are those who see his [Bellow's] fiction as the record of an inward journey, from outer to inner truth, from the confusions of discourse to the truth of the heart. For such critics, Bellow is one kind of romantic: the romantic of inner, immanent truth, of direct illumination, of the ascetic inward journey to self-knowledge" (370). It is arguable that Bellow's journey bears relevance to our collective consciousness infected with a pervasive angst as we battle these real anxieties; it is this constant fear that drives us to confront our existence metaphysically and literature has often portrayed this alienated human condition as nihilistically fashionable.

Bellow wrote in his "The Jefferson Lectures": ""

Following the first protagonist, Joseph in *Dangling Man*, who talks about his problems in order to deal with them, the internal battle that each one of Bellow's protagonists has to fight to come to accept both himself and the social reality in which he is placed forms the core of his novels. A search for and recognition of values in a given social context is the spring that sets these characters into motion. Bellow describes society, engagement, action, reason, strife and everyday reality in his novels, but the emphasis is on celebrating internals: the self, individuality, contemplation, acceptance and faith. Actually external reality becomes the reflexion or projection of the character's inner consciousness, who receives the influence of the environment and internalizes it. It is Bellow's belief, as Herzog puts it, that "there are moral realities... as surely as there are molecular and atomic ones" (*H* 221). Like his protagonist, Herzog, Bellow is "convinced that the realm of facts and that of values is not eternally separated" (*H* 133). Pifer, in the first sentence of her introduction to *Saul Bellow Against the Grain*, confirms both the recurring presence of this model character and his predisposition to interior conflict: "From his first novel, *Dangling Man* to his latest fiction, Saul Bellow has created a virtually unbroken series of protagonists doing mental battle with the world around them" (1). Opdahl also confirms Joseph as the prototype character in Bellow's novels: "Joseph embodies within himself the polarity of Bellow's later contrasting characters ... Bellow, in his first novel would return to character, and especially inner character, as the center of his fiction" (48—49).

Joseph in *Dangling Man* is a cynical young man dangling between civilian and military life, and pursues the study of the Enlightenment in an attempt to define his own values in the modern world even if he is a dilettante. At the outset of the novel, Joseph asserted the necessity of introspection, declaring it an alternative to sordid external life: "If you have difficulties, grapple with them silently .... To hell with that! I intend to talk about mine, and if I had as many mouths as Siva has arms and kept them going all the time, I still could not do myself justice" (*DM* 9).

Joseph's diary begins with a rejection of the code of "hardboiled-dom" because the code denies man's expression of an inner life, demands hard-boiled reticence, and substitutes violent action for feeling and thought. Clearly it is Bellow's own rejection of the Hemingway hero. As Chester Eisinger says,

> Bellow is turning away from Hemingwayism, away from an aesthetic of understatement which had been dominant for two decades and which was inimical to that treatment of experience which finds it necessary to discover and lay bare, with little restraint, the thoughts and emotions of its subjects. (345)

Bellow himself stated in a 1953 article on Hemingway that the struggle of the self to survive "is usually an internal struggle and Hemingway stirringly externalizes it" (Bellow, "Hemingway and the Image of Man" 338). Hemingway, Bellow contends, "felt a challenge to master himself in action and ... he was not satisfied with arriving at a satisfactory idea of his existence" (338—339). Bellow made himself clearer on the matter in his essay on the future of fiction, suggesting, as he does through Joseph in *Dangling Man*, that the Hemingway aesthetic of bald dialogue and action is no longer a viable style for an introspective fiction of ideas. Bellow wishes to restore the exposition of ideas in the novels as well as the dramatizing of them, and he apparently regarded the journal form as a suitable vehicle for the former purpose. Thus Joseph intends to vent his feelings: "I intend to talk about mine, and if I had as many mouths as Siva has arms and kept them going all the time, I still could not do myself justice" (*DM* 9)

Joseph initiates his own act of self-definition by beginning a journal. He feels compelled to assert his dignity as an individual. He seeks to bring himself to a clear understanding of the meaning and value of absolute freedom in his journal, which allows him an open form for self-expression. He starts his search in isolation "to know what we are and what we are for, to know our purposes, to seek grace" (41). He has withdrawn from work, old friends, and former polit ical ideas, is temporarily in a situation in which he is unencumbered by any external responsibilities so that he has the opportunity to turn inward, but then can find no meaningful way to use his freedom. His quest for the spirit, for an absolute value which transcends the limits of a society controlled by bureaucracy, which is an absolute quest, alienates him from his society, causing him to have "a feeling of strangeness, of not quite belonging to the world" (30). This feeling is reflected in his observations from his room which signifies for him separation from the rest of the world as well as his self-estrangement: "I, in this room, separate, alienated, distrustful, find in my purpose not an open world, but a closed hopeless jail. My perspectives end in this wall" (92). He desires the greatness and goodness implicit in spiritual freedom but ironically admits, "I do not know how to use my freedom ... because I have no resources-in a word, no character" (*DM* 12). Joseph's daily existence lacks action and change, it is filled with feelings and ideas that almost overflow their speaker.

Joseph is concerned with "defending his inner differences, the ones that really matter" (27). He wants to preserve the dignity and freedom of the self, and in doing so, cites Spinoza to his alter ego, the Spirit of Alternatives: "I recall Spinoza's having written that no virtue could be considered greater than that of trying to preserve oneself…." (167) He knows that everyone must die. He does not instruct us to graft new glands or to eat carp's intestine in order to live three hundred years. We cannot make ourselves immortal. We can decide only what is for us to decide. The rest is beyond our power. In short, he did not mean preservation of the animal.

Joseph has imprisoned himself by his quest for the absolute. Typical of the inward-turning character, Joseph casts his lot for the value of spiritual freedom, implying a rejection of society and its external values. Joseph is hostile toward his old friend Adler, who visits him and apparently has achieved some material success in life. Joseph rebuffs him by claiming their differences on the basis of outer appearances. Joseph is just as reactionary when discussing his brother Amos, who he feels has opted for materialism. Nevertheless Joseph's friend John Pearl, the artist, helps him to affirm the inner life. Joseph gives us Pearl's own words as the latter defends his art against the mundane: "I am exhilarated by the tremendous unimportance of my work. It is nonsense. My employers are nonsensical. The job therefore leaves me free" (*DM* 90). There's nothing to it. In a way it's like getting a piece of bread from a child in return for wiggling your ears. It is childish. He is the only one in the fifty-three-story building who knows how childish it is. Everybody else takes it seriously. Because it is a fifty-three-story building, they think it must be serious. It is pish, nonsense, nothing! The real world is the world of art and of thought. There is only one worth-while sort of work, that of the imagination.

Joseph responds to the words of Pearl in what we must surely regard as Bellow's own in view of what he has said in his later essays about the imagination as a source of inner life for the writer-There he is in New York, painting; and in spite of the calamity, the lies and moral buggery, the odium, the detritus of wrong and sorrow dropped on every heart, in spite of those, he can keep a measure of cleanliness and freedom. Besides, those acts of the imagination are in the strictest sense not personal. Through them he is connected with the best part of mankind. He feels this and he can never be isolated, left aside.

Pearl helps Joseph aware of the possibility of spiritual freedom as realized through the imagination-a freedom which counteracts the external world of ugly facts and circumstances. The imagination frees one, Joseph sees, by providing one a resource for an inner life divorced from the physical self and its physical limitations in society. We can only assume from Joseph's reactions to Pearl that his purpose for writing a journal is at least a feeble attempt to realize the achievement of Pearl, that is, to achieve an inner freedom unobstructed by the outside world-the freedom he ostensibly choose in the novel.

Unlike *Dangling Man*, a journalist's fragmented ideas about the historical meaning of freedom, Bellow depends more consistently on environmental imagery to explore his protagonist's inner world as he struggles toward his humanity in his second novel *The Victim*. Being human, for Bellow and his protagonist, Asa Leventhal, means simply the willingness to commit oneself to involvement with others. As one critic concisely states the issue,

> *The Victim* faces the question of our responsibility, simply as human beings, for other individual who are imposed on us by circumstances, whom we do not particularly value or respect, and with whom we are not engaged in any meaningful creative or social activities. (Davis 118)

While Bellow himself stated that *The Victim* was his first "well – made" novel in the tradition of Flaubert, several critics have gone a step further to argue for its naturalism-and with some justification since the novel is pervaded with naturalistic imagery. One of Bellow's most perceptive critics, Ralph Freedman, gives his interpretation of the symbolic relationship between the protagonist and his environment in *The Victim*, based on the naturalistic imagery Bellow uses to depict the environment as a source of the character's sensibility. Bellow delineates a naturalistic environment which coincides with Asa Leventhal's state of mind throughout the novel. Urban circumstances represent an external threat which reinforces his internal anxiety about his relationship with his world for Asa Leventhal in particular. As Bellow's prototypical Jew, one of those who is victimized by a world not of his making, Asa feels threatened by unnamed external forces. He is burdened by others' illnesses, treachery, and accusations while he attempts to lead a normal existence in a modern urban environment, which only intensifies his burden.

Environmental imagery is an artistic means for conveying Asa Leventhal's anxiety about himself in relation to the rest of the world and his subsequent realization of himself as a part of humanity. The environment is a construction of reality which imposes a value system on Asa as he constantly responds verbally and emotionally to it. Selected details of Asa's surroundings merely create a picture of the external world that corroborates his feelings. For instance, when Asa is going grudgingly to his sister-in-law's apartment to assume responsibility for his sick nephew-responsibility which he feels really belongs to his negligent brother-he finds the subway trip oppressive with the muggy heat and "gloomy yellow light" in which the fan blades turn too slowly. And then at the apartment he finds everything-the house, his sister-in-law, the sick child-oppressive: "Behind him the flat was dark; the shades were drawn and a lamp was burning amid the clutter of the dining-room table" (*V* 6—7).

Thetwo similes in the novel reflect Asa's self – concept. By refusing to be involved with Albee at first, Asa sees himself "like a bear in a winter hole" - a fitting image for one who resorts to human hibernation. Furthermore, his retreat is "like a mirror wrapped in a piece of flannel" (*V* 98). This image is equally functional, for the mirror is an object which, in order to be functional itself, must have an object for reflection. The idea suggested by the mirror is reinforced later as Asa stares at the water and sees the city buildings as the reflection of inhuman lions. Humanity, we must take it, is a possibility evoked by the antithesis of inhumanity. In other words, the mirror image symbolizes Asa's desire, not for isolation within himself, but for interaction with others in whom his own existence can be reflected. The use of a simile like the mirror is one indication that Bellow intends to portray his protagonist, despite an oppressive environment, as one searching, through his self-awareness, for a way to be human in his contact with others.

"The most important thing that happens to Leventhal," says Tony Tanner, "is that he is stirred out of his 'indifference' and 'recalcitrance' into a sense of general injustice and suffering, and thence to an awareness and confession of specific blame and responsibility" (Tanner 31). The relationship with Allbee instructs Asa in this responsibility. The urban environment Bellow depicts has the dual function of serving as the novel's setting and as an index to the protagonist's state of mind in his progress toward accommodation.

Even though Augie as the hero of a picaresque in Bellow's third full-length novel "needs little internal character development" (Opdahl, *The Novels of Saul Bellow* 78), in the first three-fourths of the novel, as Opdahl contends, "he shifts from a young man who dissolves himself in the external world to an adult who turns inward and discovers himself-and gains substance as a character" (74). Augie's journey is a quest in self-definition through independence. Augie does not seek experience for its own sake but rather as a means for finding himself in the deepest sense. "What is the true self; how navigate it through life?" (*AM* 56) Wisdom has begun to issue from experience. He must have had a feeling since he was a kid about the axial lines which made him want to have his existence on them, and as he has said 'no' like a stubborn fellow to all his persuaders, just on the obstinacy of his memory of the lines, never entirely clear. But lately he has felt the thrilling lines again. When striving stops, there they are as a gift. He was lying on the couch there before and they suddenly went quivering right straight through him. Truth, love, peace, bounty, usefulness, harmony! And all noise and grates, distortion, chatter, distraction, effort, superfluity, passed off like something unreal. And he believes that any man at any time can come back to the axial lines, even if an unfortunate bastard, if he will be quiet and wait it ou.... Even his pains will be joy if they are true, even his helplessness will not take away his power, even wandering will not take him away from himself.... And this is not imaginary stuff, because he brings his entire life to the test.

If one can remain true to these lines, Augie says, and enjoy the perspective based on experience, he will have the inner strength to pursue an independent existence. Finally Augie wants to achieve the stillness by investing himself in a foster-home academy for children "so that the axial lines can be found" (514). His final decision is based on a wisdom accumulated from all his previous experiences. His value resides in his rejections of the external values these other people try to impose on him. He has learned, like the introspective hero of Bellow's earlier novels, that it is the inner self which defines reality.

Bellow for the first time through comedy, and fantasy has externalized to a large degree the internal value of self – realization in *Henderson the Rain King*. Eugene Henderson, the protagonist in the novel, bothered by a constant inner voice crying "I want. I want," abruptly departs from America as a concrete step towards defining and realizing his values. Henderson embraces society by leaving it in order to be reconciled with it. He acts to resolve once and for all his spiritual dilemma by going to Africa: "What made me take this trip to Africa? There is no quick explanation. Things got worse and worse and pretty soon they were too complicate" (*HRK* 3). In the interview with Nina Steers, Bellow explained Henderson's motivating force for his quest, claiming that his hero seeks to avoid the anxiety over death by realizing the full and purposeful life which he has never known. This existential concern converts an otherwise comic adventure story into an introspective novel, like all of Bellow's others. "I want, I want!" becomes Henderson's theme song. It is the desire, essentially, for "high conduct," as Henderson's mentor, Dahfu, puts it. It is this motive which drives Henderson, always a bungler at home, on his spiritual quest to Africa to rid one primitive tribe of a pestilence of frogs with a home-made bomb (although he bungles this, too) and later to accept his status as Rain King in another tribe since it appears (although by coincidence) that he has been propitious in bringing the people needed rain. Both are acts to prove a purpose for the self and to achieve community with others. The whole experience provides Henderson spiritual renewal through the wisdom of his mentor Dahfu and acceptance by a community.

For Henderson the withdrawal from American society is therapeutic, and it enables him eventually to become reconciled with his own world. As Bryant observes, Henderson learns from the primitives "the desire to live . . . not the desire for immortality, but for life as it is given, with all its limits and disappointments" (Bryant 354). Thus Henderson writes his wife shortly before his return to America that his object is "to raise my spirit from the earth, to leave the body of this death" (*HRK* 284).

Herzog is Bellow's most successful attempt to synthesize idea and personal reality, as he portrays his protagonist Herzog struggling to do precisely that. The goal of Herzog: ". . . to live in an inspired condition, to know truth, to be free, to love another, to consummate existence, to abide with death in clarity of consciousness" (*H* 165) has also been the goal of all Bellow's protagonists. These, for Bellow, are the qualities of existence which give order to life. Trying to find the superior life, the protagonist is confronted with the seeming impossibility of that goal, and in the confrontation, "the issue becomes a question of whether the protagonist will reach that higher consciousness which will illumine the paradox and show him the way toward accepting and affirming it" (Bryant 342).

Joseph of *Dangling Man* asserted the necessity of introspection. Similarly, feeling an urgency to analyze his condition, Herzog has "been overcome by the need to explain, to have it out, to justify, to put in perspective, to clarify, to make amends" (*H* 2). Thus he writes numerous imaginary and never sent letters to both famous and familiar people, both living and dead, intending to struggle for order in his chaotic personal life, and hence to "construct a significant order of right and wrong, to pinpoint with unequivocal sharpness truth and falsehood" (Bryant 359). And as Opdahl rightly says of the letters, "they are at once intellectual play and a brilliant critique on the values and problems of our society" (Opdahl, *The Novels of Saul Bellow* 143). The letter writing, like the journal of Joseph, is a private enterprise and furnishes Bellow a plausible structural method for depicting his protagonist on a private quest for order and clarity, even as he lives in the present chaos of his present real world. Herzog, Bellow's spokesman,

> acclaims the values of order and connectionbetween the past and present, individuality amidst massiveness, humanitarianism, and open possibility, and disparages the state of the alienated intellectual, the poseurs of alienation and apocalyptic nihilism, and the detrimental effects of commercialism and technology on the human spirit's quest for freedom. (Sewell 194)

In striving to create order out of disorder, both Bellow and Herzog are aware of the importance of showing us our humanity through the ages. As artist, Bellow identifies with Whitman, asserting that the artist may greet his brothers in the mass and teach them their humanitarian link with the past. Similarly, Herzog as an intellectual trying to understand his present dilemma, identifies himself as a Whitmanesque figure: "You-you yourself are a child of this mass and a brother to all the rest" (*H* 201). Perhaps in *Herzog* more than in any of his other novels, Bellow asserts the value of man's individuality, his self-identity, in mass society while attacking the romantic over-evaluation of the self. As Herzog views it, it was his duty in his book *Romanticism and Christianity* to overturn "the last of the Romantic errors about the uniqueness of the Self" (39). Instead, the individual must realize himself in terms of commitment to others, as the self is discarded. This would be what Herzog perceives as "an inspired condition, to know truth, to be free, to love another, to consummate existence" (165). Just as Bellow urges the writer to fill the individual's void with an imaginative art, his fictional spokesman Herzog conceives of himself as a kind of intellectual savior for the individual:

> The revolution of the twentieth century, the liberation of the masses by production, created private life but gave nothing to fill it with. This was where he came in. the progress of civilization-indeed, the survival of civilization-depended on the successes of Moses E. Herzog. (125)

Bellow values man because of his capacity to share his humanity with others and his open possibilities for choice in adverse conditions-qualities which transcend technology, commercialism, or even intellectualism. Consequently Herzog intends in his letters and studies to counteract the negative forces at work in society, the forces which cause man to be less than his authentic self. Recalling Bellow's vehement attacks on commercialism for its damaging influence on the individual's humanity, we are not surprised when Herzog proclaims that he "will never worship the fat gods" (133) and chastises his society for its overemphasis on material goods. And it is Bellow's voice when Herzog speaks out explicitly against a technology which has helped to create a commodities-oriented society which is an intrusion on the private life. However, because the author and his character still believe in man's ability to transcend these negative forces, Bellow through Herzog rejects the stance taken by the apocalyptic nihilists and wastelanders. Denigrating the advocates of the alienation and wasteland outlooks, Herzog says in close paraphrase of Bellow's comments: "The canned sauerkraut of Spengler's 'Prussian Socialism,' the commonplaces of the Wasteland outlook, the cheap mental stimulants of Alienation, the cant and rant of pipsqueaks about Inauthenticity and Forlornness. I can't accept this foolish dreari ness" (74—75).

More expansively than in any of his other novels, Bellow has provided in *Herzog* full – blown exposition on his own basic values. Herzog's letters constitute a considerable portion of the novel as they construct the dialectic between man's fallen state and his possibilities for improvement. In order for Herzog to arrive at a realistic view of himself as a man of decline but one with potential, he must think his way to clarity in his personal life as he evaluates the present in terms of the past. While asserting the possibilities of a better life than in the past, Herzog is aware, as we have already seen, of a technological progress which enslaves man even as it frees him. What Herzog is really after is a better spiritual life for modern man. As Clayton puts it, "In a sense, Herzog is the sum of all Western civilization since the Renaissance, as if he were reflecting on his personal past. Maybe Bellow is being satirical, but he is also serious: Herzog is Representative Man fighting for survival" (Clayton 206).

Furthermore, as Mosher points out, "Most of the novel is concerned with Herzog's examination of his own past and western man's as he attempts to analyze his professional and marital failures and relate them to the history of civilization" (Mosher 25). Herzog's endless notes, jottings, and letters, constantly juxtaposed with vivid portraits of New York or Chicago, his memories of conversations with friends, and his memories of his marriage with Madeleine and their separation, show a intellectual historian who can turn inward as well as outward. Herzog, caught in the midst of wretched circumstances, tries to work his way out them by generalizing, or universalizing, his personal situation in his imaginary letters. If Herzog begins as a cerebral character, like Joseph, in an intellectual vacuum, he escapes, so to speak, out into "the streets, in American society . . . where he did his time" (303). It is only because Herzog is able to make this escape finally and see the real world of real humanity, good and evil, that he is able to reconcile the opposites of sterile intellectualism and genuine community with the world.

Sammler, Bellow's first aged and mellowed protagonist, is described by his best critic Keith Opdahl, as his "first, full-fledged hero, embodying what I take to be the virtues Bellow now believes in" (Opdahl, "Review of *Mr. Sammler's Planet*" 535). Irving Howe points out that Bellow, now himself past the middle of the journey, "has not only become a master of his own special idiom, . . . [but] he has also found his place, no longer a dangling man, as person and writer, and set forth on a stubborn, uncertain quest for the cup of wisdom" (Howe, "Review of Mr. Sammler's Planet" 106). Artur Sammler is no longer either a dangling man or even an emotionally agonized intellectual like his predecessor. He has experienced both the best and the worst, literally returning from the mass grave at Auschwitz, and has resolved all his ideologies when the novel begins. Seasoned Sammler, with personal suffering left in the past, views with acceptance the chaos of the modern world caused by the imbalance of religious faith and science and merely trying to arrive at an understanding of the conflict. Presented in his monologues, Sammler's belief in the potential of the earth, and that "There is still such a thing as a man . . . [and that] there are still human qualities" (*SP* 305), opposes the idea of man's existence being controlled by the rationality implicit in technological possibilities.

Sammler appears as Bellow's most seasoned opponent of the apocalyptic nihilists, asserting the value of order within man himself and within his present world, freed from the dictates of pure science. The critic Harris says: ". . . Sammler is fundamentally a character concerned with the act of distinguishing as a means towards the achievement of a religious faith" (Harris 239). Sammler's observation stresses the necessity for man's having a stable faith, a faith in God. It is such a faith that has salvaged him from the Nazis: "What besides the spirit should a man care for who has come back from the grave?" (233) Significantly, the religious quest culminates in the closing epiphany of the book as Sammler in "a mental whisper" consoles his dying nephew, Elya Gruner, with his faith. The realization of Sammler's religious faith resides in love for others and a sense of brotherhood as well. Sammler's personal experience at Auschwitz has taught him to seek such faith in humanity as a means of avoiding hatred and indifference in the modern mad world he finds himself in almost as a stranger.

Order for the individual or even the mass can come only with a sustained faith transcending a technology based on reason. Such is the message of an old man reminiscing and cultivating his own cup of wisdom. Sammler has known the worst and yet survives in an estranged, exotic world to give us religious epiphanies, one after another. His age, but most of all his experience and knowledge, makes him completely credible and absorbing.

Bellow has kept his commitment to society as an artist in his own right. In his first novel, he depicts Joseph as his precursor for the subsequent protagonists who pursue a private quest for inner values. In the more realistic and objective novel *The Victim*, Bellow recounts Leventhal's internal adjustment in his dilemma of entanglement with Kirby Allbee, who represents a personal threat to his self-sufficiency. Oppressive environmental imagery and naturalistic symbols helps to show Leventhal's struggle in his involvement with the concerns of another human being. Augie, who is engaged in a multiplicity of experiences with unlimited choice for realizing his individuality, accumulates wisdom to establish an internal world. Henderson, as the personification of one's disillusionment with a spiritually barren environment, seeks the spiritual rebirth in his primitive African adventures which will enable him to return to America to serve a meaningful purpose. The letters of Herzog and the monologues and dialogues of Mr. Sammler reflect Bellow's emphasis on the value of the past as a means of instructing modern man in his humanity. Through the letters, Herzog not only finds personal answers in universal problems, but, as Opdahl has pointed out, he "confronts almost every issue raised in Bellow's previous fiction . . . the reliance on an inner vision and the determination to act in the social or external world" (Opdahl, "Review of *Mr. Sammler's Planet*" 141). Sammler relies on the past "as a storehouse from which he can draw some sense of who he is" (C. Eisinger, 205). Sammler's monologues serves to answer Joseph's question-that a good man ought to live by "Feeling, outgoingness, expressiveness, kindness, heart" (*SP* 212). This, Sammler believed, is the way to achieve internal order, which is the salvation of human life.

3. Adoption of All – inclusive Attitude for a Foothold

Dangling between the civilian world and the army, which he is waiting to join, Joseph in *Dangling Man* in the state of limbo is free. He has all the time to do all the things he previously never got around to doing. Yet he feels more imprisoned now than ever before. As he says: "I, in this room, separate, alienated, distrustful, find in my purpose not an open world, but a closed, hopeless jail" (*DM* 92). To be totally and fully unattached and uncommitted is an imprisonment, as Joseph acknowledges.

What Joseph experiences in his enforced period of isolation, only broken by startling incidents and impudent noises from the outside world, of which he feels no part, is that he does not do any too well alone; that the freedom to do what likes only locks him in an agonizing, fruitless debate with his self. And the only conclusion he can finally reach is that the highest "ideal construction" to be adopted is the one that "unlocks the imprisoning self". Instead of holding on to one's self, one should stop living so exclusively and vainly for one's own sake within the claustrophobic circle. Joseph's final decision to end the period of passive waiting for his induction can be understood as his desire not to be excluded from the one major experience in which all the young men of his age will be involved, even if it means "freedom canceled", "regular hours", "the supervision of the spirit", and "regimentation" (126). He even welcomes this, for what he was unable to do in the claustrophobic isolation of his room-determine whether he has an individuality of his own or not-he might achieve if he stepped outside and joined the ranks of his fellow men.

Real freedom would seem to consist in the ability to choose that which you prefer to do. And the choice of going into the army is not an escape from freedom, but rather an exercise of Joseph's freedom. Bellow leads Joseph into the recognition that there is no such thing as abstract freedom. Freedom is relative. You are free from something, or free to do something. You have freedom of thought and freedom of movement, but suspension and stasis are not freedom. Man does not and cannot exist in a vacuum. As Joseph says, man is part of the world, whether he likes it or not. "Whatever you do, you can not dismiss it" (137). Therefore, man's freedom lies in his choice of responsibility, which confirms his relationship with society, rather than a lack of responsibility.

Joseph, isolated in his speculation on the abstract ideas, also devotes a largeamount of space in his journal to his friends. Alf Steidler is a comic, exuberant, theatrical type, a sort of bum, whose superficiality Joseph recognizes. Having been through a series of occupations, Steidler has achieved no permanent success in any of them. He has evaded responsibility as well as the army. What Steidler's presence reveals to Joseph about himself is the futility of living on the surface of things. Joseph, to an extent, identifies with Steidler. In a sense, Steidler himself is Joseph's alter ego, one who helps Joseph to see his own weaknesses more objectively. Joseph concludes: "I welcomed him at first, and I still rather like him. But I wish he would not come so often" (*DM* 150).

Abt, Joseph's former college roommate, is another of Joseph's acquaintances who instructs Joseph by adhering to ideal constructions, an existence Joseph comes to see as impractical. A political science instructor, Abt is regarded by Joseph as an individual "continually in need of being consequential" (86). According to Joseph's analysis, Abt is the antithesis of Alf Steidler. He has a driving obsession to practice greatness while the latter is concerned only with surface gestures of greatness. Taken together, however, both characters reinforce the lesson Joseph learns in the process of writing out his thoughts and conversations - that one cannot live realistically by choosing extremes in behavior or philosophy. With the aid of such characters, Joseph comes to see that his own absolute quest for pure freedom is no more a real possibility than an ideal obsession or the complete lack of one.

John Pearl, the artist, represents an important aspect of Joseph-the side he wishes us to see. If Steidler is the dilettante and Abt the idealist, Pearl affirms the imaginative life as a genuine possibility. If there is any one of Joseph's acquaintance through which Bellow speaks to affirm the inner life, certainly it is this character. He represents the value Joseph seeks, and makes Joseph aware of the possibility of spiritual freedom as realized through the imagination-a freedom which counteracts the external world of ugly facts and circumstances.

Joseph realizes that to divorce himself from the world is wrong because the world is full of wonder, with the help of the "Spirit of Alternatives" or his alter ego. The question that man must confront himself with is, "How should a good man live?" (23) It is a question Hemingway's heroes would never consider. They detest "abstract" terms. To the Bellow hero, good is not abstract. It has personal meaning, and it motivates his whole life. The question that Joseph poses to himself is a recurring theme throughout all of Bellow's works. The answer, of course, is that goodness can only be achieved in the company of man, not by isolating oneself in a room or in a drunken stupor or by going off on a safari to Africa.

As Joseph acknowledges: "The highest 'ideal construction' is the one that unlocks the imprisoning self... We are all drawn toward the same craters of the spirit—to know what we are and what we are for, to know our purpose..." (153, 4). He comes to realize that his purpose is intertwined with that of the rest of humanity. After Joseph has sent in his request to be taken into the armed services, his last words: "I am in other hands, relieved of self-determination, freedom canceled. Hurrah for regular hours! And for the supervision of the spirit! Long live regimentation!", these lines have often been interpreted as the ironic conclusion that mankind cannot long stand freedom, but equally valid is the interpretation that Joseph has said goodbye to his Ivory Tower existence of the sensitive intellectual and is ready to embrace the insensitive but vital realities of ordinary, everyday life. To Joseph the idea of a separate destiny has proved doubtful. As he reflects: "... to be pushed upon oneself entirely put the very facts of simple existence in doubt" (126). He, the Bellow protagonist, realizes that his destiny is bound up with that of his fellow men in a much more complex and mysterious way than he can account for at this stage in his life.

Bellow's decision to abandon the more closed and restricted outlook of the early novels brings as a logical consequence an enlargement of the social scene in which the characters are made to move, and heavier stress is then laid on the interaction between protagonist and historical environment. Writing *The Adventures of Augie March* is a liberation for Bellow. For the first time Bellow writes a novel in which characters, events, situations, appear by the dozen. The tightness and limitation of the earlier writing are abandoned, and instead the reader is offered a wide panorama, both in terms of space and time.

One can only speculate about the reasons which led Bellow to his new approach. All statements Bellow has made about the genesis of *The Adventures of Augie March* do indicate that Bellow was writing out of a willed effort to change, to feel freer, and probably also out of a conscious attempt to abandon what he (according to later remarks) saw as the predominant mood in literary works of the time. Here was a novel that would bring back to literature a tradition of lightness, of humor, of action—all of which twentieth century writers had seemed to forget.

Bellow's attempt at expansiveness and inclusiveness is translated into the novel in a variety of ways. In time, the plot of *The Adventures of Augie March* extends from the twenties to the post-war years. In space, though basically a Chicago novel, we move with Augie to other cities, countries and continents. The social panorama as well will include characteristic types of the times, show us Chicagoans from different origins, classes and interests. In terms of the allusion, similes and metaphors that constantly come to Augie's mind, the novel covers just about everything (the Bible, mythology, literature from different times and countries). Behind Augie's statements we sometimes very distinctly hear the voices-not of Mark Twain-but of the American Transcendentalists (Emerson, Thoreau, and Whitman). That in Bellow which made him reject darkness, closure, and limitation, makes him turn to these celebrators of cosmic optimism.

The Adventures of Augie March opens with an abundance of characters, scenes, details. The first four chapters (before Augie's years of apprenticeship with William Einhorn) are there to document a time and a way of life. Through Augie's eyes the Chicago of the Twenties comes to life. "I am an American, Chicago born" (*AM* 5) are Augie's first words, and if the urban experience, or even more specifically, the experience of immigrants in large urban centers trying to make their way into the mainstream of American society, is common to millions of Americans in the first decades of the twentieth century, Augie March is, in fact, the typical American—as typical as Whitman, whose words he constantly echoes, made himself out to be.

Augie, the picaresque hero of the novel, "is an uncommitted wanderer upon the face of earth, savoring experience for its infinite variety and cherishing his independence to seek it out where he may. He is full of the joy of living in a world where the opportunity for experiment is practically limitless" (C. Eisinger 654). And important in this process of unlimited experiment, notes Tanner, is that "in the course of Augie's various moves towards experience and moves away from regimentation and commitment, a wisdom and sense of positive values does emerge" (Tanner 50—51). Augie's inclusive experience can be reflected in the following remarks:

> Through a series of conflicts between the freedom of personal choice and the fixities of heredity and environment, Augie, representative of man in the city, touches many bases-money, power, love, travel, wisdom, other men and women-in a home-run which doesn't win the game but creates the possibilities and the limits open to character within an urbanized fate. (Crozier 22)

Augie grows up in a working-class immigrant section of Chicago, a neighborhood crowded with Jews, Poles, and Hungarians. Augie's mother is a very reticent and shadowy figure. His first major influence is Grandma Lausch, who comes to live with the family after Augie's father has deserted it. A tyrannical old Russian Jew, she teaches Augie the necessity of expedient lying when she sends him with a made-up story to the Public Health Department to get glasses for his half-blind mother. Having been persuaded that this is a mission, Augie adeptly plays the role. In her rule of Augie's family, Grandma Lausch establishes the pattern for all the other Machiavellians in the book: "With the holder in her dark little gums between which all her guile, malice, and command issued, she had her best inspirations of strategy" (*AM* 7). The one most important thing she teaches Augie is to be on the defensive in his relationship with others: "The more you love people the more they' ll mix you up. A child loves, a person respects" (9). Consequently, even while he is learning from such a person, Augie is continually saying no, refusing any commitments which threaten his independence. As the first Machiavellian in the book, Grandma Lausch is the first real test of Augie's value of an independent fate.

In this way the two sides of the urban experience—the noisy, colorful, dirty and rough immigrant section, and the more impersonal, cold, superior world outside the ghetto—are rendered in the novel. As Sarah B. Cohen points out,

> Just as Dreiser in *Sister Carrie* focused on the department store, the drummer as social type, and the telephone booth to preserve them in fiction, so Augie gives literary permanence to such places as the Palmer House barbershop with its "grand episcopal chairs" and the County Hospital dental dispensary with its "gas flamer on porcelain swivel trays." (Cohen, "Saul Bellow's Chicago" 141—2)

In Augie's childhood experiences his "larky and boisterous" nature which will remain with him throughout his later years is already revealed. Augie will consistently make use of this nature to refuse at least superficially, to be scarred by life, and go on to yet another adventure. As a child, Augie will rarely generate energy of his own, and will fall into other people's schemes. By the time Augie is twelve, Grandma Lausch has prepared his career for him; Anna Coblin, his mother's cousin, has decided he should marry her daughter; Simon finds him small jobs; Jimmy Klein, a neighborhood friend, convinces him to participate in his stealing plans. The narrative is in fact punctuated with references to what Augie feels to be a deterministic aspect in the nature of things and experiences. "All the influences were lined up waiting for me. I was born and there they were to form me..." (*AM* 46). Augie will forever come up against "one of those Machiavellis of small street and neighborhood" (6) like Grandma Lausch, who tries to dictate his life. Later on, after he has left his family and become involved in his first more permanent jobs, he recognizes that "there was something adoptional about me" (158), that he is everyone's potential adoptee. As a matter of fact, one of Augie's opening remarks gives us a clue to how he regards himself and the world: "A man's character is his fate, says Heraclitus" (5). What the novel tries to trace is the reasons that make Augie, towards the end, invert the saying and declare that "it is obvious that this fate, or what he settles for, is also his character" (553).

Augie has experienced the infinite variety of the city. Augie's adventures are an almost endless succession of contacts with a host of personalities who try to shape Augie in their image. The novel is a gallery of minor portraits of "reality specialists" who try to convince Augie of the authenticity of their private visions: Mamma, Grandma Lausch, Simon, Einhorn, Dingbat, Thea, Mintouchian, and Bateshaw. And dozens of others. Augie associates with petty crooks to big time racketeers, from prostitutes to society matrons, from simple crackpot types to true megalomaniacs. Augie says that he is around people of other kinds too. In one direction, a few who read whopping books in German or French and know their physics and botany manuals backwards, readers of Nietzsche and Spengler. In another direction, the criminals. "Except that I never thought of them as such, but as the boys I knew in the poolroom and saw also at school, dancing the double-toodle in the gym at lunch hour, or in the hot-dog parlors. I touched all sides, and nobody knew where I belonged" (*AM* 119).

In addition to the educative force of the multiple personalities that Augie encounters, Augie also runs the gamut of city jobs. He is at various times a salesman of paint, toys, razor blades, papers, and flowers. He is an apprentice to the world of shady American business, an adoptive son, a tramp, a valet, strike organizer, part-time student, book stealer, merchant seaman, immigrant smuggler, and, at book's end, a salesman for black market drugs-occupations which he apparently pursues with equal zest, exuberance and joy. The impression is strong that Augie wills himself to plunge forward into all these activities, wills himself to enjoy them, just as the novel in general stubbornly insists on proving that there should be no room to lead a disappointed life. He learns to lie, cheat, steal, connive. He learns the ways of the city in money, sex, and connections.

> Chicago-bred Augie is a servant of so many masters that by comparison, Lazarillo and Guzman are mere Iberian stick-in-the-muds. From the end of the Roaring Twenties in Chicago to the years following World War II in Europe, Augie gets himself involved in every occupation, legitimate, semilegitimate, and illegitimate. (*AM* 96)

One of the first "reality specialists" that helps shape Augie's attitude toward the city, one who begins to make Augie question and judge his experience, is Einhorn, a crippled, autocratic personality who has known both the good and bad fortunes of the city.

Augie's relationship with Einhorn probably provides Augie with some of his most valuable experiences. Einhorn is an exemplum of the dictum "character is fate." As a cripple, paralyzed from the waist down, he manages to lead a full life, conquering his paralysis. He refuses to surrender to his infirmity and considers himself a useful and extraordinary citizen. "William Einhorn was the first superior man I knew," and to Augie, now a high-school adolescent, this crippled entrepreneur is comparable to Caesar, Ulysses, Machiavelli. Einhorn may have been petty and selfish—he never wanted to accept Augie as a son—but it is to him that Augie appeals for aid after the fiasco with Joe Gorman. Einhorn does send him money, through Simon, and is upset to know that it never reached him. He is always good to Augie, as a protector though, not as a father. In dealing with Einhorn, Augie's strength of character becomes evident. He evinces a remarkable compassion towards Einhorn, helping him with his personal needs, carrying him, at Einhorn's behest, on his back to whatever destination Einhorn has in mind, and never complains about any of the menial tasks he does for this man. It never dawns on him that he is being taken advantage of, only that he is helping someone who needs his aid. This quality of compassion which Augie exhibits towards Einhorn continues throughout his life as a mark of his relationship with people.

It is again from Einhorn that Augie learns another important truth about himself. At this point, and in many later occasions, he needs other people to offer him revelations about his own personality. "All of a sudden," Einhorn remarks "I catch on to something about you. You' ve opposition in you. You don't slide through everything. You just make it look so" (123). Augie agrees and is thus forced to confront the first explicit example of a series of contradic tions that make up his character. "I did have opposition in me, and great desire to offer resistance and to say 'No!' ... No, I didn't want to be what he called determined. I never had accepted determination and wouldn't become what other people wanted to make of me" (123—124).

He learns negative values from his own brother, Simon, who is selfish, aggressive, calculating, and unhappy. Both brothers love each other, but Simon will put his own interests before those of anyone else, even when it concerns that person's welfare. It was Simon's idea to get rid of Grandma Lausch. As the oldest son, he felt Grandma Lausch was usurping his right to head the family. It is Depression-time, money is tight, and Augie is away. Simon feels he cannot afford to maintain his mother's apartment. He vacates the domicile, sells the furniture, pockets the money and sends his mother to live with neighbors, the Kreindls. From this point on, everything Simon does is egocentric. He has had a crushing defeat in love, builds for himself immunity to further hurt, and lives his life as is no one else exists, certainly as if no one else matters. In the process of adapting to his own particular version of reality he becomes a coarse, brutal, and self-destructive individual. He marries for money, tyrannizes all with whom he comes in contact, rejects Augie when Augie's actions do not appear to be in Simon's best interest. Augie recognizes Simon's shortcomings, his distortion of values, and if he does capitulate occasionally to Simon's profferings, he soon learns of his mistakes. Through it all, he never loses his sympathy and love for his brother and pities the unhappy man he has become.

Thea Fenchel is the next major influence in Augie's life. She is the most blatant of all the Machiavellian figures in her obsession with force. She carries Augie with her on an exotic adventure to Mexico to train an eagle to hunt rare Mexican lizards. Augie joins her in the project because of what he thinks is his love for her. Augie comes to realize that he is more involved with primitive force than he likes, and after he is kicked in the head by a horse, he remarks, "It takes some of us a long time to find out what the price is of being in nature, and what the facts are about your tenure. How long it takes depends on how swiftly the sugars dissolve" (362). Instead of the fulfillment and promise which Augie sought in the Mexican adventure, he finds only sordidness and infidelity. He leaves Mexico with the confession of independence from commitment to one life style as he had when he took on the adventure. As in all his other contacts with Machiavellian forces, he opts for an independent fate and thus sustains his belief in individual choice as a prime value.

Basteshaw, the psycho - biophysicist, with whom Augie was shipwrecked during the war, wanted Augie to join him in his biological experiment with cells "To understand the birth of life and be in on the profoundest secrets. . . . this is a great chance for you, not simply to rise to eminence, not just to five your intellectual powers the very highest development, but to assist in making a historic contribution to the happiness of mankind" (568). Basteshaw's idea is to tamper with genetics, create a new species so that "every man will be a poet and every woman a saint" (568). Although Basteshaw expresses ideas Augie himself has considered, he represents Augie's antithesis. For example, he tells Augie: "Everybody wants to be the most desirable kind of man" (562). The difference between the two men is the method they use in trying to achieve this standard. Basteshaw wants to change all of mankind, and Augie believes "a man's character is his fate" and rejects Basteshaw's solution for rescuing the world from the abyss of boredom. Basteshaw differs from the other "influences" which Augie has encountered in that he seeks to impose his view of reality, disallowing any choice in the matter. Augie is infuriated at the idea. He tells this madman: "I' m dead against doing things to the entire human race. I don't want any more done to me, and I don't want to tamper with anyone else. No one will be a poet or saint because you fool with him. When you come right down to it, I' ve had trouble enough becoming what I already am, by nature" (569).

Augie describes Mintouchian as "another of those persons who persistently arise before me with life counsels and illumination throughout my entire earthly pilgrimage" (534). He is a wealthy, Armenian lawyer whose diction is laced with Yiddish and Hebrew phrases, who tries to instruct Augie regarding the malice of man and his abortive attempts to overcome this malice. Mintouchian is convinced that man is duplicitous. As a lawyer, he feels he is privy to the hidden chamber of man's soul, and he takes a harsh view of human nature. But Augie tells him: "I have always tried to become what I am. But it's a frighten ing thing. Because what if what I am by nature isn't good enough? .... I suppose I better, anyway, give in and be it. I will never force the hand of fate to create a better Augie March, nor change the time to an age of gold" (542).

It is in his old friend Clem Tambrow that Augie confides about his perceptions of himself. Clem wants to use his knowledge of psychology to prey upon the weakness of others and become a vocational-guidance counselor. He would like Augie to join him. Clem's interest is not in helping people but in "clean up in this racket" (506). However, it isn't in Augie's nature to take advantage of people. He rejects Clem's offer and pursues the "axial lines of life", which involve "truth, love, peace, bounty, usefulness, harmony" (506). The stress of axial lines is on the positive aspects of life, which confirms man's humanity, rather than the negative ones that expose him as a beast. For Augie, it is in keeping with his search for an answer to the question concerning the lifestyle of a good man. Augie instinctively resists the influences, the power, that others seek to have over him. This opposition, this struggle, is a life and death contention because it involves the obliteration of personality, the erasure of the uniqueness of the individual. Augie doesn't want to become what others wanted to make of him. He doesn't want to blend into someone else's personality or be a duplicate of the next person. Augie builds his strength in his opposition to influences or powers, and his view of life as comprised of axial lines.

This desire not to settle down, to accept nothing but that which fulfills his idea of a "higher, independent fate" (440) is the cause of Augie's constant moving in and out of jobs and relationships. And he has a long series of both. "Saying 'various jobs'," he acknowledges, "I give out the Rosetta stone, so to speak, to my entire life" (31). Besides the Einhorns, Augie will work for another family, the Renlings, but when they also try to adopt him he will start looking for more independent kinds of work. He gets involved in smuggling immigrants into the U. S., becomes the caretaker of dogs belonging to rich Chicago families, steals books from university bookstores to be sold to students, becomes a union organizer, and later, during the war, a sailor on a merchant ship and black market dealer in Europe afterwards.

His relationships with women are equally "varietistic" (69). From the waitress of the hotel where he is staying with the Renlings, he moves to one of the rich guests, Esther Fenchel. When the engagement to Lucy Magnus, a millionaire's heiress (arranged by Simon, who has himself married into this rich family) is broken off, Augie takes up with Sophie, a Greek maid, the one who gets him involved in unions and strikes. But Sophie is abandoned the moment Thea, Esther's sister, appears on the scene. The affair with Thea, who takes him and a trained eagle to Mexico, is a more serious one and the whole Mexican adventure a turning point for Augie, but nonetheless Thea is replaced by

Stella, an actress. He finally marries her, but no sense of a settling down is given by the fact that Augie does get married, for towards the very end of the narrative he makes a point of revealing that his marriage is not a happy one.

The emphasis on constant action and change, of eternal movement, or as one critic has put it "the belief in energy, vitality, sheer activity as moral goods" (Guerard 584) corresponds to Augie's sense of the world as a realm of never-ending possibilities. Variety and multiplicity attract him immensely and just like Whitman who, in his days, tried to give a sense of these same qualities in American society, Augie will often catalogue in order to bring as much as he can into the picture and express his admiration for this openness:

> The students were children of immigrants from all parts, coming up from Hell's Kitchen, Little Sicily, the Black Belt, the mass of Polonia, the Jewish streets of Humboldt Park… In the mixture there was beauty-a good proportion-and pimple – insolence, and parricide faces, gum – chew innocence, labor fodder and secretarial forces, Danish stability, Dago inspiration, catarrh – hampered mathematical genius; there were waxed – eared shovelers' children, sex – promising businessmen's daughters-an immense sampling of a tremendous host, the multitudes of holy writ, begotten by West – moving, factor – shoved parents. (*AM* 132)

Augie consciously tries to reflect the same variety he sees externally in his own way of being: "I touched all sides and nobody knew where I belonged" (119); he sees himself as "democratic in temperament, available to everybody and assuming about others what I assumed about myself" (155). Through his multiplicity of experiences, Augie has accumulated knowledge of himself which is reinforced by the words of his intellectual friend, Clem Tambow: "What I guess about you is that you have a nobility syndrome. You can't adjust to the reality situation" (434).

Later in the novel, Augie makes the following statement about Chicago-Around was Chicago. In its repetition it exhausted your imagination of details and units, more units than the cells of the brain and bricks of Babel. The Ezekiel caldron of wrath, stoked with bones. . . As before the work of Egypt and Assyria, as before a sea, you' re nothing here. Nothing.

What Bellow unceasingly gives us in the novel are different, often contradictory thoughts, attitudes, perceptions, runningtogether, influencing one another, in a dialectical movement which will lead to no resolution or new synthesis. Nevertheless, human relations, in whatever form-women, acquaintances, children - are, as said, the key factor in Augie's pilgrimage.

4. Accommodation with Modern Society

Bellow is always aware of the discrepancy between the high principles and low facts he must confront and resolve as artist. Americans are sententious people and are taught at any early age to moralize. They learn it in Sunday school. In addition, they learn it from Poor Richard; at least they did so in Bellow's childhood. In Chicago during the twenties people were filled up with Poor Richard: "Little strokes fell great oaks." "Plough deep while sluggards sleep." These formulas seemed true and sound. Longfellow, whom Americans had to memorize by the yard, was also strongly affirmative: "Life is real! Life is earnest! And the grave is not its goal . . . ."

> But while this was happening, the Chicago papers reported gangland killings almost daily …. To survive such events, the moral teachings of literature had to be very strong. It might have occurred to schoolchildren as they passed from the pages of the *Tribune* to those of *Elson's Reader* that perhaps literature didn't have too much to do with life. "Give all to love," they read in Emerson. But in City Hall there were other ideas on giving, and we had to learn (if we could) how to reconcile high principles with low facts. (Bellow, "The Writer as Moralist" 58)

The gap between the real and ideal ultimately determines the imaginative process present in all Bellow's work. It is Bellow's awareness of this gap which gives his fiction its sustained tension between despair and hope. For instance, while Herzog insists on the nineteenth-century romantic concept of human dignity, he finds that merciless child abuse is a real fact of his present world. Yet this knowledge does not bring him to a dead-end despair, but to an acceptance of his world for what it is. Such is the imaginative process of Bellow's fiction through which he justifies himself as a writer in an affirmative mode. "If a novelist is going to affirm anything," he says, "he must be prepared to prove his case in close detail, reconcile it with hard facts, and he must even be prepared for the humiliation of discovering that he may have to affirm something different" (60). For the protagonist it is a psychological experience, as Clayton has demonstrated in his treatment of Bellow as a psychological novelist:

> But if Bellow is going to affirm the possibility of meaningful individual life in contemporary America, he has to affirm a changed life. If life as it is offers cause for despair and if the individual is both product and producer of this life, then the individual must be redeemed. Through his redemption society will be redeemed. So Bellow . . . affirms not the present individual and the present society but their possibilities. (5—6)

Joseph and his father recognize the deleterious effects of the street scenes upon the young child. His father blamed himself bitterly for the poverty that forced him to bring his children up in a slum and worried lest Joseph see too much. And Joseph did see, in a curtainless room near the market, a man rearing over someone on a bed, and on another occasion, a Negro with a blond woman on his lap. But less easily forgotten were a cage with a rat in it thrown on a bonfire, and two quarreling drunkards, one of whom walked away bleeding, heavy drops falling from his head like the first slow drops of a heavy rain in summer, a crooked line of drops left on the pavement as he walked.

Joseph has learned the lessons of the city street: sexuality, brutality, violence, violations of the socialtaboo of racial mixing, drunkenness, sadism. The dominant human response to such an environment is fear with its concomitant reflex to retreat. Yet Joseph comes to realize that escape into the womb - like existence of life in the six - sided box is a negation of life and human freedom. The only viable alternative to rejecting the escape into the six - sided box is to accept the world of the street. One way of accepting the real world is to assert the ascendency of art over life. John Pearl, an artist friend of Joseph's writes about his life in New York City early in the novel. John supports himself and his family by "drawing cartoon faces of bilious men and headachy office girls" (*DM* 60) for an advertising agency in a fifty-three-story office building. John writes that he is exhilarated by the tremendous unimportance of his work. It is nonsense. His employers are nonsensical. The job therefore leaves him free. There's nothing to it. In a way it's like getting a piece of bread from a child for wiggling your ears. It is childish. He is the only one in this fifty-three-story building who knows how childish it is. Everybody else takes it seriously. Because this is a fifty - three - story building, they think it must be serious. Nevertheless, Pearl thinks "'This is life!' I say, this is pish, nonsense, nothing! The real world is the world of art and of thought. There is only one worthwhile sort of work, that of the imagination" (60—61).

For John Pearl art also supplies that sense of community for which all of the Bellow protagonists yearn. He can also remain clean and free. He is there in New York, painting; and in spite of the calamity, the lies and moral buggery, the odium, the detritus of wrong and sorrow dropped on every human heart, in spite of these, he can keep a measure of cleanliness and freedom. Besides, those arts of the imagination are in the strictest sense not personal. Through them he is connected with the best part of mankind. He feels this and he can never be isolated, left aside. He has community. Whereas, Joseph just has the six - sided box. Joseph comes to know that any goodness is achieved not in a vacuum, but in the company of other men, attended by love.

Leventhal, presented as a victim of the urban environment in Bellow's second novel, lives in hot, sultry New York. The first scene in which he squeezes through the shutting door of a moving bus is a fit index to his position in that densely - packed metropolis, to his efforts to find a foothold in that tottering topsy - turvy urban world. The city of New York, with its huge crowds of people, oppressive high - rise buildings, and lurking, unnamable forces, has always been an ominous, suffocating threat to him. However oppressive the city appears to him, Leventhal works in his office, helps take care of his brother's family troubles, and tries to deal with the anti－Semite Allbee's pestering. It is through such human interaction in the city that he comes to the recognition of human commonality and human responsibility. During this long hot summer in the city, he has tried to take to heart Schlossberg's advice not to try to be more than human or to allow himself to become less than human. By accepting human limitations and life's darkness he has discovered the meaning in life and learned to come to terms with himself and with the world at large. Just as Tanner points out:

> The most important thing that happens to Leventhal is that he is stirred out of his "indifference" and "recalcitrance" into a sense of general injustice and suffering, and thence to an awareness and confession of specific blame and responsibility. Instead of timidly wrapping himself up in his too－simple concept of "good luck" he must emerge and be exposed to the problems of environmental pressure, cruel chance, mixed deservings; he must move beyond his paranoid sense of himself as simple victim and realize that there are more complex and subtler forms of "victimization." (31)

Optimism, joy of livingis the key notes in Bellow's novels. Nevertheless, Bellow (through Augie) is forced to acknowledge that there is a darkness, that the possibility of movement, of action, of engagement and disengagement, does not necessarily mean happiness like Twain. A rejection of the pessimism in mood and 'Weltanschauung' dominating his previous works did not mean a full－scale embrace of the opposite views. The tensions and ambiguities that arise from the attempts to bring together and make compatible two opposing sources of energy for Bellow's writings—in very broad but pertinent terms, to accept optimism and celebrate lightness without denying the existence of evil—and parallel issues deriving from this assumption are the basis for Bellow's writings, starting with *The Adventures of Augie March*.

Augie is willing to adapt to the "reality situation". "I will never force the hand of fate to create a better Augie March" (*AM* 504) but not if this "reality principle" or "the data of experience" (452) imply death, the giving up of hope or dreams, the denial of the world as is (as Clem Tambow and Basteshaw try to suggest).

Tommy in*Seize the Day*, like Bellow's other protagonists, must reconcile himself with the world by discarding his old selves as a series of failures and by discovering a purpose in life that transcends artificial values, and that purpose is the capacity to love his fellow man. Only by becoming the outside observer of himself, can he realize any reconciliation with his world, which comes at the point of his deepest despair when he weeps at the funeral of a stranger. Tommy's progress, says Marcus Klein, is that of "the soul through its freedom, from isolation to affirmation of ordinary life in the world" (Klein 41).

Herzog, Bellow's sixth fictional hero, comes the closest to learning to accommodate to the city. Unlike the cloistered Joseph of *Dangling Man*, Herzog moves freely about the city, experiencing the great "feast of the city," its variety, its excitements, including its sexuality. Although the city does not always satisfy, he comes to know its surfeit. As a successful academician, he has bypassed Leventhal's great fear of becoming one of the Dreiseresque city – failures. Likewise, he has escaped Wilhelm's financial ruin, and he is reestablished in American society, not wandering about the French countryside, as is Augie March. In short, Herzog has survived in a predominantly urban world and at the end of the novel has "no messages for anyone." He may not be at home in the urban world completely, but he has accepted the city and has escaped from its most destructive forces.

As we gradually penetrate the mind and personality of Moses Herzog, we begin to perceive that he, too, like Augie and Henderson, is immersed in contradictions. If Augie never really becomes aware of the workings of his mind and is allowed by Bellow simply to go on living in those contradictions and if Henderson, as instructed by Dahfu, considers himself cured once he is able to discard false and radical notions about self, reality, mortality and admit ambivalences and paradoxes, then Herzog, through his own self – examination-much more thorough, more personally relevant and less abstract than Henderson's-comes to a conscious acceptance and understanding of these contradictions in modern reality.

Citrine in *Humboldt's Gift*, as a writer from Chicago, is fully aware of his city's vulgarity and materialism. He knows that Chicago, at least for the present, cannot completely separate itself from associations with business, industry, stockyards, skyscrapers, slums, gangsters, and philistinism. Yet, for all this, Chicago remains his own turf. By taking Chicago as it is, Citrine is able to tolerate and even savor urban experiences which virtually constitute modern reality. As he admits, "There were beautiful and moving things in Chicago, but culture was not one of them.... I had accepted this condition long ago" (*HG* 66).

Citrine, not content with his lofty life as an ivory – tower intellectual, he wants to be in touch and in communion. Despite all his credentials as a scholar, a man of culture and sensibility, and a student of Rudolf Steiner, he is also a " 'Chicagoan' with a taste for low pursuits, pneumatic young women, and gangland excitement" (Cronin 272). His affection for big – city low life leads him to be mistaken for a hit man.

Citrine knows that urban America is "the great mysterious book" (*HG* 266). For years, he says, "I was too fastidious and skittish to study it closely-I had used the conditions of life to test my powers of immunity; the sovereign consciousness trained itself to avoid the phenomena and to be immune to their effects" (267). His desire to know more about real Chicago draws him close to his friend, George Swiebel, who keeps him posted about the underworld; it is George's idea that Citrine play poker with some real South Side people at his place. As a self – proclaimed "urban psychologist" (35), Citrine thinks that with "a deep no-affect belt, a critical mass of indifference" (35), a man can get along in a big American city. Rinaldo Cantabile, an elegantly dressed minor Mafia figure, whom Citrine met at a fateful poker game, is a demonic "agent of distraction" (180) from the city. Cantabile takes Citrine to places beyond a bibliophile's normal realm, such as the Russian Bath on Division Street, the Playboy Club, the Hancock Building, and an unfinished sixty-story skyscraper, and he also exposes Citrine to such people as his Radcliffe-educated wife, his gorgeous mistress Polly, a gossip columnist, an old fence dressed as a decent businessman, and a phony investor. The trips allow the "minutely observant" (134) Citrine to walk out of his book-walled sanctuary and become a city voyeur-voyager. He is gradually excited by "currents of criminality" (99) going on around him. He admits that his "American, Chicagoan (as well as personal) craving for high stimuli, for incongruities and extremes, was aroused" (99). His Chicago education enables him to accept the information about the seedy sides of the city: fancy thieving, police corruption, drug-dealing, and old lechers' scandals.

Living in a modern city like Chicago-a city noted for its criminality, violence, industrialism, and philistinism-inevitably exposes Citrine to many distractions, making it difficult for him to concentrate on his great project or meaningful work. The turbulent urban environment with its sounds, people, cars, things, smells, and sensations, always poses a great challenge to his mind and heart and body. He wishes he could stay serenely in his sanctuary. However, a writer by profession, he knows that he cannot shut himself up in an ivory tower. He needs to engage in urban experiences and to be among street people.

Essentially, Bellow has been conscious of the presence of an ideal word lying not outside but within the everyday world. The ideal world is not a heavenly Jerusalem but the earthly Jerusalem returned. The Jew returns not as an embodied soul but as a living Jew. Heaven is this world, redeemed. The Judaic sense of spiritual arrival is not a vertical journey to the heights of heaven but is attained in the horizontal immersion of the ordinary and the common. Thus we begin to understand how and why Bellow's recurring themes are closely tied not to the powerful, but to the struggling everyday: "The Jew totters between the everyday world and the miraculous one at hand" (Clayton 31). Although like many modern writers Bellow may write of alienated, burdened people, he gives them the capacity to attain inner dignity despite external restrictions and repressions. Their dignity is realized as they achieve community with others by transcending the all-important me and becoming concerned for others. It is through this very concept of character that Bellow is able to dissociate himself from the modern writers of despair, those who depict modern society as deterministic and destructive to the human spirit. By realizing his concept of characterization, Bellow feels that he can justify himself as a writer in society. As he states more than once, character delineation is the true product of the imagination.

Bellow, as the student of Judaism is aware that the sanctity of life is in direct consequence of observing and respecting the everyday ordinariness and it is in this celebration in enduring that the pious Jew understands that even a beggar can be the redeeming Prophet. Thus Bellow's characters are not inclined toward the lofty heavens but gravitate toward a sense of holiness and celebration of the common life. Just as Clayton tells us:

> And he [the Jew] has the power, at least according to the Hasidic tradition, of making the everyday actions of his life sacred by the manner in which he performs them: the zaddik teaches Torah by the way he ties his shoes, washes dishes, dances. Hasidism teaches that common life itself can be sanctified, what is can be made what ought to be. Though the piety of the Jews the redeemer will come. In Jewish fiction this duality accounts for the combination of a realistic portrayal of everyday life with a fervent idealism. (31—32)

Bellow is clearly outraged at the "crudity, disorder, ugliness, and lawlessness" of modern life, but he intends to counteract these facts with "high principles" as conveyed through the imagination and by doing so to justify the place of the writer in society. Bellow, as a Jew, understands that suffering, joy, and redemption are not worlds apart but are immediately present in the tension of daily life. Like Jew, Bellow understands redemption is possible through affirmation of life. In Bellow's first novel *Dangling Man*, Joseph asks himself, "How should a good man live; what ought he to do?" (39). This is the major question that has driven Bellow in search of moral parameters to fame his overall quest for a humanity grounded in the very essence of humility. Bellow will take character and setting, the stock elements of any literature, and manipulate them through his own imagination to dramatize the human quest for the realization of freedom, community, individual choice, order, and historical perspective.

Chapter Four Illuminations for Survival

Division, severance, and contradictions persist to the very end, yet the mere discovery of the ability to recognize holiness, beauty, and joy is enough to keep Augie going and to relate better to society. Transcendence can only be attained through submission to reality first, and then it will be overcome through involvement in the work associated with imagination, just like John Pearl's victory over the modern city.

City's ugliness, violence, its unpoetic nature, and its lack of true culture are what Charlie discovers in Chicago. Nevertheless, Humboldt, Charlie's poet friend, aims to become the Whitman of the twentieth century, to reconcile in his poetry the high and the low, art and technology, to encompass everything, in other words, to fulfill in his days Emerson's vision of the true American poet. The "problem of poetry and the inner life" in a cannibalistic, materialistic, and consumer society is the central theme in *Humboldt's Gift*, and all the other Bellow's novel. What man has to learn is how to transcend the material, and appeal to the internal side by attributing to it a new significance.

Bellow voices the prevailing belief that the basis of Jewish survival is close family ties in his novels. All of Bellow's protagonists share one quality, that is, their intense feeling of closeness and loyalty to their family, and their sensitivity to the importance of the family. There is a strong family feeling on the part of Bellow's protagonists. Family, brotherly love and friendship are consummation of the heart's ultimate need for Bellow's protagonists.

Joseph's final return to community through enlisting in the regimentation, though not without irony, manifests his realization of the dangers or ineffectiveness of alienation or isolation, and indicates Bellow's belief in how great is man's need for belonging and the extent of his sense of loss when he does not feel himself as an integral part of society. Bellow is much concerned to establish a sense of community in the city, in which man is dependent upon other men to survive.

Saul Bellow broughtwith him a world view that was life – sustaining, predicated on a belief in the inherent goodness of man and the basic significance of existence, when he made his timid, yet intrepid, entry onto the American literary scene in 1940s. Consequently, the Bellow protagonist approaches life from the optimistic Jewish perspective, and finally attains majesty of life in the reality, rather than finds only horrors. It is the writer's function, according to Bellow, to project the love of human – kind and the appreciation of the grandeur involved in man's minutest endeavors through his creativity.

1. Transcending the Reality through Spiritual Pursuit

In his non-fiction collection *It All Adds Up*, Bellow titles his opening chapter "Mozart: An Overture" in which he strives to explain, among other things, why the world should be indebted to the wondrous and mystical music of Mozart. In the closing sentences of the chapter, we can see how deeply Bellow feels about the role of art as a conduit for our deep mysteries: "In him [Mozart] we see a person who has only himself to rely on. But what a self it is, and what an art it has generated. How deeply (beyond words) he speaks to us about the mysteries of our common human nature. And how unrestrained and easy his greatness is" (14). In a later chapter titled "An Interview with Myself" in this same text, Bellow alludes to the function of art as a tonic for the soul: "The power of a work of art is such that it induces a temporary suspension of activities. It leads to contemplative states, to wonderful and, to my mind, sacred states of the soul" (84). Accordingly, in his first novel and in the words of his character John Pearl, Bellow is ruminating on the value of art: "The real world is the world of art and of thought. There is only one worth - while sort of work, that of the imagination" (*DM* 91).

In Bellow's first novel, Joseph's friend John Pearl goes from Chicago to New York to pursue his artistic career, and work at an advertising company for a living. In the fifty - three - story office building, nobody except Pearl seems to care about the drabness and meaninglessness of working there.

Pearl's letter to Joseph reveals his repugnance for New York City and his nostalgia for his home city. Pearl's nostalgia for his home city is a longing shared by almost all Bellow's heroes. As Joseph points out, what Pearl actually misses is not the present Chicago, which is no less inhuman than New York, but the familiar neighborhood around his father's house. Joseph, like Pearl, misses his childhood neighborhood in Montreal. One day while polishing shoes in his room, he suddenly falls into a Proustian - like memory of his days on St. Dominique Street. In Montreal, on the afternoons like that, he often asked permission to spread a paper on the sitting - room floor and shine all the shoes in the house. The brown fog lay in St. Dominique Street and in the sitting room, however, the stove shone on the davenport and on the oilcloth and on his forehead, drawing the skin pleasantly. He did not clean shoes because he was praised for it, but because of the work and the sensations of the room, closed off from the wet and fog of the street, with its locked shutters and the faint green of the metal pipes along the copings of its houses. Nothing could have tempted him out of the house. He had never found another street that resembled St. Dominique.

St. Dominique Street, located in a dingy slum area between a market and a hospital, was the only place where he was allowed to encounter reality. This typically Bellovian kind of memory is important to the Bellow hero, be it Augie, Herzog, or Citrine, in that it often provides an emotional anchor or brings spiritual revitalization to the troubled hero. In *Herzog*, the Napolean Street episode, an amplified version of the St. Dominique Street experience, is one of the most memorable episodes in Bellow's oeuvre.

John Pearl has not succumbed to the lure of the skyscraper, with the emotional anchor of the familiar neighborhood around his father's house. He is not taken in by the value which it symbolizes to the "adult world." Instead, John gets involved in the work associated with imagination. Joseph is attracted and fascinated to John's victory over the modern city and thinks John's work is an attractive idea. It confers a sort of life on John, and sets him off from the debased dullness of those fifty-three-story building. And thus he has escaped a trap, and can maintain himself. Joseph believes that those acts of the imagination save him.

Similarly, given the choice between acceptance of common everyday reality and the pursuit of something higher and nobler, Augie the protagonist in Bellow's third novel will (mentally or verbally at least) choose the second possibility. The "mere phenomenal" (*AM* 204) does not interest him:

> Well, now, who can really expect the daily facts to go, toil or prisons to go, oatmeal and laundry tickets and all the rest, and insist that all moments be raised to the greatest importance, demand that everyone breathe the pointy, starfurnished air at its highest difficulty, abolish all brick, vault-like rooms, all dreariness and live like prophets or gods? Why, everybody knows that this triumphant life can only be periodic. So there's a schism about it, some saying that only this triumphant life is real and others that only the daily facts are. For me there was no debate, and I made speed into the former. (204)

Augie's belief in the capabilities of man makes him a dreamer, a searcher, a man in eternal "pilgrimage". He knows he will be satisfied only if taken up into something greater than himself. He sees it as impossible to live without something infinitely mighty and great. He admires people who, despite all kinds of difficulties, set themselves apart for great ends like

> … this sheer horse's ass of a Jean-Jacques (Rousseau) who couldn't get on with a single human being, but who goes away to the woods of Montmorency in order to think and write of the best government or the best system of education. And similarly Marx, with his fierce carbuncles and his poverty and the death of children… (343)

Augie encounters several people (with whom he characteristically agrees) who call attention and criticize him for his "nobility syndrome", for his inability to adjust to the reality situation. But actually Augie fully acknowledges the presence of a "darkness" from the beginning. Seeing external reality as an emblem for subjective states, Augie makes the following comments on darkness. There's a dark Westminster of a time when a multitude of objects cannot be clear and they' re too dense and there's an island rain, North Sea lightlessness, the vein of the Thames. That darkness in which resolutions have to be made - it isn't merely local; it's the same darkness that exists in the fiercest clearnesses of torrid Messina. And what about the coldness of the rain? That doesn't defeat foolishness in its residence of the human face, nor take away deception nor change defects, but this rain is an emblem of the shared condition of all.

Confronted with the dark reality, Augie is forced to make adaptations in his philosophical views, and does it without any trouble. On several occasions Augie defends the point of view that reality is already created and that it has to be accepted as is: "everyone tries to create a world he can live in, and what he can't use he often can't see. But the real world is already created" (394). It is also one of the basic Jewish beliefs that transcendence can only be attained through submission to reality. Living everyday reality with "vitality, simplicity, directness" rather than "seeking to penetrate beyond reality in a mystically contemplative manner" (Buber 40—1) is in itself an act of faith, and source of inexhaustible joy.

In a book entitled *Mystic Trends in Judaism* Arnold Posy explains that:

> There is a firm belief in Hasidism that man is capable of recognizing the holiness and exalted beauty there is in every thing, of comprehending the absolute unity that exists even in division, in severance, in contradictions, in dismemberment, in what appears to be the error of Being. (140)

This is a surprisingly fitting description of Augie March's world. Division, severance, contradictions persist to the very end, yet the mere discovery of the ability to recognize holiness, beauty, joy is enough to keep Augie going. It is in this sense that Augie can invert Heraclitus' aphorism and declare that a man's "fate, or what he settles for is also his character" (*AM* 533).

Bellow puts in *Humboldt's Gift* what he had already declared, in an article published in the *Chicago Daily News*, about his relationship to Chicago:

> I have had a love and hate attitude towards Chicago for nearly 50 years. I am greatly attached to it, and greatly estranged from it as well. Often and from the very first, Chicago gave me a sense of painful emptiness or discontinuity. Its great energy uncomfortably demanded participation. (Bellow, "A Writer Looks at Chicago Culture" 11)

Chicago also provokes a double reaction from the protagonist of the novel, Charlie. If on the one hand it is perfect illustration of the "overwhelming phenomena" that tire him out, he is yet also undeniably attracted to its high-voltage energy.

Yet, when Charlie participates in this Chicago reality, what he most discovers is the city's ugliness and violence, its unpoetic nature, and its lack of true culture. In addition to these eminently negative feelings toward the contemporary city, Charlie also sees cannibal phenomena. He constantly refers to his lawyer as "cannibal Pinsker." There are, in fact, "bitter hardfaced and cannibalistic people" (*HG* 114) everywhere. Cannibalism is also the subject of the film script Humboldt and Charlie had written together. It is in fact Humboldt who introduces the motif when he explains what success in America can lead to: "I don't suppose you've read about the Cannibal Society of the Kwakiutl Indians... The candidate when he performs his initiation dance falls into a frenzy and eats human flesh. But if he makes a ritual mistake the whole crowd tears him to pieces" (13).

Thus Chicago, "clearly the representative American city" (Bellow, "Off the Couch by Christmas" 674), also stands as a metaphor or illustration for Bellow's feelings about the problem of art in America: Chicago with its gigantesque outer life contains the whole problem of poetry and the inner life in America. You can look into such things through a sort of fresh-water transparency in Chicago. The problem of poetry and the inner life in a cannibalistic, materialistic, consumer society becomes the central theme in the novel. James Fenimore Cooper was probably the first American writer to allude to the problem. And more than a hundred years after Nathaniel Hawthorne listed the failures or absences that, for his particular sensibility, explained the difficulty of writing in America, it is easy to find that the American artist is still confronted, if not with exactly the same, at least with related forms of barrenness. In the preface to *The Marble Faun* (1860), Hawthorne wrote:

> No author without a trial, can conceive of the difficulty of writing a romance about a country where there is no shadow, no antiquity, no mystery, nor anything but a commonplace prosperity, in broad and simple daylight, as is happily the case with my dear native land. (Hawthorne V)

Some years later, Henry James, in his book on Hawthorne, considerably expended this list:

> ... one might enumerate the items of high civilization, as it exists in other countries, which are absent from the texture of American life, until it should become a wonder to know what was left. No state, in the European sense of the word, and indeed barely a specific national name. No sovereign, no court, no personal loyalty, no aristocracy, no church, no clergy, no army, no diplomatic service, no country gentlemen, no palaces, no castles, nor manor, nor old country houses, nor parsonages,

not thatched cottages, nor ivied ruins: no cathedrals, nor abbeys, nor little Norman churches; no great Universities nor public schools-no Oxford, nor Eton, nor Harrow, no literature, no novels, no museums, no pictures, no political society, no sporting class - no Epsom nor Ascot! (34)

And in 1975, in a self interview published in the *Ontario Review*, Bellow creates a modern version of these complaints: "no tea at Gertrude Stein's, no Closerie de Lilas, no Bloomsbury evenings, no charming and wicked encounters between George Moore and W. B. Yeats... no literary world, no literary public··· ours is not a society which creates such things" (Cronin, *Conversation with Saul Bellow* 117—118).

It seems to be more than a coincidence that these three novelists expressed exactly the same kind of disappointment and attributed the failure to the country in which they were trying to produce their art. Living and writing at moments in which a definite change towards a greater emphasis on industry and technology could be felt, Hawthorne, James, and Bellow react by calling attention to the hardships that the American artist has to face. In *Humboldt's Gift* Bellow carries this problem to its extreme development. With the advantage of another century of American history, Bellow now has enough perspective to be able to denounce America not only for being unfavorable to the arts by placing too much emphasis on external aspects, but for consequently creating a society which actually devours its artists, a society in which money controls the arts and the imagination, and in which even success is measured on a Dow -Jones scale.

At the very beginning of *Humboldt's Gift*, Charlie Citrine, the protagonist, thinks back on his career as a writer, and by recalling the condemnatory words of the late Von Humboldt Fleisher, the poet who has exerted such a strong influence on him, Charlie begins the series of explanations and justifications that run through the book: "Humboldt held the money against me... And money wasn't what I had in mind" (*HG* 2). Charlie goes on explaining what he wants is to do good. And this feeling for good goes back to his early and peculiar sense of existence-sunk in the glassy depths of life and groping, thrillingly and desperately, for a sense, a person keenly aware of painted veils, of Maya, of domes of many -colored glass staining the white radiance of eternity, quivering in the intense inane and so on. He is quite a nut about such things. Humboldt knew this, really, but toward the end he could not afford to give Charlie any sympathy. He only stressed the contradiction between the painted veils and the big money.

The material and the ideal, money and art, success and failure-these are the sets of opposites hovering in Citrine's mind. It is obvious that Charlie Citrine stands for Bellow himself, or any other young writer who leaves home (in this case, the Mid-West) in the thirties or forties to look for opportunity and partake of the intellectual excitement of New York City, and that Von Humboldt Fleisher is a representative of the group Irving Howe later called the New York Intellectuals. In fact, the similarity between Humboldt and Delmore Schwartz was noted as soon as the novel came out. Charlie, like Bellow, is a successful writer, both in terms of fame and monetary returns: he has twice been awarded the Pulitzer Prize, he has been made a Chevalier of the French Legion of Honor, he is invited to White House dinners, and he makes a pile of money. On the other hand, Humboldt, whom Charlie considers a real genius, has met only with temporary success. He is an avant-garde writer, the first of a new generation, he is handsome, fair, large, serious, and witty, and he is learned. "The guy had it all" (*HG* 1). However, in the late Forties he started to sink and Charlie watches his decline: from drugs and drink to shock treatments, to "loony bins", to his death in the sixties "in a dismal hotel off Times Square". This is the fate Humboldt illustrates, and the one Charlie will try to analyze, understand and escape.

In this history of the fate of the artist in America, Humboldt is just one more example in a list of consumed poets. After all Humboldt did what poets in crass America are supposed to do. He chased ruin and death even harder than he had chased women. He blew his talent and his health and reached home, the grave, in a dusty slide. He plowed himself under. Okay. So did Edgar Allan Poe, picked out of the Baltimore gutter. And Hart Crane over the side of a ship. And Jarrell fell in front of a car. And poor John Berryman jumped from a bridge. And Bellow makes it clear who is to blame, and what the logic behind the whole pattern is. For some reason this awfulness is peculiarly appreciated by business and technological America. This country is proud of its dead poets. It takes terrific satisfaction in the poet's testimony that the USA is too tough, too big, too much, too rugged, that American reality is overpowering. And to be a poet is a school thing, a church thing... So poets are loved, but loved because they just can't make it here. They exist to light up the enormity of the awful tangle and justify the cynicism of those who say, "If I were not such a corrupt, unfeeling bastard, creep, thief, and vulture, I couldn't get through this either. Look at these good and tender and soft men, the best of us. They succumbed, poor loonics" (103).

Charlie thus accuses Humboldt of allowing himself to repeat this cycle. Beginning in poverty, the son of immigrants, "Born (as he insisted) on a subway platform at Columbus Circle, his mother going into labor on the IRT" (*HG* 115), Humboldt gradually "makes it" in the cultural life of New York City. Humboldt's aim has in fact been to become the Whitman of the twentieth cen tury, to reconcile in his poetry the high and the low, art and technology, to encompass everything-in other words, to fulfill in his days Emerson's vision of the true American poet, as Whitman had tried to fulfill Emerson's ideal in the 19th century.

Humboldt loved literature and intellectual conversation and argument, and loved the history of thought. A big gentle handsome boy he put together his own combination of symbolism and street language. Into this mixture went Yeats, Apollinaire, Lenin, Freud, Morris R. Cohen, Gertrude Stein, baseball statistics, and Hollywood gossip. He brought Coney Island into the Aegean and united Buffalo Bill with Rasputin. He was going to join together the Art Sacrament and the Industrial USA as equal powers. . . . He wanted to be magically and cosmically expressive and articulate, able to say anything; he wanted also to be wise, philosophical, to find the common ground of poetry and science, to prove that the imagination was just as potent as machinery, to free and bless humankind.

In the next sentence in the passage Bellow reveals the cause of Humboldt's failure: but he was out also to be rich and famous. And from Charlie's point of view, Humboldt thus sells out. The success of his Harlequin Ballads starts him on the road to disaster. More and more will he look for material pleasures and comforts (money, girls, drink, etc.), and take advantage of what the affluent American society can offer him. Eisenhower's victory over Adlai Stevenson (a possible savior of the arts) in the fifties distresses him and probably encourages him to obtain even more material advantages out of the system. He involves Charlie in a scheme to get an endowed chair at Princeton; he accepts money from big business corporations which, supposedly, should help advance the arts. But having yielded to these false gods, his decline follows immediately. Imagination and creativity are thwarted. No new poetry results from a financially secure life. Instead of becoming the Whitman of his days, Humboldt illustrate the perils that result from the "marriage of the dollar and the soul," "the might of money and the entanglement of art with it" (329), and ends up as bum living in a flophouse in Manhattan.

The problem is that Charlie, despite Humboldt's example, has also "made it." He is apparently a successful man of letters, whose play *Von Trenck* was a hit on Broadway, an important public figure who flies over New York with Senators Javits and Robert Kennedy to attend a fancy luncheon party. His expensive clothes, his Mercedes Benz, his visits to the Playboy Club and luxurious restaurants also prove it. Humboldt himself had warned Charlie of this possibility: "I have vertigo from success, Charlie. . . It'll happen to you too. I tell you this to prepare you" (11). In the letter written before his death, Humboldt shows that he is aware that his warning had not been heeded. Charlie has indeed followed his steps too closely. As Humboldt's fame declines, Charlie, the disciple, starts on his road to success, spurred mainly by the play *Von Trenck*, whose pro tagonist is evidently based on Humboldt.

Soon after his success, Citrine feels his grip on life slipping. He thinks he knows what is wrong: his time and energy are too much taken up with devising means to cope with hostile poets, crooks, ex-wives, demanding mistresses, lawyers and the IRS. Charlie is going through a double crisis. His powers as a writer seem to have left him. He is also losing all his money in a divorce suit and in the attempt to start a journal with a friend. Thus, at least temporarily, Charlie's fate seems to be identical with Humboldt's. Maybe America doesn't need art and inner miracles. It has so many outer ones. The USA is a big operation, very big. "The more it, the less we" (*HG* 5). At the moment, Charlie becomes aware that he has indulged in the same material pleasures that led Humboldt to his ruin. In one important respect Citrine does not differ from Humboldt and so many of his other compatriots: he too has "the American craving for high stimuli", the insatiable drive to find fulfillment of the satisfactions which life, as they feel, owes them. Citrine should "take the vow of poverty", for his own good. There would be "no more Renatas, no more erotic life, and no more of the exciting anxieties associated with the erotic life" (235). And although Citrine agrees with Durnwald that "the only manly life was a life of thought", it is his body whose needs stand between him and his pursuit of the higher life, needs that find fulfillment in such acquisitions as his silver Mercedes, "the loveliest of machines", his money, prizes, recognition, and mistresses. The fact that he is at the present moment unable to write and sees his money slip away from him makes him conscious, moreover, that he has reached a decisive point in his life, a crossroads in which he can either follow the road that took Humboldt to disaster or escape it by maintaining the Emersonian "original, fresh self" (329) to follow the great poet and fulfill the mission that Humboldt had failed to carry out.

In a world in which "brotherly love is corrupted into sexual monstrosity" (282—3), in which individuality and the "heavy weight of selfhood" (9) make everyone fear death, in which body, money, power, technology, business-all things external-are overemphasized, man has to learn how to transcend the material, and appeal to the internal side by attributing to it a new significance.

Just as soul and spirit leave the body in sleep, they could also be withdrawn from it in full consciousness with the purpose of observing the inner life of man. The first result of this conscious withdrawal is that everything is reversed. Instead of seeing the external world as we normally do with senses and intellect, initiates can see the curcumscribed self from without. Soul and spirit are poured out upon the world which normally we perceive from within-mountains, clouds, forests and seas. The external world we no longer see, for we are it. The outer world is now the inner. Clairvoyant, you are in the space you formerly beheld. From this new circumference you look back to the center, and all the center is your own self, is now the external world... There is a star world within us that can be seen when the Spirit takes a new vantage point outside its body.

Life and death will then also acquire a new meaning. Imagination and creativity will flow again, "Imagination must not pine away... It must assert that art manifests the inner power of nature" (107). Mankind must recover its imaginative powers, recover living thought and real being, and no longer accept these insults to the soul, and do it soon. When this is accomplished, mere identities will once more be transformed into true entities. "A significant man is an entity. Identity is what they give you socially" (301). As a true entity people have the power to cancel the world's distraction, activity, noise, and become fit to hear the essence of things.

Mankind must recover its imaginative powers, as Citrine acknowledges. It is not easy to achieve this, when people are offered so many exciting material and sexual enticements which modern city life allows us to satisfy so easily and readily. Citrine's story records the fight against the insidious powers of distraction that have colonized modern consciousness. The essence of things, then, is not to be found in the world of distraction, the world of the Simkins, Cantabiles, and Renatas, but in the world beyond this world, the spiritual world. As Citrine concludes, the only trustworthy medium to spiritual world is eventually the artist, through whom "a mysterious power" works, which enables him to hear what is essential. It is his product, the work of art, which, provided it is genuine, will embody this essence, and thus constitute "a matter of the spirit". What consequently guarantees the growth of the spirit is the continuing activity of the artist, an activity which, as Citrine's final decision to give up his glamo rous jet-set existence makes clear by implication, can only be pursued in a spirit of dedicated sincerity and ascetic denial, qualities generally accorded to members of a priesthood. Bellow himself as the artist proves that the growth of the spirit, as exemplified by his own oeuvre, can be an exhilarating venture, from which the richly funny, the bizarre and the incongruous need not be excluded for it to remain an activity profoundly serious in its aim, while at the same time gratifying enjoyable in its execution.

As Humboldt nears his death, he revives his sanity and casts away rational orthodoxy. He comes to reassert the power of the imaginative soul. He refuses to let the imagination be engulfed by the materialistic, pragmatic, and rationalistic world. All this is clearly manifested in his gift to Citrine. Citrine reads Humboldt's loving, posthumous letter with avidity. He is moved to tears as he reads along. The letter ends with a significant sentence: "We are not natural beings but supernatural beings" (347). Although the letter is only a prelude to Humboldt's gift, it testifies to Humboldt's power as an imaginative poet. Writing with "end-of-the-line lucidity" (373), he reiterates the importance of the imagination, the love of the good and the beautiful, and the passion for literature. It is indeed a valuable legacy to Citrine and to the world. The box office success of the movie created out of a scenario by Humboldt and Citrine proves that art still has a power to instruct, to delight, and to move people.

When Citrine hears of the death of his old friend, he is shocked, but he is even more shocked by the obituaries that appear about him and which turn him from the public amusement he had become into "the prominent literary intellectual, a salon personality", Humboldt had been denied to be in life. Only of the dead does the world seem to have any use, and genuinely outraged Citrine realizes that he has come into a legacy, demanding him to achieve what Humboldt had failed to do: to vindicate and restore "the credit and authority of art, the seriousness of thought, the integrity of culture, the dignity of style" (249). Roused from a "deep snooze that lasted for years and decades" (306), Citrine once again understands what his own interests really are, interests which are those of the poet, the artist, in whose soul a voice sounds "which has a power equal to the power of societies, states, and regimes"; a power "to cancel the world's distraction, activity, noise", to enable man to become "fit to hear the essence of things" (312).

It is Humboldt, the failed poet, acting from the grave, the man whom Citrine, as he now realizes, had never stopped loving, and who strengthens Citrine in his determination to complete his renewed search for the old feelings of spiritual fulfillment. In particular Humboldt's farewell letter, which moves Citrine to tears, is of crucial importance. By attempting to recover this "original self", Charlie can begin pursuing his true goal to restore his imaginative powers, to gain the strength to fulfill his mission, and to transform him, with the help of Humboldt's money, into the Whitman of his age. Now he is only simmering, still, and it would be necessary at last to come to a full boil. He has business on behalf of the entire human race-a responsibility not only to fulfill his own destiny but to carry on for certain failed friends like Von Humboldt Fleisher who has never been able to struggle through into higher wakefulness. His very fingertips rehearse how they would work the keys of the trumpet, imagination's trumpet, when he gets ready to blow it at last. The peals of that brass would be heard beyond earth, out in space itself. When that Messiah, that savior faculty the imagination is roused, finally we could look again with open eyes upon the whole shining earth.

After Humboldt and his mother are reburied next to each other at the last scene in the novel, Charlie walks away from the grave. It is April, and his discovery of an early spring flower makes rebirth, the possibility of eternal renewal, become Charlie's last thought:

> "What's this, Charlie, a spring flower?" "It is. I guess it's going to happen after all. A warm day like this everything looks ten times deader."
>
> "So it's a little flower," ... "They used to tell one about a kid asking his grumpy old man when they were walking in the park, 'What's the name of this flower, Papa?' and the old guy is peevish and he yells, 'How should I know? Am I in the millinery business?' Here's another, but what do you suppose they' re called, Charlie?"
>
> "Search me" I said, "I'm a city boy myself. They must be crocuses." (471)

The theme reminds of Whitman ("I bequeath myself to the dirt to grow from the grass I love/If you want me again look for me under your boot-soles"). There is something in man which is important to continue: the spirit, however "cheated, outraged, defiled, corrupted, fragmented, injured", but still the spirit. Since the spirit's most attractive and powerful expression is through art, through culture in general, it seems appropriate that the two main protagonists of the book should be artists: Von Humboldt Fleisher, famous poet and man of letter; Charlie Citrine, his one-time protégé, admirer and best friend, equally famous, be it as playwright, biographer, critic and essayist. By dealing specifically with the problem of the two artists, who have an early exhilarating and successful start, Bellow shows how they come to despair of the possibility of keeping the spirit alive, of retaining a sense of artistic values in a society which abounds with commercialism and materialism, and lacks spiritual life. *Humboldt's Gift* is Bellow's most self-reflexive text, a testimony and an accusation, an explanation and a justification of the difficulties of achieving what Bellow sees as the highest end of art: transcending the reality through spiritual pursuit.

Like his predecessor Citrine, Albert Corde, the protagonist in Bellow's *The Dean's December* (1982), an ex-journalist of the Paris *Herald Tribune*, is an artist, that is, a man of words but not merely of words. Like Citrine, he realizes that it is only the pursuit of the life of the spirit which renders human life truly human, and in order to fight the degradation of the spirit which underlies the moral crisis of the West, he has to withdraw from the powers of distraction furnished by public life. Exchanging his journalistic activities for those of a professor, Corde, too, turns his back on the mass media that produce and cater to the modern consciousness, a consciousness which, as he believes, is basically a false, reduced consciousness: it receives reality in a distorted form as a world of "false description and non-experience". It is a world that lends itself to manipulation by the powerful, the people who by readily accepting it as the only existing world, derive from this their justification to exploit it ruthlessly to their own advantage.

Corde knows this world, as he knows the people who feel at home in it, some of whom he even likes and appreciates. He nevertheless entertains serious doubts about its reality which proves beneficial to a few only while condemning a large segment of mankind to a sub-human lumpen existence. This, Corde believes, must never be accepted, and one of the crucial questions dealt with in the novel is how to combat this modern consciousness, how to transform it, so that it will be capable again of recognizing to what extent reality comes to us in distorted forms.

One way of achieving this is to go back to the great sources of human thought and feeling, to the Platos, the Vicos, the Hegels. Thus journalism could regain the solidity of real human experience and rid itself of faddish trendiness. Facts could be given as facts again, divested of the dissociative generality they acquired when uttered through the public media. One should become "the moralist of seeing".

Corde's own efforts at *Harper's*, however, prove far from successful. He wants to show how the American ideas of liberty, equality, justice, democracy and abundance are pounded into dust. His articles are more like the public denunciations than "matters of the spirit" guaranteeing the growth of the life of the spirit (the artist's ultimate aim, as Citrine had recognized). Originally meant to be "period pieces, picturesque, charming, nostalgic" (*DD* 101), they turn out too "raw" to anybody's taste. His stark descriptions of the horrors of prison life, the broad-daylight rapes and robberies, the sexual acts committed in public places; of the Tailor Homes where people, afraid to go at night to the incinerator drop on each floor, flushed their garbage down the toilet, and where young men were getting on the top of the elevator cabs, opened the hatch and threatened to douse the people with gasoline and set them afire, these descriptions offended the politicians, the businessmen, the professions and the government alike. These articles alienate not only the people he tries to reach but also those whose support he needs to effect changes in modern consciousness: the politicians, the businessmen, the professions. Corde realizes that if he is to achieve what he wants to achieve, to continue his moral crusade in Chicago, his approach should be different. It will be mainly a question of language, he concludes, and in believing this, Corde shows himself a firm adherent of the idea that the way we arrive at what we call reality is the way we articulate our world, and that if there is something wrong with our sense of reality, it is because there is something wrong with the way we articulate the world. Proceeding from this basic idea, which confirms the Bellovian belief that what renders human life truly human is the life of the spirit, language being both exclusively human and mental, Bellow has turned *The Dean's December* into a powerful statement about the deplorable condition of the life of the spirit in the West. It is at the same time a moving statement so far as it gives expression to Corde's agony in convincing himself that what is wrong with the way we articulate the world is not simply aesthetic (Corde being a professional man of words), but profoundly moral.

Applied science, engineering technology may be today's powers of darkness, "which had poisoned land, air, water, the forests, the animals, the cities and our human cells" (140), but not because there are these disciplines but because the pure scientists have not really understood science. If they had, they would have realized the morality and poetry implicit in its laws. But not only have the scientists failed, the humanists, too, have flunked the course. They, too, have shown themselves ignorant of science, though not in the sense the pure scientists have. They have been weak because "they have no conception of what the main effort of the human mind has been for three centuries and what it has found" (228). Corde, then, does not believe in the purely materialistic bit. If there is something wrong with man's humanity, the cause lies in the nature of his spiritual life, not in something external.

Corde, an earnest, brooding, heart-struck, time-ravaged person, with his moral desires and taking up the burdens of mankind, believes that poetry has the strength "to rival the attraction of narcotics, the magnetism of TV, the excitements of sex, or the ecstasies of destruction" (187), a suggestion proving again that Corde firmly holds to the liberal humanist belief that culture is not simply embellishment but a vital force in shaping man's moral being. The great sources of human thought and feeling lend depth and scope to Corde's search for a meaningful life to reject the powers of distraction in public life. Corde has to relinquish the sheltered life of the lecture room and library and go out into the streets to retain his sense of integrity. To feel fully human Corde, and all the Bellow heroes needs the great sources of man's cultural heritage to renders human life truly human.

2. Consummation of the heart's ultimate need

All of Bellow's protagonists share one quality, that is, their intense feeling of closeness and loyalty to their family, and their sensitivity to the importance of the family. There is a strong family feeling on the part of Bellow's protagonists. Bellow voices the prevailing belief that the basis of Jewish survival is close family ties in his novels. In the words of Rabbi Louis Isaac Rabinowitz, "The constant insistence upon the value of the family as a social unit... had the result of making the Jewish family the most vital factor in the survival of Judaism and the preservation of the Jewish way of life, much more than the synagogue or school" (Family). Religion brings the family members together during the Sabbath and holidays. Religion also helps preserve the basic hierarchal structure of the family, in which the father occupies the position of patriarch. The mother, on a rung lower, ministers to the needs of the family. After Jew's immigrating to the new world, their family tie is easily maintained when they live in a world hostile to them. The mutual suffering of members of society, their antagonism to the perpetrators of their troubles, forces them to turn inward, to cement the communal bond.

Judaism is a family-oriented religion. At the present time, family life in general is undergoing a crisis and the overall societal picture influences religious patterns. The once "solid Jewish family" finds itself now in a crisis situation, mirroring society as a whole. Bellow reflects this occurrence when he presents his protagonist. Actually, in a sense, the family becomes, for Bellow, a metaphor for religion, with the father representing God, the mother, religion, brothers a bisexual humanity (because Bellow's protagonists have no sisters, except Tommy Wilhelm in *Seize the Day*.)

The one strong family bond that is evident in Bellow's works is that between brothers. It affirms the social responsibility inherent in the communal brotherhood of man. It also depicts a specific family bond that is indissoluble. It is a bond based upon a protective instinct that the older brother displays to his younger siblings. It reflects the biblical attitude that each man is his brother's keeper and is also a comprehensive statement concerning the nature of society or humanity. Joseph in *Dangling Man* quarrels with his brother, Amos, but the rift does not last long and is soon mended. They are of differing economic levels and differ in their social perspectives, but the brotherly bond is very strong and overrides all other considerations.

Familial relationships are very important to Augie in *The Adventures of Augie March* from the very beginning . When Grandma Lausch wants to institutionalize Georgie, Augie is very upset because it connotes the breakup of the family. He recalls: "After that we had a diminished family life, as though it were care of Georgie that had been the main basis of household union and now everything was disturbed" (*AM* 63). Though Georgie's going to the institution brought about the breakup of the household, Aguie always maintains closeness to his family. He visits Georgie when ever he can. He visits his mother in the home for the blind whenever he is able to. Augie's true family feelings are depicted in his relationship with his brother Simon. There are times when Simon behaves in a despicable, boorish, and for a brother, unconscionable manner. Augie reacts, initially, with hurt feeling, but he always acknowledges his love for Simon and is never, at any time, angry with him. Augie says, in his own jargon: "I was a sucker for it too, family love" (243). This feeling always remains with Augie. As a mature individual he looks forward to being a family man, both as a foster parent in a school which he will set up and as an actual parent resulting from his own marriage. When Augie is in Europe with Stella after the war, he reflects: "I would have preferred to stay in the States and have children" (584) and "my hopes have settled themselves upon children and a settled life" (591). Simon visits Augie in Europe and he says: "I love my brother very much. I never meet him again without the utmost love filling me up. He has it too. . . " (595)

In *Herzog*, Bellow presents a much more complete picture of a family than in any of his other works. The hierarchal structure of the traditional Jewish family is presented in the flashbacks that deal with Moses' childhood. Jonah Herzog, Moses's father, although he is a gentleman in Russia, is a failure as a provider in Montreal. Nevertheless, to his family he is a "sacred being, a king" (*H* 183). When he returns home beaten, bloody and penniless from his abortive attempts to run whiskey across the border, Sarah, Moses's mother comforts him, bathes his wounds, and watches over him silently after she put him to bed. She never utters a word of reprimand, other than suggesting that he give up this means of livelihood. Sarah, indeed, represents the typical Jewish mother: she is self-sacrificing, doting, and devoted. She maintains the stability of the home and sees to it that everything runs smoothly. Jonah is not a provider, but the family is well-fed anyway and kept clean. Her children are sent to the best schools; her daughter takes piano lessons, while the boys study more serious subjects. She even provides entertainment for the children by pulling them on their sleds in the Montreal snow in the wintertime, unmindful of the cost to her own health. She seems content in her position in the hierarchal structure of the Herzog family and attempts to perpetuate it by acquiescence and repetition.

So Herzog develops a strong family feeling from his childhood. His family is a cohesive one. All pitches in to help as a family unit. He recalls fondly how he and his brothers pasted Johnny Walker labels on the bottles to help their father. His mother's brother used to help them out financially, whenever possible. His father's sister, Zipporah, would scold his father for his weakness, his lack of business acumen, and his unrealistic approach to life, but this is an integral aspect of family life, caring, sharing, and scolding. This feeling of family solidarity remains with the Herzog children. When Moses needs help, he could always count on either of his brothers, Shura (diminutive of Alexander) and Willy. He loves his brothers. But his love for his brothers extends beyond the periphery of his immediate family. He learns from his family the necessity of becoming involves with others, that "brotherhood is what makes a man human" (333), that compassion is a necessary component of life.

At the beginning of the novel, when Herzog is on his way to Grand Central Station to catch a train to Martha's Vineyard, he remembers how, when he was a child, all holidays would begin with a train ride. Annoyed now at the traffic and heat, "the buses spurting the poisonous exhaust of cheap fuel, … the cars crammed together, . . . the racket of machinery and the desperately purposeful crowds" (44), Herzog thinks nostalgically of the family outings: "the basket of fruit. . . the St. Lawrence. . . the summer fields …" (45). The passage also clearly foreshadows the novel's pastoral ending:

> But that was forty years behind him. Now the train was ribbed for speed, a segmented tube of brilliant steel. There were no pears, no Willie, no Shura, no Helen, no mother. Leaving the cab, he thought how his mother would moisten her handkerchief at her mouth and rub his face clean, he had no business to recall this, he knew, and turned toward Grand Central in his straw hat. He was of the mature generation now, and life was his to do something with, if he could. But he had not forgotten the odor of his mother's saliva on the handkerchief that summer morning… All children have cheeks and all mothers spittle to wipe them tenderly. (45—46)

To Herzog these things matter a great deal. He will not stop thinking about the past; he will not feel free from this personal shaping force, until all memories, even the most painful ones, are dug up.

The Herzogs of Napoleon Street keeps a boarder, named Ravitch. Ravitch's family, his wife, and two children, remain in Russia, and he is working with the hopes of saving enough money to be able to send for them. They are lost during the Russian revolution. Consequently, Ravitch drinks his sorrows away and returns to the Herzog household drunk and disorderly every payday. Jonah Herzog complains, but he pities him and helps him to bed. This lesson in compassion, in brotherly involvement with other human beings, is one that Moses Herzog never forgets.

Another quality that is apparent in Bellow protagonists is compassion. Augie is called a "man of feeling" (*AM* 483). Every crucial event causes him to break into tears. He is moved by the fate of those with whom he associates, and he feels their sorrow as if it were his own. Augie's compassion for people goes beyond his relationship with his family. It extends to all others with whom he comes in contact. It extends to Grandma Lausch who is never considered part of the family but rather as an intruder, one who transcends her role as boarder and attempts to assume control of the March family. It works until the March boys are old enough to realize what is going on. They view her as a usurper, making decisions that rightfully belongs to their mother and inverting the roles so that, in essence, she becomes the mother and Mrs. March, her housekeeper. They appeal to Simon to change the situation, and Simon, disregarding the needs of the mother, puts her into a home for the aged. It is Augie, however, who does all for her. He helps her pack, brings her to the Home, and helps her get settled. As he says: "My heart went soft for her" (105). And he is truly grief-stricken at the news of her death. "That was a shaft! It went straight and cold into my bowels, and I couldn't bring up my back or otherwise move, but sat bent over. Dead! Horrible to imagine the old woman dead. . . . I shed tears with my sleeve over my eyes" (197).

Augie's compassion is sometimes detrimental to himself, such as when he helps Mimi Villars. He and Mimi are next-door neighbors in the same rooming house. Mimi is in trouble. She has become pregnant by her lover, a married man, and decides to have an abortion, but needs Augic's help. Augie does not agree, but does not judge, her decision concerning an abortion. He knows that she needs help and is ready to help her. At this time, he is going with Lucy Magnus and is contemplating marriage. Augie's involvement with Mimi has the external appearance of the guilty lover attempting to comer up his misdeed. Augie realizes that this could ruin his relationship with Lucy, but he cannot allow Mimi to fend for herself. He helps Mimi; he saves her life, and Lucy breaks up with him. Augie learns that the quality of compassion exists only in a minority of humankind and those who do not possess it are usually incapable of recognizing and appreciating this trait in others. But he cannot, nor does he desire, to change his nature.

In Mexico, he gets involved with another woman, because she appeals to his sense of compassion. Stella entreats Augie for assistance, claiming that her life is in danger. He helps her leave Mexico, but his aid causes the final break with Thea. In both instances, his compassion is seemingly harmful to himself. But he does what he does from an acute sensitivity to others and never regrets it. Ultimately, he marries Stella. At the time, however, each woman jealously suspects his compassion for another woman thereby terminating a relationship.

Augie's compassion extends to animals also. He is in love with Thea and goes along with her wild scheme of training an eagle to hunt iguanas. Yet instinctively he disapproves of it. He considers the idea of training a powerful beast to prey upon a defenseless creature as inhumane and unnecessary and is relieved when the small creature strikes back and even wounds the giant eagle. He soon realizes that it is Caligula who needs compassion. He is a giant eagle but in an unnatural situation and, therefore, resists the training when it becomes dangerous to himself. Thea thinks he is a coward and has no more use for him. Augie, however, sees the humanity inherent in the situation. A creature, no matter how big he is, will instinctively recoil from being hurt. Thea makes no allowances for humanity's frailness; Augie's compassionate nature sympathizes and empathizes with the frailty of all creatures.

In *Humboldt's Gift*, Naomi Lutz, Charlie's girl friend of his youthful days in Wisconsin, tells him: "Doc (her father) told mother that your whole family were a bunch of greenhorns and aliens, too damn emotional, the whole bunch of you" (*HG* 288). She continues: "But you people all loved each other. You were like real primitive that way. Maybe that's why my father called you greenhorns" (289). Charlie accepts the proposition that sentimentalism belongs to the Old World and part of becoming American was learning to control one's feelings. He tells Naomi that his father became an American too and so did Julius. They stopped all that entire immigrant loving. Only he persisted, in his childish way. His emotional account was always overdrawn. He never has forgotten how his mother cried when he fell down the stairs and how she pressed the lump on his head with the blade of a knife. And what a knife—it was her Russian silver with a handle like a billy club. So there you are. Whether it was a lump on his head, or Julius's geometry, or how Papa could raise the rent, or poor Mama's toothaches, it was the most momentous thing on earth for all of family members. He never lost the intense way of caring—no, that isn't so. He is afraid the truth is that he did lose it. . . . But he still required it. That's always been problem.

The Old World Jew, living in the close quarters of the ghetto, was, of necessity, involved in the life of everyone within those boundaries, and everyone's problems were treated as one's own, i. e., momentously. American society is more open and diversified. Consequently, Americans are egocentric, tend to keep to themselves and are reluctant to get involved with others, especially if they are not compelled to do so. People who are not involved personally are usually not involved emotionally. Bellow treats this isolationism as a loss, inevitable, but deleterious to society, nevertheless.

Charlie is sentimental. He cries about Humboldt; he cries when Renata leaves him. Charlie has strong family feelings. When he hears that his brother, Julius, is about to have a heart operation, he postpones his plans to go to Europe, much to the chagrin of Renata, and goes first to Texas to be with Julius. The meeting is an emotional one for Charlie. Although Charlie is divorced, he has very strong feelings for his daughters, Lish and Mary. He loved Menasha, the boarder in the Citrine home when they were children; he loved Szathmar, his lawyer and childhood friend. In addition, he loves Pierre Thaxter, the aristocratic mountebank, who has the ability to keep Charlie smiling while conning him out of his money. Charlie is also beneficent. He is not as wealthy as was Elya Gruner, but he is very generous with his money when he has it. He keeps his promise to Waldemar Wald—both a moral and charitable act—and shares the proceeds that he gets from "Humboldt's Gift." He also reburies Humboldt and Humboldt's mother in Valhalla Cemetery (an act of reverence for the dead). To a remembrancer like Citrine, Chicago means his childhood, adolescence, and adulthood. Growing up in a closely-knit Jewish immigrant family, he has strong family feelings, which weigh heavily in his choosing to settle in Chicago. As his ex-wife Denise often declares, he moved back to Chicago because his parents were buried there.

Moreover, Citrine cherishes his old-time school chums; to him, they are "a sacred category" (38) and he is noted for his "terrible weakness or dependency on early relationship" (38). Through his Chicago friends, he not only gets to know parts of the city condition normally beyond his realm but also indulges in acts of recall and shares advice, assistance, and friendship. A writer by profession, Citrine knows he is in an unremitting paradox-he needs to stand back from, and yet shares in, the struggle of human life itself. Citrine's family moved to Chicago's West Side in the twenties, where he grew up and received his education. Like other Bellovian heroes, Citrine is terribly nostalgic and tries to justify his hysteria-like keenness in recollections by arguing that "Love made these things unforgettable" (*HG* 330) and "Plato links recollection with love" (348). He remembers that he played softball with Polish kids under the EL tracks, that at eight he spent Christmas in a TB ward, and that he spent a blizzard night with his first sweetheart, Naomi Lutz, in her father's office.

Growing up in Polish Chicago in the twenties, Citrine comes from a closely-knit Jewish immigrant family. They were so closely attached to one another that Naomi's father, Dr. Lutz, called the Citrines "a bunch of greenhorns and aliens, too damn emotional" (298). Citrine remembers that they very much cared about one another: "Whether it was a lump on my head, or Julius's geometry, or how Papa could raise the rent, or poor Mama's toothaches, it was the most momentous thing on earth for us all." (299). Citrine is persistent in his love for his school chums and old-time acquaintances. To him, they are "a sacred category" (37) and he enjoys their company and love. His feeling toward them verges on "family feeling."

Citrine is generous to his friends. He lends money to his lawyer friend Szathmar to buy a condominium. He entrusts money to his journalist friend, Pierre Thaxter, and becomes a sort of patron to his art. Although he suspects that Thaxter is conning him, he is extremely fond of him; as he says, "I love Thaxter, whatever he does" (74). To him friendship is more important than money: "Didn't I, myself, aim at magnanimity, and wasn't friendship a far bigger thing than money?" (242) Citrine's celebration of brotherly love culminates in his intricate relationship with his late blood – brother, Von Humboldt Fleisher. In Chicago, he constantly thinks about Humboldt, "a precious friend hid in death's dateless night, a camerado from a former existence (almost), well – beloved but dead" (110). To Citrine, Chicago is a perfect place to remember him: "In Chicago Humboldt was a natural subject for reflection. Lying at the southern end of the Great Lakes … Chicago with its gigantesque outer life contained the whole problem of poetry and the inner life in America. Here you could look into such things through a sort of fresh – water transparency" (9). His memory becomes all the more poignant when, engulfed in all sorts of troubles, he is blessed by Humboldt's gift which removes many of his problems.

Citrine has a fierce love for his city Chicago. No matter where he is, in Madrid or in New York, he, like Augie, is always thinking about his home city. He chose Chicago, instead of other places, to settle in because of his loyalty to his past, his dead parents, and his city. Chicago, a symbol of his roots, is his own turf where he can feel at home.

Bellow's protagonists, growing up in a closely-knit Jewish immigrant family, share intense feeling of closeness and loyalty to their family. They value the strong family bond and the brotherly love, which affirms the social responsibility inherent in the communal brotherhood of man. Their family bond and brotherly love also extend to people around them, which is reflected in their compassion for those who need help. Family, brotherly love and friendship are consummation of the heart's ultimate need for Bellow's protagonists, who are family-oriented. Family becomes, for Bellow, a metaphor for religion, which is undergoing a crisis, but is still the foothold of human life.

3. Restoration of Community to Counteract Chaotic Modern World

It is instructive that Bellow does not encourage dwelling in the Wasteland as an option but suggests an alternative. It is not difficult to notice the influence of *The Old Testament* which Bellow studied from since as a boy: "It may be more difficult to reach the whirling mind of a modern reader but it is possible to cut through the noise and reach the quiet zone. In the quiet zone we may find that he is devoutly waiting for us. When complications increase, the desire for essentials increases too" (Bellow, The Noble). It is paradoxical too that Bellow suggests it is in the location of the quiet zone that we will find this spiritual connection verses the clamor of community. While Bellow believes in the significance of the individual, he also advocates a return to society, an affirmation of human possibilities. As Marcus Klein shows in his brilliant *After Alienation*, contempo rary American literature also swings between the poles of alienation and accommodation; the hero is fearful of losing his identity yet longs for a union of self and society. Perhaps the most intense champion of the individual in American literature is also the most intense "accommodationist": Whitman is able to sing both of the dynamic, non-conforming individual and of the union of such indivi dualists into a community of love.

Bellow depicts an alienated hero trying to find his way towards community in so much of his fiction-*Dangling Man*, *The Victim*, *Seize the Day*, and *Henderson the Rain King* to indicates how great is man's need for belonging and the extent of his sense of loss when he does not feel himself as an integral part of society, either civilian or military. Joseph of *Dangling Man* gives up his civilian life to wait for the army induction center to remember its intention to call him. During these eleven months' waiting, Joseph withdraws more and more into his own isolated world. He seldom leaves his "six-sided box" and he loses contact with most of his friends. He tries to fill up the empty, lonely days of waiting. He reads the newspaper from cover to cover, reluctant to put it aside, missing not a word. Joseph is forced to admit to himself that he does not know how to use his freedom.

Far from bringing him the freedom to pursue his quest for how "a good man" should live, his enforced seclusion intensifies his sense of alienation to such a pitch that he loses touch with reality. He begins to act strangely, "not like Joseph", getting involved in exacerbating quarrels and humiliating fist fights. Reflecting on the city scene leads him to admit that he is closely tied to his fellow citizens and acknowledges that it is undeniably to his interest to do that, because he is involved with them; because, whether he likes it or not, they are his generation, his society, and his world. People are figures in the same plot, eternally fixed together. He is also aware that their existence, just as it is, makes his possible.

What Joseph realizes at the end of the novel is that it is impossible for him to conduct the quest through the self only, that one must break the solitude of the self, one's self-imposed isolation, if one is to retain one's sense of reality and purpose. Joseph's reappraisal of his identity must, as he feels, take place by stepping outside the small circle of friends and family, by joining the ranks of his fellow men, by exposing himself to the cruder but vital realities of the outside world. He cannot escape the society in which he is born and the challenge it poses. His declaration of a shared humanity with others, however temporary or fanciful, is unmistakable. This testament of the common brotherhood of man is what all Bellow protagonists pursue.

Bellow believes that the human spirit must have been the same in all principal ways and that all men are drawn into the "same craters of the spirit" (*DM* 26). Thus arises one of his "ideal constructions": his longing to build "a colony of the spirit", a group whose covenants forbid spite, bloodiness, and cruelty, because "the world was crude and it was dangerous and, if no measures were taken, existence could indeed become-in Hobbes' phrase, which had long lodged in Joseph's mind-'nasty, brutish, and short'" (27). As Gilbert Porter points out, "What he [Joseph] wants is a form of utopian Brook Farm to set over against the harsh realities of Work War Ⅱ, which threaten both his personal identity and his private vision" ("Is the Going Up Worth the Coming Down" 23). At the end of the novel, his final move to return to community through enlisting in the regimentation, though not without irony, manifests his realization of the dangers or ineffectiveness of alienation or isolation and his decision to stop living exclusively and vainly for his own sake. Just as he acknow ledges that any goodness is achieved not in a vacuum, but in the company of other men, attended by love.

Bellow's subsequent works continue this image of a man who pendulously moves through life, longing to grasp at meaningful relationships. It is not a specifically Jewish image, but it is appropriate to the Jew who attempts to assimilate into the American community, only to find himself vacillating between insignificant alliances and attitudes.

Because of Asa's experience with Allbee he knows that he is linked to other men, that each man is perhaps the victim of every other as well as the victimizer of the other, although unwittingly, as in Asa's case. It is the unknown means by which the victimization takes place, never knowing when or how.

> Is there anything you want? There are a hundred million others who want that very same damn thing. I don't care whether it's a sandwich or a seat in the subway or what. ... Look at all the lousy men's the world was made for and I share it with. Love thy neighbor as thyself? Who the devil is my neighbor? I want to find out. Yes, sir, who and what? Even if I wanted to hate him as myself, who is he? (*V* 194)

This demand to know one's neighbor, to discover a relationship between oneself and others, is both Asa's quest and that of the urban habitants who tries to find a new set of relationships to replace the face-to-face relationships of the small town which have been destroyed by the metropolis. Asa, with an unusual but refreshing acceptance of the urban mass, replies, "Don't be so noisy.... I can't help it if the world is too crowded for you, but pipe down" (*V* 194—195). This acknowledgment, rather than denial, of the urban masses is a great leap forward in Asa's and Bellow's coming to terms with the city. As Tony Tanner puts it,

> "In this novel Bellow is again probing down into the problem of what the self owes the self and what the self owes the rest of the world; to what extent should a man permit himself to be limited by the claims of other people; where does the privilege of individuality run up against the responsibilities of inter-relatedness?" (Tanner 27)

Although Leventhal refuses to shoulder the whole responsibility for Allbee's ruin, he does take Allbee into his home when he learns that Allbee is so down and out that he has been evicted. Leventhal takes a decisive step toward integration into the society of man. Leventhal is also involved in his brother's family trouble. His first trip to Staten Island shows his moral seriousness: he wants to help his relatives, although he realizes that leaving his work in the middle violates his sense of conscientiousness and may result in his losing his job. His nep hew Mickey is not seriously ill, but Leventhal feels sorry for the baby because of his mother's suffocating and foolish "love" and his father's irresponsible and neglectful absence. He resolves to commit himself more to his brother's family. Leventhal does his best to help his brother's family and to make amends to his nephews for his past neglectfulness. Leventhal's family feelings awakened by the visit trigger him to make his trips to Staten Island almost a routine in the following weeks. He even tries to make amends by taking his older nephew Philip for an outing in Times Square and in the city park and zoo. His trips between Manhattan and Staten Island thus mark his deep moral commitment to his brother's family and his genuine love for his nephews.

In addition, the parent-child relationship is also fundamental in Judaism because it is recognized that the survival of Jewish life depends on this bond. The tradition of honoring one's parents remains a vital aspect of the Jewish child's life, throughout the ages, down to the present time.

Bellow reiterates the commitment to society, and the feeling of social responsibility in all his works. This is also one of the important Jewish qualities. The Jewish Sage, Hillel, says: "do not separate yourself from the community" (Goldman, *Saul Bellow's Moral Vision* 111). In *The Adventures of Augie March*, Augie's social responsibility is evident in his immense involvement with others, which, of course, is reflected in his compassionate and sensitive nature. Augie never withdraws from people, regardless of the setback he may encounter at the time. His comment regarding Rousseau stresses the importance of man's recognition of himself as a social creature, and notes that the only way he can affect society, if that is what he seeks to do, is in its midst, not by withdrawal and objective recollection.

Onecan only understand and respond to society's needs if one is a vital part of the community because the ideal is very far from the real. Augie's dream is to establish an "academy foster-home" to care for children, to teach them, to help them. Augie is a happy social creature who refuses to lead a life of "quiet desperation" or even just a disappointed life. He is never arrogant, cruel, misanthropic, or unloving.

Occasionally, a sense of community overtakes urban man, even in the Dantesque underworld of the subway in *Seize the Day*-all of a sudden, unsought, a general love for all the imperfect and lurid-looking people burst out in Wilhelm's breast in the dark tunnel, in the haste, heat, and darkness which disfigure and make freaks and fragments of nose and eyes and teeth. He loves them. One and all, he passionately loves them. They are his brothers and sisters. So what does it matter how many languages there are, or how hard it is to describe a glass of water? A moment of brotherhood, of connection, a momentary thing, and an involuntary thing, flickers for a moment in the subway; then it dies. That Bellow has Wilhelm reduce the sense of community to such an embarrassing and involuntary response speaks painfully for the degradation of the human spirit.

Herzog also longs for the sense of community, hints of which come to him in isolated moments. Little epiphanies which keep alive the sense of community appear even in such debased surroundings as the subway-Herzog dropped his fare in the slot where he saw a whole series of token slighted from within and magnified by the glass. Innumerable millions of passengers had polished the wood of the turnstile with their hips. From the scene rose a feeling of communion-brotherhood in one of its cheapest forms.

Sammler enjoys being with people, for all their idiosyncrasies and perversions. The relationship with them affirms the human bond. He fully believes in the sacredness of life, and, like the protagonists of Bellow's other works, he is concerned with the preservation of the dignity of the individual.

Citrine is persistent in his love for his school chums and old-time acquaintances. Among his Chicago friends, George Swiebel and Richard Durnwald are closest to him. George is a link to Citrine's good old days in Chicago. Their friendship goes back to the fifth grade. An ex-actor, George has wide connections with varieties of people through his previous experiences in the theatre, Hollywood, radio, TV, and journalism. A contractor now, he is in contact with people from all walks of life. For years he has been Citrine's "self-designated expert on the underworld" (*HG* 39) and has kept him informed about criminals, whores, racing, the rackets, narcotics, politics, and syndicate operations. Despite his present occupation as a contractor, George knows "his Ibsen and his Brecht" (46) and in South Chicago he is identified with Bohemia and the arts, with creativity, and with imagination. A down-to-earth, practical, warm - hearted, genial, nature - worshipping, health-conscious, outgoing Chicagoan, George is a true friend Citrine can count on. George shows his genuine friendship when Citrine has to go abroad to escape his Chicago troubles. He says to Citrine that he' ll be standing by Citrine. Cable him from anywhere and he' ll arrive. The friendship is mutual; Citrine loves him, too.

Citrine's friend Durnwald is another Chicagoan who is "well up among the pure." Although he has been out of the city-at the University of Edinburgh for half a year-he is constantly in Citrine's mind. Citrine's respect and admiration for him is without irony or ambivalence: in crude Chicago Durnwald, whom he admires and even adores, is the only man with whom he exchanges ideas. Except Durnwald, none of "the mental beau monde of Chicago" (59) interests Citrine. Durnwald's serious, analytical, cool, rational, disciplined character serves as a foil to Citrine's romantic, eccentric, passionate, impulsive, and metaphysical propensities. Despite their different interests and inclinations, they are good friends. Significantly, Durnwald, absent throughout the novel in the present, is unable to extend his rational and sensible advice to Citrine in trouble.

Citrine realizes that America is an overwhelming phenomenon and his Chicago is predominantly a city of distractions. He has tried in vain to withdraw from the clutter-ridden city into his own self. He feels that he is unable to grasp the "vivid actuality and symbolic clarity" (260) of the city and to reach a state of equilibrium in which "the listening soul... can hear the essence of things and comes to understand the marvelous" (306). Fortunately, Citrine's life in Chicago is a little more tolerable because he has received brotherhood, love, sympathy, advice, assistance, and support from his friends there. Like other Bellow heroes, Citrine knows that goodness cannot be achieved in isolation and that universal brotherhood should be celebrated. With his friends, Citrine has formed a Whitmanesque "new city of Friends" against the attacks of the brutal, and impersonal physical city. Though the "new city" built by Citrine and his friends is not as strong as Whitman dreamt it, it at least drives away part of the craziness, savagery, ugliness, and alienation of the city.

Man is closely related to his fellow creatures. Bellow's heroes are all traditional men who cherish the traditional values of family and community. Bellow is much concerned with establishing a sense of community in the city. His characters reject the dead-end of the alienated self. They are forced, consequently, into a quest for establishing a relationship with others in the urban complexes. This quest for community is central to Bellow's work. It is interesting that the sense of community his characters search for is not the product of a nostalgia for an earlier small-town community. Most of his characters have known only the city and have no past rooted in the small-town experience. Bellow seems to assert as an article of faith that community is necessary if one is to be a true citizen of the city. In the country, man is dependent upon God's providence. In the city, man is dependent upon other men, and this is what makes man so vulnerable. Whether the exact relationship is discoverable or not, urban man is still related to his fellow man. There are quite a few of moments in the lives of Bellow's characters when they sense a common brotherhood and these moments keep alive their effort to restore community in modern reality.

4. Persistence in Affirmation and Hope in the Harsh Modern World

Bellow, in his works, voices the Jewish opinion that man, with all his imperfections, is basically good. The ideal is not the transcendence of human nature but the refining of its essence. That is why all Bellow's protagonists search for an answer to the question: "How should a good man live?" The quest of Bellow's protagonist is for a method of coming to terms with his own nature in a universe that denies him his own essence.

The Bellow protagonist approaches life from the Jewish perspective, which is optimistic, which firmly believes that it is a sin to neglect the pleasures of life which are also God-created. Consequently, the distinctive Jewish characteristics of the Bellow novel are its candid joie de vivre and its comic treatment of otherwise somber situations. Bellow's protagonists finally attain majesty of life in the reality, rather than find only horrors in the reality. Bellow relentlessly ridicules the proponents of "nada" existence, those nihilistic writers who suggest that man is nothing; life is meaningless, no more than a game of chance or a "dirty trick".

Until the early 20th century, the American literary scene was heavily dominated by the pessimism of such authors as Dreiser, Hemingway, and the early works of Faulkner. These men were strongly influenced by the mode of naturalism, which is profoundly pessimistic, as a world view. It confirms man's helplessness against the overwhelming forces of the universe, and it is reflected in literature by its tone of frustration, despair, and hopelessness. The period of the forties in 20th century was a period of transition, which saw the end of the Second World War. After coming so close to annihilation, and almost approaching the reality of the abyss during the war, the public needed a literature of hope and optimism, a literature that would restore dignity to man and a value to his life. This was the period in which Bellow made his timid, yet intrepid, entry onto the American literary scene. Saul Bellow brought with him a world view that was life-sustaining, predicated on a belief in the inherent goodness of man and the basic significance of existence.

Augie in *The adventures of Augie March* is certainly a protagonist not shutting himself away from life, but meeting it head-on with enthusiasm. He refuses to lead a disappointed life. Therefore, his character becomes his fate. He views everything positively and does not take minor setbacks seriously. He shows this quality at age nine, when he makes mention of the conflict he has with the Polish youth of the neighborhood at the beginning of the novel.

> Andwhile we're on that side I'll mention the Poles—we were just a handful of Jews among them in the neighborhood. . . . And sometimes we were chased, stoned, bitten, and beat up for Christ - killers, all of us. . . . But I never had any special grief from it, or brooded, being by and large too larky and boisterous to take to heart. . . . (*AM* 11)

Augie does have experienced a lot of setbacksthroughout his life. Nevertheless, he does not dwell on them, but to look forward to the future. The setbacks are disappointments, but they do not shape his life. From the disappointment of the institutionalizing of his brother, George, to losing his job with Einhorn during the Depression, to leaving the Renlings because they were smothering him, to his disillusionment with Lucy Magnus, and his failure with Thea, Augie continues to search for a "fate good enough." And even when he thinks he has found it, but it eludes him again, he continues to look forward to the time when it will be within his grasp.

What we do notice is that Augie is not formed by his environment or his adventures. He has the resiliency or opposition to resist them. The disappointments do not make him bitter, but he refuses to become what others wanted to make of him. He "never had accepted determination" (*AM* 130). Augie has the ability to resist the familial, social, and economic influences that besiege him. In the novel, Augie says: "All the influences were lined up waiting for me. I was born, and there they were to form me, which is why I tell you more of them than of myself" (*AM* 46). However, Augie has opposition, he wants to search for a fate that is peculiar to him and does not allow external forces to determine his fate, and then his own character will decide his destiny.

Augie is a man who enjoys life, and relationship with other people, even those that are not of long duration, and has a positive outlook concerning existence. These are qualities almost all of Bellow's protagonists possess, some to a lesser or greater degree.

> By portraying a vitality and color that is antithetical to 'normalcy' and yet is the very fabric of our nation, Bellow celebrates America at the same time that he rejects false values .... He argued for accommodation not by the usual indirect means of an alienated hero, but by a forthright example of engagement .... Having progressed from Joseph's rejection of the world to Leventhal's qualified acceptance, Bellow now made another leap, rejecting Flaubertian polish and despair to create a rough-hewed, energetic new world. (Opdahl, *The Novels of Saul Bellow* 71)

The passage typically reflects another outlook on Chicago than that seen through Joseph-a hearty love that Bellow holds for his rearing place. Although Bellow wrote *Augie March* during his extended foreign travel, he avows a love for the place:

> For it was Chicago before the Depression that moved my imagination as I went to my room in the morning, not misty Paris with its cold statues and its streams of water running along the curbstone.... A descendant of Russian -Jewish immigrants, I was writing of Chicago in odd corners of Paris and, afterward in Austria .... To speak of rootless or rooted persons is all very well. No man needs to bother his head about the matter whose emotions are alive. We are called upon to preserve our humanity in circumstances of rapid change and movement. I do not see what else we can do than refuse to be condemned with time or place. We are not born to be condemned but to live. (Bellow "How I Wrote Augie March' s Story")

Clayton says, *The Adventures of Augie March* was Bellow's attempt "to catch the spirit of America [as] part of a tradition going back to Emerson's 'American Scholar' address and, concretely, to the local colorists, to the identification with America by Walt Whitman .... " (88) The following passage-taking up Augie's first words in the novel, "I am an American," -with its Whitmanesque listing, indeed affirms the possibilities of life, freedom, and multiplicity in America as it describes Augie riding in the City Hall elevator with bigshots and operators, commissioners, grabbers, heelers, tipsters, hoodlums, wolves, fixers, plaintiffs, flatfeet, men in Western hats and women in lizard shoes and fur coats, "hothouse and arctic drafts mixed up, brute things and airs of sex, evidence of heavy feeding and systematic shaving, of calculations, grief, not caring, and hopes of tremendous millions in concrete to be poured or whole Mississippi of bootleg whiskey and beer" (*AM* 39).

Bellow's statement on how he wrote *Augie March* expresses the central value of the novel which the exuberant, uninhibited style and open form support- "We are not born to be condemned but to live." "To live" means for Bellow, and for Augie, to be an individual following one's own instinct, to realize an independent fate, whatever it may be. Thus Augie's transposition from "a man's character is his fate" (3) to "this fate, or what he settles for, is also his character" (514). As Norman Podhoretz puts it, "Bellow attempts to create a new idiom that could express the intellectual's joyous sense of connection with the common grain of American life … [and one that suggests] that individual fulfillment is still possible in this fluid and rather rootless society of ours." (Podhoretz, "The Adventures of Saul Bellow" 110)

Augie's belief in the worthiness of man is epitomized in what he calls "the axial lines of life" - "I have a feeling…about the axial lines of life, with respect to which you must be straight or else your existence is merely clownery, hiding tragedy..." (*AM* 472) When striving stops, there they are as a gift... Truth, love, peace, bounty, usefulness, harmony! And all noise and grates, distortion, chatter, distraction, effort, superfluity, pass (ed) off like something unreal. And he believes that any man at any time can come back to the axial lines, even if an unfortunate bastard, if he will be quiet and wait it out... At any time life can come together again and man be regenerated... He will be brought into focus. He will live with joy. Even his pains will be joy if they are true, even his helplessness will not take away his power, even wandering will not take him away from himself, even disappointment after disappointment need not take away his love. Death will not be terrible to him if life is not.

The Canadian-born, Russian, Jewish-American Moses Herzog often tries to establish the validity of the statement made by Emerson, and which he had used in his high-school commencement address: "The main enterprise of the world, for splendor... is the upbuilding of a man. The private life of one man shall be a more illustrious monarchy... than any kingdom in history... " (*H* 198). Indeed, Herzog's words are Bellow's own as he disparages "the commonplaces of the Wasteland outlook, the cheap mental stimulants of Alienation, the cant and rant of pipsqueaks about Inauthenticity and Forlornness" (75). Clearly the comic spirit of *Henderson The Rain King* is a counterattack for such outlooks. This exuberant comic novel is Bellow's reaction to the nihilistic and wasteland writers whom he has castigated on numerous occasions. As Bellow stated in *The Great Ideas Today* essay, the comic spirit is "the spirit of reason opposing the popular orgy of wretchedness in modern literature." (Bellow, "Literature" 171) Henderson rejects precisely the "commonplaces of the Wasteland outlook" and the nihilism which he sees in America by retreating to the natural world of primitive spontaneity and community in Africa: "I am a true adorer of life, and if I can't reach as high as the face of it, I plant my kiss somewhere lower down" (*HRK* 150). Thus while a fantastic African journey may cause us first to view *Henderson* as Bellow's most atypical novel, it becomes his most typical attempt to be affirmative, in a thematic sense. Henderson's vitality and reaction against a "depressive temperament" are apparently Bellow's own, if we consider his statement in an interview concerning the novel: "But perhaps writing *Henderson The Rain King* stirred me more than writing any of the other books. I felt the sheer pleasure of release from difficulty, and I suppose this may have something to do with my mental constitution." (Galloway, "An Interview with Saul Bellow" 21) In the same interview Bellow struck at the heart of the novel's concern, suggesting the basic value which moves Henderson from America to Africa and thus establishes him as an opponent to the nihilists: "But I suppose things have become so bad that one can state the modern crisis in a single proposition: either we want to continue living or we don't. If that's the case, curiosity if only that compels me to say that I want to continue living" (21).

When Herzog speaks to a friend who proves to be a rhetorician of nihilism claiming that men "loathe the daily bread that prolongs useless existence," Herzog refutes his position as emphatically as he later claims in his closing imaginary letter to a former professor that "we must get it out of our heads that this is a doomed time, that we are waiting for the end, and the rest of it, mere junk from fashionable magazines" (*H* 316—317). Herzog is "convinced that the extent of universal space does not destroy human value, that the realm of facts and that of values are not eternally separated" (*H*106). At the very end of the novel, it is one of the signs of Herzog's recovery that he is interested in fixing the house, re-organizing his kingdom.

Life on the moon seems to provide a way of dealing with the problem of vast multitudes. It is also a nihilistic expression of escaping the human condition. The aged Sammler, survivor of the Holocaust, with the knowledge that six million of his brethren have been killed, is not pessimistic. He still believes that the earth is "a glorious planet" (*SP*125) even though "everything was being done to make it intolerable to abide" (125) on it. He feels that mankind cannot be other than what it is. It cannot get ride of itself neither by means of transcendence nor by "universal self-destruction" (215).

Sammler, having experienced both the best and the worst, literally return ing from the mass grave at Auschwitz, believes that religious faithmust be sustained by the recognition of the self as a worthy creation of God-the only self-image by which man can live authentically and an image that is threatened by the application of scientific rationality in the modern world. The self must be free to pursue its private quests-a principle supported by all Bellow's fiction: "We see what is before us, the present, the objective. External being makes its temporal appearance in this way. The only way out of captivity in the forms, out of the confinement in the prison of projections, the only contact with the eternal is through freedom" (*SP* 57). As Bellow's most seasoned and tested protagonist, Sammler is his most credulous exponent for the individual's continuance. Back from the verge of death, Sammler can reaffirm this position with the prospect of future technological threats before him:

> It is charged against the Christian that he wanted to get rid of himself. Those that brought the charges urged him to transcend his unsatisfactory humanity. But isn't transcendence the same disorder? Isn't that also getting rid of the human being? Well, maybe man should get rid of himself. Of course. If he can. But also he has something in him which feels it important to continue. Something that deserves to go on. It is something that has to go on, and we all know it .... The spirit knows that its growth is the real aim of existence. (SP 235—236)

The Bellow protagonist, constantly beleaguered by devastating personal problems, walks—at times, limps—through life, laughing and crying, but never defeated and always as a member of society. Life is a wondrous experience to be enjoyed by the living in the company of others, and this is the guiding principle of Bellow's heroes.

Dean Corde publishes articles in *Harper's* on the deterioration of urban life in Chicago and pressed murder charges against two Blacks, who bound, gagged, and pushed one of the Dean's students out of a window to his death. Based on his conscience and sense of duty, Corde the moralist demands justice for the victims in spite of all the agitations and protests.

Corde, a native son of Chicago, like Augie, Herzog, and Citrine, is strongly attached to his city. He especially cherishes his memories of Old Chicago's lovable neighborhoods. His reunion with his old pal Spangler in Bucharest gives him not only "the pleasure of nostalgia" (*DD* 123) but the opportunity to explore the motives behind his writing the *Harper's* articles on the deterioration of urban life in Chicago. In an exotic city, two journalists from Chicago indulge in reminiscences of the good old days of poetry and feeling they shared in high school in the thirties. Corde recalls that they were drawn to each other because of their passion for poetry and literature: "Of course it was Swinburne, Wilde, Nietzsche, Walt Whitman, in high school. Perfumed herbage, intoxicating lyricism and lamentation, rich music, nihilism and decadence had made them pals" (74). In a city noted for its gangsters and stockyards, its industry and business, their love of poetry and philosophy was indeed odd.

Corde returned to Chicago ten years ago in his mid-forties after a successful career as a journalist for the Paris *Tribune*. He chose to become a professor in Chicago because of his allegiance to his city, on the one hand, and his desire to reorient himself in the classics, on the other. After "a twenty-year interruption by 'news', by current human business" (208), he decided to give more attention to Baudelaire, Rilke, Montesquieu, Vico, Machiavelli, Plato, Thucydides, and Shakespeare.

After a ten-year's dormancy, Corde decides to walk out of his ivory tower and see first hand what is happening in his city. Originally he plans to write about the Chicago that he knows, focusing on "personalities, scenes, feelings, tones, and colors" (219). However, as he probes into the present Chicago, his original plan begins to take a twisted turn. As he discovers, the city that is is not the city that was: Chicago is not "the old town anymore" (125). While collecting materials for the articles, he finds at once "wounds, lesions, cancers, destructive fury, death" (223). Chicago is the "contempt center" of America, filled with chaos, insanity, violence, sexual anarchy, and moral decay. Corde's essays begin with picturesque, charming, nostalgic recollections, ending up with animadversions and exposes. He does not mean to attack-as he says "I' m attached to Chicago-I am speaking quite seriously" (131)-but he writes cutting polemics denouncing Chicago's criminal-justice system, the corruption of local judges and lawyers, and the violent, primitive conditions tolerated in the Cook County jail. He fills his articles with "disobliging remarks about City Hall, the press, the sheriff, and the governor" (13).

Corde does not want to yield to nihilism. Corde's true purpose is to awaken his fellow citizens' conscience and make them look at reality without recoil. Corde does not see his articles on Chicago as attacks on his city. He writes them not "because of the opportunities it offers for romantic despair, nor in a spirit of middle-class elegy or nostalgia" (182), but because he wants "to prevent the American idea from being pounded into dust altogether. And here is our American idea: liberty, equality, justice, democracy, abundancy." (135). Corde tries to justify his incorporating poetry and philosophy into his essays. Since reality does not exist "out there" - "It began to be real only when the soul found its underlying truth" (295)-Corde decides to "pass Chicago through his own soul" (294—295). To him, as to Bellow, "without art, it is impossible to interpret reality" (Roudane 280). Thinking about virtue and vice, Corde maintains that in a crisis such as this we should use our imagination and poetry, for "perhaps only poetry had the strength 'to rival the attractions of narcotics, the magnetism of TV, the excitement of sex, or the ecstasies of destruction'" (207).

Not intimidated by the criticism and hatred of his colleagues, readers, and fellow Chicagoans, Corde will continue to write because he believes in his own sense of existence and his obligation to defend civilization. As he says, "I was speaking up for the noble ideas of the West in their American form. . . . 'This is your city-this is your American democracy. It is also my city. I have a right to picture it as I see it' " (136). Corde is Bellow's "best balanced hero" (Cohen, Joseph 53). Like other Bellow heroes, he is in quest of equilibrium in the city, but unlike them, he is a wise observer and brave moralist who demands justice and wants to right wrongs.

Bellow creates an internal protagonist in his novels to carry out private quest for inner values, resulting in the contemplation of the fundamental questions, which Bellow himself as an artist raises in one of his essays: "Why were we born? What are we doing here? Where are we going?" (Bellow, "The Writer as Moralist" 19) Bellow's questioning of the purpose of human existence in modern society suggests the importance of personal values in his novels, to which external social values remain largely subsidiary. This concern in Bellow's fiction conforms to Jerry Bryant's assertion that "The overwhelming moral and metaphysical preoccupation of the western mind in the twentieth century is the integrity of the individual, because that is where reality and value are deemed to lie" (Bryant 284). In this respect John Clayton is most accurate in his observation that Bellow "stands as a spokesman for our culture, as a defender of the western cultural tradition" (3).

Bellow is concerned that modern writing has presented a negative and destructive view of man. Bellow suggests that the negative should be diminished and the positive accentuated. Over and over again, Bellow stresses that the writer's problem is perspective, that he must present a more positive approach to life, based upon a love-relationship with humanity and a belief in the value of existence. It is the writer's function, according to Bellow, to project the love of human-kind and the appreciation of the grandeur involved in man's minutest endeavors through his creativity.

Saul Bellow wants desperately to affirm the value of human existence, the possibilities of meaningful life in this civilization, the dignity and beauty of the individual. We have seen Bellow's struggle against the denigration of the individual. Bellow wants Herzog to be a "marvelous Herzog" (*H* 93); he wants to consider men as "a little lower than the angels" (Bellow, Distractions 14). In his works, Bellow portrays his characters as achieving a degree of self－fulfillment in American society despite its negative pressures.

Conclusion

Beginning his writing career in the mid-forties of the twentieth century, Saul Bellow represents a post-modern writer-that is, a writer whose fiction has turned away from a concern with social values to embrace the inner values of the individual. As an inward-turning writer, Bellow rejects alienation and nihilism and affirms the values inherent in individuality. He places premium value on the individual who is capable of realizing himself through commitment to others, through the multiplicities of experience to attain perspective, through spiritual self-renewal as a means to social service, and through internal order as the way to external order.

Bellow is a moralist as he believes all writers should be. He is concerned with the question of "What is man?" and his answer reveals an attitude which is positive, affirmative, optimistic. His views, stemming from the tenets of Judaism, become the themes and perspectives of his fiction, and they in turn, affect the tone, character, and style of his works. Bellow's overall approach to life is affirmative and optimistic. He deals with social responsibility, the lifestyle of a good man, brotherly love, the uniqueness of the individual, and the dignity and divinity of man in his nobles. These ideas as themes of his works come from Bellow's Jewish background and his knowledge of the Old Testament.

The Bellow hero tries to assert his sovereign self. Believing in the nobility of man, he cannot accept the belittling or annihilation of self. But the Bellow hero also realizes the dangers of self-estrangement, which is imprisoning and limiting. Caught in such a frightful dilemma, the Bellow hero tries to achieve equipoise between preserving one's selfhood and relating oneself to others. In the end, he is always drawn back to the human conditions, discovering that "any goodness is not achieved in a vacuum" (*DM* 61). With his mind bent on becoming a good man, he chooses to be among his fellow citizens because brotherhood is what makes a man human. Each of Bellow heroes progresses from his guarding his self to his breaking out of his self and eventually to his embracing of human communion.

In many of his essays, Bellow emphasizes that the writer should look at life steadfastly and tries to write as authentically and faithfully as possible. As an artist living in the city, Bellow always looks at the facts of the city without recoil and tries to redeem the ugliness and chaos of the city with his art. His aesthetic view is similar to that expressed in Keats' famous epigram, "Beauty is truth, truth beauty." He believes that truth in its intensest moment can become beauty.

That is why he has never avoided looking at the evil and seamy side of modern society, nor has he easily succumbed to the wasteland outlook.

All Bellow's central characters are urban-bred and urban-oriented and face more or less the same existential problems. They keep asking: How should one orient oneself in a modern city which is characterized by chaos, madness, ugliness, philistinism, and cultural nihilism? How can one retain one's sovereign, autonomous self under the weight of an oppressive and maiming mass urban society? How does one relate oneself to others when alienation, fragmentation, materialization, and mechanization are in ascendency? How can one achieve serenity, spontaneity, dignity, and humanity in a fast-moving, frenzy-bent, wastelandish urban construct? How can one maintain equilibrium between self and society? These are demanding questions with which Bellow heroes -from Joseph to Dean Corde-have to come to grips in their quest for order, equanimity, and the meaning of human existence.

Despite Bellow's ambivalence toward the city, the Bellow hero has to accept it as part of reality. It is mainly in the city, amidst the crowd, alone in solitude, or during conversations, that the Bellow hero gains sudden illuminations about man's place in the city, in the world, and in the universe. Although he uses Chicago and New York City as the settings for almost all his novels, Bellow is not a parochial writer. In fact, his oeuvre, which combines "the human understanding and subtle analysis of contemporary culture," is a mirror that truthfully reflects the reality of society.

Despite the degradation, clutter, dismalness, and annoyances he sees in the modern city, Bellow knows that only by the transcending power of poetry, art, or imagination, can man save himself, the city, and the whole civilization from decay or destruction. Here he is very Blakean. In *Dangling Man*, John Pearl, Joseph's artist friend, contends that "the real world is the world of art and of thought. There is only one worthwhile sort of work, that of the imagination" (*DM* 90—91). Like Citrine in *Humboldt's Gift*, Bellow admits that he is "sentimental about urban ugliness" (*HG* 72), but he, like Citrine, decides to ransom "the commonplace, all this junk and wretchedness, through art and poetry, by the superior power of the soul" (*HG* 72).

Because of his recognition of the dangers of being shut in, his sense of duty, his family feelings, his moral conscience, or his entanglements with people around him, the Bellow hero walks out of his solipsistic, cell-like room and becomes a city voyager. Walking on the street or riding on the ferry, subway, or bus, in a taxi or in a car, the Bellow hero continues to read the text of the urban reality. Through his observations and musings during city voyages, the Bellow hero comes in direct contact with the reality and gains first-hand urban experience. Like his author, the Bellow hero is ambivalent toward the city because of its simultaneous desolation and vitality. At times terrified by the chaotic condition of the city, the Bellow hero embraces pastoral aspirations and longs to go out of the city for fresher air and solace. Despite his occasional idyllic dreams, however, the Bellow hero never considers living in the country a viable option, because escapes from the city dose not solve his problems. As clearly demonstrated in *Augie March* and *Herzog*, living in the countryside does not yield the happiness, transcendence, or tranquility the Bellow hero expects.

Thus the Bello hero either remains in the city or returns to the city after a brief flirtation with pastoral ideals. Oppressed by the present city, the Bellow hero likes to indulge in memories of the old city where he enjoys closely knit family life and congenial neighborhoods. However, remembrances of city past cannot obliterate the grim realities of city present. The Bellow hero has to accommodate himself to it, however terrible it is. Drab as the modern reality is, the Bellow hero tries to find moments of transcendence. At times, he does find beauty in the ugliness of the city. Most important of all, through human interactions he feels part of humanity and learns to accept his fellow citizens as "his brothers and his sister" (*SD* 92). Despite the turbulence and agitation of the chaotic city, the Bellow hero never gives in to despair or nihilism.

Bellow has the most powerful mind among contemporary American novelist, or at least, he is the American novelist who best assimilates his intelligence to creative purpose. So in Bellow's ostensibly autobiographical novels, the typical Bellow hero is male and often an intellectual, a scholarly or literary figure, like Bellow himself and has frequently been taken as mouthpieces for Bellow's own views. He is anxious about self, "concerned with exploring its inward claim, which may be our salvation or the real source of our suffering." (Bradbury 29) Bellow turns away from Hemingwayism in the opening paragraph of *Dangling Man* by portraying Joseph who will expose his inner life through introspection. The Hemingway hero is the strong, hard-boiled athlete who can shoot his opponent but is "unpracticed in introspection", and he is also bored with life, and preoccupied with death. Nevertheless, each of Bellow's novels focuses on the mental experience of the protagonist who searches for the true self and true freedom. In fact, his protagonist's mental struggles represent Bellow's own subtle understanding of the real self in the modern world. His spiritual exploration of accommodation of the self in modern urban world is partly Bellow's own speculation on the fortune of the whole human kind. Dean Corde actively demands morality and justice in a city which seems devoid of positive moral values. He tries to uncover the truth that is hidden under the debris of falsehood. The ultimate reason for Corde is his deep attachment to Chicago: he wants to rescue the city from decay through poetry, art, and the imagination. Only by finding the axial lines of life and living by them, by finding the wisdom of life in the recognition of darkness of reality, by breaking out of one's self, by achieving universal brotherhood, by reinvigoration ethical values, and by upholding moral initiatives, can man save himself and the modern reality from decay.

Bellow's emphasis on love, feeling, imagination, and brotherhood leads him to criticize vehemently the so-called "modern public consciousness," which exemplifies itself in indifferent-bystander attitude, bogus culturalism, wastelander's mentality, and nihilistic philosophy. When moral depravity and wayward behavior follow in the wake of the blind pursuit of material and sensual enjoyment, when human dignity is severely ravaged, when rationalism, existentialism, and pragmatism are in vogue, when apocalyptic visions about the future of civilization prevail, it is most significant that Bellow, one of the best novelists of this century, persists in writing about common feelings shared by humankind, in rejecting the cant of pessimism and nihilism, and in believing in the power of poetry and the imagination.

Essentially a realist, Bellow, like Joyce, is a "chronicler of the city" (Schwartz 20). As he say, "Every novelist is a historian, a chronicler of his time" (Brans 67). His realistic description not only yields a faithful picture of the American society but gets really close to its contemporary facts. For instance, *Augie March* delineates vividly the cityscape and life style of Chicago in the thirties and forties. Through his examination of a cross-section of life in New York City during the sixties, Bellow records his honest vision about the Holocaust, the Moon exploration, and the counter-culture of the sixties in *Mr. Sammler's Planet*.

Bellow's novels focus on the individual, the options available to him, his preferences and judgments, and his capabilities in dealing with his present predicament. His characters may grumble, lament, fret, and complain, but they do not despair about the future. He is a Jewish protagonist, who espouses a Jewish philosophy, unconscious though it may be, and maintains a nostalgic relationship to Judaism. He is an intellectual, who tries to subsume his knowledge of Judaism into a general intellectual framework, to work out a remedy for the chaotic modern urban world. Within this generally optimistic, at times ebullient, attitude, Bellow presents a picture of the American-Jewish community, the progeny of the immigrant generation, which has labored to assimilate itself into the mainstream of American life.

According to the Nobel committee, Bellow portrays "a man who keeps on trying to find a foothold during his wanderings in a tottering world, one who can never relinquish his faith that the value of life depends on dignity, not its success, and that truth must triumph at last" in his novels. The typical Bellow hero keeps on trying to find a foothold, so that he may be reconciled with this tottering world, by pondering deeply over self-knowledge and self-definition, and by insisting upon finding the dignity of the self.

Bibliography

Alexander, Edward. *Classical Liberalism and the Jewish Tradition.* New Brunswick, New Jersey: Transaction Publisher, 2003.

Alfer, Robert. *Rogue's Progress: Studies in the Picaresque Novel.* Cambridge: Harvard University Press, 1964.

Alter, Robert. "The Stature of Saul Bellow." *Midstream* Vol. 10, No. 4 (Dec. 1964): 3—15.

Atlas, James. *Bellow: A Biography.* New York: Modern Library, 2000.

Bach, Gerhard. *The Critical Response to Saul Bellow.* Westport, CT: Greenwood Press, 1995.

——and Gloria L. Cronin. *Small Planets: Saul Bellow and the Art of Short Fiction.* East Langsing, Michigan: Michigan State University Press, 2000.

Baeck, Leo. *The Essence of Judaism.* N. Y.: Shocken Books, 1948.

Bakker, J. *Fiction as Survival Strategy.* Amsterdam: Editions Rodopi B. V., 1983.

Bell, Daniel. "Sensibility in the60's." *Commentary* 51 (June. 1971): 63—73.

Bellow, Saul. "A Word From the Writer." *Fiction of the Fifties.* ed. Herbert Gold. Garden City, N. Y.: Doubleday, 1959.

——. "A Writer Looks at Chicago Culture, 'This Furious Spirit Which Builds Up and Pulls Down'". *Chicago Daily News.* Saturday – Sunday, November 11—12, 1972.

——. "Culture Now: Some Animadversions, Some Laughs." *Modern Occasions.* (Winter, 1971): 177—178.

——. "Distractions of a Fiction Writer." *The Living Novel: A Symposium.* ed. Granville Hicks. New York: The Macmillan Co., 1957.

——. "Facts that Put Fancy to Flight." *The New York Times Book Review* 11 Feb. 1962.

——. "Hemingway and the Image ofMan." *Partisan Review* Vol. 20 (May –June, 1953): 338—342.

——. "How I Wrote Augie March's Story." *New York Times Book Review*, 31 Jan. 1954: 3.

——. Introduction, *Great Jewish Short Stories.* New York: Bell Publ. Co., Inc., 1963.

——. *It All Adds Up: From the Dim Past to the Uncertain Future: a Nonfiction Collection.* New York, N. Y., U. S. A.: Penguin, 1995.

——. "Keynote Address: Inaugural Session of the 34 Session of the International Congress of Poets, Playwrights, Essayists and Editors," *The Montreal Star*, 25 June 1966, Special Insert.

——. "Laughter in the Ghetto." Rev. of *The Adventures of Mottel the Cantor's Son*, by Sholom Aleichem, *The Saturday Review* 30 May. 1953.

——. "Literature." *The Great Ideas Today*. New York: Encyclopedia Britannica Inc., 1963. 135—179.

——. "Machines and Storybooks," *Harper's*, 59.

——. "Mystic Tradition and the American Novelist: Saul Bellow Talks to Jim Douglas Henry," *The Listener*, 81 (22 May 1969), 705—07

——. The Nobel Prize in Literature 1976 - Lecture. The Nobel Prize Committee, Stockholm, Sweden, 12 Dec. 1976.

< http: //nobelprize. org/nobel _ prizes/literature/laureates/1976/bellow -lecuture. html >.

——. "Off the Couch by Christmas." *The listener* 20 Nov. 1975: 674—675.

——. *Recent American Fiction*. Washington: Library of Congress, 1963.

——. "Some Notes on Recent American Fiction." *Encounter* 21 (Nov. 1963): 22—29.

——. "The Creative Writer and His Audience." *Perspectives USA* 9, Autumn 1954.

——. "The Sealed Treasure." *The Times Literary Supplement* 1 July. 1960.

——. "Skepticism and the Depth of Life." *The Arts and the Public*. ed. James E. Miller and Paul D. Herring. Chicago: University of Chicago Press, 1967. 13—30.

——. "The Thinking Man's Wasteland." *The Saturday Review* 3 Apr. 1965: 20.

——. "Where Do We Go from Here: The Future of Fiction." *Saul Bellow and the Critics*. ed. Irving Malin. New York: New York University Press, 1967. 211—220.

——. "A Writer fromChicago." In *The Tanner Lectures on Human Values*. Ⅲ, 1982. ed. Sterling M. McMurrin. Cambridge: Cambridge UP, 1982.

——. "The Writer as Moralist." *The Atlantic Monthly* 211 (Mar. 1963): 58—62.

Bercovitch, Sacvan. *The Cambridge History of American Literature* (Volume 6 Prose Writing, 1910—1950). Cambridge: Cambridge University Press, 2002.

Bloom, Harold. *Saul Bellow*. New York & Philadelphia: Chelsea House Publisher, 1986.

——, ed. *Saul Bellow's Herzog*. New Haven, CT: Chelsea House Publisher, 1988.

Bothwell, Etta K. *Alienation in the Jewish American Novel of the Sixties*. Rio Piedras, Puerto Rico: Editorial Universitaria, 1980.

Bradbury, Malcolm. *Saul Bellow.* Meltheun, London & New York, 1982.

——and Sigmund Ro. *Contemporary American Fiction.* London: Edward Amold (Publisher) Ltd, 1987.

Braham, Jeanne. *A Sort of Columbus: The American Voyages of Saul Bellow's Fiction.* Athens, Georgia: University of Georgia Press, 1984.

Brans, Jo. "Common Needs, Common Preoccupations." *Critical Essays on Saul Bellow.* ed. Stanley Trachtenberg. Boston: G. K. Hall, 1979. 57—72.

Brauner, David. *Post－war Jewish Fiction: Ambivalence, Self－explanation and Translantic Connection.* New York: Palgrave, 2001.

Bryant, Jerry. *The Open Decision.* New York: Free Press, 1970.

Buber, Martin. *Hasidism.* New York: Philosophical Library, 1948.

Budick, Emily Miler. *Ideology and Jewish Identity in Israeli and American Literature.* Albany, New York: State University of New York Press, 2001.

Clayton, John Jacob. *Saul Bellow: In Defense of Man* (2nd edition). Bloomington: Indiana University Press, 1979.

Cohen, Joseph. "Saul Bellow's Heroes in an Unheroic Age." *Saul Bellow Journal*, Vol. 3, No. 1, 1983: 53—58.

Cohen, Sarah Blacher. *Saul Bellow's Enigmatic Laughter.* Urbana, Ill.: Univ. of Illinois Press, 1974.

——. "Saul Bellow's Chicago." *Modern Fiction Studies*, Vol. 24, No. 1, Spring 1978.

Cronin, Gloria. *Saul Bellow's Rejection of Modernism* (Doctoral Dissertation). Brigham Young University, 1980.

Cronin, Gloria. et al. *Jewish American Fiction Writers: An Annotated Bibliography.* Garland, 1991.

——. *A Room of His Own: In Search of the Feminine in the Novels of Saul Bellow.* New York: Syracuse University Press, 2001.

——and Ben Siegel, eds. *Conversations with Saul Bellow.* The University Press of Mississippi, 1994.

——and L. H. Goldman, eds. *Saul Bellow in the 1980s: A Collection of Critical Essays. East Lansing.* Michigan: Michigan State University Press, 1989.

—— and Blaine H. Hall. *Saul Bellow: Annotated Bibliography.* New York & London: Garland Publishing, Inc, 1987.

Crozier, Robert D. "Theme in*Augie March.*" *Critique* 7 (Spring－Summer, 1965): 18—32.

Culler, J. *On Deconstruction.* Beijing: Foreign Language Teaching and Research Press & Cornell University Press, 2004.

Cunliffe, Marcus. *American Literature Since* 1900. New York: Peter Bedrick Books, 1987.

Davis, Robert G. "The American Individualist Tradition: Bellow and Styron." *The Creative Present.* eds. Mona Balakian and Charles Simmons. New

York: Doubleday and Co., Inc., 1963. 111—141.

Detweiler, Robert. *Saul Bellow: A Critical Essay*. William B. Eerdmans Publishing Co, 1967.

Dickstein, Morris. *A Mirror in the Roadway: Literature and the Real World*. Princeton, N. J.: Princeton University Press, 2005.

Dutton, R. R. *Saul Bellow*. Twayne Publisher, 1982.

Eisinger, Charles. "Saul Bellow: Love and Identity." *Accent*, Vol. 18, No. 3, Summer 1958.

Eisinger, Chester E. *Fiction of the Forties*. Chicago: Univ. of Chicago Press, 1963.

Eliot, Emory. *The Columbia History of the American Novel*. New York: Columbia University Press, 1991.

——. *Columbia Literature History of the United States*. New York: Columbia University Press, 1988.

Emerson, Ralph W. "The American Scholar." *The Portable Emerson*. eds. Carl Bode, Malcolm Cowley. New York: Penguin Group, 1981.

Fiedler, Leslie. "Saul Bellow." *Prairie Schooner* 31, Summer 1957.

Fischs, Daniel. *Saul Bellow: Vision and Revision*. Durham, N. C.: Duke University Press, 1984.

Fischs, Harold. *New Stories for Old: Biblical Patterns in the Novel*. London: Macmillan Press Ltd, 1998.

Frye, Northrop. "Fables of Identity." *The Archetypes of Literature*. New York: Jovanovich Publishers, 1963.

Fuchs, Daniel. "Saul Bellow and the Modern Traditon." *Contemporary Literature*, 15 (1974), 67—89.

——. *Saul Bellow: Vision and Revision*. Durham, NC: Duke University Press, 1984.

Galloway, David. *The Absurd Hero in the American Fiction: Updike, Styron, Bellow, Salinger*. Austin & London: University of Texas Press, 1970.

——. "An Interview with Saul Bellow." *Audit*, Vol. 3, No. 2, Spring 1963: 19—23.

——. "Moses – Bloom – Herzog: Bellow's Everyman." *The Southern Review* 2, Winter 1966.

——. "Mr. Sammler's Planet: Bellow's Failure of Nerve." *Modern Fiction Studies* Vol. 19, No. 1, 1973: 17—28.

Geismar, Maxwell. "Saul Bellow: Novelist of the Intellectuals," in *Saul Bellow and the Critics*. Ed. Irving Malin. New York: New York University Press, 1967.

Glenday, Michael K. *Saul Bellow and the Decline of Humanism*. London: Macmillan Press, 1990.

Gold, Herbert. "Fiction of the Fifties." *Hudson Review*12, Summer 1959.

Goldman, L. H. "Saul Bellow and the Philosophy of Judaism." *Saul Bel-*

low in the 1980*s*: *A collection of Critical Essays*. Ed. Gloria Cronin and L. H. Goldman. East Lansing, Mich: Michigan State University Press, 1989. 51—64.

——. *Saul Bellow's Moral Vision*: *A Critical Study of the Jewish Experience*. New York: Irvington Publishers, 1983.

Goldman, Liela. *Affirmation and Equivocation*: *Judaism and in the Novels of Saul Bellow* (Doctoral Dissertation). Wayne State University, 1980.

Gross, Beverly. "Review of*Mr. Sammler's Planet.*" *Nation* 9 Feb. 1970: 153—155.

Guerard, Albert J. "Saul Bellow and the Activists." *Southern Review*, Vol. 3, No. 3, July 1967.

Guerin, W. L. et al. *A Handbook of Critical Approaches to literature* (4th edition). Beijing: Foreign Language Teaching and Research Press & Oxford University Press, 2004.

Gullette, Margaret Morganroth. *Safe at last in the Middle Years*: *The Invention of Midlife Progress Novel*: *Saul Bellow*, *Margaret Drabble*, *Anne Tyler*, *and John Updike*. Berkeley, Los Angeles & London: University of California Press, 1988.

Harp, Louis. *In the Mainstream*: *The Jewish Presence in the Twentieth - Century American Literature*, 1950*s*—1980*s*. Westport, CT: Greenwood Press, 1987.

Harper, G. L. "The Art of Fiction," *Partisan Review*, 9: 65 Winter 1966.

——, ed. "Saul Bellow." *Writers at Work*. New York: Viking Press, 1967. 177—196.

Harper (Jr.), Howard M. *Desperate Faith*: *A Study of Bellow*, *Salinger*, *Mailer*, *Baldwin*, *and Updike*. Chapel Hill: The University of North Carolina Press, 1974.

Harris, James N. "One Critical Approach to*Mr. Sammler's Planet.*" *Twentieth - Century Literature* 18 (Oct. 1972): 235—250.

Harris, Mark. *Saul Bellow*: *Drumlin Woodchuck*. Athens: The University of Georgia Press, 1980.

Hassan, Ibab. *Radical Innocence*: *Studies in the Contemporary American Novel*. Princeton: Princeton University Press, 1973.

Hawthorne, Nathaniel. *The Marble Faun*. New York: The New American Library, 1961.

Heifetz, Harold. *Zen and Hasidism*: *The Similarities Between Two Spiritual Disciplines*. Hoboken, NJ: KTAV Publishing House, 1978.

Hollahan, Eugene. *Saul Bellow and the Struggle at the Center*. New York: AMS Press, 1966.

Howard, Jane. "Mr. Bellow Considers his Planet." *Life Magazine* 3 Apr. 1970: 57—60.

Howe, Irving. *Classics of Modern Fiction*. New York: Harcourt, Brace and World, Inc., 1968.

——. *Herzog: Text and Criticism*, New York: The Viking Press, 1976.

——. "Introduction." *A Treasury of Yiddish Stories*. New York, 1954. 1—71.

——. "The New York Intellectuals." *Commentary* 46 (Oct. 1968): 29—51.

——. "Odysseus, Flat on his Back." *The New Republic* 19 Sept. 1964: 57—60.

——. "Review of Mr. Sammler's Planet." *Harper's* 240 (Feb. 1970): 106—108, 112.

Hyland, Peter. *Macmillan Modern Novelists: Saul Bellow*. London: Macmillan Education Ltd., 1922.

——. *Saul Bellow*. London: Macmillan Press, 1992.

International and Pan - American Conventions, *The Holy Bible* (Revised Standard Version), Second Edition. Nashville: Thomas Nelson Inc, 1971.

James, Henry. *Hawthorne*. Ithaca, N. Y.: Cornell University Press, 1975.

Josipovici, Gabriel. *The Lessons of Modernism and Other Essays*. London: The Macmillan Press Ltd, 1977.

Kakutani, Michiko. "Heartbreak and Humor." *New York Times* [New York, N. Y.] 7 Apr. 2005, Late Edition (East Coast): E. 1. 15 Apr. 2009

Kazin, Alfred. "The Earthly City of the Jews." *Bright Book of Life: American Novelists and Storytellers from Hemingway to Mailer*. Boston: Little, Brown and Co., 1973. 127—138

——. "My Friend Saul Bellow." *Saul Bellow: The Man and His Work*. ed. M. A. Quayum and S. Singh. New Delhi, India: B. R. Publishing, 2000. 3—12.

Kerbel, Sorrcl. *Jewish Writers of the Twentieth Century*. New York & London: Fitzroy Frederick Unigar Publishing Co, 1983.

Kiernan, Robert F. *Saul Bellow*. New York: Continuum Publishing Company, 1989.

Klein, Marcus. *After Alienation*. New York: World Publishing Company, 1964.

Kramer, Michael P. *New Essays on Seize the Day*. Cambridge: Cambridge University Press, 1998.

Kulshrestha, Chirantan. *Saul Bellow: The Problem of Affirmation*. New Delhi: Arnold - Heinemann Publishers (India) Pvt, Ltd, 1980.

——. "A Conversation with Saul Bellow." *Chicago Review*, Vol. 23, No. 4, 1972.

Kunitz, Stanley, ed. *Twentieth Century Authors*, First supplement. New York, 1955.

Leaman, Oliver. *Evil and Suffering in Jewish Philosophy*. Cambridge University Press, 1995.

Liptzin, Sol. *The Jew in American Literature*. New York: Bloch Publishing

Co. Inc, 1966.

Liu, Wen -song. *Saul Bellow's Fiction: Power Relations and Female Representation*. Xianmen University Press, 2004.

Longinus: "On the Sublime." *Critical Theory Since Plato*. Ed. Hazard Adams, Orlando: Fl. Harcourt Brace, 1992. 75—98.

Mahadevan, Usha. From Verbalization to Non - Verbal Awareness: A Study of Saul Bellow's Herzog. ed. Bhongle, Rangrao. *Contemporary American Literature: Poetry, Fiction, Drama & Criticism*. New Delhi: Atlantic Publisher and Distributors (New Delhi), 2000.

Marcus, Steven. "Reading the Illegible: Some Modern Representations of Urban Experience." In *Visions of the Modern City*. Ed. William Sharpe and Leonard Wallock. New York: Columbia U Proceedings of the Heyman Center for the Humanities, 1983.

May, Lary. ed. *Recasting America: Culture and Politics in the Age of Cold War*. Chicago: University of Chicago Press, 1989.

Miller, Ruth. *Saul Bellow: A Biography of the Imagination*. New York: St. Martin Press, 1987.

Mosher, Harold F., Jr. "The Synthesis of Past and Present in Saul Bellow's Herzog." *Wascana Review*, Vol. 6, No. 1, 1971: 28—38.

Murdoch, Iris. "The Sovereignty of Good Over Other Concepts." *Aesthetics: The Big Questions*. Ed. Carolyn Korsmeyer. Malden, MA: Blackwell, 1998. 196—201

Nadon, Robert J. *Urban Values in Recent American Fiction: A Study of the City in the Fiction of Saul Bellow, John Updike, Philip Roth, Bernard Malamud, and Norman Mailer* (Doctoral Dissertation). University of Minnesota, 1969.

Nair, R. Ramchandran. Citrine's Transcendental Quest in Humboldt's Gift. ed. Bhongle, Rangrao. *Contemporary American Literature: Poetry, Fiction, Drama & Criticism*. New Delhi: Atlantic Publishers and Distributors (New Delhi), 2000.

Newman, Judie. *Saul Bellow and History*. London: Macmillan Press, 1984.

Oates, Joyce Carol. "Imaginary Cities." *Jaye and Ann Chalmers Watts*. New Brunswick: Rutgers University Press, 1981. 11—33.

Opdahl, Keith Michael. *The Novels of Saul Bellow: An In Introduction*. University Park and London: The Pennsylvania State University Press, 1978.

——. "Review of*Mr. Sammler's Planet* by Saul Bellow." *Commonweal* 91 (13 Feb. 1970): 535—536.

Ousby, Ian. *A Reader's Guide to* 50 *American Novels*. London: Heinemann Educational Books Ltd, 1981.

Pifer, Ellen. *Saul Bellow Against the Grain*. Philadelphia: University of Pennsylvania Press, 1990.

Pinsker, Sanford, *Jewish - American Fiction* 1917—1987. New York: Twayne Publishers, 1992.

——. "Sustaining Community of 'Reality Instructor': The City in Saul Bellow's Later Fiction." *Studies in American Jewish Literature* 3 (1979): 25—30.

Podhoretz, Norman. "The Adventures of Saul Bellow." *Doings and Undoings*. New York: Farrar, Strauss, 1964.

——. "The New Nihilism and the Novel." *Doings and Undoings*. New York: Farrar, Strauss, 1964. 163.

Poirier, Richard. "Bellows to Herzog." *Partisan Review* 32, Spring 1965.

Porter, M. Gilbert. "Is the Going Up Worth the Coming Down: Transcendental Dualism in Bellow's Fiction." *Studies in the Literary Imagination*, Vol. 17, No. 2, 1984: 19—38.

——. *Whence the Power:? The Artistry and Humanity of Saul Bellow*. Coulumbia & Missouri: University of Missouri Press, 1974.

Posy, Arnold. *Mystic Trends in Judaism*. New York: Jonathan David Publishers, 1966.

Qiao, Guo - qiang. *The Jewishness of Isaac Bashevis Singer*. Bern: Peter Lang, 2003.

Quayum, M. A. *Saul Bellow and American Transcendentalism*. New York: Peter Lang Lewisburg: Bucknell University Press, 1981.

Roth, Philip. *Shop Talk: A Writer and His Colleagues and Their Work*. Boston & New York: Houghton Mifflin Company, 2001.

Roudane, Matthew C. "An Interview with Saul Bellow." *Contemporary Literature*, Vol. 25, No. 3, 1984: 265—280.

Rovit, Earl. *Saul Bellow: A Collection of Critical Essays*. Englewood Cliffs, N. J.: Prentice - Hall, Inc, 1975.

Ruland, Richard and Malcolm Bradbury. *From Puritanism to Postmodernism: A History of American Literature*. New York: Viking Penguin, 1991.

Russell, Marianne. "White Man's Black Man Three Views." *CLA Journal* 17, 1973.

Samuel, Maurice. *The world of Sholem Aleichem*. New York, 1956.

Schwartz, Edward. "Chronicles of the City." *New Republic* 3 Dec. 1956: 20—21.

Scott, N. A. Jr, *Three American Moralists: Mailer, Bellow, Trillling*. London: University Of Notre Dame Press, 1973.

Selden, R. ct al. *A Reader's Guide to Contemporary Literary Theory* (4th edition). Beijing: Foreign Language Teaching and Research Press & Pearson Education, 2004.

Sewell, William Jacob. *Literary Structure and Value Judgment in the Novels of Saul Bellow* (Doctoral Dissertation). Duke University, 1974.

Shaked, Gershon. *The Shadows Within: Essays on Modern Jewish Writers*. Philadelphia & New York: The Jewish Publication Society, 1987.

Showalter, E. *A Literature of Their Own: British Women Novelists from Bronte to Lessing*. Beijing: Foreign Language Teaching and Research Press & Princeton University Press, 2004.

Siegel, Ben. "Artists and Opportunists in Saul Bellow's*Humboldt's Gift.*" *Critical Essays on Saul Bellow.* ed. Stanley Trachtenberg. Boston: G. K. Hall, 1979. 158—174.

——, ed. "Saul Bellow and the University as Villain." *The American Writer and the University.* Cranbury, NJ: Associated University Presses, Inc, 1989.

Simmons, Maggie. "Free to Feel." *Quest*, Feb. - Mar. 1979, 31.

Steers, Nina. A. "'Successor' to Faulkner?" *Show* 4 (Sept. 1964): 38.

Steinberg, Milton. *Basic Judaism.* N. Y.: Harcourt, Brace and World, Inc., 1947.

Tanner, Tony. *Saul Bellow.* Edinburgh: Oliver and Boyd, 1965.

Todorov, Tzvetan. "Poetry and Morality." *Salmagundi* 111 (Summer 1996): 68—74. 29 Oct. 2007. 21 Sept. 2009

Trachtenberg, Stanley. *Critical Essays on Saul Bellow.* Boston: G. K. Hall & Co, 1979.

Wagner-Martin, Linda. *The Mid-century American Novel*, 1935—1965: *a Critical History.* New York: Wayne Publishers, 1997.

Walden, Daniel. "The Resonance of Twoness: The Urban Vision of Saul Bellow." *Saul Bellow: The Man and His Work.* Ed. M. A. Quayum and S. Singh. New Delhi, India: B. R. Publishing, 2000. 133—150.

Wasserman, Harriet. *Handsome Is: Adventures with Saul Bellow.* New York: Fromm International Publishing Corporation, 1997.

Wieting, Molly Stark. "The Symbolic Function of the Pastoral in Saul Bellow's Novels." *Southern Quarterly* 16 (1978): 359—374.

Wilson, Edward. *Rev. of Dangling Man. The New Yorker* 1 Apr. 1944: 78.

Wilson, Jonathan. *Herzog: The Limits of Ideas.* Boston: Wayne Publishers, 1990.

Wirth-Nesher, H. and Michael P. Kramer. *The Cambridge Companion to Jewish American Literature.* Cambridge University Press, 2003.

Wisse, Ruth R. *The Schlemiel as Modern Hero.* Chicago: University of Chicago Press, 1971.

Zhou, Nan-yi. *Toward a New Utopia: A Study of the Novels by Saul Bellow, Bernard Malamud and Cynthia Ozick.* Xiamen University Press, 2005.

中文参考文献

阿巴·埃班著:《犹太史》,阎瑞松译,北京:中国社会科学出版社1986年版。

阿丁·施坦泽兹著:《阿伯特——犹太智慧书》,张平译,北京:中国社会科学出版社1996年版。

艾伦·布鲁姆著:《走向封闭的美国精神》,缪青、宋丽娜等译,北京:中国社会科学出版社1994年版。

埃马纽埃尔·勒维纳斯著:《塔木德四讲》,关宝艳译,栾栋校,北京:商务印书馆2002年版。

柏拉图著:《文艺对话集》,朱光潜译,北京:人民文学出版社2000年版。

布斯著:《小说修辞学》,华明译,北京:北京大学出版社1987年版。

C. P. 斯诺著:《两种文化》,陈克艰、秦小虎译,上海:上海科学技术出版社2003年版。

常耀信著:《美国文学简史》(英文第二版),天津:南开大学出版社2003年版。

戴卫·赫尔曼著:《新叙事学》,马海良译,北京大学出版社2002年版。

丹尼尔·霍夫曼著:《美国当代文学》,北京:中国文艺联合会出版公司1984年版。

董衡巽著:《美国文学简史》(修订本),北京:人民文学出版社2003年版。

杜小真著:《存在和自由的重负——解读萨特的存在和虚无》,济南:

山东人民出版社 2002 年版。

F·R·利维斯著：《伟大的传统》，袁伟译，北京：生活·读书·新知三联书店 2009 年版。

弗洛伊德著：《摩西与一神教》，李展开译，北京：生活·读书·新知三联书店 1997 年版。

傅有德著：《现代犹太哲学》，北京：人民出版社 1999 年版。

郭继德著：《20 世纪美国文学：梦想与现实》，北京：外语教学与研究出版社 2004 年版。

郭继德编：《美国文学研究》第 2 辑，济南：山东大学出版社 2004 年版。

郭继德编：《美国文学研究》第 3 辑，济南：山东大学出版社 2006 年版。

海伦·加德纳著：《宗教与文学》，江先春、沈弘译，成都：四川人民出版社 2003 年版。

黄明哲等著：《梦想与尘世——二十世纪美国文化》，北京：东方出版社 1999 年版。

黄铁池著：《当代美国小说研究》，上海：学林出版社 2000 年版。

科林·威尔逊：《局外生存》，吕俊、侯旬群译，南京：译林出版社 2000 年版。

拉曼·塞尔登：《文学批评理论——从柏拉图到现在》，刘象愚、陈永国等译，北京：北京大学出版社 2000 年版。

利奥·拜克著：《犹太教的本质》，傅永军、于健译，济南：山东大学出版社 2002 年版。

列夫·舍斯托夫著：《狂野呼告》，方珊、李勤译，北京：华夏出版社 2004 年版。

刘洪一著：《犹太名人传——文学家卷》，郑州：河南文艺出版社 2002 年版。

刘洪一著：《犹太文化要义》，北京：商务印书馆 2004 年版。

刘洪一著：《走向文化诗学》，北京：北京大学出版社 2002 年版。

罗德·霍顿、赫伯特·爱德华兹著：《美国文学思想背景》，北京：人民文学出版社 1991 年版。

马丁·布伯著：《论犹太教》，刘杰等译，济南：山东大学出版社2002年版。

马克斯·韦伯著：《新教伦理与资本主义精神》，彭强、黄晓京译，西安：陕西师范大学出版社2002年版。

麦金太尔著：《追寻美德——伦理理论研究》，宋继杰译，南京：译林出版社2003年版。

毛信德著：《美国小说发展史》，杭州：浙江大学出版社2004年版。

摩迪凯·开普兰著：《犹太教：一种文明》，黄福武、张立改译，济南：山东大学出版社2002年版。

聂珍钊："作为方法论的文学伦理学批评"，《文学理论前沿》（第二辑），王宁主编，北京：北京大学出版社2005年版。

诺曼·所罗门著：《犹太教》，赵晓燕译，沈阳：辽宁教育出版社1998年版。

欧文·豪著：《父辈的世界——东欧犹太人移居美国以及他们发现与创造社会的历程》，王海良、赵立行译，上海：生活·读书·新知上海三联书店1995年版。

潘光、陈超南、余建华著：《犹太文明》，北京：中国社会科学出版社1999年版。

齐宏伟著：《心有灵犀：欧美文学与信仰传统》，北京：北京大学出版社2006年版。

钱满素著：《美国当代小说家论》，北京：中国社会科学出版社1987年版。

乔国强著：《美国犹太文学》，北京：商务印书馆2008年版。

乔国强著：《所要来的都是虚》，北京：北京出版社1999年版。

秦小孟著：《当代美国文学——概述与作品选读》（中册），上海：上海译文出版社1995年版。

让—保罗·萨特著：《存在与虚无》，陈宣良等译，北京：生活·读书·新知三联书店1987年版。

让—保罗·萨特著：《存在主义是一种人道主义》，周煦良、汤永宽译，上海：上海译文出版社2005年版。

荣格著：《人，艺术和文学中的精神》，孔长安、丁刚译，北京：华夏出版社 1989 年版。

荣格著：《心理学与文学》，北京：生活·读书·新知三联书店 1987 年版。

芮渝萍著：《美国成长小说》，北京：中国社会科学出版社 2004 年版。

萨克文·伯科维奇著：《剑桥美国文学史》（第七卷，散文作品 1940 年～1990 年），孙宏主译，北京：中央编译出版社 2005 年版。

申丹著：《叙述学与小说文体学研究》（第二版），北京：北京大学出版社 2001 年版。

帅培天等著：《圣经文学词典》，成都：四川人民出版社 1996 年版。

苏珊·桑塔格著：《反对阐释》，程巍译，上海：上海译文出版社 2003 年版。

特里·伊格尔顿著：《后现代主义的幻象》，华明译，北京：商务印书馆 2002 年版。

童明编：《美国文学史》（英文本），南京：译林出版社 2002 年版。

王宁、顾明栋著：《诺贝尔文学奖获奖作家谈创作》，北京：北京大学出版社 1987 年版。

王诜著：《世界著名作家访谈录》，南京：江苏文艺出版社 1995 年版。

王守仁著：《新编美国文学史》（第四卷），上海：上海外语教育出版社 2002 年版。

王运熙、顾易生著：《中国文学批评史》，上海：上海古籍出版社 1985 年版。

吴富恒等编：《美国作家论》，济南：山东教育出版社 1999 年版。

雅各·瑞德·马库斯著：《美国犹太人：1585～1990》，杨波、宋立宏、徐娅囡译，徐新校，上海：上海人民出版社 2004 年版。

杨仁敬著：《20 世纪美国文学史》，青岛：青岛出版社 2000 年版。

叶舒宪著：《文学与人类学》，北京：社会科学文献出版社 2003 年版。

张京媛著：《新历史主义与文学批评》，北京：北京大学出版社 1997 年版。

周南翼：《贝娄》，成都：四川人民出版社 2003 年版。

Fiction by Saul Bellow

A Theft. New York; The Penguin Group VikingPenguin Inc. , 1989.

Dangling Man. Harmondsworth: Penguin Books Ltd, 1985.

Henderson the Rain King. New York: Penguin books Ltd, 1982.

Herzog: Text and Criticism (edited by Irving Howe), New York: The Viking Press, 1976.

Herzog. New York: The Viking Press, 1964.

Him With His Foot in His Mouth and Other Stories. New York: Pocket Books, 1985.

Humboldt's Gift. New York: The Viking Press, 1975.

More Die of Heartbreak. New York: The Penguin Group VikingPenguin Inc. , 1988.

Mosby's Memoirs and Other Stories. New York: Penguin Books, 1982.

Mr. Sammler's Planet. Harmondsworth, Middlesex: Penguin Books Ltd, 1978.

Ravelstein. New York: The Penguin Group Penguin Putman Inc. , 2001.

Seize the Day. Harmondsworth, Middlesex: Penguin Books Ltd. , 1988.

The Adventures of Augie March. London: Penguin Books Ltd, 1988.

The Bellarosa Connection. New York: Penguin Books, 1989.

The Dean's December. New York: Pocket Books, 1982.

The Victim. Harmondsworth, Middlesex: Penguin Books, 1978.

ToJerusalem and Back: A Personal Account. New York: Penguin Books, 1985.

汉译本

《奥吉·马奇历险记》（上、下），宋兆霖译，河北教育出版社 2002 年版。

《更多的人死于心碎》，李耀宗译，中国文联出版社 1992 年版。

《更多的人死于心碎》，姚暨荣、林珍珍译，河北教育出版社 2002 年版。

《挂起来的人》，袁华清译，中国社会科学出版社 1987 年版。

《何索》，颜元叔、刘绍铭译，今日世界出版社 1971 年版。

《赫索格》，宋兆霖译，漓江出版社 1985 年版。

《赫索格》，宋兆霖译，河北教育出版社 2002 年版。

《洪堡的礼物》，蒲隆译，陆凡校，江苏人民出版社 1981 年版。

《洪堡的礼物》，蒲隆译，河北教育出版社 2002 年版。

《晃来晃去的人/受害者》，蒲隆译，河北教育出版社 2002 年版。

《集腋成裘集》，李自修等译，河北教育出版社 2002 年版。

《今天过得怎么样》，郭建中等译，浙江文艺出版社 2003 年版。

《绝望·奋斗——奥基·马区历险记》，原元，齐志颖译，宋芯荃校，陕西人民出版社 1992 年版。

《口没遮拦的人》，郭建中、王丽亚等译，河北教育出版社 2002 年版。

《拉维尔斯坦》，胡苏晓译，译林出版社 2004 年版。

《塞姆勒先生的行星》，汤永宽，主万译，河北教育出版社 2002 年版。

《偷情/真情/贝拉罗莎暗道》，段惟本，主万译，河北教育出版社 2002 年版。

《勿失良辰》，王誉公译，湖南人民出版社 1981 年版。

《像他这样一个知识分子》，李桂蜜译，时报文化出版社企业股份有限公司 2003 年版。

《耶路撒冷来去》，王誉公，张莹译，河北教育出版社 2002 年版。

《雨王汉德森》，冒名渚译，河北教育出版社 2002 年版。

《雨王汉德森》，卞宇理译，今日世界出版社 1979 年版。

《院长的十二月》，陈永国、赵英男译，河北教育出版社 2002 年版。

《只争朝夕/莫斯比的回忆》 王誉公、孙筱珍、董乐山译，河北教育出版社 2002 年版。